NIGHT'S END

A WEREWOLF SUPERNATURAL THRILLER ADVENTURE

NIGHT'S CHAMPION
BOOK THREE

RICHARD PARRY

CONTENTS

THE THREE FACES OF FATE

NIGHT'S END

The Riders have come. The world is running out of time.

Vampires have hunted werewolves to the brink of extinction. Now, **Val and Danny, the last of their kind, are done running.** Their final stand will take them to the **City That Never Sleeps**, where the heart of their ancient enemy beats in the shadows.

But their foes are not just vampires. **Kaylan Gleicher is Death itself, and with her brother Pestilence, they lead the vampires as Riders of the Apocalypse.** Created to drain the world dry, they are forces of **destruction**, not mere creatures of the Night. Even Adalia's gifts pale in the face of **beings forged to end all things.**

Their only hope? A fallen vampire with secrets of his own. Trusting an enemy may be their only chance to stop **Judgment itself.**

The Night's Champions have fought monsters before... **But this time, they're up against the end of the world.**

YOU'RE AWESOME

You could have picked any book, but you chose this one. That means a lot.

Your support keeps independent authors like me forging ahead, writing the stories we love (and hopefully, the ones you love too). Whether you're here for the characters, the worldbuilding, or just a little escapism, thank you for being part of this journey.

You. Kick. Ass.

ROLL FOR NARRATIVE
WHERE WORLDBUILDING AND OVERTHINKING COLLIDE

Love stories that linger in your brain long after The End? Ever wonder why some books hit like a natural 20 and others critically fail their way into the 1-star abyss?

Join *Roll for Narrative*, my hub for sci-fi and fantasy lovers. I explore storytelling like a rogue casing a dungeon, review movies, books, and games, and dish out writing tips like a chaotic-good bard with a grudge against bad prose. No spam, just good stuff.

Join the quest:
https://rollfornarrative.parrydox.com

For Jane; everyone should have a Jane. Carlisle is my eternal gift to you.
And for my Rae. I must be very heavy to keep carrying after all this time.

OVERTURE

The Russian stood in front of him like this kind of thing happened every day. Like being in front of a vampire was a thing that a man could get used to. Like he didn't really care how this turned out — maybe they could hit the bars after, shoot some pool, but they'd need to agree on what kind of drinking they'd be doing.

Dragomir liked that about him.

Of course, drinking could come later. Right now, they were in a shack, tucked between two warehouses. The lighting outside was poor, which was the idea, and the lighting inside wasn't a lot better. It didn't bother either of them. They were friends with the dark. It wasn't palatial accommodation — two chairs stood on either side of an old table. The table's sole purpose was holding some papers, which the Russian had ignored. The floor was bare concrete, the walls corrugated steel. There was no one else with them, because other people would lead to mistakes, and mistakes would lead to dying. Dying, if done at the wrong time, would undo everything. So here they were, just the two of them, in a worn-out neighborhood full of worn-out people, after dark.

"Dragomir Balan," said the Russian. "You are my good friend, *da?*"

They clasped arms, Dragomir feeling the strength there. It'd be useful not to forget that — not the sheer physical presence of that grip, but the man that stood behind it. To come this close to someone who could end your life took — well, it took some serious balls. In Dragomir's experience — his very, *very* long experience — that kind of ball quotient didn't come out of training, or the gym, or having your pet rabbit run away. It came out of everyone you'd ever known dying, horribly, and that sort of thing was a useful asset.

"I am," said Dragomir. He pulled the Russian closer into a hug. "Thank you ... thank you for coming."

"Is nothing," said the Russian. He stepped away, looking around the small room. Probably trying to work out which wall was the best one to punch through if they needed an exit. It's what Dragomir had done ten minutes ago. Dragomir noticed that the Russian hadn't sat at one of the stools set at the rickety table in the middle of the room, or even looked at the papers resting there. He was more of a man of action, this Russian, even after all this time. "Was in neighborhood."

"Since when did you live in the Bronx?"

"Since Tuesday," said the Russian. He sniffed the air. "Storm. Is coming."

"I can't ... I can't really tell when you're joking," said Dragomir. "Of *course* a fucking storm is coming. It's why you're here. To, uh, bring the rain. Look, I'll get you a room. At a nice place for a change."

"I am here," said the Russian, "to kill everyone, but most of all those that need killing. I am here to die. I do not care about nice places."

"Yeah," said Dragomir. "It's my plan, remember?"

"I remember," said the Russian. He pressed against the thin tin wall of the shack, the metal flexing slightly. "You were followed. Did you know?"

"I'm always followed," said Dragomir. "Kaylan's got plans for me. Most of them involve a box buried six feet under."

"I remember," said the Russian. "Kaylan, who wants to end everything. Before you were made, I," and he slapped his broad chest, "saw her raise her sword at Golgotha. She and her brother Maynor. Before they wore those names, they—"

"I know what happened," said Dragomir. Something nagged at his chest, an old pain, the well-worn path in his memories leading him there often. "I was there too. Just ... not quite ready, as you say."

The Russian looked at him, then sighed. "You will see her again soon, my friend. Kaylan? She cannot keep you from your Viorica. Not forever."

Dragomir clapped his hands together. "Well, this conversation's turned dark. What have you learned since Tuesday?"

"The Night is here," said the Russian. "They have tracked your kind to this marvelous city. But nothing else, *da*? They do not know where you live. Who you are. What your names are, or how to find you. Not like me." He gave Dragomir a bright smile, full of perfect white teeth. "They are hunting."

"We must help them," said Dragomir. "They cannot do it alone."

The Russian shrugged. "Maybe so. Maybe not. Do not underestimate the Night."

Dragomir thought about that for a while. "I'm not sure it's about my estimation skills, my friend. It's about a horde of unholy monsters that were designed to end the world. They ... *we* ... were *manufactured*. Two thousand years ago, to end the world when the apocalypse didn't come."

"Apocalypse wasn't meant to come," said the Russian.

"There's disagreement on that theory," said Dragomir. "If it wasn't for Liselle and Josef, we wouldn't be in this fine shack together. Anyway, it's not just the Night. They brought friends."

"Friends?" said the Russian. "The Night has ever walked alone." He pointed at himself with a thumb. "Like me, *da*?"

"Well, no," said Dragomir. He leaned his arms on the table to the sound of old metal creaking, and started flipping through the papers. Dossiers, a collection of stats and numbers and photographs that showed a little of the *what* but none of the *why* or *how*. "Actually, they're completely different, as near as I can tell. Here." He held up one dossier, a head-and-shoulders shot of a fit woman in the top right corner, a number of vital statistics detailing a military history, a *career*, that she'd left behind. "This one. Major Jessica Pearce. Discharged. Pretty clean run through the ranks, lots of medals, bet her dress uniform looks like someone threw a fruit salad at it. You know what the file doesn't say? Her reasons for leaving her promising, successful military career to join a bunch of ... of *werewolves*."

"Is not sensible, *nyet*," said the Russian.

"Not fucking sensible, no," said Dragomir. "You know what they call her? The Lost Warrior."

"I think," said the Russian, "that you have found her, *da*?"

Dragomir gave a snort. "Yeah. Okay. What she lost was her kid."

The Russian frowned for a moment. "Is difficult. The Night, it can collect the needy. Those who need protection. It is weakest when burdened by the frail."

Specialist with a fifty calibre sniper rifle, commendations out the ass. On the ground when that zombie shit hit Chicago — wouldn't call that one weak. Maybe it was a matter of perspective — when Dragomir had lived for over five thousand years maybe he'd have the Russian's point of view. "What about this one then?" he said, pushing another dossier in the Russian's direction. "Retired firefighter. Rex Aubrey."

The Russian leaned closer to read the papers. "'The Guide?'" He gave Dragomir a glance. "Is seeing eye dog?"

"I don't think it's literal. Managed to corral them all to the right place at the right time," said Dragomir. He flipped over another dossier. *The Shield.* "What about this one?"

The Russian tapped the photo. "*Da.* This one, yes. She is made of burnished metal. She will not break."

"I hope not," said Dragomir. "File says she's been in hospital a lot since meeting the rest of them."

"And yet," said the Russian, "not broken, *da*?"

"I guess," said Dragomir. "The Good Right Arm?"

The Russian squinted at the photo, then laughed. "Is like seeing old friends, these papers. Leaves nothing to imagination, *nyet*? John Miles." He frowned, like he was remembering something. "I ... I am not sure, I admit it. It is like he serves no purpose, but..."

"But," agreed Dragomir. "Let's look at these two and I'll save the best for last." He pushed two more files towards the Russian. The man looked at them, then finally sat down on the chair by the table.

"The Knight," said the Russian, "and his Sword." He traced a finger over the photo of Valentine Everard, then made his hand into a fist. "I do not like this, Dragomir Balan. This one should be dead."

"She probably should too," said Dragomir, pointing at Danielle Kendrick's photo. "But here. One more." He shuffled the dossiers, looking for the last one. A young woman, the photo grainy through distance and speed. She hadn't been on the grid, not a decent image of her on file in any system they controlled. They'd grabbed this one shot as she was getting into a car, her face turned towards the photographer. Her eyes looked right out of the page. "The Prophet."

The Russian became still, then he reached a cautious hand out towards the papers. Unclipped the photo of the young woman, held it up to the light. "Adalia," he said, sounding like he was tasting the word, savoring it. "Adalia Kendrick. So ... lost."

"That's where you come in," said Dragomir.

"I am sorry," said the Russian. "My English. Is not always the best, *da*? You think—"

"I think," said Dragomir, "that there's a bunch of bloodsucking assholes who are *right now* trying to get the information I have on this table. They are *right now* trying to capture her," and here, he snared the photograph of Adalia from the Russian, slapping it back down on the table, "so they can continue what they started. To end the world."

"They didn't start it," said the Russian. "*You* didn't start it."

"Semantics," said Dragomir. "Kaylan and Maynor started it. Made us, to finish it. If you can't get the Apocalypse to happen organically, you got to make your own luck, right? I guess in a way it's nice having a purpose. Avoids the whole mid-life crisis. Only problem here is the purpose is *ending the world*, which leads me to my therapist every week."

"Therapist," said the Russian. "Is expensive?"

"I'll give you his card later," said Dragomir. "Look, the thing we need here is some focus."

"You need guardian angel," said the Russian. He laughed, showing those perfect white teeth. "I am not angel, Dragomir Balan. I am weapon."

"Today," said Dragomir, "you're an angel. The world needs one."

"I am ... broken, Dragomir," said the Russian.

Dragomir leaned forward. "*She* needs one," he said.

The Russian was silent for a long time. The noise of the city beyond the walls came to them in muted tones, the blare of a horn turned into something softer, almost gentle. Dragomir waited, because he was used to time, and the passage of it, but also because this man was his friend, perhaps his only one, and they were planning to die, together. A little waiting wouldn't hurt. The Russian seemed to collect himself, pulling thoughts together as many people would sweep dust into a pan. "I am no angel," he said again. "But for her, I will try."

"We're going to save the world," said Dragomir.

"I do not think so," said the Russian. He tapped the photo of Adalia Kendrick. "I think she will save the world."

"Again, semantics," said Dragomir. "The plan is working. The Night is here. The vampires are all trying to find them. I've ... given a nudge. To an old friend of theirs. Sam Barnes. Head of Biomne."

"I know Biomne," said the Russian. "They tried to capture the Night." He laughed. "Was where it all started."

"Everyone knows Biomne," said Dragomir. "What everyone *doesn't* know is that we've got Sam's kid. That's providing a certain level of pressure on the man. He's already been in contact with the Night. They're going to meet him. Tomorrow."

"I will be there," said the Russian.

"No you won't," said Dragomir. "You will be finding Adalia Kendrick."

"They are not ready to fight *vampiry*," said the Russian. "They will need—"

"They'll be fine," said Dragomir. "The second thing I've done is, hell, where is..." He rifled through the papers again, pulling out Major Pearce's dossier. "Here we go. Jessie, here," and he tapped the papers, "has been sniffing around, trying to find us. So I've let it slip that there's a young vampire they can capture. What they do with him is ... up to them."

"You, the great Dragomir Balan, are leaving something to chance?" The Russian's eyes were wide with astonishment. "Tell me is not so."

"Sometimes," said Dragomir, "you gotta roll the dice. Also," and here, he fished out the Knight's dossier, holding up the photo of Valentine Everard, "this man. Given a choice, what do you think he will do?"

The Russian looked at the photo for a long time. "I think he will die," he said, but there was no satisfaction in it.

"I think you might be right," said Dragomir. "But I think he might die *for* something. And that's all we need."

CHAPTER
ONE

"What the hell is this?" Carlisle leaned on the pitted wood of the bar with an elbow, holding up the glass with her other hand. "There some kind of world shortage of gin?"

"You're working," said Danny, draining her third beer.

"I don't want to be tense when I'm working," said Carlisle, frowning into her glass. "Is there any alcohol in here at all?"

"It's what a single shot tastes like," said Danny.

"Doesn't taste like much," said Carlisle. "I don't think there's any risk of this becoming a habit."

Danny spared her a sideways glance. "You told me to make sure you didn't have too many before—"

"Hell," said Carlisle, "I remember what I said. I didn't mean I wanted to drink water." She brushed off some of the rain that lingered on the dark leather of her jacket, then flicked her hand to dry it. "There's enough of that outside."

"Relax," said Danny, starting on another beer.

Carlisle gave her a hard stare. "That's what the gin is *for*."

"I've been here for an hour," said Danny. "You don't know what waiting even means. Besides, he's not late. Yet."

You're nervous, Carlisle. You get cranky when you're nervous. "I hate waiting."

Danny shrugged, leaning back against the bar. She tugged on Carlisle's sleeve. "Here's number seven."

"Seven what?" said Carlisle, watching as a man walked towards them. Confident swagger, like his balls were so big he couldn't easily get his legs together. Carlisle wanted to punch him in the face almost immediately. She took a drink from her gin instead.

"Evening, ladies," said the man, the confidence in his walk making it to the smile on his face. "Can I—"

"Fuck off," suggested Carlisle.

The man's smile flickered slightly. Carlisle could almost see the thoughts going through his head. It'd be something like, *hey, this is unexpected*, or *maybe my fly is undone* or *these bitches are lesbians*. He rallied though, the smile coming back on in full force. "Well, it's a bit early, but—"

"Hey," said Danny. "You look like you're from out of town." She held out a folded pamphlet to the man.

"What's this?" he said.

"It's a map," said Danny, unfolding it. She pointed to a section near Times Square, circled in fat red pen. "See this point here?"

The man was still smiling, nodding along with it now. "Yeah. Yeah, I see it."

"I'd like you to go there," said Danny.

"To meet you?" said the man, his smile coming on brighter. Carlisle could almost smell the optimism pouring off him.

"No," said Danny. "I just want you to go there. Fuck off."

The man's smile snapped out like a candle flame in a hurricane, and he turned on his heel and stalked off.

Carlisle watched him go, then took another sip of her gin. "You had six more like that?"

"Not exactly like that," said Danny. "But similar. I'm running out of maps."

She still looks thirty, thought Carlisle. *Or twenty-five in good light.* "Let's hope Sam gets here before you bruise every ego in Manhattan."

The door at the front of the bar opened, a man ushered in by both the huge doorman — *is he technically a bouncer if he's big enough to block out the sun?* — and the rain in equal measure. Carlisle recognized the man immediately. He was a little older, a little thinner, but still the same Sam. Two men followed him in, both pretty big pieces of machinery, which made Carlisle frown a little. Even when Elsie Morgan was heading Biomne, she didn't have hired muscle following her around. Their jackets didn't fit quite right — *probably packing a little heat in a shoulder holster* — but the tailoring was otherwise immaculate. *Top shelf* pieces of machinery, then.

"I don't like those guys with him," said Danny.

"You don't have to like them," said Carlisle. "Remember, the last time he saw us his company's super-important secret base had been burned right down to the foundations. By us. It'll make him feel a little more relaxed."

"Maybe he should have a gin too," said Danny.

Sam saw them, inclining his chin and starting to make his way through the room. It was early, the night outside still fresh and new, but the bar was still filling up. When Sam made it to them, he held out a hand. "Detective."

Carlisle winced. "It's just Carlisle," she said. She shook his hand.

"I know," said Sam Barnes. "But you are what you are." She could feel something in his grip, a little like a cross between desperation and hope. Carlisle heard the catch in his voice.

She smiled, letting his hand go. "Truth," said Carlisle. *This man was in your corner when no one else was.* She — *they* — needed to find out if he was able to be saved, or if he was lost. "You remember Kendrick? Uh, I mean, Danny?"

"Ms. Kendrick," said Sam, shaking her hand in turn. He frowned. "Where is Mr. Everard?"

"You know," said Carlisle. "Important wolf stuff. You want a drink? Only, don't let her," and she jerked her head at Danny, "order for you. You'll get a glass of water with ice in it."

Sam didn't do the usual *allow me* or *I'll get one of my lackeys to get it*. He just nodded, and gave a small smile. "I'd like that."

They found a table — its availability helped along by the presence of Hulk and Gigantor — drinks arriving straight away. The table was round and small, tucked along the back wall of the bar. Hulk and Gigantor — whose names turned out to be Ben and Ernesto — turned their backs to them, watching the crowd. Giving them some space. Or, if you were the paranoid type, making sure no one heard something that would need to be ... cleaned up.

"Excuse the presence of Ben and Ernesto," said Sam. "They're not for you."

Danny's eyes flicked between the muscle and Sam, the muscle and Sam. "They're not?"

"Ms. Kendrick," said Sam, "last time we saw each other, you jumped out of a research building many floors up. A fall that would certainly kill a normal ... *person*. At the time, you were ... a little larger, if memory serves. I very much doubt that either Ben or Ernesto would be much use against you."

"Then what are they for?" Danny leaned closer. "*Who* are they for?"

Sam's eyes, nothing involuntary in the look at all, moved to Ben, then to Ernesto, and finally back to Danny. He sighed. "I'm sorry. This was a mistake. I shouldn't have agreed to come."

"Then why did you?" Danny leaned forward an inch, maybe two. "Sam, we've been hunting something—"

"How is Charlie?" said Carlisle.

Sam's eyes narrowed. "What did you say?"

"Charlie. Your kid." Carlisle played with the straw the fool bartender had put in her gin, then tossed it on the table. It was blue plastic, in her experience useless for stirring and drinking both. "He's got to be ten years old."

"Eight," said Sam, who looked like he wanted to say something. The man swallowed, then said, "He's fine. Detective? Why did you come?"

"You were in town. We were in town. Seemed a good reason to catch up — on old times," said Carlisle. "Remember that time when we all went out and played pool for hours?"

About fifty emotions went across Sam's face, then he nodded. "Yes," he said. "I remember. Pool. Except I didn't know the rules — I'd never played. Still don't, really. Know the rules, that is."

Carlisle pushed her glass away. "I can teach you," she said. She looked at Danny. "We can teach you."

Danny said nothing. She knew they'd never played pool with Sam Barnes. She started making slow circles on the table with her beer bottle, the knurled bottom making a grinding sound against the wood.

"I don't think ... I don't think I can play anymore, Detective." Sam shrugged, then stood. "Well, it's been a pleasure."

"Sure it has," said Carlisle.

Sam looked to Danny, looked to her like he wanted to shake her hand or hug her or run away or all three. "Ms. Kendrick."

"Sam?" said Danny. Her voice was soft. "Sam, you take care of yourself, okay?"

He gave a harsh laugh, something nasty in it. "That's all I do these days." He shuffled towards the back, Ben and Ernesto flanking him.

"That was weird," said Danny, after a moment.

"Not really," said Carlisle. She lifted up Sam's glass, the whiskey hardly touched. She flicked aside the coaster, finding the paper she'd seen him slip under it. Creased, worn like it had been folded and refolded many times.

"What's that?" Danny picked the paper up, unfolding it with

care. She smoothed it out on the table between them. The text on it was to the point.

Know that we have your son Charles. Know that he will come to no harm if you do as we say. We are keeping him safe, and safe he will remain as long as you do as we ask. If you speak to law enforcement, he will die. If you talk to this world's media, he will die. If you seek help of any kind, he will die.

We are not without gratitude. Do as we ask, and you both shall know wealth and power everlasting. This will be handed to Charles on his twen-tieth birthday. Until then, he shall remain our ward, learning our ways. He will be your successor in all things. What you sow, he will reap.

Carlisle's eyes met Danny's over the table top. "You know what this means?"

Danny's lips pulled back from her teeth, baring them in what was definitely not a smile. "We've found them."

"I'm glad," said Carlisle, "because otherwise I'd have felt bad about what was about to happen to Ben and Ernesto."

"I know, right?" Danny frowned. "Still. I'm surprised at how easy this has been."

"It's not been easy," said Carlisle. "We had to get that clown Miles a job, remember? Interviews, dressing nice, trying not to talk. It was tough."

Danny smiled at her. "Right. Well." She stood up, smoothing the front of her jacket. "Time to get to work." Her eyes had found a reedy man towards the front of the bar. Danny nodded at him. "That one, I think."

"How can you tell?" Carlisle adjusted the back of her jacket, feeling the comforting weight of the Eagle at her spine. The sidearm still had her back. It always had her back.

"He's looking for someone," said Danny. "Like, really looking. And he's ... unhealthy. I don't know. It's been a long, long time. And ... Melissa? It wasn't even me. I don't know if I'm remembering this right."

Carlisle looked over at the man. Danny was right, the man *was* unhealthy. If she'd seen him elsewhere, she'd have thought he was in dire need of a burger and fries, probably supersize, washed down with a jumbo fat Coke, no ice. The guy was thin, like he didn't make eating a habit. His complexion was washed out, leaving him pale, reedy. What really got her humming was the look in his eyes, a kind of fanaticism she hadn't seen except that one time she'd had to face down a guy with a bomb strapped to his chest, another to a little kid he'd held in front of him like a shield.

That had been a bad day.

The reedy man saw them. Or really, if Carlisle was being honest, he saw Danny. Completely ignored Carlisle, eyes skipping right over the top of her like she was just a piece of furniture. Carlisle could almost see the wheels moving in the guy's head as he sized up Danny, whether to come on over and start some shit or walk the fuck away. If she was being honest with herself, Carlisle was hoping for *walk the fuck away*. Danny and Everard had talked about what these freaks were, what they could do.

If Carlisle hadn't been on the ride with them so long, she'd have called them crazy. She swallowed, looked up at Danny, and said, "I think you're remembering it right. Go kick his ass."

Danny rolled her shoulders and strode forward. The reedy man took one look at her and made a break for the door at the front of the bar. Which was more or less expected. They'd prepared a contingency for that.

The reedy man didn't run, more like he flowed around people. They'd look away, or lean forward, or spill their drink, or a dozen other things at just the right time to let him move right towards the bar's main door. Right towards Valentine Everard.

As far as contingencies go, he wasn't a bad one to have. Everard was brushing the water from his coat. The reedy man looked around him, back towards the rear exit where Carlisle and Danny were, then to the front, blocked by Everard. *Caught.*

He bared teeth at them, teeth that were just too damn long, then grabbed a passing waitress. She had a moment to say something —

it might have been *hey* or *watch it, asshole* — before the reedy man sank those teeth into the flesh at her neck. There was a bright spray of red as he sucked at the waitress, the life leaving her like water down a drain. Just like that, she was gone. Color bloomed in the reedy man's face, a flush of power as the waitress's blood gave him vigor.

The screams hit like a wave, people panicking as they surged away from the reedy man. Bouncing off walls, off each other, surging for any exit. Carlisle watched as they streamed around Everard, not moving him at all — he was like a rock.

"*Come*," said the reedy man, hard voice carrying as he turned to Everard. "*Come and die.*"

CHAPTER
TWO

When Sam Barnes hit the alley behind the bar, he was moving at a jog. Ben had a hand — *large, meaty, controlling* — on his arm. Ben's other hand was on Sam's shoulder, steering him like he was a supermarket cart. Ernesto was up front, leading like a snowplow. He shoved aside anything that got in their way: people, doors, furniture. It made the short trip outside feel like a couple of rounds in a bumper car.

The speed of their journey wasn't the surprising part. Sam had been herded by these guys, or others like them, before. What was surprising was how quickly they stopped.

The alley was dark, and the rain made it even harder to see. It took Sam's eyes a moment to adjust to the light cast by the single naked bulb above the exit. There were two people waiting in the alley, standing next to Sam's black limo like they owned it. Of his driver there was no sign, just the limo, engine on, idling with the quiet grumble that came with owning a Maybach. The doors were shut, windows tinted for privacy, and Sam wished, oh how he *wished* he was safely inside that, a few blocks or miles or cities between himself and what was probably going on in the bar behind him.

"Move." It was Ernesto, of course. The man wasn't eloquent; no matter how hard Sam tried, the man never opened up. Frugal with English, like it was a precious resource that could run out if you over-used it.

"Son," said one of the people waiting in the alley, squaring up against Ernesto. "Son, it's not going to be that kind of day for you."

Sam's eyes were adjusting, feeding him the details. The two people were as different as chalk and cheese. The one who'd just spoken was an older man, maybe complaining about his upcoming sixtieth birthday, but with shoulders and arms that spoke of the ability to tear coins in half. The other was a woman, a compact slenderness that came with being a gymnast. He was wearing comfortable clothes, an inexpensive jacket and slacks that came off the rack at Gap. She was wearing fatigues, but good ones like she'd found Bergdorf's army surplus outlet. A cap sat on her head, her hair pulled into an efficient ponytail out the back.

The screaming hit Sam then, the noise coming from the bar behind them. He closed his eyes, swallowed once, and then opened them again. "Would you please move? We have to go."

"You'll go all right," said the older man, a kind of certainty in his voice that you felt when holding a rock. "But not with these guys."

Ernesto laughed. "Little man," he said, slapping a fist the size of a ham into the palm of the other. "I will bust you open like a piñata."

"Sure," said the older man again, "that's one way. The other way is we all take a nice ride in this car together. Sounds like something bad is happening behind you, and I think we'd all like to miss what's going on in there."

Ernesto had passed his two-word, or two-sentence, or whatever-it-was rule. He stepped forward, reaching for the older man. The woman, who hadn't moved a micron until this moment, stepped in, all efficient moves and hard angles. Her hand shot out, grabbed Ernesto's wrist, and twisted. Ernesto's entire frame spun through the air around the pivot of his wrist, and he hit the ground like a dropped safe. He didn't even groan; he was out cold.

"Hey," said the older man. "I had that."

"You talk too much," said the woman.

Sam saw that Ben's mouth was open, his eyes moving between Ernesto on the ground and the man and woman arguing in front of them. Ben let go of Sam, reaching into his jacket for the weapon he carried.

It would take less than a second for the weapon to clear the holster. Sam had counted off the *one Mississippi* in his head before, never making *two Mississippi*. Before the gun saw the dim light of the alley, the older man was in front of him, hand on Ben's elbow, other hand companionably inside his jacket.

"Son," said the man, "let's not do something we'd both regret."

Sam watched as Ben struggled to pull his arm free, muscles straining against the fabric of his jacket.

"Son," said the man again, this time through clenched teeth, "what we have here is a failure to communicate. I'm real sorry about this." And with that, he brought his knee up into Ben's groin. As Ben grunted, falling forward, the old man slammed his forehead into the bridge of Ben's nose. There was a crunch, and Ben went down.

Sam looked between the two of them. "I don't carry much cash," he said. He knew it was a dumb thing to say, but his lips were working without his brain in any kind of control. "I mean. Money."

"In the car, Barnes," said the woman.

"What Jessie means," said the man, "is that we'd take it as a personal favor if we could escort you out of here." He nodded towards the bar, the screams having faded away. "I don't think anything good is happening in there. Do you? Besides. We've got an old friend you need to meet."

This is … this is actually surreal. Sam looked between the two of them, then at the limo. He closed his mouth before speaking — hadn't even realized it was hanging open. "An old friend?"

"Sure," said the man. "Now get in the car, like the lady asked."

The woman — Jessie — was holding one of the doors open. He walked over, feeling like this was some kind of dream, and slid into the black leather comfort of the Maybach. Jessie swung herself in beside him, pulling the door closed as the older man got in the driver's seat up front.

"Hello, Sam," said a new voice. Sam's eyes adjusted — tonight's theme was poor lighting — and he saw a young woman, green hair, lip piercing. "It's so good to see you again."

"Hi," said Sam. "I don't mean to be rude, but it's been a rough night. Who are you?"

The wall near the exit to the bar exploded in a shower of bricks, Danny Kendrick flying through. She bounced off the outside of the Maybach, the car rocking with the force of it. Sam caught sight of her yellow eyes through the tinted windows, heard her yell at them in a voice no human throat should have made. "*GET. MOVING.*" And then she ran back inside.

Sam swallowed, looked at the girl with green hair, then back out the window of the Maybach. "Was she ... was she grinning?"

Jessie slapped the glass between her and the older guy. "Rex? It's time to go."

The older man — Rex — had that very same thought, at the very same time. The Maybach was roaring, peeling out of the alley in a wreath of tire smoke.

Sam's heart was pounding, and he kept looking out the back window for pursuit. They had a few moments. *But they'll be coming. They always come.*

"It's okay," said the young woman. "They'll be busy for a while. My Mom's on it. And Val."

Sam blinked. "Adalia?"

Adalia smiled at him. "Yes, Sam Barnes. And I would like to make a trade."

~

"No trades," said Sam. "No ... do you realize what you've done?" And then he sat in silence, his fist held clenched at his mouth, knuckles white.

The Maybach moved through the city — after the initial frenzied escape — quiet and smooth as any limo should. The car only started to look out of place as they hit the Bronx, the gentrification of the city giving way to decaying buildings, brownstones more black and gray than anything else. Sam hadn't been up this way since he was a kid. It hadn't improved with time. It was always people's eyes that had stayed with him. They stared out from faces lacking hope as the luxury of the car slipped past them in the lightening predawn.

He cleared his throat. "Why are we here?"

Adalia had been watching him. "It's safe," she said.

He barked a short laugh. "Not for me. I come down here dressed the way I am, in this car, I take one step outside and I'm rolled for my wallet, watch, and probably shoes as well."

"Oh," said Adalia, "that. That's not what I'm talking about." She turned away from him to look out the window. Sam noticed that Jessie sat close to the younger woman, some part of her attention never far from Adalia.

Sam rolled her words over in his head for a while. "What are you talking about?"

"Them," she said. "You know. The ones who have Charlie." She said it like she knew Charlie, not *Charles* or *your son* or *you remember that kid you had*, just a simple *Charlie*. Like, like, hell, like she'd sat down and played Lego with him, building a starship or race car or one of the other six impossible things Charlie could imagine up before breakfast on any given morning.

He leaned forward, and almost in sync Jessie leaned forward too. She eyeballed him. "Watch it there, chief."

Adalia placed a hand on Jessie's arm. "It's okay, Jessica. He's just scared."

"That's what I'm worried about," said Jessie. "Scared men do stupid things." She raised her voice. "Isn't that right, Rex?"

"Don't pull me into this," said Rex, from the front. "Don't—"

"Have you seen him?" said Sam. He knew the words tumbled out of him in a rush like he was four years old, but he could feel the desperation in him, a kind of bubble that was almost ready to pop. "Have you talked to him?"

Adalia watched him for a few moments. "Not in the way you mean," she said.

Sam could taste the bitterness of his words. "Then you've doomed him," he said. "He's going to die. You've got to let me go. You've got to let me..." He ran down then, feeling the futility of it. He was trapped here in this car with these *psychos* and because of them, his little Charlie was going to be killed.

She crooked an eyebrow at him, then turned her head towards Rex. "Stop the car."

"Say what?" said Rex. "We're almost—"

"Stop the car," She said again. The Maybach's speed dropped to zero, halting at the side of the road. Crumbling buildings watched from either side, the lighting giving them faces of judgment. Adalia looked at Sam, then opened the door for him. "Go."

Sam looked out the open door, then at Adalia. "What?"

"Go. You're not our prisoner."

"I'm ... what?" Of *course* he was their prisoner. They'd taken him from Ben and Ernesto, and bundled him up in his car, and...

Wait.

"I'm not your prisoner," he said.

"That's right," said Adalia.

"This is my car," he said.

"Right again." She was nodding at him, encouraging.

"You ... took away my jailers." Sam thought about Ben and Ernesto, and the others before them, the stone-faced men who'd filed through his life. Watching what he did, what he said, where he went, hell, even what he wrote in his corporate emails.

"Sam Barnes," said Adalia, her voice harder than a human's should be. "Sam Barnes, hear me. You can take the door. The easy route, the soft step away from this car and back into the world you know. You will wear the comfortable shackles of your hidden prison. You will see your Charlie again. But he will never be as you remember him. He won't laugh and smile and run in the sun, because his soul will be lost. Or you can stay here, in this car. You can hear what we have to say. You can try to fight with everything you have. You will lose your kingdom. You will change the world. You will save your Charlie's soul. Now choose."

There was a stillness in the car, like the world was waiting. Sam looked at Jessie, saw her hard eyes, but something in them that might have been pity. Saw the back of Rex's head, the man waiting for his answer, hands easy on the wheel. Turned his head back to Adalia, saw her outstretched hand still held towards the door. "Will he die?"

Adalia closed her eyes for a moment, tilting her head to the side. Her brow furrowed in concentration before she opened her eyes again, looking at him. *Through* him. "Hard to say. It's not clear."

"So you're telling me," said Sam, "that if I stay here in this car, Charlie might die."

Jessie leaned forward in her seat, grabbing a fistful of Sam's shirt, tie, and jacket. She hauled him forward, so close that he could smell her, sweat and leather and cordite. "She's saying, asshole, that Charlie is *gone*. He's lost. You step out this car, and he'll never be *your* Charlie again. He'll be *theirs*. You stay here, you stay with us, and there's a chance you can hold your son again. Your living, breathing son. She's giving you a chance, you dumb sonofabitch, to save the one thing that—"

Jessie was cut short, Adalia's hand on her shoulder. Sam could see the muscles in Jessie's jaw working, but it was Adalia who spoke. "It's okay, Jessica. He needs to choose. *He* needs to *choose*."

Sam fell back into his seat as Jessie let him go. He smoothed the front of his jacket. "You're crazy," he said. "You're all crazy." He started to get out of the car, even had one hand on the sill of the door when Jessie spoke again.

"His name was Gabriel, and I chose wrong." Sam heard the pain in her words, and that held him still for a moment. "He was the most perfect thing in this world. Your Charlie still has a chance. If you walk away from here, he's lost to you forever."

Sam looked out at the street, the soft pink of dawn starting to lean into the orange of real sunlight. He thought about Charlie, about how that kid of his loved to laugh. How he hadn't heard that sound for a long time now. His fingers clenched around the door frame, and he looked back at Adalia. "He might die."

Adalia nodded. "He might." She shrugged. "He might live, too. Actually, if my mom's involved, he's got a better chance of living than dying. But I can't be sure."

"You're not making this easy."

"It's not about making it easy," she said. "It's about making it right."

Sam Barnes looked at her for another moment, then let go of the Maybach's door frame. The door closed with a *clunk*, and he let out a breath he hadn't known he was holding. "Tell me everything," he said.

The Maybach slipped away from the curb, purring into the quiet dawn of a new day.

CHAPTER
THREE

Liselle picked her way through the street, glass crunching under the red soles of her Louboutins. She'd mastered the stiletto heels, walked with an almost magical ability that meant even here, in this shattered New York city street, she never put a foot wrong.

She took in the scene as she walked. There, a car overturned, all windows shattered, the roof flattened down. Her fingers traced along brickwork pocked with bullet holes, some of the dry dust and mortar wisping out, hungry for her touch. A utility pole was snapped at the base, debris strewn out along a line that led to fragments of the pole itself. She looked at the line drawn by the debris, traced the point of origin back to the bar.

There wasn't much left of the front of it, just some crumpled metal and fragments of wood that might have been tables, and could just as easily have been chairs. No people alive, a few bodies lying in their final release, some eyes staring, some closed. It was always the way: the dead forgot all their pride and purpose. The empty vessels of humans would drown the world before the end.

She shook herself. *Not yet. That's why you're here.*

Her feet *crunched* over more glass as she stepped inside. There were, a miracle in and of itself, still lights on. Another miracle: a man was here, working the bar. Or trying to work, without any customers — moving a cloth across the surface, cleaning away shattered bottles and spilled liquor. She took in the concave shape of a wall where something — something large — had been thrown with great force. Liselle stepped across the body of a woman who'd been taken, the blood gone from her body. Her name had been Candice Marshal. Her daughter, Susan, was not yet awake as the city stumbled from dawn into day. Candice's mother, Theresa, named after Theresa of Avila, waited for her daughter to come home from working the late shift. Candice Marshal would never come home again.

"We're closed," said the man behind the bar.

Liselle looked at him, took in the broad shoulders, a face that looked like it loved to smile, but perhaps under better circumstances. She gestured to the broken frontage. "The door was open."

"Yeah," said the man, "about that. Look, and I don't want to be the asshole here, but I just need to say that tonight's been one of those nights. You know the ones, where there's people dying everywhere, guns firing, I mean for Christ's sake, it was intense."

"You're still here," she said, sliding into a stool across from him, the faux fur of her coat making no noise. "It sounds like a night to remember."

"Sure," he said. "Sure. Look, since you're still here, do you need a drink?"

"Do you have Midas Touch?" Liselle looked at the shattered glass from broken bottles strewn across the room. "I guess you might be low on stock."

"Dogfish Head?" The man turned behind him, freeing a bottle with a distinctive blue label. He looked around for a while before saying, "Do you need a glass? Because that might be a little tricky."

"It comes in a glass," said Liselle. She took the bottle from him, took a pull, her eyes closing as she savored the flavor. "That's good," she said.

"Sure," said the man, again. "It's not really my thing. Beer's a beer, wine's a wine, and that thing is—"

"Something in between," she said. "I know. I remember. They're wrong, though."

"Say what?" The man blinked at her.

"It wasn't Midas's tomb," she said. "It was Gordius's." She closed her eyes. "He was a gentle man, for his day." She took another sip. "This tastes of a better time."

"It tastes like ass," said the man, "but each to their own."

She laughed. "You don't … you're not worried about what happened here tonight?"

"It's my job," said the man. "People come in, I pour them drinks. I don't really get worried about that."

She blinked at him, then laughed again. "And … the other events from this evening?"

"Oh," he said, "you mean when everyone started running and screaming. I'll admit, it's cut down on the number of tips I got. But I'm waiting."

"Oh," she said, looking at him over the top of her bottle. "Waiting. For what?"

"Well," he said, "I'm no expert, but I'd have expected the police to turn up at some point. So those guys, for a start."

"They won't be coming," said Liselle. "Not today. Not for this."

"Yeah," said the man, "I figured."

"You did?" She was momentarily surprised, realized the feeling had been creeping up on her during the conversation until it collected into this moment. The barman, this *man*, had a drink that hadn't been common for over two thousand years. This *man* was relaxed in the face of what had happened, and more: he was alive. "Tell me your name."

"Well," said the man, "normally that's not how you ask someone out."

Liselle almost snorted her drink through her nose. She picked up the small paper napkin to dab at her lips, and perhaps to hide her smile. "I ... I wasn't."

"No, it's cool," said the man. "Women of today, you got to lead the conversation. I get it." He made a fist and pumped the air. "Girl power, right?"

"I'm ... did you just call me a *girl*?" Liselle wanted to be offended, but that wouldn't have felt right. There was a light inside this man, something she caught a glimpse of out of the corner of her eye. She could see it through his skin, and she hadn't ever seen anything like that. The color of his soul, perhaps, although she'd never seen its like in a million other humans.

"Hey, I don't judge," said the man. "You don't roll with the gender binary, we can work with that too."

"I ... what?"

"Another?" said the man.

"What?" she said again, feeling a little out of place. After all this time, someone made her feel unsteady, *unlinked*, and it was delicious.

"Your drink," said the man. "You're empty. And that impresses me, because you couldn't pay me to drink it and you just sucked it back like you were siphoning gas."

Liselle looked at her empty bottle. "I could do another."

Another bottle appeared on the bar. The man put aside his cloth. "Your accent. It's neat, but I can't place it."

"That's..." Liselle felt the grin on her face, and she didn't want to stop it this time. "That's not how you ask a girl out."

He laughed, and there it was, that wonderful smile. Like his face was born to hold it. "I ... I don't know. Was I?"

"You were," she said.

"Right," he said, and then looked at his hands. "I'm a bit out of practice." He turned around, rummaging through the stocks behind him, and pulled out a beer of his own. It was a Peroni, a beer she judged good by the standards of today. "I think we should do the name thing."

"The name thing?"

"You tried. Before," he said, making a gesture with his bottle that might have meant a moment ago, or might have tried to encompass the world. "You did it wrong, remember?"

"So I did," she said. "I'm waiting for someone."

"Ah," he said. "Who?" Not *he must be a lucky guy* or *what the hell have we been doing for the last ten minutes,* just *who.*

She was going to answer when the sound of the motorcycle rolled through the open front of the bar. Loud, he was always loud. *Josef.* He was riding something with a Harley Davidson label on the side of the engine. They both turned to the front of the bar as Josef kicked the stand of his Harley down, leaning the bike over with a practiced air, and started a slow, confident walk through the open front towards them. His short boots — crocodile skin, unless she missed her guess — crunched over broken glass. Josef was wearing a sleeveless vest, the muscles on his arms a thing to catch the eye. The vest was open at the front, no shirt, showcasing a lean physique. *Hard* was what Liselle thought whenever she saw him. *Hard,* and maybe *hungry* too.

"Him," said Liselle.

The barman looked Josef over, a practiced eye used to gauging the competition. "You could do better."

She wanted to laugh, tried to stop herself, then let it out anyway. She covered her mouth with a hand. "It's ... it's not like that."

The barman nodded. "Sure," he said. "Sure."

Josef walked up to them, looked at her, then at the barman. "Who's this?"

"We hadn't got that far," said the barman. "Two drinks in, still don't know her name."

"No," said Josef, some of that *hard* and *hungry* coming into his voice. "You don't."

The barman winced. "That's cold. Interest you in something frosty to loosen up?"

"Beer," said Josef. "Something American."

"Miller it is," said the barman. He slid a bottle across to Josef. "I don't know how you can do that to yourself."

Josef eyeballed the barman for a moment. The barman looked back, nothing challenging in it, standing like a rock in the face of that stare. Josef turned to Liselle. "We've got work to do."

"You're late," she said. "I've been working already."

Josef looked at her, then at the barman, then back at her. "Really."

"Really," she said, letting some steel into her tone. "It happened. Here." Liselle tapped a finger against the top of the bar for emphasis.

Josef leaned back, and she could see some of the tension he'd been holding ease out. "There are no bodies." She knew he didn't mean the bodies of the humans. He meant the bodies of the Night.

"That's because ... they survived," said Liselle. "Josef, they're *alive*."

"You," said Josef to the barman. "What did you see here tonight?"

The barman stared at Josef for a minute, then turned slowly to Liselle. "You want to get out of here? Since, you know, 'it's not like that.'"

She felt the warmth hitting her cheeks — *I'm blushing, by the Father, I'm* blushing — and looked down at her beer. "I can't," she said, meaning, *I want to.*

"As a small ... what would you call it, incentive," said the barman, "I will tell you two things." He held up two fingers, as if there were an audience to keep count.

"Two?" she looked up, met his eyes.

"Liselle," said Josef, "we don't—"

"Yeah," said the barman. "First up, I'll tell you my name, and we'll do it right this time. Second, I'll tell you what happened here tonight. So Captain Action here—" and he jerked a thumb at Josef without looking at him "—can relax a little."

"Yes," said Liselle, knowing she should have said *no*.

"Great," said the barman. That smile came out again. "Let's start again, okay?"

"Okay," said Liselle. "I'm Liselle. Liselle Vitols." She held out a hand.

The barman looked at her hand, then reached out his own. She felt the warmth of his skin in her palm as they shook, the easy strength of his hand, and felt that thrill of the brightness inside him as their skin touched. "John," he said. "I'm John Miles."

CHAPTER
FOUR

Val crouched by the edge of a dumpster, a big old worn piece of metal. The smell coming from it was exceptional, which bothered him for more reasons than the obvious. It was probably easier to hide in an alley filled with a ... magnificent, horrendous *stench* when you didn't have such a great sense of smell. That was the thing about these creatures, if Val's borrowed memories were right: they were strong, and fast, and could see in the dark like goddamn walking Starlight scopes, but their smell wasn't for shit, and their hearing wasn't much better either. Strong and fast, check, rest of senses, basically non-existent. It's what made it possible, in a set of particular circumstances, to sneak up on one. He was really, really counting on that set of memories being right. Otherwise, tonight was going to go from bad to worse. Still, the setup had worked. It had made the creature go here, to this alley. This perfect, beautiful alley with such a horrible dumpster.

It hides from us.

The creature had run in here moments ago, Val hot on its heels. He felt the—

Paw and claw. Feet across the bare earth, mother moon above us.

—thrill of the chase, the hunt, but also fear. The last time he'd fought one of these ... well, it wasn't *him*, for a start. It was Volk, and Volk's memories were a scramble of inconsistencies wrapped up with a heavy dose of crazy. But if Volk's memories were to be believed—

I remember also.

—then a single one of these creatures was more than a match for him. Even if Val *changed*, it wouldn't be enough. They were that strong, that fast.

There was a small ace in the hole. Volk's problem, near as Val reckoned, was that the man had never worked in a team. Always going it alone, running from friends, running towards the dark. Val and Danny had talked long about what they'd do when they found one. The ultimate goal was to capture one, but that was several levels above base survival. A dead one would do just fine for a start. No one had pulled these things apart to find out if the insides were full of meat or cotton stuffing.

Tonight was a test.

They were going to pass. He knew. He knew it in his blood, could feel it in his hands, taste it in the air. He knew it because Danny—

Pack mate.

—ran at his side. His friends, his *family*, had his back. Time to pay back that trust.

Time to save the world.

There was no blood leading into the alley — these things wasted nothing, he'd watched this one suck that waitress dry like she was a cold beer on a hot day, not a drop left in the bottom of the glass. Val knew when he killed things, when the Night was free, there was always blood. Everywhere. But these things used blood like some kind of freaky battery, and they didn't need a napkin to avoid getting a stray drop on their clothes.

The odor of the dumpster meant he couldn't find the thing by smell, and the fuckers didn't have the common decency to have a heartbeat. Mark One Eyeball it was, then. Although, if he was being honest, it was more like a Mark Twelve Eyeball; the Night gave him all the edge he needed.

Look for what is absent. Look for what you cannot see.

He peered around the edge of the dumpster, the cold metal touching his face. Down the alley, doorways were staggered, alcoves allowing easy hiding. Easy, except for the lights, often just a naked bulb, that shone above them. One of the doorways stood dark, the bulb gone, leaving the alcove in shadow.

There.

Val flipped the lid of the dumpster open. Black plastic bags, a kid's tricycle, an old sewing machine ... he pushed items aside until his fingers found wood. He pulled it out, found himself holding a broken leg of a table. Val hefted it, felt its weight, touched his fingers to the splintered end.

Good enough.

"Hey," he said to the empty alley. It felt like all of the city was quiet around him, a hush that was as out of place in New York City as snow in Hawaii. "Come on out. You don't really have a lot of time, do you?" He cocked his head sideways, looking at the lightening sky. "I'd say you've got maybe a half hour to get into whatever hole you crawled out of before you're fresh out of options." He tapped the table leg against his pants. "We'd like to talk."

A soft chuckle, full of velvet, came to him from the shadowed doorway. "You want to kill me," said the creature, "or you want to die."

"Uh," said Val, "no. We really just want to talk. You were the one who wanted to start killing."

A shoulder came out of the gloom, leading the rest of the thing. *Christ, it just looks like a man. Nothing more.* Nondescript. Forgettable. Except for the way it walked, moving like his skin held a panther, not the sinews of a human.

This is no human.

"Is that," said the creature, gesturing with a hand at the table leg, "for talking?"

"Hell no," said Val. He held up the table leg. "It's for beating the stupid out of you. I call it, I dunno, sort of a backup plan."

"You think that piece of wood is going to slow me down?" Val could see the thing's teeth as it smiled across the alley. Those teeth held promise.

Val spun the table leg in his hand. "No, I'm going to slow you down. This is more for dramatic effect."

There was a shrug from the thing, then, "What questions?"

"What are you?" Val didn't take his eyes off it. "Where do you come from?"

"We're the darkness," it said, "that lives in your soul. We come from your fear."

Val frowned. "Fuck *right* off," he said, "with that mumbo-jumbo. I've had enough of that shit. Five years ago? We had to deal with this ass clown Talin. He spoke like that. Got real boring, real fast."

The creature blinked at him. "What?"

"Okay," said Val, "let's try a different tack. Why are you here?"

"To end the world," it said.

"Figures," said Val. "That problem seems a little bigger than you."

"We are many."

Val *tsked*. "You know that's not true. You're a few. If you were many, you'd have sucked this city dry. You can't stop eating, can you?"

The thing stepped out of the doorway fully, it's fingers curled into half fists, like it wanted something to rend. "You know what it's like to be hungry."

"Yeah," said Val, "but I don't know what it's like to be so damn stupid."

"You talk large for such a small ... *dog*," it said.

"Oh hell no," said Val, with a laugh. "I'm only talking like this so she could get behind you."

"What?" said the thing, a fraction of a second before Danny slammed her fist into its back. The force of the punch sent her fist right through it, her bloody hand coming out its chest. She ripped her hand back, a spray of blood spattering the ground accompanied by the sound of fat rain. Danny held up her prize, a piece of spine covered in clots of meat. Her eyes were a bright, bright yellow, her lips pulled back from her teeth in something that was half snarl, half raw joy. *The end of the hunt.* Val could feel it too as the thing dropped to the alley floor like a puppet with its strings cut.

It worked. The goddamn plan had *worked*. He almost whooped, the high of being *alive* making his nerves hum.

Val knew they didn't have a lot of time. Not just because of the dawn, but because the wound was already healing. The thing on the ground was keening, the pain must have been incredible, but the bleeding was slowing. He leaned down over it. "You killed five people on your way here."

"Yes." It looked at him with red eyes. "They are fuel."

"They're *people*," said Val. He tapped the table leg against the alley floor. "And you're an experiment."

Danny sniffed the air. "We need to hustle." She wiped her bloody hand against her jeans, then pulled out her phone. She walked away, dialing.

"Experiment?" The thing looked at Danny's receding back, then at Val. "You will all *die*."

"Hah," said Val. "You tried that before, didn't you? Thought you'd knocked us all off. Thought—"

"We wiped the face of the Earth of your wretched kind," it said. "You are nothing."

"Still here," said Val, pointing a thumb at his chest. "I'd say that's more than nothing." He looked up at Danny. "We good?"

"She's coming," said Danny, waving a hand at the creature. "Do the thing."

"What thing?" said the creature beneath Val. The wound was almost closed, but its skin was sallow. It would need to feed, he could see it in the thing's face. The way its nostrils flared as it scented him. *Him.* As if—

35

We are not for hunting. We are not prey.

"Right," said Val, raising the table leg. He gripped it in both hands, then drove it through the creature's chest. Through its heart. It screamed, veins along its neck, veins in its *face* bulging out. The scream felt loud enough to bring the very heavens down. Then ... it died. Something just switched off inside it, the life force within gone. The body fell back to the alley floor, head bouncing once against the cold concrete. In death, the thing's face was still, almost peaceful. Its teeth, those too-long teeth, receded back into its jaws. It could now be just about any other guy.

Any other *dead* guy.

A car pulled into the mouth of the alley, lights bright. Val held a hand up in front of his face, wincing. The driver's door opened, Carlisle stepping out. She walked over to them, shoulders relaxing as she saw them both. "Christ," she said. "I almost worried." She held up a black plastic bag. "Let's get this guy sealed in a blanket."

They smoothed out the body bag on the floor of the alley, big *CORONER* letters in white on the outside. Val had never thought, not in a million years, that he'd be stuffing a corpse into a sack in a New York City alley at five in the morning. But here he was. Never say never, right?

They lifted the body into the bag, Carlisle sealing the zip with practiced ease. She stood, then arched her back. "Ready?"

Danny nodded, and she and Carlisle each grabbed a side of the bag. Val smiled to himself. He knew that Danny had strength enough to Popeye cans of spinach — hell, they both did — but sometimes it was about letting other people help where they could. Letting them be useful. He loved that about her, the way she did it naturally. He had to work at it a little harder.

Pack for Pack.

The body folded into the trunk, Carlisle slipped back behind the wheel. She wound down the window, the whine of the electric motor audible over the idling engine. "See you guys back at the ranch?"

"Sure," said Danny. "We've got to ... you know."

"I know," said Carlisle. "Be safe."

"Always," said Val. He watched the car reverse out of the alley, Carlisle driving off into the thickening traffic.

"Just one," said Val. "That was just *one*." He wiped his face, smearing sweat and grime across his forehead with the back of his arm. "Man."

"I know, lover," said Danny, her fingers touching his ever so lightly. Her eyes had lost their yellow brightness, but her face still held something wild. "But we got one."

Val looked up at the fingers of the dawn as the light stroked the sky. "We got one." He gave an unsteady laugh. "We need to ... go back and check."

"Yes." She nodded, then reaching up a hand to stroke his face. "So we're safe."

So that Pack is safe.

"I..." Val slowed his thoughts. "I'm still having trouble processing this."

"Just say it," she said.

"I hate saying it," he said.

"Vampires," she said. "They're *vampires*. And now ... now, we've found them. We've drawn them out. We're hunting *them*."

He nodded, looking at the pool of blood on the ground. The dawn's light touched it at the side, and there was a flicker of flame as it charred. As the sun rose, even its weak early light was enough to erase the remains from the Earth. They turned around, together, to retrace their steps, leaving the flames of the burning blood behind them.

Vampires, here, in New York City. Still, nothing much surprised him these days.

CHAPTER
FIVE

"What we've got here," said Rex to the room at large, "is a basic failure of marketing." He held up his Pop-Tart as evidence. He hadn't looked away from the Pop-Tart when Val entered. "See?"

Val gave the room a quick look-over: Rex on the couch, Jessie across from him, limbs sprawled out every which way, head back, eyes closed. A nervous Sam Barnes had looked up as Val had kicked the door open, his face holding that half hopeful, half *I'm done* expression you see in cancer wards. A big TV perched at the edge of their ring of furniture, looking down like a judge. It looked like it was playing some CNN feed, but the volume was off. Adalia was away from them, huddled in a booth against the wall, twin snakes of white coming from the headphones under her green hair to the tablet she was using. The space felt like a diner that had bred with an Internet cafe, one where the designer had thought *industrial chic*.

"I see," said Val. "Hold that thought." He closed the door again, walking back outside to Carlisle's car. "Looks fine."

"Define 'fine,'" said Carlisle, stubbing a toe in the dirt.

"Rex is complaining," said Val.

"We're good to go," Carlisle said. She dug an elbow into Danny's ribs. "Try to at least look like you're working hard this time." She walked with Danny to the rear of the car, gave a quick scan of the street, then popped the trunk. They started to manhandle the body bag out.

Val turned back to the warehouse they were calling home. More than *calling*, it had been their base for a year or more. John had called it a *lair*, then a *den* after Carlisle had threatened to punch him in the face. Den was fine. Den meant home.

Pack.

Val closed the trunk after them, locked the car, then jog-stepped past them to hold the warehouse door open. The door was old, the surface pitted with rust, a few spots of lichen here and there, but under the surface it was strong. Carlisle and Danny shuffled through after him, and he let the door swing closed.

Smoke was seeping through the zip of the body bag, the dead vampire inside starting to fall apart. The depravations of time could only be kept at bay while they were — alive? half-alive? — and this one was all the way dead. Carlisle and Danny moved out through a door towards the rear of the big open space, back to where the garage was.

Garage. Well, it was something, that's for sure. A collection of ... resources. They'd been stockpiling for a while. Val remembering the conversation with a smile.

"The way you win a war is deodorant," said Jessie.

"I'm not sure I follow," said Rex. "I thought it was guns."

"Guns by themselves aren't that useful," said Jessie. "I mean, yes, you need them. But you need soldiers to hold them."

"With you up to that point." Rex had held up a hand, ticking things off on his fingers. "Guns, bullets, soldiers." He held up three fingers, then pointed to where his little finger remained curled. "Don't see where deodorant comes in."

"Well, it's more like what gives you deodorant," she'd said. "Supply lines. Resources. Run out of fuel, can't drive the car, right? When you're

out of deodorant, you've got a basic failure in supply. We're fighting a war, and we need to make sure we're well-resourced."

They had deodorant, and many other things besides. A few vehicles, weapons, a little money. Sam might be able to help with that last one.

"Hey," said a voice, pulling Val back to the here and now. Speak of the devil — *Sam*. "Uh."

"Hey, Sam," said Val, face splitting into a grin. "How you doing?" He crossed to the other man, grabbing his hand in a shake.

"Yeah," said Sam. "Uh."

"Right," said Val. "I figured it would be something like that. You got any specific questions, or do you want to just see where this conversation goes?"

"Uh," said Sam again, looking at his hands before clearing his throat. "You know, when I was a kid, we had stories. All kinds of stuff, knights, dragons, and yeah, vampires, and werewolves. When Elsie … When Miss Morgan had pulled that crazy Russian out of the ice, I thought it was just another one of her reclamation projects. But … but it's real. Werewolves. Vampires."

"Dragons are real." Danny's voice carried across the space, causing Sam to turn to face her. She'd come back in, Carlisle slipping into the room behind her. The door to the garage closed with a *clunk*. Danny looked at Val. "Knights, too."

"Uh," said Sam, then gave his head a small shake. "What?"

"Pretty much everything you know of this world, the constants you hold true, are a lie," said Rex. He held up the Pop-Tart, now half-eaten. "Like this."

Jessie didn't open her eyes. "What's wrong with your breakfast?"

"Well that's it, isn't it, right there," said Rex. "It's not a breakfast. It's not even really food. And yet, somehow, I can't stop eating this one."

"What's the flavor?" Jessie had started swinging a leg back and forth over the side of her chair.

"So," said Rex, "you know? I think it's root beer."

"Your problem," said Jessie, "isn't that everything's a lie." Her eyes still closed, she raised a finger. "It's that you make bad choices."

"Hey," said Rex, "that's—"

"A good segue," said Val, looking to Sam. "I'll bet this isn't how you figured your day was going to go."

"It doesn't matter," said Sam. "She," and here, he nodded in Adalia's direction, "said that you'd get my boy back. My Charlie. They've taken my company, Mr. Everard. Biomne. They took my son to make that happen."

"Yeah, they'll do that," said Val, rubbing his jaw. "For what it's worth, they pretty much do it to everything. Like a virus."

"Like a pestilence," said Adalia. She didn't look up, just kept typing. "I didn't say we'd get Charlie back. I said we'd save Charlie. His soul. I told him we'd make it right. I told him we'd tell him everything." She finally looked up, eyes holding Val's for a second. "Maybe you should tell him everything."

"Sure," said Val. "Sam, here's where it's at. The world used to be full of a bunch of cool stuff. Magic, and pixies, and fairy dust." He tapped the side of his head. "I remember."

"You ... remember?" Sam's face had that *I-think-you've-been-hit-in-the-head-once-too-often* look. "You grow up in a really weird part of the world?"

"Oh," said Val. "I haven't got to the best part. It's better if I show you." He closed his eyes for a second, reaching back. Far back, to a different self, a life that had gone before. He found—

The quiet of the crowd, the hush itself was a platform, a stage of a kind they had made that sat under the tired wood he stood on. They'd drawn his cart in here just as the rains were falling, asking for a scrap of shelter in exchange for a show. The mandolin sat on a chair at his side, strings waiting for the touch of his fingers. A story, that's what he'd give them. A story of a man who was attacked, the Night striding strong into his camp—

"You figure yourself a strong man, a man who leads a company," said Val. "You figure wrong. Don't really understand how it works in your head, now that's between you and God. What I do know is that you're a strong man because you want to stand here, right here, right now, for your boy. For your son. It's your family that makes you strong. Why," and here, he started to walk around Sam, his voice carrying, the pitch lowering, "it's that strength that makes you stand here while the piss wants to run down your legs, makes your legs weak, makes you want to run and cry and a hundred other things. Am I not wrong?"

"I—" Sam swallowed. "No. Yes."

"You, Sam," said Val, stepping close, a hand on his shoulder, "carry the faith of a father. It holds you up, makes you strong, gives you purpose. Fuck your company. You hear me?"

"I hear you," said Sam.

"Fuck *them*," said Val, leaning close. "Fuck those mother*fuckers*."

"Yeah," said Sam. "Fuck them!"

Val stumbled back, that past self stepping out of his head. The orator gone, he reached for another, one much closer. "*Vy nesete sud'bu vsekh lyudey*, Sam."

Sam blinked, took a step back. "I..."

Val shrugged. "I know, right?" He looked across at Danny. "How'd I do?"

"Gave me shivers," said Danny. She was near, silent steps bringing her close. "Sam, do you understand? We carry the memories of everyone taken into the Night before us. A long line stretching back through time. We carry their abilities. We can do what they do."

"So," said Sam, "you can remember?"

"That's what I said," said Val. "I get it, it's a lot to take in. But I need to tell you everything."

"Oh *shit*," said Adalia. "Shit, shit, shit." She crammed her tablet into a canvas messenger bag, the side of it rich with hand-drawn artwork. Her headphones got tangled, and she tugged them free. "*Shit*."

"What is it?" Danny took a step towards her daughter, then stopped. Val could see the internal dialog playing across her face, the

42

one where Adalia said *you don't have to protect me all the time* and Danny said something like *yeah I do*, and then they'd not speak for the next two days.

"I'm late for work." Adalia sighed, shoulders slumping. "Fucking *shit*balls. Not *again*."

"Oh," said Val, "I thought maybe vampires had come in and started eating your face. You know, because of how you were talking."

Adalia rolled her eyes at him. "Remember our talk about the value of hard work, and being a normal kid in a normal society? You gave it to me about," and here she counted off on her fingers, "I'd guess four years ago. Was it four?"

"Near enough," agreed Val.

"Well, I got a job," she said, "because of that. And my boss, because you know he's an asshole, this asshole says to me, 'Ady' — you know he calls me 'Ady?' right? — he says to me, 'Ady, I need you here on the till at opening. There's a hundred people who'll work for less and all of them own a watch.' He said that, to *me*." She patted her pockets, pulled out her phone and checked the time. "Shit!"

"Sounds to me," said Val, "like you're learning all the important lessons about normal society. You'd best get to work."

Adalia stormed out, her middle finger cranked high and pointed in Val's direction. The door slammed behind her, and he shrugged, turning back to Sam. "Where were we?"

Sam was looking between the door, to Val, to the door, to Val again. "You ... just let her go out?" He swallowed. "It's not just the vampires! They own people. Everywhere. They've got a PMC — not Ebonlake, this is a different private military company — on the payroll."

"Yeah, so about telling you everything. Adalia, she's a little special," said Val, then stopped, frowned, and looked around. "Where the fuck is John?" He pulled his phone from his pocket to check for missed texts. At least he hadn't smashed this one; he was going through about three phones a week. Jessie had tried to make him feel better about his three-phones-a-week-habit by telling him that ditching burners was good practice when operating in enemy territory.

One missed text. From John. *Hot chick*. Not, *I'm alive,* or *At the police station,* but *Hot chick*. Val rubbed one hand over his face.

"What is it?" said Danny.

"Ten to one," said Rex, "he's on a date."

"I'm not taking those odds," said Jessie. "More like one to one, he's on a date."

"Wait," said Sam. "Mr. Miles? He's still with you?"

"What do you mean by, 'with?'" said Danny.

"Do I need to go get him?" Carlisle was doing something in the kitchen area — stove, refrigerator, coffee machine tucked against the wall — that smelled like coffee. Val was going to have to fix that problem before it started; she made horrible coffee. He was sure it was something about every police academy everywhere: a stolid, base requirement to delete everything you ever knew about making coffee, replacing it with a love for too-strong instant shit. Maybe they put a chip in their brains? No wonder they all got ulcers.

"Stop," said Danny. "Stop making coffee. Val will do it." She looked at him. "Won't you, baby?"

"What's wrong with my coffee?" said Carlisle.

"Everything," said Jessie. "Jesus, even in Afghanistan we had better coffee than what you make, here, in a city, with all the resources our wonderful society has. I've had coffee strained through a Marine's underwear that tastes better than what you make."

"Sometimes," said Carlisle, pointing a spoon at Jessie, "you say hurtful things."

Val looked at Sam, saw the look of blank comprehension on his face as he watched the conversation bounce around the room. "You okay?"

"You're all crazy," said Sam. "You're all crazy, and my Charlie's going to die."

"Hey," said Val. "No."

"No?" Sam pulled at his collar, loosened a button. "How can you be sure?"

"It's what I do," said Val. He looked around. "What we do."

"Adalia, she said he might die."

"Yeah," said Val.

"But you're saying he won't."

"Yeah," said Val, again.

"Who do I believe?" Sam looked around, Jessie's eyes finally open and looking at him, Rex with his half-eaten Pop-Tart. Danny, arms crossed, and Carlisle, half-way through making coffee, as if there were a point she was trying to make by it. Back to Val. "Who do I trust?"

Val thought about that. "I'd say, you got to trust yourself until you get to know us, and then you can work out if we're the kinds of people who can be trusted."

"And ... let me get this straight, one of you, John Miles, Mr. Miles is currently out on a date?" Sam's throat worked. "While Charlie is..." and then the words ran right out of him, and he sat down on the floor right there, five thousand dollar suit and all.

Carlisle walked from the kitchen over to Sam. She crouched down. "Sam?"

His face was blank, more shock than anything else. "Yes?"

"Sam, I'm going to give you just the highlights. Because this asshole," and she jerked a thumb over her shoulder at Val, "takes too long and misses the important bits. Vampires came along, a kind of apex predator that only hunts at night. They pretty much fucked everything, even the other apex predators who also only hunt at night." She looked meaningfully at Danny, then back to Sam. "They're destroying the world. And how they do that, Sam, how they do it is that they take the children of powerful men and women. They hold them to ransom until they're grown up, making those powerful men and women do what they want. After those children are grown, kind of *indoctrinated*, you see, right then they get turned. Into new, baby vampires. Who then run those companies for all eternity." She swallowed. "What you need to know, really, is that Charlie is on his way to being dead and eternally damned at the same time, and he'll do it right over the top of your dead body. These assholes," and she jerked a thumb at Val over her shoulder again, "are set on stopping them."

"Why?" said Sam. He looked around the room.

Val crouched down to Sam's level, looked the man in the eyes, felt the hot snarl come—

We *are not for hunting*. We *are not prey*.

—to his face. "Because it's not right. *They're* not right. They have torn everything right from the world. But also ... Sam? I need to be honest with you. It's because the world is *ours*." He stood back up. "Also, we'd be worse than them if we didn't. We have the strength, and the means."

"There's ... there's only two of you," said Sam, looking between Danny and Val. "There are hundreds of them."

"Technically," said Val, "there are seven of us, but I get your point. There are two werewolves here."

"How are you going to win?" Sam looked lost.

"Because it's us," said Val.

Sam looked around the room, then levered himself to his feet. Carlisle stood with him, held a hand out but he waved it away. "I get that now's probably the time most people would say something like, 'We're screwed.'"

"Most people would," agreed Val.

"You're going to kill all the vampires, and I'm going to help you," said Sam. "What do you need?"

CHAPTER
SIX

It was funny the things you remembered, after all the years had passed. Some things you couldn't get away from. He'd been an odd child, he knew that, always too serious — a black-haired waif that moved around the feet of his parents, looking out at the world with wide, dark eyes. He'd been given a serious name, after all: Maksimillian Kotlyarov. He loved the name, the weight of it, the length of it, how it sounded when spoken aloud. His mother had tried to call him *Maks*, but he'd refused to answer to it, a deaf dog when the whistle blew. The fad had subsided, and Maksimillian had remained. She'd said to him once—

He screwed up his face. What was her name? What was his mother's name?

He couldn't remember. Too many names, too many faces. No matter.

She'd said to him once, *One day, Maksimillian, one day a pretty girl will call you Maks, and then what will you do?*

He'd looked back at her from his three feet off the ground and said, *I will tell her my name is Maksimillian.*

She'd laughed, of course. But it had always rankled, this thought that someone would have a right to call him something else. He'd tried telling his mother that, and she'd laughed harder.

Maksimillian looked over the edge of the fire escape, taking in the people hurrying below him. A woman there was wearing fur. So gauche, in this day and age. It was real fur, not some faux mixture of plastic fibers designed to evoke an emotion. A man was with her, carrying a briefcase. Now a briefcase, there was a thing from out of time, from when all the men in entire world bustled about with those black cases held firm in a hand, as if the annual reports and lunches inside were priceless jewels.

He was happy that the day of the briefcase seemed mostly behind them. Except for the odd fossil, a relic of a past age, like this man. Perhaps the couple, that woman with her coat and the man with the briefcase, were like Maksimillian. Perhaps they were also lost in time. Maksimillian pulled the collar of his coat up around his neck, sturdy sheepskin attached to faded denim. He'd loved blue jeans as soon as he'd seen them. He'd missed the entire denim revolution when he was on ... *vacation* ... for all that time, but when he'd got back to the world he'd worn them pretty much ever since. The honesty of the fabric appealed to him, but its real benefit was stealth. Blue jeans and a black jacket let him hide him among the numerous *proletariat* of the world, living in plain sight among all those faceless slaves.

Ah. There she was. The woman came into his eyeline a block or so away. A normal man wouldn't have picked her out among the hundreds of people already clotting up New York's busy avenues, but this one was special. He could feel her presence from here, his eyes drawn to her not through his gifts but hers. Green hair, shoulders held in a way that spoke of anger, or frustration. She moved at a brisk pace.

Maksimillian understood anger.

Truth, though, the woman with the green hair didn't hold real anger. She held the anger of tiny things, of being in a hurry with a hundred people in your way, of a late subway car, of lights and traffic that just weren't going your way. Anger, but not the same anger as when your entire family were killed before your eyes, your people lost, your village razed, your mother...

Enough. That didn't really happen.

Did it?

He got so confused sometimes, the years that crushed him down like a hundred mountains. No man was supposed to live this long. How could he remember what had happened to his mother when he couldn't remember her name?

The woman with the green hair made it to her destination, a Starbucks much like any other Starbucks. Nothing extraordinary about this one except for a particular counter worker with green hair. She had a canvas bag — no soul-dead black briefcase — slung over a shoulder, and she was talking with a man at the door. His whole attitude said, *I want you inside but you have to persuade me*. The manager then, a tiny man on the inside. After an animated exchange — perhaps they were short-staffed, so he would make an exception, but *this is the very last time* — she was ushered inside. The manager's hand lingered on her shoulder as she moved inside, causing Maksimillian to frown. Perhaps this morning was the morning Maksimillian Kotlyarov would have a spiced pumpkin latte.

He swung himself over the fire escape's railing, clambering down the outside. The old metal creaked, a few people underneath him looking up as he descended. Most walked on. *New York isn't a city that rewards the curious*. As he arrived at street level, a final swing off the ladder dropping him to the sidewalk, he saw a few people were taking photos of him with their phones.

Cameras, now there was a thing. Who would have thought you could have a device that could capture the face of your mother for all time? He wished he'd had a camera back then, wished that they'd been around to help him remember important things. Wished that these photographs had been around for longer than their meager two hundred years.

He crossed the road to the Starbucks, shouldering through the crowd. Humans were so … *tiny*. Still, some of them were important, he had to remember that. His mother had said he, Maksimillian, was important; and she'd been right. He apologized to a man who he'd almost knocked over, helped him with his bag — this time, a one of the new styles, a *messenger bag.* Maksimillian turned the name over in his head. Clearly the people buying them weren't messengers, and yet there it was. It wasn't that English was a funny language, it was that people — any language, every language — were funny in how they used their words.

The door of the Starbucks opened, the warm inside, with its smell of coffee and promised breakfast, surrounding him. He saw a family — no, not a family. There, a man and a woman had children's strollers, but for the little dogs with them. *Amerikantsov.* As if a dog couldn't walk. As if a dog needed one of the four arm chairs the couple were using.

Maksimillian joined the line, looking at the menu behind the counter. For less than five dollars he could have a coffee, for a few more dollars one of their fine breakfast treats. He was in the mood for something with sausage; it had been a cold morning on the fire escape and he hadn't eaten since—

Hot blood, the spray fine and red.

—he shook his head again. Those were not the thoughts he should be having here, in front of the woman with green hair. As if conjured, he found himself at the front of the line, face to face with her. Despite what Dragomir had said, had asked for, Maksimillian knew: he'd been waiting for this, this moment, this meeting for what felt like a thousand years. What should he say?

"What do you need to make your day better?" She scrubbed a hand through her hair, smoothing out a curl or two. Her name badge said *Ady.* It wasn't her name, it wasn't what her name was *supposed* to be.

"I am sorry," he said. "But what?"

"You know. Coffee. Food." She jerked a thumb at the board above and behind her.

"Ah," he said. "I am thinking, this is not your name." He pointed at her name badge.

"Eyes up, buddy," she said, but there was a hint of a smile at her lips.

"*Da*," he said, looking up. "See, is no one called Ady. Is name of aunt, or small dog. Is not name for beautiful woman." Maksimillian thought for a moment. "Your boss, he is asshole?"

She laughed. "Strictly speaking, that might be true." She looked over his shoulder. "Look, I'd love to do the asshole game, you know, find out which one of our bosses is the bigger one. I'd win. You know it, I know it. We both *know* it. The thing is," and she leaned forward over the register, "there's about a thousand people behind you, and sooner or later one of them is going to get thirsty and want one of our fine, fine frappucinos. So, sir, would you like to order something?"

"*Da*," he said. "I would. A spiced pumpkin latte. Your website, it claims they are delicious."

"Pumpkin spice latte," she said.

"I am sorry," Maksimillian said, "but that is what I said."

"No," she said. "You asked for a 'spiced pumpkin latte.' The board," and here she jerked her thumb behind her again, "clearly calls them a 'pumpkin spice latte.' The order is important."

Maksimillian frowned. "Is important?"

"Yes," she said. "God only knows what you'd get if you really ordered a spiced pumpkin latte." She was writing on the side of a paper cup. "Anything else?"

"A fine breakfast of sausage," he said. "Perhaps double the size an ordinary man would order."

"An ordinary man, huh?" She looked at him over the edge of the cup. He wondered what she saw. Perhaps a young man, no grey in his hair. One with dark eyes. She might have noticed that he hadn't had time to shave in a day or two, but that was fashionable these days. She might have seen the casual way he dressed. But above all, he hoped she saw his smile. He could swear he saw an answering smile

51

on her lips, just the hint of it. "You look like a sausage, cheddar, and egg kind of guy. Am I not wrong?"

"You are not wrong," he said, grinning. "You know me, *da?*"

"No," she said, "but I know you want two of those. Coming right up..?" She left the sentence hanging, like a question.

He waited a moment, then leaned forward. "*Da.* Two." He started counting bills out onto the counter.

"No," she said again, pen poised, the fat black tip waiting. "A name for the order."

"Maksimillian Kotlyarov," said Maksimillian. "Is good name, for good breakfast."

"Maksimillian Kotlyarov," she said, "is never going to fit on this cup, assuming I can spell that bad boy."

"Hey asshole," said a man behind Maksimillian. "Just give the lady a name. Fucking Chewbacca, whatever. We're dying of hunger here."

Maksimillian felt the smile freeze on his face, turned around. There was a man, slightly shorter than most, slightly heavier than he should be, this last detail most noticeable in this city of short, *thin* people. He was wearing a light suit, and — *of course* — a messenger bag. Maksimillian felt like he should—

Rend this tiny thing. Feast.

—reach out and snuff this man from the world. He felt the grin tightening on his face, his fists clenching. Then, he thought about the woman with green hair, her cup held ready, waiting for this name. *His* name. He relaxed. "Am sorry. Is English, no? Very ... you say 'complicated,' *da?*"

The other man looked up at Maksimillian, cleared his throat, and swallowed. "Hey," he said, putting a nervous laugh behind it. "Don't sweat it. She just needs a name."

Maksimillian reached out, the other man cringing, but Maksimillian only smoothed the man's jacket. "There. Your jacket, was crooked. Is better now." He turned back to the woman with green hair, her pen still poised, her posture saying *bored, bored, bored.*

Maksimillian thought he heard the man behind him say *Fucking Russians*, and he felt he was losing the moment. "Maksimillian Kotlyarov," he said to her, "is the only name I have."

She looked him up and down. "Maks," she said. "You're a Maks." With quick strokes of her pen, it was made so, the countless years of his life carrying a heavy name nothing in that moment, that one moment his mother had predicted.

He swallowed, then nodded. "*Da*. Is good? This Maks?"

"It's great," she assured him. "The best part is that it lets you move along over there," and she pointed with her chin, "so this next gentleman can order."

"*Da*," he said. He was about to step away, then said, "Is only fair. You give me new name, I do same for you. You are no Ady."

"You're damn right there," she said.

"I give you," he said, "Adalia. Is your name."

"How..." She blinked at him. "How did you know?"

"Like ... famous sculptor. His name..." Maksimillian frowned. "Ah. Michelangelo. He saw man," and here, Maksimillian held his hands up, pantomiming a rough shape of a person, "inside rock. He would let man out, *da*? Is same. Inside," and here, he pointed at Adalia, "is your shape of person. Is Adalia."

"Okay, Maks," said Adalia. "Well, thanks for letting my name out. It appreciates it. Now, could you do me a favor and move along?"

"*Da*," he said, catching one last smile from her.

Maks. Who knew that he could change such a big thing after so long? Maksimillian went to wait for his breakfast with the faintest hint of hope in his step.

CHAPTER
SEVEN

It had been such a long night, but Liselle didn't mind. If she were being honest — *by the Father, I'm on a* date — she didn't want it to end. The man, John Miles, sat across from her, his strong shoulders and easy smile catching her eye. They were in a ... she guessed it would be called a 'diner,' the kind of place that was open more than it was closed. John had led her here, not to a bar, not to a restaurant, but a *diner*. A couple of menus were spread on the table in front of them, stacked condiments to one side. The Formica of the table was worn, but in a happy way, and she let her fingers rest on the surface. She felt as if a thousand thousand people had been here, been content here with simple food and easy conversation.

There was something different about a man who tried to impress over waffles.

The walk here had been accompanied by talk of everything and nothing, she couldn't even remember what, but she did know that they hadn't spoken a single word about what had happened back at the bar, about the dying, about the vampires, and about the other — the Night — that must have been there.

"You want coffee?" John hadn't looked at his menu.

"Of course," she said, "but I'm not sure if this place will do 'coffee.' It will do some kind of liquid with caffeine in it, which might be colored black."

"Oh, they do coffee all right," said John. "The pancakes are good too."

"I haven't had pancakes in..." Liselle trailed off, thinking about it. "It must be over twenty years."

John looked at her for a moment. "Couple of comments come to mind on that one." He nodded to himself, as if making a list. "First, were you a zygote? Jesus Christ, but you must have been barely out of preschool." Liselle felt the warmth come to her face at the compliment. "Second comment, and not in priority order, is how can you go twenty years without pancakes?"

She thought about it. Last time—

The streets of Khorramshahr burned, vehicles and people blazing after the rain of munitions. Liselle looked at the ruins of the table she'd been sitting at, the newspaper open in front of her. Josef had promised her a City of Blood, something to flush the pestilence from hidden burrows, but all he'd given her was death.

Her breakfast, half-eaten, was a plate of Western-style pancakes. They were ruined now, dirt and debris and crumbs of concrete and plaster mixing with the fake maple syrup. She wiped a hand through her hair, looking at the death around her. The room was shattered, crushed inward by the massive hand of the explosion right outside the window, and the humans who'd been here with her were flung around like insects, their faces showing nothing other than surprise, if there was a face left at all. She reached a hand out to pick up a chunk of concrete, her fingers finding the edges rough and hot — still carrying the fiery heat of the explosion that had broken it — and turned it over. Looked at the body of a man underneath.

Josef was behind her. "Just like you asked."

"Did I?" She looked at him. "Did I ask for this?"

"You're getting too attached to Liselle." He shrugged. "You know that. The real you, that's who asked. Not this shell."

Liselle gave her head a tiny shake, her smile feeling brittle. Who was she, to be here with this man, after what she'd done? She didn't deserve it. But she couldn't make herself stand up, not yet, so she said, "They ... weren't very good."

John watched her for a moment. "Yeah," he said, "okay. Well, your face looks like you're sucking on a lemon, so I'm guessing it was more than the pancakes. I tell you what."

"What?"

"I, John Miles, will order the pancakes. You should get something else, and ... look, I'm not saying it's going to happen, but if you like the way the pancakes sit on the plate, you know, the way they smell, maybe I can share." He sat back. "Least I can do."

"That's a big sacrifice," Liselle said, her smile coming back, the memory of Khorramshahr fading in face of the light peeking out of this man. Sometimes it was there, sometimes it wasn't, or perhaps she just couldn't see it all the time. She picked up a menu. "I think I'll have the waffles. Just to do my part." She kicked off her Louboutins under the table, looked up as the waiter arrived. She knew it was wrong, but she couldn't make herself take an interest in this man with his order book and fake smile and *ma'am* and *sir*. She'd seen a million like him before. But John Miles, this ordinary-but-not-ordinary man was looking at her, something expectant in his look. She wanted to live up to that expectation, so she picked up the menu. "Are the waffles good?"

"Ma'am, the waffles are heaven sent," he said. The lettering stitched to his shirt said *Luke*, and she wondered if he knew anything about the gentle doctor from Antioch who'd made the name popular. "You want a coffee with that?"

"I ... I *need* a coffee," she said. "Black."

"Like the night," he agreed, turning to John. "How about you?"

"Hell," said John. "Give me the pancakes, maybe four. I'd like bacon, eggs over easy, some of your famous potato hash, sausage, and a single slice of toast."

Their waiter looked up from his order book. "Just one slice of toast? You don't want two?"

"Diet," said John.

Liselle laughed. "John Miles," she said, "that is not a low-calorie breakfast."

"Diet," said John, "and today is a cheat day." He looked back at their waiter. "It'd be great if you could bring me a coffee so large it's embarrassing. You know what I mean? And a little cream."

"I know what you mean," said Luke. "A coffee it takes two people to carry, coming right up."

The waiter left, order book tucked into the back pocket of his jeans. Liselle watched him go, waiting for ... what? Distance? Time? "So, do you cheat?"

John watched her across the table. "Not in any way that counts." He shrugged. "Depends what you mean. Cheating is just an excuse to do the shit you were going to do anyway, like eat a breakfast for four people."

"Sugar," she said.

"Sure," said John. "What?"

"Do you take it in your coffee?" Liselle paused as the waiter arrived, a simple cup for her, and a cup plus a carafe for John.

John nodded his thanks at the waiter and poured himself a cup. He reached across the table, grabbed the sugar from the island of condiments, and spooned two generous piles of snowy white into his cup. He seemed to be thinking for a moment, then picked up the cream and stirred it in. "I take pretty much everything in my coffee," he said. He took a sip, fought a grimace, and said, "This is not as amazing as I ... well, it tasted better inside my head." He looked at the carafe.

"You're not ... you're not selling it to me," she said. She tasted her coffee. It wasn't amazing, but it was far from the worst she'd had. A little sugar would definitely help.

"Why are you here?" said John.

"You were going to tell me—"

"Oh, sure," said John. "So what happened was this vampire, right, this vampire comes in, and my buddy Val and his girl Danny beat the hell out of him. Actually, it was a little more even than that, two on one I thought it'd be easy, but shit, those fuckers can fight, right? Carlisle, she was there too, shot it a few times, and then they all ran off." He took another sip of his coffee, fighting a wince again. "That's not what I meant."

Liselle blinked at him. She had expected ... something else, some form of struggle extracting the information. She realized, with a faint touch of surprise, she had expected John Miles to lie to her, to play some kind of game. Their breakfast arrived, plates and plates of it, buying her a little more time to think. As their waiter left, she tried the waffles. Crisp, and light. Perfect. "I'm here because I ... need something."

"Information." John was working on his breakfast like a lumberjack. He spoke around a mouthful. "Right?"

Yes, she should have said. *Just the information.* "No." She sighed. "John, do you know what it's like to live forever, or as near as it as counts? But on the day you'll die, the day it all ends for you, it'll be because you've helped kill every human everywhere?"

"No, I don't know about that." He thought for a moment. "Doesn't sound cool, though."

Not, *I understand, Liselle*, or, *Man, that sounds bad.* Just, *No.* "I don't know either, not all of it. Not yet. But I will."

"Sure." He put his knife and fork down. His voice got a little softer, a little gentler, and she saw that beautiful light inside him flare for a moment. "You still haven't answered my question."

Liselle picked at her waffles. She wanted to say, *I'm here because I need someone*, or, *What is that light inside you? It comes and goes. Can't you see how bright you can be? Can you shine all the time?* But she didn't. People didn't say things like that, not over breakfast. "They want to kill you all," she said.

"Yeah," he said. "We know. You want to know the neat part?" When she nodded, he smiled, like the sun coming out. "We're going to kick their *asses*. Just absolutely monster those throwbacks, you know?"

She laughed at the audacity of it. "You … John Miles, I don't know what you are, but I don't think you're a match for a vampire."

"That's what the last guy thought too," said John, before his smile flickered a little, the light inside him going out. "Before the sky fell."

Liselle didn't know what made him falter, but she wanted to. "What happened?"

"Wasn't vampires," he said. "First time, just some PMC and an evil megacorp, the usual kind of first world problems. Second time, this whole bunch of black magic, I guess you'd say voodoo—"

"*Vodou*," she corrected.

"Sure, voodoo guys, so they come all the way over here, and I don't mean from Brooklyn, I mean from over the sea, and they try and, I dunno, maybe steal the Night. The Night, you know about that?"

"Yes," she said.

"Figures," he said. "Didn't work. Stealing the Night."

"No, it wouldn't," she said. "It's a singular force."

"Right," he said. "Did you know? My best friend, he's a werewolf."

She gaped at him for a moment. "You are friends with the Night?"

"So I guess, that's why we're going to kick their asses." He sighed, picking up his knife and fork again. "Because we need to. Because no one else is going to. Because we can."

"You…" She picked up her cup, then put it down again, leaning forward. "You … *can't*."

"Says who?" He gestured with the fork at the room around them. "The Universe?"

By the Father. "Why are *you* here, John Miles?" Sometimes the light inside this man made him hard to look at. In his words, not arrogance, but certainty. "What do you want?"

"A few good times, before the end." He frowned. "Cold beer on a hot day. What's Melissa say? Champagne and happiness. But you mean, here, in this diner?"

"Here, in this diner," she agreed.

He smiled. "Just breakfast," he said. "I think we both need a little breakfast."

Just breakfast. It had been such a long time since she'd had the time for *just breakfast.* Liselle picked up her knife and fork, suddenly hungry, suddenly starving, wanting to eat it all, to experience it, like it was the first meal of her life. *Just breakfast* was okay. It was … amazing. Liselle Vitols sat across from John Miles, and talked, and laughed, and talked some more, until the sun was high in the sky and the events of last night seemed so far away.

CHAPTER
EIGHT

Val sat in the back of the van, Danny across from him. It wasn't the kind of van with lots of windows and seats. It was the kind of van with no windows, a couple bench seats, and a cage. The cage was the important part, and he hoped they'd made it right.

"It'll be fine," Jessie had said, wrench in her hand, grime smudged on one cheek. "Those steel bars are as thick as my arm."

"It wouldn't slow me down for long," said Val. "Not if, you know." He made clawing motions with one hand.

"What, if you put a sock puppet on one hand?" She eyed him critically. "I hadn't, well, maybe I'm being hard on myself, but I feel a little foolish for not thinking they might have a sock puppet."

"No. Jesus. I meant——"

"I know what you mean," she said. "Couple of things. First, I think this would slow you down. This is stainless, precipitation hardened, and since you're asking, it's been a bit of a big deal to make it. You know, here." She gestured with the wrench at the room around them. "This isn't General Dynamics."

"Could General Dynamics make it stronger?" said Val. "We could go there."

"Second thing," she said, "is that you'll be surrounded by all that sunlight."

"At least," said Val, "for as long as it's daytime."

Whatever it was, it was heavy. Danny and he had wrestled it in here together, and the van sat low on its shocks, shocks Rex had modified for just this reason. Val still felt every bump and jounce as they'd rumbled through midtown New York.

"Something about this broad daylight thing is bugging me," said Rex, to no one in particular. He was sitting behind the wheel up front. "It might be all the people who are staring at us."

"It's Times Square," said Jessie, who sat beside him. "They're not staring at you, they're just staring."

"I guess ... well, maybe that's the point," he said. "We're in Times *Square*." He drew a triangle in the air with a finger. "Technically not square in shape. More like three sides, about a million people a side, cameras everywhere."

"No second chances," said Val. "We've—"

Hidden in the dark.

"—stayed underground for long enough. Now we—"

Hunt.

"—take these assholes."

It was, all macho bullshit aside, a ballsy plan. Break into the Renaissance hotel, grab the vampire staying in 2602, and get him back out to the van. Put him in the cage, drive like hell, hope the cops didn't come.

That last one was pure fantasy. The cops were going to come. It's whether they were *the* cops, or *their* cops. The vampires had control of just about everything, everywhere, which made it a little difficult. The thing was, it'd be helpful — just this once — if the cops were *their* cops. Far more likely to try and resolve this off the books. Off the books was good. Off the books meant no jails. Probably meant no SWAT in Times Square, because that would leave a trail on YouTube a million clicks wide, and probably at least one front page article no matter how many newspapers the bloodsuckers had in their pockets.

Time to test the theory. He gave Danny a little nod. She gave him a nod back, red curls bouncing, holding up the black polythene bag, then pushed it into a knapsack. She kicked the back door of the van open, Val following her onto the street. Yellow cabs surrounded them, people everywhere. Not just people but tourists, cameras and selfie sticks and gaping. They moved like zombies, eyes up, the pan handlers moving among them with the usual *lost my leg in the Gulf* or *it's the GFC, man, those fucking bankers took my house* stories. Val pushed the doors of the van closed, looking up at the Renaissance. The popular hotel reached for the sky, a stubby hand held up in surrender. He walked with Danny on the sidewalk, moving at a brisk pace towards the entrance.

"It feels good," he said.

She gave a tight grin back. "Not hiding," she said. "Hunting."

Hunt. Kill.

"Hunting," he agreed. "Nervous?"

"Shaking like a tree in the wind," she said, holding out a hand. It was steady as a rock.

"Me too," he said, feeling the thrill of the upcoming events in his step, his feet feeling lighter than air. "I love you."

She stopped, grabbed his face, and kissed him hard. "I love you." She kissed him again, then let him go. "Let's go bag some big game."

They put in their earpieces, tiny things Jessie had got through her network, milspec comms that didn't have a fat wire hanging down from your head. Battery life wasn't for shit, but they wouldn't be here that long. "You hear me?"

"I hear you, you clown, because we're three feet apart." Jessie's voice, coming through his earpiece loud and clear. Also from behind him.

Val looked back, saw Jessie get out of the van, her cap pulled low. She was carrying a case, fat and black, and gave him a nod before jogging across the street to the blare of horns and *watch it, asshole* or *you crazy, lady? You gone get killed.* She disappeared into a building across the street; the front was covered in a catwalk, getting its own impossible makeover. It wasn't tall enough to see into level 26 of the Renaissance, but that was kind of the point. Val and Danny wouldn't need help on 26. They'd need help — *maybe* — when they hit the street. The building Jessie had vanished into was low, squat, ordinary, *invisible*, right next to some kind of comedy place and a store pushing dollar gifts of the moment.

It was pretty hard to find a place that was invisible around Time Square, and Val had to wonder if this was some kind of elaborate trap. The kind where the bloodsuckers knew you knew, right, and so they just sat there waiting. It wasn't impossible. They'd talked about it, and Carlisle had called it an *overdeveloped paranoia reflex* and Rex had said it *didn't really matter because the damn sun is up*, which more or less made the point for everyone. If the sun weren't up, a trap would be ... pretty scary. Sun up? Just normals, that's all. That could get exciting, but in a roller coaster kind of way, as opposed to an *oh-God-oh-God-we're-all-gonna-die* kind of way.

The entrance to the Renaissance opened, taking them from New York summer heat that made your clothes stick to you five minutes after putting them on into a cool, quiet lobby. There was the usual: reception desk, concierge who was already gravitating to them like iron filings to their magnet, a bunch of octogenarians with too much luggage who were staring around them without really knowing where to go.

"Sir," said the concierge, "how may—"

"I'm good," said Val. "I'm here to see a friend."

The concierge didn't even pause. "Of course. If you give me your friend's name, I can call—"

"I'm good," said Val, holding up his phone. "Called him already. Just gonna wait for him here."

"Very good, sir," said the concierge, losing interest as the opportunity to glean a tip vanished. Times Square tended to feel a little ... *transactional*, that was the word.

Val looked at Danny. "What's the play?"

"You're always so ... wait here," she said.

"I'm always so what?" he said.

"Just wait here," she said, striding through the lobby, past the dark glass and low tables and ostentatious—

This world is old and sick and fat.

—light fixtures in the roof. What would you even call those damn things? They hung from the ceiling like elongated teardrops, like some kind of ooze frozen in time. Not the kind of thing Val would want to sit under. The almost biological shapes of those light fixtures made him uneasy, but if he was being honest, being anywhere around vampires made him uneasy as well. He looked up as Danny came back towards him, a couple of bags with her. She tossed him one.

"Stealing?" He frowned.

"Borrowing," she said. She nodded towards the elevators. "C'mon."

They walked towards the elevators, using standing guests as human sight barriers between them and any hotel staff. They made the elevators without incident, and Val nodded at an older couple, faces so tan they looked like upholstery. "Hey," he said.

"Hey," said the guy, older, voice pegging him in maybe his sixties. His wife was grinning like it was her first time at the fair.

Val watched Danny do the same sums he was doing, felt her hold his arm. "We're here for our honeymoon," she said.

"Oh," said the woman, nodding. "We're here for our anniversary. Forty years."

"That's gorgeous!" said Danny, a little high-school-prom in her voice. She patted the air with a hand. "Did you ... did you get married here?"

"Oh heavens, no," said the woman, with a conspiratorial wink. "Bert wanted to elope."

Danny covered her mouth, making a tiny gasp. "Bert, you devil."

Bert grinned at them. "Where you folks from?"

"We're kind of traveling at the moment," said Danny. She tugged on Val's arm. "Mike here, well, Mike is an adventure photographer, so we travel a lot. But after our last trip to Africa—"

"Oh my," said the woman. "Africa?"

"I know, right?" said Danny, bouncing on her feet. "It's so exciting."

The elevator arrived with a chime, Val holding the door for the other couple. "Where you folks from?"

Bert nodded his thanks as he entered the elevator after his wife. "Jean and me, well, we moved about some too, but we've retired in Florida."

"Retired?" said Danny. "You must have done so well for yourselves, you're both so young."

Jean laughed. "Oh, dear, you're so sweet."

"Darn it." Danny patted her pockets. "Mike, baby, I've left my card in our room."

Val patted his own pockets. *Follow her lead.* "I ... *darn.* I left mine with—" and he groped through his mind, *Bobby* being too close to *Bert* "—Andy. He took some of our bags on ahead." He looked at Bert and Jean. "Our son. We, uh, eloped as well." He faced Danny again. "It's no problem, we'll just call him down."

"Don't be silly," said Jean, swiping her card against the elevator. "Just press your button, dear."

Danny put a hand on Jean's arm. "Thank you *so* much. Andy will probably have his headphones on anyway."

Val stabbed the number 26, the elevator's door's closing with a cultured rumble. Val agreed to tell Bert and Jean about Africa over a drink later before the couple got out. The elevator doors slid closed behind them, and Danny relaxed with a sigh. "Give me vampires any day."

"'Mike?'" said Val. "Do I look like a Mike?"

"Hang on," said Danny. "I think all that gushing made me throw up a little in my mouth."

"Right," said Val, then, "thanks."

"You'd have hit someone," she said.

"I know," said Val.

"And the police would have come," she said.

"I said thanks already," said Val, as the doors to 26 opened onto soft carpet and silence.

"We're not ready," said Danny, "for the police to come." She gave him an affectionate kiss on the cheek, then walked out on to 26, dropping her ... *borrowed* ... bag on the carpet. He smelled the air, something old and decayed underlying the scents of carpet cleaner and bleach. There was a faint smell of blood, the subtle hint of it recirculated a thousand times around the floor by the air conditioning.

Death is here.

"I know, buddy." Val cocked his head. "Nice and slow." He dropped his own bag, the need for that camouflage gone. They padded on the carpet, two predators in a nest of vipers. "I got to wonder," he said. "Why the Renaissance?"

"It's a nice enough hotel," said Danny. "It's right in Times Square. If you were a bloodsucking motherfucker, you'd probably want take-out within walking distance, right?"

"Right," said Val. They looked around. They were on a standard floor hub, elevator doors yielding to a corridor. Left was just a couple of rooms, and Val dismissed them without even checking the numbers. *Too close to the main traffic area. It'd want something quiet, private, a killing box with a view.* Right it was, then. They rounded the corner, then Val said, "'Darn?'"

"It seemed the best word for the situation," said Danny, eyes forward. "There." Dark wood, a door like any other, near the end. Fire escape stairs led down at the end, a convenient second route if the thing needed to run. Room 2602. No different, from the outside, from 2601 across the hall, except a lot more killing had happened inside. There was a sign hung from the door handle, and Val picked up the black card. *Don't even think about knocking*, it read, *History being made.* He snorted, handed it to Danny. She read it, tossed it aside. "See? Nice enough hotel. Someone's got a sense of humor."

Val knocked on the door. He reached back into his mind, to that time—

He stood on the stage. The motley crowd sat, hushed, expectant, before he burst into his next ribald song. The accent he used was borrowed from a laborer he'd met on the road, all hard sounds said the wrong way. The accent was the people of this crowd, and they loved that he was one of them.

—when he'd had an ordinary house, Baitan keeping him from falling into a complete pit of mess. He remembered the sound of her voice, how the lilt of her Filipino accent was wonderful to listen to. He put that into his voice. "Housekeeping," he said. *Room service* wouldn't have been right ... vampires didn't order a burger to their room, unless they wanted to eat the delivery service itself.

No response. He looked at Danny for a five count, then knocked again. "Housekeeping," he said, but louder.

"Fuck," came a voice from inside, muffled by the door. "I've got the fucking ... what's it ... fucking *Do Not Disturb* sign out, asshole."

"No English," said Val. "Housekeeping."

He heard with his perfect ears someone walking across the carpet, the sound so quiet an ordinary human wouldn't hear it. No heartbeat. No problem.

Well, maybe a little bit of a problem. It was still a vampire — a young one, sure, but all teeth and hunger and killing.

Enemy of Pack.

Val felt his lips pull back from his teeth as the door opened. A man stood there, pale, shirtless, the look of annoyance-turning-to-anger melting into surprise. "You're not—"

Danny's fist caught him in the face, teeth shattering and knocking the thing back in a tumble. He rolled back into the room, hitting a low table, crushing it to kindling. Val and Danny slipped into the room, Val pulling the door closed while Danny ran past the fallen vampire to the windows. Dark, heavy curtains shut out the world.

Shut out the *sun*.

She reached a hand up, fingers curling into a fist in the fabric. And paused. Waiting.

Val crouched down in front of the fallen vampire. Danny's fist had done a good job, the thing's front teeth gone. They'd grow back in a few minutes, sure, but until then his options for a refill were limited. "Hi," he said. "I'm Val."

"You're dead," said the vampire.

"Give it a tug," said Val.

"What?" said the vampire. Danny twitched the curtain. A beam of pure white light left a spear through dust motes in the air, and the thing ducked down, covering its eyes with a scream. "Fuck! Stop! Fuck!"

Val looked at Danny, and she closed the curtain again. "Hi," he said again. "I'm Val."

"Sure, Val, whatever," said the thing.

"And you are..?" Val frowned. He softened his voice, but not in a friendly way. "It's usually polite to introduce yourself back."

"Right," said the thing. "Jeremy. Jer. Or ... well, Jeremy."

"Jer," said Val, "is what your friends call you?"

"Sure."

"Do I fucking *look*," said Val, teeth bared, "like a *friend*?" He knew his eyes would be bright yellow, felt his voice gain the texture of the monster...

We are one. We are the same.

...champion inside him. The Night was right. They *were* the same. Now, more than ever.

The vampire looked up, actually *looked* at Val, for the first time since they'd come into the room. Saw the vampire's eyes scan his face, saw the dismissive attitude of the everliving damned fall away as it recognized him, really understood what he was. "You're ... we ended you *all*." Val waited for a moment. The vampire — *Jeremy*, for fuck's sake what kind of vampire name was that anyway — blinked, then said, "Well, okay. Clearly we missed one or two."

"Do you know why I'm here?" said Val.

"You want to kill me," said Jeremy.

"No," said Val.

"Uh," said Jeremy. "You're here for the view?"

"We're here," said Val, "to give you a small chance to be useful to the world again."

"I can't tell you about them," the creature — *Jeremy*, goddamn it, his name was *Jeremy* — said.

"Fine," said Val. "That's not what we want. Jeremy, let me be honest with you. We didn't find you by accident. We already know about them."

"You do?"

"We do," agreed Val. "What we're hoping for is a ... little more science." Jeremy laughed, bloody teeth stumps looking a little less jagged than before. Val kept going. "We want you to tell us how you work."

"I'm a vampire, bro," said Jeremy. "Like in the books."

Val sighed. "We both know," he said, "that's not true. Anyway, it doesn't matter."

"It doesn't?"

"No," said Val. "Here's how it's going to work. I see three outcomes."

"Three outcomes," repeated Jeremy.

"Exactly three," said Val. "In the first one, your teeth finish healing, and you think you can take us. You do your thing." He blinked yellow eyes at Jeremy. "You hope the Night is what you've been told, what you remember, and that little you — a fresh, young, baby vampire, new in your powers and basically weak as a kitten — can take both of us. You hope that will happen before Danny," and he nodded towards Danny, and the window with the sun at its back, "pulls that curtain opens and turns you into a fire hazard."

"I don't like option one," said Jeremy.

"Cool," said Val. Jeremy shifted, and Val reached out a hand, palm outstretched. "Jeremy? Don't fucking move. Seriously." Jeremy settled a little, and Val pulled his hand back. "The thing inside my head? It really, really—"

Rend this tiny thing. Destroy it, and all its kind.

"—*really* wants an excuse to visit a world of hurt on you. You hear what I'm saying?"

"I get you," said Jeremy. "What's option two?"

"Option two," said Val, pulling the black bag folded under his jacket, "is that you get in the body bag, we carry you out, take you back to our lair, and experiment on you." The problem with these vampires was that they sounded *just like people*. It was ... *difficult* to not see some base humanity there. And if you saw that, you took pity on it. Then you died.

They have killed us all. We are the last.

Then again, race memory helped a lot to overcome any residual squeamishness.

"Okay," said Jeremy, "what's the real option two?"

"Sorry. You're getting in the bag." Val shrugged. "I don't have an option three, but if it's any consolation, we won't really experiment on you. Much."

"Much? What the fuck does that mean?" Jeremy looked back at Danny, saw her smile, and shuddered. He turned to Val. "I don't like option two much, Val, if I'm being honest."

"Would it help," said Val, "if I told you why?"

"You want to kill us all," said Jeremy.

"Not really," said Val.

"What?" said Jeremy.

"I've got a, what would you call it, a kind of *deal* going on with ... the Universe," said Val. "Something was done a very long time ago, before either of us were born. It made the world wrong. Dragons, Jeremy. Do you know you mother*fuckers* killed all the dragons? They were magnificent." He paused. "It wasn't really your fault, as near as I can tell, any more than you can blame grass for being green."

"We don't have much time," said Danny. "This wasn't part of the plan."

"Hold up," said Val, looking at her. She saw that *I've got to try* look, and her eyes softened just a little. He turned back to Jeremy. "You get me, Jeremy? Grass, and being green?"

"No," said Jeremy.

"So the thing is," said Val, "about ten years ago I was bitten. Crazy part is I don't even remember it. I was in a, what would you call it, an alcohol-induced coma at the time. Now a part of me, it's grass, and it's green. All the time. It is what it is. I am ... what I am."

"Oh," said Jeremy. "And all this greenery," and here, he made a tiny and slow, oh-so-slow circular movement with one of his hands, "is me."

"The problem with an analogy is if you torture it enough, it loses all its shape," said Val. "But sort of. You can't help being you. You were ... bitten, as well."

"Right," said Jeremy. He gave a harsh laugh, something that said *I know why you hate me, because I hate myself too.* "What about it?"

"The deal I've got going on with the Universe," said Val, "is that we get to put it right. The *terms* of the agreement are more ... flexible."

"What the hell does that mean, Val?" Jeremy looked at Danny again, then back at him. "I'm not seeing what you're saying."

"We want," said Val, "to remove *vampires* from the world. We don't really want to remove the people they once were."

Jeremy looked at him, long and slow, then said, "Hand me the bag."

～

"It doesn't really look like a roll of fabric," said Danny. "It looks like a torn-off piece of curtain with a dead body in it." She nudged the edge of the bundle containing Jeremy with her toe. They'd wrapped his body bag with the curtains from Jeremy's room, but body bags had that characteristic bend in the middle. Couldn't mistake it, they were riding down 26 floors in an elevator with a body ... in a body bag.

"Hey," said Jeremy, voice muffled from the inside.

"This part of the plan," said Val, "was always going to need a little more speed than style."

The elevator chimed, opening onto the Renaissance's lobby. There was the usual small crowd waiting for the next elevator, and the people started to enter before what they saw pushed them back like an invisible hand. Val could see it in their faces, the look of *surely not* or *is that..?* or *what the* actual *fuck* playing out in similar ways. Val bent over, picked up Jeremy's half-bag-half-curtain tube, and stepped out after Danny.

She set a brisk pace ahead of him, murmuring *excuse me* or *pardon me* or, in one case, *move it, asshole* as she made a path for them. The main doors of the Renaissance were ahead of them. They'd made it.

Val said, "You still with us, Jeremy?"

"I'm cool," said Jeremy. "Don't hole the bag. I'd be less cool then, you know?" He was hard to hear, if you had normal ears, but Val could make out what he was saying just fine.

The same concierge they'd seen less than twenty minutes ago sped over. "Is that ... are you..."

"My buddy," said Val, "wasn't in."

The concierge looked at Jeremy's tube, back at Val, and back at the tube. "I'm going to have to call someone—"

"Call whoever the hell you like," said Danny. She started to move towards the exit.

The concierge reached for the radio clipped to the back of his belt. "Security?" He frowned. "I've got—"

Danny moved like oiled smoke, stepping behind the man, and yanked the radio from his belt. She held it up, crushed it to fragments of plastic and metal in one hand, and let the pieces fall to the tiled floor of the lobby with tiny *tinks*. She nodded at Val. "Let's go."

"Let's," said Val.

"What's going on?" said Jeremy.

"Concierge wanted a tip," said Val.

"That guy is totally obvious about it," said Jeremy. He sounded scared, and Val would be too. He tried to imagine being inside a piece of black plastic, the only thing shielding you from fiery oblivion a thin sheet of polythene and a shred of fabric and the trust of a stranger who had every reason to want you dead.

Val hefted Jeremy to shift his weight against his shoulder. It's not that he was particularly heavy, it's that carrying a body was just damn awkward no matter how strong you were. Like trying to carry a mattress with more personality. "We're almost out," he said. "We'll be gone in just a couple of minutes. If things get crazy, try not to panic or try to get out of the bag."

"Why would they get crazy?" said Jeremy.

Out through the tinted glass of the main doors, Val saw two squad cars pull up in a shroud of tire smoke, lights on, sirens going, cops pouring from their sides like a small army of ants. Danny looked back at him, then said, "I got this."

"Val?" said Jeremy. Val felt him squirming inside the bag-curtain supercombo. "What's going on?"

"It's cool," said Val. "Danny's going outside to make a path."

"A path? Through what?" There was a pause, then Jeremy said, "Danny's the hot woman?" Val adjusted his load a little too vigorously and heard Jeremy give a small *ooof*. "What'd I say?"

"Stop talking for a second." Val watched as Danny walked out the main doors, cops swarming all over the place. There was a gunshot, glass exploding in the front of the Renaissance. The bullet hadn't even touched her, she'd just taken a small step sideways. She let the movement continue right up to a car at parked out front, squatted down, and grabbed it. Val could see her strain, the car lifting up, before she put some pepper into it, the car falling on its side with a *crump* of deforming metal. She reached up and steadied it with a hand, leaning back to stop it tipping over. There was a pause, then the gunfire started, but she just dusted off her hands and looked back at him with a *come on* look.

Val grinned. A car was probably a good enough barrier, visually or otherwise, for a quick jog to the van. Danny was already running ahead of him, making the back of the van without any visible effort. Val ran out of the Renaissance, Jeremy shouting something, and it was as Val got to the lee of the tipped car he thought, *shit — these assholes are just going to follow us.* He didn't really want to kill them, but—

They stand against our Pack.

—there was a certain argument that could be made for that approach because they'd just started shooting. No *freeze asshole* or *this is the police* or *we have you surrounded,* just bullets and a lot of noise. Which called into question the whole authenticity of their uniforms. Carlisle would have pitched a fit. Val looked at Danny, hefted Jeremy's tube, and tossed it through the air to her. He heard Jeremy yelling as he sailed across the distance, cut short with another *ooof* as Danny caught him, slinging him into the back of the van. Val looked at her, wanted to tell her to get moving, but there wasn't time.

He looked at the tipped car, braced his foot against it, and pushed. The vehicle toppled with a groan of metal and the rainy tinkle of crushing safety glass. It gave a pause to the action, firing stopping for a moment. He saw cops ducking low, refilling weapons that were dry, shouting at each other, and generally being disorganized. Not cops, then. He looked around, took in the traffic stopped dead — *nothing so unusual about that in New York City* — and people running and screaming around. A man's body was spread out in the street at the edge of the fire zone, blood pooling around him. *Definitely not cops.*

That was a little unusual for New York City, no matter what you read online.

"Hey!" said Val. "I don't know how you guys think this is going to end, but—"

Two of the "cops" started firing on him, and Val ducked down in behind the tipped car. Val tapped his earpiece. "You with me, Jessie?"

"Jesus," she said. "Don't tap it, it sounds like a really clumsy horse inside my head. It's not a Star Trek communicator. You just speak. Like I'm doing."

"Bullets," said Val, "are all around me. I'd rather not ... uh. You know."

"Hulk out, I know," she said. "You remember what we talked about?"

"The *Street Fighter* thing?" Val closed his eyes, put his forehead to the metal frame of the car in front of him. "Do we have to?"

"We had a deal, Everard." Her voice was crisp, professional. "I'm up here on overwatch, you're down there in the mud. The way we make them miss a step—"

"I remember," he said.

"Say it then."

"The way we make them confused," said Val in a brief lull, "is to make them afraid."

"Give me your best *Hadouken*," she said. "I can see people with their phones out. This will be on YouTube inside sixty seconds. Psychological warfare, one Millennial at a time."

"I still don't know why it has to be *Street Fighter*." Val wiped sweat from his face.

"This only works if you do what I say," she said, "and I'm telling you to do a *Hadouken*. You pick the target." Her voice crackled in his ear. "I need the practice."

"Are you ... is this *boring* you?" Val tapped the earpiece again. "Tell me you're bored."

"A little," she said. "Hey. You'll be famous, and not for turning into a hideous beast that eats people this time. Trust me. And don't hit the damn earpiece again, or I'm going home."

Val sighed. *What the hell.* He waited for a pause in the firing, grabbed the edge of the car, and pulled himself up. There was one "cop," complete with pedophile mustache, who was leveling his sidearm at Val. The shot rang out, but Val twisted sideways, then reached his arms back behind him. He let the twisting motion turn him around, both palms facing the other man, and shouted, "*Hadouken!*"

The silence lasted maybe half a heartbeat, then the man's chest exploded in a shower of gore. His body toppled to the ground. Val looked at his hands, then back at the fallen man.

"Not bad for a first try," Jessie's voice said in his ear. "You have to really want it though. I didn't feel it."

The "cops" were looking at Val, then they all ducked down as one. Val heard *what the fucks* and *how the hell did he do that* and even one guy who said *was that, was that fucking* Street Fighter. Val bounced on the balls of his feet, loosening his shoulders. "Which one of you assholes wants the next one?"

"I'll take it," said a burly man, standing up. He had a gun the size of a Howitzer in his hand, and started to level it at Val.

The movement came easier this time, Val twisting back fast and smooth, then returning his torso back the same way, palms out. "*Hadouken!*"

The burly man's head disintegrated in a shower of meaty chunks, his gun clattering to the asphalt.

The others looked at that, then scrambled for a car. One made the passenger seat before Val's next *Hadouken* collapsed the windshield and the man's face at about the same time, bloody pieces of safety glass showering in and out of the car. His body fell outside of the car. The last two men were in the car, one behind the wheel, and he was already hammering the gas before his door was closed. The car started to peel away in a scream of tires, rubber smoke filling the air.

"Last one," said Jessie.

"Gas tank," said Val, then he did one more *Hadouken*. The back of the squad car exploded, the fireball lifting the rear up and tumbling the car end over end to land on its roof, smoke and fire and metal raining down around it.

"That's a wrap," Jessie's voice was calm, cool. Professional. "Nice work, Ryu."

"I was ... more of a Ken guy," said Val.

"They're ... aren't they the same thing?" Danny's voice cut across the conversation.

"No," said Jessie. "They're rivals. And friends. It's complicated."

"Let's go," said Val, taking a last look at the burning car, the tossed and crumpled remains of men. "You coming down now?"

"On my way," said Jessie.

Val shrugged, then walked towards the van. He looked inside, Jeremy safe in his tube, tube tucked into the metal cage. Danny waiting in the back, animal tension still radiating from her like heat from a furnace. He waited until he saw Jessie approaching from across the street, then slipped in beside Danny, closing the rear doors of the van.

Our Pack is strong.

"Yeah," he said. "When we work together."

Together. All of us, for all of us.

CHAPTER
NINE

Maksimillian watched the woman with the green hair—
She could join our Pack.
—leave the Starbucks, holding a bag and a harried expression. Neither sat right on her. Maksimillian had watched a hundred million people over the long years of his life, and he had grown to know with mechanical accuracy, like one of those very expensive watches made by the *Shveytsarskiy*, when people were right or wrong.

Not right as in, whether they had the correct answer, but right as in, whether they were comfortable in their own skin. The woman with the green hair wasn't happy in her own skin. The green hair might even have been a piece of it, an attempt to be more right than wrong, but the bag was the giveaway.

It wasn't that it was a messenger bag. That wasn't the problem here. The problem was that she was carrying a bag, through the streets of New York City, dodging people, rushing, trying to make the subway. She was carrying a bag, and she should have been carrying the world instead. That, right there, was what Maksimillian Kotlyarov—

She gave us a new name.

—saw in her steps as she hurried along. In his hands he turned the paper cup that she'd given him, long since empty and cold, and looked at where the tip of her pen had carved his new name in fat black lines. She hadn't written *Max* like he was some kind of *Amerikanskaya.* She had written it as *Maks*, like she knew how that heavy old name he'd worn for so long was supposed to start in mother Russian. Like she could see into the heart of him, see who he was, and keep something special about him just as she had remade him in an instant.

Why was she hurrying? Perhaps she was running late, her shift brimming over its allotment of hours, her own Pack waiting somewhere, worried, in this city of *izvergi.* They were right to be worried, because they were hunted. The orange ball of the sun had fallen below the lip of the horizon, the remaining light in the sky a burnished red. None of the sun's radiance hit the ground, and now was when the *vampiry* would come out. When her biggest need for a guardian angel would come. The *vampiry* didn't need to fear anything until the coming of the next terrible dawn. And there — right *there* — Maksimillian picked out the two people in dark clothing following her, a man with his hair done in a purple Mohawk, the woman with eyes blackened like a panda's. It wasn't the way they looked that gave them away, it was the way they moved, weaving between the people around them like predators. Always finding a place to stand where there was none. And when there was someone there, that person would move, shy away from them instinctively, like the hare hid from the fox. Both wore black leather coats — *they have all been watching the same movies, da?* — and Maksimillian could tell from the way the leather moved, the way it clung to them, that it was not made from the skin of a bull. More seams than large sheets of hide would need — this had been put together from smaller prey. They walked the streets, wearing the skins of their kills. They walked after the woman with the green hair.

They walked without fear, this close to sunset. Kaylan had made them strong, and powerful, and with that strength and power, they had lost their fear. Kaylan would want the woman with the green hair to change the *vampiry*, to allow them to be fearless in the sun as they were fearless in the dark.

He would teach them fear.

He swung down from his fire escape, tugged his jacket straight, and moved after them. After the two people who hunted—

We are not for hunting.

—the woman with the green hair. It was easy to follow, pulled along in this sea of people, deep ocean currents of them as they surged along, into the darkness of the subway. He couldn't keep the green hair in view, not all the time — she might go around a corner here, or be lost in a surge of people there. It didn't matter. He knew her scent, a trail laid out in breadcrumbs of vanilla and coffee and the rich smell of a young woman's hair. Maksimillian followed, just another man trying to get home.

We have no home. We destroyed our own Pack.

He shook his head. Maksimillian hadn't killed his own Pack. He couldn't do that any more than water could be fire. It would be wrong, impossible, like breathing rock. He listened again for that inner voice, the voice that had been there since before everything else. It felt like it had ridden just behind his eyes forever, as all the ages of men had come and gone and left nothing but crumbled ruins as the faint footstep of their passing, a print in sand to be washed away at the next tide.

It said nothing, did nothing, and so Maksimillian kept walking.

The subway platform was packed, close, a mass of people. The Mohawk and the Panda pushed through, trying to get to the woman with the green hair. She was oblivious, headphones in, still looking harried, phone in hand. Probably a message for her Pack, or perhaps just changing the tunes piped into her ears. He would make sure she got on her subway car, and that these two did not. He could feel the arrival of the car, the rumbling under his feet, the *skree-skrit* as the subway car clattered against the tracks, well before anyone with normal ears could. The blast of air and noise as it arrived at the station didn't make any of the people here look up, not a hint of surprise as this magical car came to take them home.

We have no home.

Maksimillian's hand found the elbow of the man with the Mohawk as people churned about them, pushing on to the already crowded subway cars. The man whirled, tried to yank his hand free, but Maksimillian kept his grip like iron. "A moment, friend." He let his teeth show, perhaps as a smile. Perhaps not.

The man looked down at his hand, then at the Panda woman, then at the woman with the green hair. His face was so pale, so much time since it had seen the sun. "You—"

"*Da*," said Maksimillian. "You think, this is crazy man on subway, like other crazy men. That I ask for loose coins like *nishchiy*, try to buy a small meal. Or alcohol, to make the night warmer."

"What?" said the man.

The subway station was emptying, water down a drain. Maksimillian smiled wider. "You have come here for her."

Mohawk looked to Panda. "Go. Get her." He turned back to Maksimillian, eyes narrowed. He tried to pull his arm free again. "You're making the last mistake you'll ever make."

Maksimillian nodded, as if he was agreeing. "*Da*. I have made many mistakes." He watched Panda hurry towards the subway cars, to capture the woman with the green hair. Dragomir had said that couldn't be allowed.

"You—"

"But I do not think this is one of those," said Maksimillian. "I think that this," and he gestured with his free hand to the emptying station around them, "is first right thing I've done in long time."

Mohawk gave his arm a violent tug, pulling free at last. The leather of his coat ripped, leaving Maksimillian with just a torn fragment in his hands. Maksimillian lifted it to his face, breathed in the scent of it. It had been a person once, this leather a part of their skin. Soft. He let it fall to the ground. He reached out his hands, grabbed the front of Mohawk's coat, and twirled the man like a dance partner. The other man's feet slipped across the concrete as Maksimillian spun him, let him go to sail through the air, colliding with Panda as she was making the subway car. They both went down in a tangle of limbs, the subway car's doors hissing shut with a *thunk* no more than six feet in front of them.

Both were on their feet in a moment. Panda looked to Mohawk. "We need to get her."

Mohawk shook his head. "I think ... this is more important." He pulled a gun from under his coat, pointing the weapon at Maksimillian. "You're strong, *friend*."

"*Da.*" Maksimillian shrugged. "I think there is question you must ask. Knowing what you know so far. The strength, *da*, but also, how do you say it, being in right place at right time. With all of this, what am I?" Maksimillian clenched his fists, almost stepped towards them until he saw a flash of green hair through the subway car's windows. He pulled back behind a column, the tiles covered in small scrawls of mindless graffiti. He rested his head against it.

She must not see us. She must not know us.

He waited a few moments for the car to pull away, the noise fading off into a distant rush of speed. Always hurrying, these *Amerikanskaya*, even their machines hurried. He frowned. *What am I?*

Maksimillian took a step out from behind the column, and Mohawk fired. Maksimillian turned, and spun, and ducked, the bullets missing, until Mohawk's weapon clicked dry. He enjoyed the dance so much he could almost ignore the panicked terror that hit the commuters around him, like a light switch as soon as the first shot sounded. The remaining people on the subway platform started screaming, running anywhere but *here*, fear making them blind, terror making them careless. He smiled across the now empty subway platform. "Is another ... point of fact, *da*?" He patted himself down. "Not one shot hit, and you, you are good shot. You are *fast*. And still. Here I am. I have question, just as you think about mine."

Mohawk was looking from the gun to Maksimillian, back to the gun. "What?"

Panda's eyes were wide, her mouth open slightly. She closed it with a snap around teeth that were too large to be *human*. "We should go."

"Fuck, no," said Mohawk.

"Really," said Panda. "There's no problem with regrouping—"

"There's *every* problem with regrouping," said Mohawk. "You know what they're like. What *she's* like."

"No, but I've heard," said Panda. She held a hand out towards Maksimillian. "But this asshole here, well, he wasn't in the mission brief."

"May I," said Maksimillian, "ask my question?" They both turned to look at him, saying nothing, so he continued. "Why you make coat from their skins?"

"Why shouldn't we?" It was Panda who answered. "Why shouldn't we make a coat from your hide?"

"It seems ... ah, this English, is hard, *da*?" Maksimillian thought for a moment. "Impractical. That is the word. Take so many people to make one coat, and the leather, it is weak."

Panda blinked, looked at Mohawk, then looked back. "What?"

"It is just..." Maksimillian snapped his fingers. "A single cow for a coat. Efficient. And the leather would be strong. I see," and here, he gestured at his eyes, "that the coats you wear flow very well. Is like that movie, with the very pretty woman. *Underworld*, *da*? You want to be like her. Is that the reason?"

"You are crazier than a Klansman at a white sale in June, aren't you?" said Mohawk. "Won't save you."

We are not right. We are wrong.

Maksimillian squinted his eyes closed for a second, opened them again. "*Da*. I think you are right. About the crazy part. So many things go on in my head, it is hard to know what is real. But I think I know one thing. One tiny thing, so small, is almost insignificant."

"And what's that?" said Panda, cocking her hip, her voice almost a lazy drawl. Trying to talk some courage back into herself. Maksimillian had seen it before. It never helped. Not really.

The station was empty, distant shouts still sounding, but not drawing closer. No *politsiya*. No people, and not one person in particular, not a hint of green hair anywhere. Not *her*. Maksimillian almost relaxed, smiled. "The thing — the tiny thing — is that you are baby *vampiry*, *da*? Infants." He rolled his shoulders. "You do not have all of the things that make you special."

"Are you ... Russian?" Mohawk frowned. "What the fuck kind of word is, '*vampiry*?'"

Maksimillian thought for a moment, then held his hand out. He wiggled it in the air *so-so*. "More or less. Mother Russia is old, but I remember when she was born."

Mohawk's smile faded, and he leaned forward, taking a deep breath of the air around Maksimillian. "You smell ... alive."

"*Da*." Maksimillian smiled at the man, encouraging.

"But you say you're centuries old."

"*Da*." Maksimillian clapped happily. "You will get there. Keep going."

"You're not one of us." Panda stepped closer. "So what are you?"

"See?" said Maksimillian. "Baby *vampiry*." He shrugged. "You are," and he gestured at her face, her makeup, and then at Mohawk's hair, "a sign of your times. The punk years, *da*?"

Fight.

Panda bared her teeth at him, her fangs showing pale and white. But it was Mohawk that spoke. "Yes."

Kill.

"Then you have lived long enough for men." Maksimillian closed his eyes for a moment—

They must all DIE.

—then looked at Mohawk. "Is time. Time for you to be … finished."

Mohawk's fangs were out, and he took a single step towards Maksimillian. Maksimillian read the intent of that movement, how it would have turned into another step, a fist to the face, a hand in the back of his hair, teeth to the neck. He almost wanted it, almost wanted his eternal Night to end—

They made us kill our Pack.

—and then snarled, a hand punching out. It was an overpowered swing, all rage and hate, catching Mohawk in the chest. The creature flew back across the station's platform, the *crack* of crushing bone overlaid by the fragmenting sound of breaking masonry. Panda was already leaping at him, and he caught her rush with open arms. *Catch each wrist, just so, and hold the teeth away. It is the teeth, Maksimillian Kotlyarov, that will be the end of you. The only thing that can really hurt.* They strained against each other, her bared fangs snapping in his face, and he felt his breathing go ragged, heart bright and fierce in his chest. They were strong, these baby *vampiry*, stronger than he remembered, but it had been such a long time, so many years since he'd fought one. So many years since he'd felt the pain, and the fear, and the hate, and the anger. The anger, that was what he needed.

THEY MADE US KILL OUR PACK.

He screamed at the thing, felt a burst of strength that came with the rage, and smashed his forehead into the bridge of her nose. It wasn't enough to do anything but distract, but distraction was enough. Her strength eased up for a moment and he managed to unbalance her. A moment later, he slammed her into the ground, the concrete of the platform cracking underneath Panda with the force of the throw. She was clawing about, fingers cutting into the pavement, furrows through the stone, but his grip was—

Stronger than rock. As eternal as the Night.

—firm, a knee in her chest, and he arched back, slowly, so slowly, against the massive strength she had. The strength given to her by the deaths of many. But he was stronger, stronger now with all his hate and rage and the *memory of blood in his mouth as he killed his family* and the terror of being alone. He snarled, felt a pop as her shoulder dislocated, and the thing beneath him screamed. Maksimillian kept pulling, harder, and harder, wanting to make the screaming stop, as his Pack's screaming had stopped, pulled until her arm pulled free from her torso in a spray of dark wet. It smelled—

Ancient. Rotted. Bad meat.

—like a thing dead already, and he threw the arm away. The creature beneath him was mewling, and he hit it in the face, and then again, and again, until there was nothing left of Panda, nothing left at all to remind him what she used to be, someone else's Pack.

He stood up, blood and viscera coating his arms, his chest. He looked around the platform, felt the snarl that wasn't a smile on his face, turned his yellow eyes towards Mohawk. The man was already standing, pulling his broken torso back into some semblance of shape.

"You ... killed her."

"How can you kill a thing already dead?" said Maksimillian, his voice thick. He stalked towards Mohawk, then paused. Mohawk's passage had crushed a bench, leaving splinters of wood and metal, and Maksimillian reached down for a piece of wood. "*Nyet.* But she is not dead."

"She looks pretty fucking dead to me!" Mohawk reached out a hand, the end falling loosely down as the broken elbow failed to support it. "Look what you did to her!"

Maksimillian moved back towards Panda's body, the blood, the smell of death, and held up his stake of wood. He drove it—

Through the heart.

—into her chest, and the body gave one last convulsion. It would have screamed again if there had been enough working parts to make a noise, but it just slumped back down in a wet *slop* of its own remains.

"Now," said Maksimillian, "the creature is dead."

"What ... what *are* you?" said Mohawk. He was trying to back away, eyes looking for an exit. The station was full of ways out, but none of them fast, except for the subway's tunnels.

What am I? Maksimillian could feel the rumbling of another train coming, and smiled. "I am Maksimillian Kotlyarov."

"That's a name, a fucking *name*, not a *thing*," said the creature. "*What* are you?" Then it looked around, turned, and sprinted towards the station's tracks. Even normal hearing could pick out the sound of the train coming, and the thing thought it could use the train as a distraction.

Maksimillian reached down, picked up a piece of broken stone about the size of a fist. He lined up the throw, thinking about how it would be if The Bambino threw. Babe Ruth was one of the first five members of the Baseball Hall of Fame, known for his pitch and his swing, and Maksimillian would do him proud.

The creature had almost made the tracks, the train coming into the station in a blast of light and noise. Maksimillian could see from the way the creature moved, from the way he'd watched a thousand thousand people run away, that it was about to jump, to leap the track in front of the train, use the machine as a barrier. Maksimillian wound his arm back and threw.

The chunk of stone flew straight and true, catching Mohawk in the back just as he was about to jump. It wasn't much, but it put him off-balance, and the man stumbled, rather than jumped, in front of the train. He didn't even scream as the train rolled over the top of him, and Maksimillian knew there'd be nothing but fragments of clothing and teeth left. Hard to identify a body from a size 10 shoe.

He picked up another piece of wood anyway. Being thorough, that was important.

He nodded to himself, looked at the bloody mess that had been Panda, and then walked towards the train. People were screaming, more people now, people who'd just arrived on that train, the driver no doubt in shock at having run someone over. Other people would come, there would be questions, and Maksimillian needed to be far away from here before that happened.

Time enough to finish the job first. He kept walking, then realized he hadn't answered Mohawk's last question. He looked around, at the panic, the fear, and smiled.

We are the Night.

"I am Maksimillian Kotlyarov, and I am the Night."

CHAPTER
TEN

John Miles *(01:01): Melissa*
    (01:01) Melissa
    (01:01) Yo, Melissa. It's John.

CARLISLE (01:02): I cn seee tht.
    (01:02): What time

JOHN MILES (01:02): It's like one in the morning.
    (01:02): That's not important. I need help.

CARLISLE (01:03): Yr rigt. I kill yo.
    (01:03) you.

JOHN MILES (01:03): I met this girl.

. . .

CARLISLE (01:04): I'm turnng my ph of.

JOHN MILES (01:04): Melissa?
    [Message can't be sent]
    (01:04): Melissa?
    [Message can't be sent]

⁓

JOHN MILES (01:05): Hey Val
    [Message can't be sent]
    (01:05): Val
    [Message can't be sent]
    (01:05): Val
    [Message can't be sent]
    (01:06): Val
    [Message can't be sent]

⁓

DANNY (01:07): Don't even ask.

JOHN MILES (01:07): It's a big problem.

DANNY (01:08): Melissa told me. You're on a date. I'm turning my phone off.

JOHN MILES (01:08): Danny?

[Message can't be sent]

～

JOHN MILES *(01:09): Hey Adalia*
(01:09): Don't turn your phone off.

ADALIA *(01:10): I don't tink it turns off Uncle J*

JOHN MILES *(01:11): Has Melissa spoken to you*

ADALIA *(01:11): Melissa? Y would?*

JOHN MILES *(01:12): No reason*
(01:12) I need some help.

ADALIA *(01:12): R U n a fite*

JOHN MILES *(01:12): No*

ADALIA *(01:13): R U n jail*

JOHN MILES *(01:13): No*

ADALIA *(01:14): iz it bout a 3:o)*

. . .

JOHN MILES *(01:14): ...*
    (01:14): What the fuck is 3:o)

ADALIA *(01:14): girl*

JOHN MILES *(01:15): Not specifically*

ADALIA *(01:15): I'm turniN on DND*

JOHN MILES *(01:15): Wait*
    (01:17): I think the devil herself is here
    (01:18): Adalia?
    (01:19): Adalia?

ADALIA *(01:20): We're almost ther*

JOHN MILES *(01:20): We?*

ADALIA *(01:21): Melissa's w me*

JOHN MILES *(01:21): But how*

ADALIA *(01:21): sumtimz seein the futR iz fun*

ELEVEN

Liselle pulled the sheet off and felt the light of the moon wash over her bare skin. The floor to ceiling windows of her apart- ment — which continued here, into her bedroom — gave an impressive view. It wasn't the view of the ground she wanted, but of the sky. The Father's works still made her marvel, and that's why she didn't want the world to end. *Not yet.* There was so much beauty.

Her feet made no noise as she left her bed, leaving the man there — *so much beauty* — sleeping. Her apartment was large by the stan- dards of this city, with a view — for those who cared — of the park that sat in the center of it. Moonbeams hung in the air, the light almost blue. Liselle moved into the space she'd reserved as a living room. She never used it, never even had people here, until now. She looked around the room, the expensive furnishings, the comfortable couches and chairs, the rare art, and frowned.

She hated it. Hated it all, these tiny trinkets. Funny how all it took to see the baubles for what they were was *just breakfast*.

Liselle paused. No, that was wrong. It wasn't *just breakfast* any more than she *hated these things*. She saw these things for what they were: trappings laid about so she could try and ignore ... the rest.

The endless loneliness. By the Father, but she'd been so alone for so very, very long.

Her living room was attached to the kitchen; a balcony bared itself to the sky through large bi-folding doors of glass. The main entrance to her apartment was in this room, and it sat ajar, the darkness of the corridor outside an open invitation.

She sighed. This was going to happen sooner or later. Liselle reached down to the low glass table in the center of the lounge, opened the wooden case that held her cigarettes, and picked one out. The smooth smoke of the Davidoff curled into her lungs as she lit it, a long tongue of flame banishing the blue of moonbeams for a moment.

Liselle breathed out, clicked off the lighter, and crossed her arms across her chest. "I didn't say you could come here."

A shape, just a smudge of shadow, detached itself from the wall, resolving into a woman. She was so pale, so porcelain perfect. Long black hair fell like dark water around her face. But it was the eyes that caught most people's attention. Those eyes that could see into the souls of men. "You didn't say I couldn't, either."

"Kaylan," said Liselle, "that's because I said I didn't want to see you again. I've kept up my side of that."

Kaylan shrugged. "Now I know. I won't come back."

"Thank you," said Liselle. She gestured with her hand at the box on the table. "Cigarette?"

Kaylan walked forward, picking out one of the Davidoffs and helping herself to the lighter. She inhaled the smoke, her eyes closed with pleasure. "You still keep good things, Liselle."

"Yes," said Liselle. Not *if you like these things why do you want it all to end* or *I should strike you down where you stand.* Just *yes.*

It didn't matter — Kaylan heard what she meant. "Sister, we shouldn't fight. We were *made* for this."

"This is an old argument," said Liselle. "We're not going to resolve it here, while you stand dressed in the skin of men, and I stand naked before the Father."

"You noticed." Kaylan fingered the collar of the long coat she wore, the soft leather whispering around her. "I quite like it. It's so ... *nouveau chic.*"

"They are *his children*!" Liselle waved her cigarette at the window, at the world that waited beyond. "You dress yourself in the skins of his children, Kaylan. You don't think he'll notice?"

"Of course he'll notice," said Kaylan. She turned to look at some of Liselle's art. "He's got big plans, remember?"

"The first and the last," said Liselle. "Kaylan Gleicher and Maynor Coen, trying to bring an end to the world. I don't think that was his plan."

"Do you presume to know?" Kaylan looked back at her. "It seems quite clear to me. He made four of us to do a job, and you and that dreary, boring Josef Hackett aren't doing your part." She thought for a moment. "That's not fair. Josef is doing his part. Conflict is everywhere."

"You reap what he sows," said Liselle. "But he's not doing it for you."

"I know," said Kaylan. "He's still put out that we didn't ask him to join the club."

"I don't think that's it," said Liselle. "You know as I do that as long as hate lives in the hearts of men, there will always be War. How did he put it? 'Job for life.'"

"Indeed." Kaylan took another pull of her cigarette. "Were you upset? That we didn't need you?"

Liselle snorted. "You needed me. You tried to make them just the right level of hungry, but instead they're starving. Always wanting more."

"That's just them being *human*," said Kaylan.

"Perhaps," said Liselle, then, "Kaylan, why are you here?"

"I wanted to see," said Kaylan, "and now I've seen."

Liselle gave a throaty chuckle. "Oh, sister. I see."

"There is nothing to see."

"They're ... they're actually doing it." Liselle thought for a moment. What had John Miles said? *So I guess, that's why we're going to kick their asses. Because we need to. Because no one else is going to. Because we can.* "And you don't know who they are. You thought ... you thought it was *me*."

Kaylan crushed out her cigarette. "It might not be you, but you know who it is."

"I know," said Liselle. She laughed again. *Because we can.* "I'm laughing because I thought he was crazy."

"Who?" said Kaylan.

"But he's not, is he?" Liselle flicked ash from her cigarette.

Kaylan was in front of her, faster than thought, her hand around Liselle's throat. "*Tell me a name.*" Her eyes had gone pale, so pale in her pale face, all color draining from them, and they stared at Liselle with unblinking purpose.

Liselle swayed back, grabbing at Kaylan's hand with her own. She struggled, but Kaylan had always been stronger, stronger even than Josef, she was the last one of them, the bringer of the end, the—

"Ladies," said John Miles. "How we all doing?"

Kaylan's hand dropped from Liselle's neck like it had been burned, leaving Liselle gasping. Liselle reached a hand up, felt her neck, coughed, but Kaylan had already moved on. Moved towards John Miles.

No. Liselle straightened herself, made to jump at Kaylan, but saw her sister had already stopped. Kaylan was looking at John Miles, her posture speaking astonishment. "You are ... just a *man*."

John looked down at himself. He was wearing one of Liselle's silk robes, far too small on him, the hem only coming down mid-thigh. He looked back up at Kaylan, then said, "But *what* a man, amirite?" Liselle noticed that he held a bundle of fabric in one hand.

"You ... how..." Kaylan looked back at Liselle, then at John again. "You are *just a man*."

"Hey," said John, "so a couple of things. First up, anyone want some coffee?"

Both Kaylan and Liselle looked at him, not speaking. He nodded at them. "Great. Coffee for three, coming up. Babe, where's the coffee?"

Liselle pointed a hand at one of the cabinets over the sink.

John nodded, but didn't move towards the cabinet. "Second thing," he said, "is that I find that when I'm being strangled by someone, or something, or, you know, werewolves, right? You just don't know how they're going to act on any given Sunday. Anyway, what I was thinking is that it's really bad to be strangled when I'm not wearing any clothes."

"What?" said Kaylan.

"The third thing," said John, walking towards Liselle, "and I know I said 'a couple of things' like there were only two, well." He stood in front of Liselle, shaking out the fabric bundle — another one her robes. It was her favorite one, like somehow he'd known. She remembered getting it as John whispered the silk around her shoulders, the pattern of the dragon that wound its way through the silk falling free to lie against her side. She remembered the dragons, had wanted to be free like them. It was because of them that she wore the robe often. A reminder of what she wanted. Or a reminder of what she was. Or a reminder of what she could never be. "Hey," said John, his voice low and just for her. "It'll be okay."

She shook her head, but didn't say anything.

"What is," said Kaylan, "this impressive third thing?"

"Oh, that," said John, turning around. He moved into the kitchen, getting out the coffee can, some cups. "Anyone take sugar? I take cream and sugar, so you know, it's cool."

"The. Third. Thing." Kaylan was gritting her teeth.

"Normally, well, normally Carlisle's the one who delivers news like this," said John, looking straight at Kaylan, "but you're a huge, and I mean cavernous, truly epic scale, whale-sized cunt."

"You can't speak to me like ... *you are just a man!*" Kaylan was angry, she was actually *angry*, and it made Liselle laugh. Again.

John looked up at the sound, and smiled, that wonderful smile. "That's it," he said. "That's the sound we want."

"You're … you're…" Kaylan stopped. "Is this some kind of joke?"

"You're right, it is," said John. "I make terrible coffee." He shrugged. "My buddy Val, he's got this whole cinnamon thing going with the coffee. I don't know how he does it. He was trying to tell me, you know, a recipe, but when I do it, it tastes like a mixture of apple pie and burnt ass."

Kaylan turned from John to look at Liselle. "Is this *buffoon* the one who is … no." She shook her head. "He can't be."

"Can't be what?" said John. He was tipping boiling water into the French press, giving it a swirl as he poured. "The coffee really will be bad." He stared at Kaylan for a minute. "You're a cream-no-sugar kind of woman, aren't you?"

Kaylan hadn't stopped looking at Liselle. "He doesn't have the power, the *strength*, to fight them. You let this *shell* you wear," and here, she gestured at Liselle's body, "guide you like you're some kind of rutting *whore*. You've forgotten who you are. We both know," and here, she turned back to John, "that the only way to hurt you is to hurt *them*."

Father, no. Liselle started forward, but Kaylan had the head start, was already moving towards John. One hand on the countertop, her feet swung up and over, that black coat flapping like wings, and then she had a hand around *his* throat. Kaylan lifted him off the ground, and Liselle was too far away, she was still too far, she wasn't going to make it, saw Kaylan's hand pull back—

"*STOP.*" The voice cut across them all, halted motion, thought, purpose. It was hard and strong; Liselle had heard a voice like that only twice before. Once, at the beginning, and then once more when she'd met a kind young man with gentle eyes and a gentler soul. He'd turned her away as she'd offered to sweep the Romans aside like chaff on the wind. And then he'd died, and she'd been lost ever since.

Liselle stumbled, watched as Kaylan dropped John Miles and staggered. Liselle looked towards the voice, saw a young woman with green hair standing in the door of her apartment. Her face was pale, color leeched out from fatigue, but she steadied herself with a hand on the door frame.

"*Kaylan Gleicher, I tell you this once. You will go from this place. You will not harm the man named John, of the house Miles.*" The woman with green hair — *so young, so frail, so strong, so ancient* — started at Kaylan, eyes hard. "*Do you hear me?*"

Kaylan stared at her, and laughed. "You can't command me, child. I collected His only son's soul. Your words—"

"*Kaylan Gleicher, you* will *go from this place.*" The woman with green hair strode forward, the room feeling too small to hold her. Her lips twisted into a smile. "*Or ... would you like to make a trade?*"

Kaylan's lips pulled back from her teeth in a snarl. She stood tall, tension pulling between the two of them. It felt like the charge before a storm, the air smelling of ozone. A crack ran up one of the windows, slowly at first, then with a *snack* the pane popped in a shower of glass. Kaylan didn't even blink. "You don't know what you're—"

The French press smashed against the side of her face, scalding coffee and glass and metal raining down. It startled Kaylan, and she took a step back — *she calls mine a* shell *but she's wearing one too* — wiping her face. Thunder rumbled outside, and for just a moment something *else* stood in Kaylan's place, something tall and frightening, with pale eyes. It was like a shadow superimposed over her.

A bullet took her in the shoulder, then another in the chest, a final one tearing away Kaylan's jaw. The sound was impossibly loud in the room, the firearm shouting defiance at Kaylan, and she stumbled back. Through the windows, more broken glass falling like hard tears. The gun spoke again, a hole punching through Kaylan's stomach. Another shot and her hand tore away. A final boom from the weapon and Kaylan's shell tumbled over the side of the balcony, and then she was gone, falling from sight.

Lightning arced from the sky, the light so bright, so close, the air smelling of power and melted metal and burnt stone. Liselle looked away, held her hand up in front of her face, but the lightning struck on, and on, and *on*. Bolt after brilliant bolt came from the sky, hitting with force enough to shake the earth.

Silence.

"Enough fucking talking," said another voice into that absence of sound. Liselle blinked away the after images to take in another woman, short leather jacket below hair pulled into a practical tail. She held a gun, and Liselle could see it for what it was. *The Eagle*.

"Hey," said John, looking at the broken window, then back at the two newcomers. "Took you long enough."

"For Chrissakes, Miles," said the one with the gun. "You're lucky her phone was even on."

"She's a Millennial," said John. "They never turn their phones off." He started walking, not looking like he was really moving at all but managing to cover the floor of her living room at speed. Liselle could see in the way he held his shoulders that he was worried but not wanting to look worried; it might have fooled anyone who hadn't spent a thousand lifetimes looking at people. He made it to the woman with green hair just as she began to topple, caught her in those strong arms — *is this what jealously feels like? I don't think I like it* — and held her.

"Hey," he was saying to her. "Hey. It's okay."

"Miles?" The voice of the woman with the gun had turned sharp with worry. "What's wrong with her?"

"Too much partying," said John, scooping up the woman with green hair like she weighed nothing at all. There was surprising bitterness in his voice. "Too many stupid uncles." He carried her to Liselle's couch, laid her down. "Hey, Adalia. It's okay. It's okay."

"You keep..." The woman with green hair — *Adalia* — licked her lips. "You keep saying that, but you know, it doesn't feel okay. You ever fought with someone about a hundred times your weight?"

"Anton the Ape," said John.

"What?" said Adalia.

"Guy I wrestled with when I was, I dunno, it must have been ten years old. Something wrong with him, he was shaving at the age of eight." John smoothed back Adalia's hair. "But yeah. Thanks."

"It's what family's for," said Adalia, then closed her eyes. Out, asleep, gone. *Family*, thought Liselle, and felt that green clenched fist around her heart relax.

"Miles," said the woman with the gun, "start talking."

"Yeah," he said. "Okay." He stood up, but was still looking down at Adalia. "Yeah. So."

The woman with the gun took four strides towards him, wrenched him around by his shoulder. Liselle thought she was going to hit him, real fire in her eyes, and John stood there like he wanted her to, like he thought he deserved it. After a moment, the woman with the gun grabbed him close, her hug fierce. "Don't ... I was..." The gun was still in her hand, Liselle watching it. She thought, *Wouldn't this be fine, if the gun went off after all the action was finished?*

John pulled the woman free. "It's okay, Melissa."

"Call me," she said, "fucking *Carlisle*." Liselle heard no malice in her voice, an old joke shared between friends who knew each other better than lovers. Carlisle pulled herself free, straightened her jacket, then looked at the gun she still held. Without taking the eyes off it, she said, "Who's that?"

"Oh," said John, "hey, yeah, that. Melissa—"

"Carlisle," said Carlisle.

"—this is Liselle. Liselle, this is my friend Melissa." He rubbed a hand through the hair at the back of his head. "She's kind of a hardass. Sorry she shot your sister."

Liselle took Carlisle's hand, felt the true iron in the grip. "It's a pleasure to meet you," she said.

"Yeah, great," said Carlisle. "Now that's done, who the hell did I just shoot?" She seemed to notice for the first time the robe John was wearing. "Nice bathrobe. It really sets off the highlights in your hair." She thought for a moment. "Why didn't Adalia's ... *thing* ... work with that crazy who went out the window? Why was there a lightning strike, and Miles, this is the really important question I need an answer to, why was there a lightning strike that lasted for like a minute? That didn't seem like a natural fucking weather phenomenon."

"I went on a date," said John, as if that explained everything.

Liselle laughed. Because, more or less, it kind of did.

Carlisle frowned. "I don't think I understand."

"It's when two people, see, they get together, and they—"

"I know what a date is, Miles," Carlisle said.

"You said you didn't—"

"I am confused," said Carlisle, "about why you're in a woman's bathrobe in an apartment over the Park. I am confused about why I had to shoot someone tonight, which I'll agree seemed like the right thing to do at the time, but I feel like I'm missing the ... *start* of the whole thing. I am confused," she said, "about why you're here in this very fine apartment instead of back at the bar, where we went to such an effort to get you a job, feeding my old comrades at the five-oh some nice misleading statements that would throw them off our tracks for a few more days."

"About that," said John. "It's not what—"

"It's my fault," said Liselle.

They both looked at her. Then Carlisle looked at the gun in her hand, said something that sounded like *hell*, and put it away.

"Baby," said John, turning to Liselle. "There's a few things I've learned in life—"

"A precious few," said Carlisle.

"—but one of them is that it's usually my fault."

"The police won't bother you," said Liselle.

"How do you figure that?" said Carlisle. "Earlier on, a bunch of people in a bar died." She swallowed. "There's a bit of a thing going on here too with some woman dead outside on the sidewalk, so I'm figuring that they'll be along shortly to find out why she jumped, and they're going to find," and here, Carlisle gestured at the blood on the ground, mixed with the remains of the French press and the coffee it had held, "a crime scene. Eventually, that will lead to questions that, on any given day, I'd feel uncomfortable being involved in, but we don't have the fucking *time* right now."

"The police won't bother you," said Liselle, "because they are controlled by the vampires."

"That was a scenario we'd considered," said Carlisle, "but it does kind of imply that *vampires* might come along afterward instead. And given a choice between a few uncomfortable questions down at the station, and being surrounded by legions of things that want to drink my blood and turn me into an unholy monster, I'll take the station." She started to pace.

"They won't come here," said Liselle.

"Why not?" Carlisle paused her pacing. "Seems like we've lit a big sign in the sky that said, 'Free lunch here.'"

"Because I'm here," said Liselle.

"Baby," said John. "Baby, and don't take this the wrong way, but just before your sister had you in a stranglehold, and then she got to me, and it doesn't look like she even lifts, but she was *strong*." He opened his mouth, closed it again. "What I'm trying to say—"

"You're trying to say," said Liselle, looking at him, "that you think they could take me."

He considered. "That's more or less it," he agreed.

"Kaylan," said Liselle, "is my sister. My sister ... they're afraid of her."

"It's a family thing?" Carlisle frowned. "And you're using 'is.'"

"I'm sorry?" Liselle looked at the other woman.

"'Is,'" said Carlisle, "not, 'was.' Present tense. Usually, when someone's taken a dive out the window and left a crater and a bunch of hamburger, you'd refer to them in the past tense. Normally I'd be a little more ... sensitive to the situation, but you seem pretty chill about the whole affair."

"Kaylan's not gone," said Liselle. She looked between them, the man with the beautiful light inside him, and the Shield that stood at his side. Should she trust these two? Should she tell them about her family? Could they really fix things? So many had tried, so very many, and Liselle had seen them all fail.

That's why we're going to kick their asses. Because we need to. Because no one else is going to. Because we can.

Liselle knew she shouldn't have taken this man to her bed, but it had seemed so right. It didn't just *seem* right — it *was* right. *By the Father, but it feels so good to be human. How can Kaylan want to end this?* It felt good, and natural, and everything that this world was meant to give to its people. Love, and happiness, and life. She nodded to herself, then turned to the broken window. Dawn would be here within a few hours, light cascading like a slow waterfall over the city.

"Baby?" John was behind her, a touch at her elbow, his scent all around. She closed her eyes, breathed it in. It was forbidden. It was wonderful.

Kaylan rode the lightning so she could begin again. She put a hand over his. Liselle felt the weight of the words before she said them, the despair welling up inside her. The things she must say, should say, mustn't say, could never say. She licked her lips, closed her eyes for a moment. If this beautiful man stayed with her, no matter that he thought he could fix it, he would surely die. And she couldn't let that happen. This one human, this one, perfect man, this one at least she could save. She opened her eyes. "I think ... I think you better go."

CHAPTER
TWELVE

"She went out," said Rex. He sighed. *Too damn old for this shit. Was too old five years ago, and I haven't got any younger.* "She went out with *Carlisle*."

Danny was staring at him, the same way she'd been staring at him since she'd come out wearing a bathrobe and a frown and found her daughter gone, smoke on the wind. If Rex was being honest, he was a little worried too, but what was he supposed to do? The kid channeled the power of the Universe. It's not like *he* had any kind of special powers to keep her to a curfew. It's not like she couldn't just change the wind to stone or cats into dogs or whatever the damn Universe-power-thing let her do.

"Rex," said Val, "you know that we're hunting vampires, right?"

"I do know that," said Rex. "It keeps me up at night."

"Cool," said Val. "You know that vampires are out at night, right?"

"It's a part of the lore I'm familiar with." Rex rubbed his face. *Too damn old. Vampires, for Chrissakes.*

"And you let," said Danny, "my daughter go outside. At night. Where there are vampires. By herself."

"With Carlisle," said Rex. "She was with—"

"Melissa," said Danny, "is not really up to this." She sat down on the couch, put her head in her hands, ruffled her hair, and sighed. "It's not that she's not capable, it's that—"

"It's that we're just normal," said Jessie, coming in from her room. Rex knew she called it her *rack*, like she was getting a *little rack time*. Rex took a double-take: first damn time he'd seen Jessie wearing a bathrobe in as long as he'd known her. Always, always she wore her clothes like some kind of uniform, always pressed, always neat, and Rex didn't know who else had time to iron their denim but it wasn't him. "We're just people, right?" She started rummaging around the kitchen. "Rex, where's the coffee pot?"

"It's in the—" Rex started.

"I'm going out after her," said Danny, rising from the couch.

"The thing about people," said Jessie, "is that they can do amazing things if you trust them."

"Vampires are a bit above Melissa's pay grade," said Danny. "They are fast, and strong, and they terrify me. *Me*. I'm a *werewolf*, Jessica. I can tear the door off a car or run faster than a train, and they scare me."

"I get that," said Jessie, putting some grounds into the coffee pot. "I was scared, too. I was scared when I was deployed to a place with no family, nothing but sand, IEDs under every rock. I was scared when they told me that my son was dead. I was scared when we went out yesterday to get the creature we're keeping in the cage out the back. What I'm not scared about is whether Carlisle has this one. She'll make it work."

Danny looked uncertain.

That's my cue. Rex ran a hand over his chin, feeling the stubble that was one hundred percent grade-A silver. "Danny," he said. "Danny, weren't you the one who said she should get a 'real job?'" *Like this isn't the realest job in the whole world.* "You've got her working at Starbucks."

"So she can learn about how things work," said Danny. "Anyway, that was Val's idea."

"Right," said Rex. "It was Val's idea, and he—"

"Hey," said Val, a startled expression on his face. "Don't put me in the middle. I didn't—"

"The thing is," said Rex, "it was a *good* idea."

"It was?" said Val and Danny, together.

Jessie winked at him from the kitchen, so Rex pushed on. "She's learning about people. You know, she talks to me, probably because I'm so close to death's door any secrets have a finite time to live. You know what she said to me last week? She said that she doesn't use it anymore."

"That's it," said Danny. "I'm—"

"She doesn't use her gift," said Rex, "because everyone she meets has a, hell, I'm not saying this right, but some kind of thing that makes them hard to deal with. Baggage, I guess you'd call it. So she doesn't look to the future, or the past. I'd doubt she even looks both ways when crossing the road anymore. She doesn't use her gift because the world's full of noise, and you've got her working at Starbucks, where there's nothing but people with their noise. And you know, she's doing it anyway, because you asked her to. Not told her, mind, because you couldn't *tell* that kid what do to even with the best of intentions. You raised her right, to be true and strong, and tonight she found a chance to be what she was made for again. She's not making caramel lattes, she's out there, fixing things. That's her *real job*." He stopped talking, felt like a clock that had wound down. "That's what I think, anyway."

"I..." said Danny. She looked lost.

"Hell," said Rex, "I've probably said too much. I'm an old man who can't sleep at night. Wrong place, right time. I just happened to see her go outside, that's all. You know what she said?"

"No," said Danny.

"She said," said Rex, "that she'd be back in time for breakfast. So she could go to work." He paused. "At *Starbucks*."

Danny sat back down again. "Oh," she said. "Why was Carlisle awake?"

"She wasn't," said Rex. "Or, I don't know, not at first. She came out here with that damn hand cannon and asked where they were going. Looked angry."

That put a small smile on Danny's face. "Okay," she said. "Okay."

"Not really," said Rex. "She looked like she was going to shoot someone. I didn't want to give her an excuse."

"Do you know," said Val, "where they were going?"

"Yes," said Rex.

"Where?" said Danny.

"I'm not telling," said Rex, feeling vaguely like he was channeling his long-past five-year-old self.

"You're ... what?" said Danny, leaning forward.

"I'm not telling," said Rex, "because you should trust her."

"I trust Melissa," said Danny.

Rex looked at her for a moment. "Not Melissa," he said. "That's not who I meant." He wanted to say, *kid's got to make her own way*, or, *your kid's got real fire in her*, or even, *don't sass me, girl*, but he didn't. He sat there, still as midnight.

Val looked like he wanted to say something, so Rex shot him a look. He hoped the look said something like *not now*, rather than *come punch me*, because the man was mostly calm but there's no way Rex wanted to wrestle a tiger before breakfast. Hell of a way to go out. Rex sighed. "Look," he said. "I don't want to tell you how to raise your kid—"

"But you're going to anyway," said Danny.

Rex chewed that one over. "More or less."

"I get it," said Danny. "I still want to go after her, but I ... shouldn't."

"Right," said Rex. "Great."

"I've got just one question," said Val. "Where's John?"

Now that's *a question*. Rex coughed. "On a date, I think." Not —

strictly speaking — a lie. Not full quality truth either. Good enough for now. "You remember, right?"

"Still?" said Val. "That's a long date."

"Sure," said Rex. "Who wants coffee?"

Jessie winked at him, started pouring. Chalk one up for *normal people*.

THE THING in the cage stared out at Rex. *Damnedest thing, vampires, werewolves, and you thought you'd spend your twilight years in a home slapping the asses of pretty nurses.* Rex shook himself, took a couple of deep breaths, and walked towards the thing. *Rex, Rex, Rex: you know you shouldn't think about ...* him *that way. He was a person once. Named Jeremy.* "Hungry?" He took a sip of his coffee.

Jeremy's eyes opened, and he licked his lips. "I could eat."

Rex walked across the gloom of the garage to the double doors of the refrigerator. "How much you need?"

"Not much." Jeremy thought for a second. "You know, I've never measured it."

"Well, son," said Rex, "that's kind of what this is about. Finding out things."

"Let's start with one bag," said Jeremy. He looked across the room at the black body bag. "What's with the stiff?"

"Uh," said Rex. "I think that's, uh, well."

"You wanted something to experiment on, and then I got here," said Jeremy. "That about it?"

Rex rubbed his chin, nodded. "That's about it."

"Won't work," said Jeremy. "I don't mean me. I mean the guy in the bag. Doesn't work that way."

"Son—"

"I'm not trying to be a dick about it," said Jeremy. "I'd far prefer you to experiment on whoever that asshole was. But open the bag."

"Uh—"

"Look," said Jeremy. "You got to start somewhere. Just open the bag."

What the hell. Rex walked over to the black body bag, grabbed the zipper, and yanked. The plastic peeled open, smoke pouring from the side along with a charnel reek. The remains in the bag were ... *ancient.* Charred, and where they weren't charred, rotted. "Uh," he said, then stepped back, covering his nose.

"Yeah." Jeremy looked out from behind the bars. "When we die ... well, shit catches up on us. How about that food?"

Rex looked at the mess in the bag, then back to Jeremy. "You're hungry?"

"I've killed literally hundreds of people," said Jeremy. "*Murdered* them. It's not fun, okay, but a man's got to eat. So, you know. I'm used to it, I guess."

Rex nodded, walking back to the refrigerator, then opened it. Cool white light spilled out around his feet. There was a digital read-out, big red letters with 42.8 glowing red. *Temperature's still fine.* He snagged a clear plastic bag, the blood on the inside a healthy red. There was a label stuck to it, a bunch of barcodes and a big AB+ right in the middle. It had a tube coming out, coiled like a big flexible straw. "You ... hell, son." Rex let the refrigerator door close. "Hell. This is, well, what I want to know is whether I need to warm it up."

"That'd be nice, actually," said Jeremy. He pushed fingers through his hair. "Look, I don't want to gross you out, but if you give it to me like that it's a little sludgy. Sticks to the throat, you know? Warm, it's..."

Rex looked at him. "More authentic."

Jeremy sighed. "I don't really like it any more than you do," he said. "The difference is that I have to do it. You just have to watch it."

Rex took the blood to a small microwave, tossed it inside, and punched a few buttons. The machine beeped back at him, then hummed.

"Not too much," said Jeremy. "People aren't boiling on the inside."

"I gave it twenty seconds," said Rex. "Twenty seconds sound good to you?" He sipped at his coffee again. Damn, but he wished Val had made it. Jessie made coffee like she was still out in the desert hunting insurgents. Served a purpose, had caffeine in it, but lacked a little soul. Val, though, the man made coffee like some kind of Zen master, and the cinnamon was *inspired*.

"Sure," said Jeremy. "You know, I could do it myself."

"No way," said Rex, "that I'm opening the door of that cage."

"Oh," said Jeremy, then paused as the microwave beeped. "I meant, if you put the microwave in here. But thinking about it, you'd also need to put that big ass refrigerator in here, and I don't think it'd all fit."

"Yeah," said Rex. "I guess." He fished the blood out of the microwave. *There's a thing. You're microwaving someone else's blood, and you're about to serve it to a vampire. It's not too late to check into that nursing home.* "It doesn't feel too hot."

"People aren't," said Jeremy. "Ninety eight point six."

"Figures," said Rex. "Warm summer day."

"Warm summer day," agreed Jeremy, holding a hand out through the bars. "Toss it over."

Rex looked at the bag, then at Jeremy's hand. "Son, we don't work like that here." He walked on over, close to the bars, and held up the bag.

Jeremy took it, then leaned back away from the bars. "You like taking risks?"

Snagging an old camp chair, Rex sat down in front of the cage. He took another sip of his coffee. "Not particularly."

"Coming up to a hungry vampire," said Jeremy, "would be *risky*."

"Sure," said Rex. "I'll write that one down." He took another sip of his coffee.

Sitting down in his cage, Jeremy shook the bag, plumped it, then stuck the tube in his mouth. He sucked, the blood moving down the straw, turning the clear plastic red. He drained the bag, scrunched the plastic up, and sighed. "You're pretty fearless."

"I'm not fearless," said Rex. "I'm terrified."

"You're sitting on a fold-out chair with a cup of coffee, in a dark room with a vampire. You look ... well, if you don't mind me saying, you look fearless."

"Son," said Rex, "I was thinking. You know, about what it'd be like if I found myself in a cage, locked away, sunlight scorching the outside of this big old building. You know, if I was a vampire, you see? Not a lot of safety outside, nowhere to run. And then I was thinking, you know, about what it would be like if that big old building just so happened to be owned by a werewolf Pack. I don't know your history, don't really care, if I'm being honest, and I like being honest. Hell, my wife used to say I was too honest." He took another sip of the coffee. It was growing on him. "But let's say those werewolves were my sworn enemies, for thousands of years. Wanted to snuff me out and were just looking for an excuse. And when they grabbed me, out of a nice safe hotel, a thousand people all around, and took me away in broad daylight, and *got away with it*, well, I was thinking all those things might add up to me being terrified."

The vampire in the cage — the real beast behind this kid Jeremy's eyes — looked out at him. Those eyes glinted in the gloom like mirrors. "You don't know anything about fear. This is nothing."

"Okay," said Rex.

"This isn't ... in a hundred years, I'll still be here, and you'll be dust."

"Okay," said Rex, again.

"Do you understand?" said Jeremy, and Rex could swear he could see that kid come back out from behind those vampire eyes. "Do you know?"

"No," said Rex. "Not really."

"Of course not," said Jeremy, his voice bitter.

"But," said Rex, "I'd like to learn."

"What does it matter?" said Jeremy. "You want to kill me or cure me. You think I'm an oddity, a science experiment. It can't be cured. God, if it could be cured..."

"God," said Rex. "You leave God to us."

Jeremy blinked at him, then leaned forward in his cage. "Do you know how they work?"

Rex thought about that for a minute. The *they* that Jeremy mentioned had to be Vampire High Command or something, that was obvious. But how High Command worked, well, no. He opened his mouth, then closed it, thinking some more. Finally, he said, "No. Son, I wish I did."

"They come to you," said Jeremy, "when everything's completely fucked. When there's no damn light in the sky in the middle of the day, you know?" His voice turned quiet, harsh, tinged with self-loathing. Rex had heard enough of that in his time to recognize it instantly. "They offer a way out. An eternal rescue. No more being afraid." He gave a brittle laugh.

"What was it?" said Rex. "You on the run from some big bad? Trouble with the law?"

"No," said Jeremy. "My girlfriend, see, she had stage four cancer. You know," he said, rubbing his face, "they use *stages*, this word that sounds all nice and measured, like it's a process they can manage. Fucking doctors. They don't manage anything. Stage four, it's a term for, 'you're fucked and you're going to die.'"

"Okay," said Rex. He took a sip of his coffee, but found it had gone cold and bitter.

"So we're in the hospital, and Vi—"

"Vi?"

"Vi," said Jeremy. "My girl." A small smile lit his face for a moment, a memory of something better. "Vi, she was beautiful. Not like, pretty, I mean yeah, she was pretty. But she was nice. I was more of a downtown kind of guy, if you know what I mean. Vi, she was all uptown." He sighed. "It was a while ago."

Rex thought about his own wife, dead and gone. "Son," he said, his voice soft. "It doesn't matter how long ago it was."

"Right," said Jeremy. "So, Vi, she's dying. She's just skin and bones in that hospital bed, all kinds of tubes coming out of her.

Doctors say she's got a week if we're lucky. A week. You know what you can do in a week? Nothing. So you start talking, and you talk until the words run out, and then you just start crying."

"That sounds about right," said Rex. "That sounds about what I remember, too."

Jeremy tossed him a sharp look. "You lost someone too?"

"Hey," said Rex. "This isn't about me. I'm not the one in a cage. Fearless."

"Fearless," said Jeremy. "That's right. That's me. Big ol' fearless." He sighed. "They came to me on the second night. There were two of them. I don't know why they needed two. Maybe because it's a peer pressure thing. So they come to me, and they say they want to give me a gift. They say they can make me live forever, and get this, I can give the gift to Vi. She'll live forever too. Cancer, gone. And all I got to do, they say, is never go back outside in the daylight."

"They didn't want anything else?" said Rex. "No favor? No special task?"

"No," said Jeremy. "A gift, they said, had to be freely given. And freely taken. Like the Muppet I was, I took it. I damned myself." He grabbed the bars of the cage. "Right there, right then, in the back ass-end of this hospital, they stripped the life out of me, drained me dry, and breathed new life back into me. I woke up, I saw the world after I'd died. You want to talk about being terrified, being terrified is dying. Dying, and knowing that's the end. And then, just like that, you come back."

"Just like that?" Rex swirled the dregs of his coffee.

"No, not really." Jeremy frowned. "You're thirsty. *Hungry*. Man, you're so damn hungry. Like you want to eat a hundred Big Macs."

"Not really a MacDonald's kind of guy," said Rex, "but I get you."

"Except," said Jeremy, as if Rex hadn't said anything, "you can't. You can't eat, or drink. It makes you sick. And you've got these teeth, these big fucking teeth in your head, and you wonder what they're for. And the two guys, they're gone, they're gone and there's no one to tell you anything, and a doctor, a young doctor comes around the corner, and you tear his throat out, and you drink, and oh, oh, it's sweet, it's so *good*, it's like you can't stop, and then, and then he's dead. This doctor, this guy who came to see if you're okay, he's dead, and you killed him. And you go up to see Vi, your beautiful Vi, and she sees you, and she screams, and you're still hungry, man, you're still hungry, and you don't understand why..." Jeremy gave a sob, red tracks of blood tears running down his face. "You don't understand why," he said, again.

"Son," said Rex, "I'm so sorry."

"What for?" said Jeremy. "You didn't do anything. Nobody did anything. Nobody except me."

Rex thought about that for a while, letting the silence stretch between them. *Old man, you need to say something. You need to make this right.* But there wasn't any putting this right. Not really. Not ever, not unless they won. Not unless they fixed the world. He stood up. "I don't know much about that," he said. "Oh, hell. Son, I know about death. I know about losing people I loved, more than I loved myself, more than I loved life. I know about that. But not your kind of pain." He leaned close to the bars, crouching down on knees that were stiff with age. "I'm not even going to say we're going to make it right, because that's a promise I can't make. Just an old man, past my use-by date."

Jeremy looked out at him with those vampire eyes, mirrors in his face. "So why are you here?"

"Because we want to try. Because we can. Because we want to help." Rex fished into his pocket, pulled out a big metal key. "I can't help your Vi. Hell, I don't even know if I can help you. Only one who can do that is you. But if you want to help, you need to come on out and join us." He tossed the key to the vampire, then stood up.

Jeremy held the key, looked at it like it was a piece of hope itself. "You're letting me go?"

"Hell, son," said Rex. "Sure. You can go. But I hope you don't." He turned his back on Jeremy, stretched his back. *Damn old bones.*

"Hey," said the vampire. There was a click of a lock, the sound of metal on metal as the cage opened. "Hey."

Rex turned around, slowly. Saw the face of this kid who'd been damned, saw the bloody tracks of tears. *You've finally done it, old man. You've let a beast free and he's going to kill you.* "Hey," he said.

"I don't know your name," said the vampire.

Rex held out his hand. "Rex," he said.

The vampire shook itself, became Jeremy again. Took his hand. "Good to meet you." He thought for a second. "Rex, like a dog?"

Rex smiled. "Like a fucking Tyrannosaurus," he said. "Come on out and meet the team."

"Who," said Jessie, "let the vampire out of the cage?" She was sipping a cup of coffee, probably her third or fourth — tricky to tell, because you could pour a couple pots into that girl before she began to twitch. Always calm. *Rex,* she'd said, *your heart really gets going when artillery's coming down like hot rain. Coffee just tastes good.*

"Uh," said Rex. "I—"

"I used my hypnotic powers to convince him to open the cage," said Jeremy. He was still wiping bloody tears from his face.

"You what?" said Rex.

"Kidding," said Jeremy.

"You can do that?" said Jessie.

"I said I was kidding," said Jeremy. He was still standing in the doorway to the garage, feet right on the border of the gloom. His eyes glinted as he looked out at the room full of people and sunlight. "I didn't use my hypnotic powers on him. Because, you know, I don't have hypnotic powers. You guys watch too many bad movies."

Danny and Val hadn't said a word, just watching them across the room. Val stepped forward a pace, stopped himself, then with visible effort said, "I'm going to make some coffee." He was looking at Jeremy. "Do you drink coffee?"

"No," said Jeremy. "Just the good stuff."

Val nodded, moving towards the coffee pot like he wanted to twitch right out of his skin. He picked up the pot, swirled it, then looked at Rex. "I'm having trouble with this."

"I said I was going back to talk to him," said Rex.

"It looks like you did more than talk," said Val. "He looks like he's ready to go on a vacation with you."

"I find it difficult to travel," said Jeremy, "because some asshole always opens up the blinds on a plane, and then it's all fire and screaming."

"Can you," said Danny, "step into the room some more?"

"There's a lot of sunlight out there," said Jeremy. "Unlike hypnotic powers, that one's not a myth. It's all bad. Very bad."

"For you," she said.

"I'd like to think," said Jeremy, "that it'd be bad for all of us. Since we're getting along so well."

Val sighed. "Sorry," he said. "I'm ... sorry."

There was a moment of quiet, then Jeremy said, "Don't be. Did you mean it?"

"Mean what?" Val was putting some coffee and cinnamon into the pot.

"That you wanted to fix this." Jeremy gestured to himself.

"Son," said Rex, "he—"

"Yeah," said Val. "Whatever it takes."

"Well," said Rex, "I reckon—"

"Then you need to know," said Jeremy, taking a couple of cautious steps into the room, "how it all works."

"Super speed?" said Jessie.

"Yes," said Jeremy.

"Cool," she said.

"Super strength?" said Rex. He paused. "No. I'm not saying 'super strength' like this is some kind of comic book."

"What do you want to call it?" said Jessie.

"I'm warning you here," said Val, "that she taped me doing a fake *haudoken* in broad daylight."

"I like comic books," she said. "I used to send them to Gabriel. Keep a copy for myself, and we'd read them together over the SatCom. I'd be more worried about your use of the term, 'taped.' You're more in touch with the kids of today than that, Val."

"Who's Gabriel?" said Jeremy. He stepped around a beam of sunlight streaming in through a window, his pale, pale skin almost shining with it as he got close.

"I want to know more about the super strength thing first," said Danny. Rex had almost forgotten she was there, she'd been so still. Like a stone. Like a predator. Like she was waiting for something. Rex looked at her, the way she held her shoulders, the way her eyes were so very focused on Jeremy. *Like she's waiting to kill something.*

"Hey," said Rex. "Danny? Can you not kill Jeremy? Until after coffee, at least."

"We can always get another one," said Danny. Rex was pretty sure she didn't mean *another coffee.*

Silence held in the room for an awkward ten seconds or more. Rex ran a hand over the stubble on his jaw and sighed. "Not like this one," he said at last.

"Ignoring the quality of this particular vampire," said Jessie, "it's actually difficult to get them."

"We're funny that way," said Jeremy. "In other news, *this* particular vampire more or less let you take him in. I'll admit, the punch in the face took me by surprise, but there was any amount of time—"

"You're just a baby vampire," said Danny. "You're not quite ... *ripe* yet."

Jeremy sighed. "That's true," he said.

"Wait," said Rex. He thought about it for a minute. *Vampires. Living dead, sure. But don't the dead just ... stop?* "What, you've got to spend a little more time on the tree? Son, and don't take this the wrong way, but son, I thought you were dead."

"Not really," said Jeremy, looking sad. "Okay, look. Yeah. I'm dead. I was taken about ten years back—"

"Wait one second," said Jessie. "Maybe this will go better with more coffee, but our intel said you were a fresh one. Newborn, if you like. Ten years?"

Jeremy threw himself down on one of the couches, ran a hand through his hair, then looked at his shoes for a minute. "Where'd you get the intel?"

"I'm going to paraphrase a really complicated investigative process for a second. We followed a trail of Instagram posts from teenagers," said Val, "to Times Square. Where we assumed you were eating them all. Then we had a source corroborate what we thought, point us at a particular room. And there you were."

"Like I said," said Jessie. "A source."

"What source?" said Jeremy.

"A confidential one," she said. "Called himself 'BloodFriend92.' We've spent a lot of time in conspiracy chat rooms weeding out nut jobs from genuine leads."

"Okay," said Jeremy. "The terminology, right, it doesn't hang together in quite the same way as you'd expect. My, I guess you'd say kind, my kind, we live … we're around for thousands of years. Thousands. You play video games?"

"Of course," said Jessie.

"No," said Danny.

"Sure," said Val. "Bit of a Civ guy, myself."

"Great," said Jeremy. He looked at Rex. "What about you?"

"I'm not sure what you're asking, son." Rex felt like he was about to get caught in another conversation where the generation gap hurt.

"I guess it doesn't matter," said Jeremy. "In video games, you level up, right?"

"Is this an analogy?" Rex frowned. "I think I need that coffee as well."

"Jesus," said Val. "Look, it's ready." He started pouring into cups. He looked at Jeremy. "You sure you don't drink coffee?"

"I used to," said Jeremy. "Loved it. Doesn't agree with me now."

"Is this part of the video game thing?" said Rex.

"No," said Jeremy. "I can't stretch the analogy that far."

"Great," said Rex, taking a cup from Val. The smell of coffee and cinnamon was divine. Say what you would about the kid, but he made a mean brew. "Leveling up."

"What? Right." Jeremy frowned. "So, you usually do stuff, conquer kingdoms or kill bad guys, level up, and can do more general badassery."

"Like a promotion," said Rex.

"Okay, so the reason I didn't use *jobs* as analogy is because, most jobs, you don't kill people to get promoted." Jeremy frowned, looked sideways at Jessie, then said, "Uh."

"Yeah, we haven't been properly introduced," said Jessie. "I'm Jessica Pearce." She paused, gave Rex a smile. "My friends call me Jessie."

"Military?"

"Not anymore."

"Cool," said Jeremy. "With a few minor exceptions, most jobs don't give you promotions for killing people. And, Jessica? I hope to earn the right to call you Jessie."

"It's just we've all had jobs," said Rex, the bit between his teeth now. "The analogy might have worked better."

"For the love of..." Jeremy sighed. "Okay. It's a job. You've got a job, and you do great at it, and you get a promotion."

"With you so far," said Rex.

"And in some jobs, you need to do certain things to get a promotion. Pass an exam. Do a little overtime." Jeremy frowned. "You need to not do anything wrong."

"What could a vampire do," said Danny, her coffee untouched, "that is considered *wrong* by other vampires?"

"Meat of the issue, I'll agree," said Jeremy. "It's not so much what they consider wrong, although that's part of it. It's what's wrong *about* it. Right, so you spend a lot of time going around killing people to survive. I guess you have some experience with that."

"Not like—" said Danny.

"Sure," said Val. Rex watched a look pass between them, saw the softening of Danny's face.

"And once you've got the knack of it, because let me tell you, sucking on someone's neck like it's a straw is not a natural thing, not something we learned at *my* dinner table when I was a kid, you've got to do other things. Each person you kill, it makes you stronger. A little at a time. Hardly enough to notice, but some of those other guys who are a thousand years old? They're pretty buff." Jeremy paused. "You need to make another."

"Vampire?" said Danny.

Rex held up a hand. "Son, let me get this right. Making another one of you is an exam, and if you don't—"

"Or won't," said Jeremy.

"—then you don't get a promotion?" Rex mulled it over. "I guess I got to ask, son. What's at the end of the promotion?"

"Next level, right?" Jeremy looked around. "You ever wonder why it's so hard to catch a vampire?"

"Apart from the super strength and speed?" Rex looked at Jeremy with what he thought was a hard look. "No."

"Bats," said Jeremy.

"What?" said Rex.

"It's not actual bats," said Jeremy.

"Bats that aren't bats," said Rex. "Son, you need to start making sense."

"It's a level-up, or, keeping with the boring job analogy—"

"I never should have let you out," said Rex. "I'm regretting letting you out."

"—a significant promotion, with more responsibilities." Jeremy looked around. "You have to earn the right to change."

"Into bats," said Jessie.

"It's not bats," said Jeremy. "I just figured you knew about the vampire/bat thing."

"Seen some movies," said Jessie. "If you don't turn into a cloud of bats, what is it? Mist?"

"No," said Jeremy. "Locusts."

"I can see why you didn't lead with that," said Rex. "So you change into a swarm of locusts?"

"Not me," said Jeremy, "because I haven't *turned* anyone. But sure, pretty much ninety-nine point nine percent of all vampires can do it. And yeah, you got to earn the right."

"That," said Val, "could be a problem."

"You think?" said Jeremy. He leaned back on the couch.

"And they get stronger the more they kill," said Danny.

"Yeah," said Jeremy. "Doesn't count if it's not a death, so those bags of blood you got out the back wouldn't do it. It's why we're not big into blood banks, as a general rule. Also, it's like eating water crackers without any cheese or wine."

"How the hell," said Jessie, "are we going to fight a bunch of people who can turn into swarms of locusts?"

"I've got some thoughts on that," said Rex. "Jeremy, do you like to fight?"

"Not really," said Jeremy.

"Too bad," said Rex.

CHAPTER
THIRTEEN

B y the time Carlisle opened the front door, she wanted to strangle someone. Or hit them really hard. It didn't really matter to her who that person was, but it felt like it should have been Miles. Miles, who was carrying Adalia like some kind of drunk prom queen. At least Vitols had let him put his clothes back on before she'd thrown them out.

Carlisle didn't blame her. She wanted to throw Miles out of any room she was in within about five minutes as a general rule, couldn't imagine the impulse reducing after a roll in the hay with him. That thought alone made her shudder.

It'd taken hours to get back across the city. The three of them made a conspicuous trio. An unconscious woman with green hair carried by a man who looked lost and confused, accompanied by another woman who looked like she wanted to kill anyone who looked at them sideways. There weren't any cabs, of course, not ones that wanted to take a passenger who looked black-out drunk and thus might throw up in the back of their car. Uber was a risky proposition because it left a digital thumbprint, and digital thumbprints were dumb when fleeing from a possible crime scene, and/or going back to your top-secret lair. To make matters worse, Miles had wanted to buy beer on the way back. *Beer.* Because that was the most important thing right now, *of course.* Manhattan wasn't the size of Kansas, but it was big enough and far enough away from the Bronx that she'd worked up a blister and a hot rage by the time they finally got a ride.

It was the hot rage that had burned their first chance at a ride. A woman in a minivan had pulled over, asked if they'd needed a ride, and Carlisle had said — her mouth engaging about ten seconds before her brain — something like *Do you think? No, we're just out for a walk.* And the woman had pulled away, the minivan speeding away in the morning's light.

Miles hadn't said anything, which was probably for the best.

Some hero passer-by had stopped, this time a guy in a truck, some kind of removal company, and given them a ride most of the way. He'd been nice enough, and the ride was bearable because Miles had continued to not say anything.

Now they were back at the base — *it's not a base, Carlisle, it's a warehouse* — and she was trying to get her thoughts together before they went in, but her brain still hadn't got a hold of her yet and she'd just opened the front door. She took in the scene — Barnes standing to the side of the room, arms crossed. The sparring mats were down on the floor, furniture pushed to the side, and Rex was trying to referee some kind of match between Danny and a man she didn't know.

That had best not be the fucking vampire. They had best not have let the vampire out of the fucking cage.

Everard was looking hot and sweaty but also happy, which was a thing she noticed happened to him more these days, especially when he fought. Carlisle figured he was making peace with God or the thing inside him or both, and that was fine, but she didn't need him to be so happy right now that she had a blister. He was about to say something, but she held up a hand. "I need coffee, Everard, and I need some quiet time. I need some breakfast. And I need to know who that motherfucker is," she said, pointing at the man she was sure was a vampire.

It wasn't that vampires — or this probably-a-vampire, in particular — looked different. It was that the windows had been taped over, sunlight kept at bay. It was the way his eyes glinted like mirrors, the way he looked at them all like they were … *options*. Food. Or something.

John stepped in, right on her heels. Danny took one look at Adalia and rushed over.

Carlisle held up her hand again. "She's fine, Kendrick."

"She doesn't look fine." Danny took Adalia from Miles like the young woman weighed no more than a feather pillow.

At least Adalia's condition looked like it had sucked some of the happy from Everard, and Carlisle hated herself a little bit for enjoying it. Still, *he* hadn't had the night she'd had. "We had a bit of a run-in."

"With who?" This from Rex. Which was good, the old guy could be counted on to not lose his cool even in some pretty exciting situations.

"No clue," said Carlisle. "I honestly have no clue."

"I went on a date," said Miles. He was making his way towards the kitchen. Moved around Barnes with a nod, the usual Miles ease-of-life smoothing his passage.

"Miles," said Carlisle, "if you're about to make coffee, don't."

"I—"

"Because," said Carlisle, "you're the only person in the world who can make instant wrong. I asked Everard for a coffee."

"You did?" Everard was looking confused, but everyone did when Miles was in the room.

"I did," said Carlisle. "And I asked for breakfast. And while that's happening, while you're doing your magic in the kitchen, we need to talk. But before any of that shit, I need to know who this asshole is." She pointed at the probably-a-vampire. Again.

"I'm—" started the probably-a-vampire.

"What happened to Adalia?" said Danny.

"She's fine," said Carlisle.

"She's unconscious," said Danny.

"Kendrick," said Carlisle, "it's been a long night. Long morning, too. I've walked about halfway between Manhattan and here, I've got a blister the size of Staten Island, and since being woken up by our resident circus clown Miles at about three in the morning, I'm tired."

"I told them," said Rex, "that—"

"The thing is," said Carlisle, "that Miles didn't even wake me. You know how it is, being the Shield of the fucking Universe, right? Something's going on, and I get a little nudge. I was already awake by the time Adalia's phone buzzed, I'd called a cab and everything. We were ready to leave before Sleeping Beauty had even woken up. She's, and I'm being serious here, going to be fine, because if she wasn't I'd be going berserk, and as you can clearly see I'm *fine*. Just like she is. Kendrick, put the woman down."

Danny seemed to realize she was still carrying her daughter, and laid Adalia on a couch at the side of the room.

"That's what I said," said Rex. "What I was trying to tell them earlier was—"

"What I still need are the same fucking three fucking things," said Carlisle. "I don't want to overstate the situation, you know it's not really my way, but as I see it I could use a coffee, some breakfast, and a name. For that guy. Right there." She pointed at the probably-a-vampire. *Again.*

"I'm Jeremy," said the probably-a-vampire.

"Great, Jeremy." Carlisle sighed. "Don't take this the wrong way, but I can't tell if I'm pleased to meet you. Because, well, because I'm pretty sure you're a vampire."

"I'm a vampire," said Jeremy.

"Who," said Carlisle, choosing her words carefully, "let you out of the cage?"

"It's not like that," said Everard. "It's—"

"Everard," said Carlisle, "you better be making a pot of coffee while you're talking."

"Yes ma'am," said Everard, automatically. She could see the wheels going around in his head as he checked himself, then checked himself again. Probably a thought like *wait, what?* and then settling on *whatever, coffee is good.*

All eyes in the room did a slow swivel towards Rex. He looked around, did a quick double-take, then said, "Hey. Now, c'mon. We weren't going to leave him in the cage."

"We were," said Carlisle, "going to use the vampire as a lab rat. You know, because they control all the corporations, drink the blood of the innocent, and are generally not nice. And we needed intel."

"You don't need intel," said Jeremy. His eyes caught Carlisle's attention. Little pieces of polished glass, that's what they looked like, no color, just pale mirrors glinting at her across the room. "You need someone to pray for you. Because we don't just drink the blood of the innocent. It's not that we're *not nice.* We rule the world, fool. You're our food. You're nothing. You're beneath us. The things we've done to people, you don't know even the tiniest part. You think you know suffering? We'll show you suffering. We'll end your rag-tag little cabal like it never was, erase it from existence like everything else that's stood before us. You think that, what, a couple of werewolves makes you unique? *We destroyed all the other werewolves.* We ate them, like a snack, it didn't take us long at all. Just a few years, and they're gone, and you're *all going to die.*"

The Eagle was in her hand without a thought, roaring at the vampire, but he wasn't *there* where she was shooting. He moved around her shots as she squeezed the trigger, just like she'd seen Danny do, or Everard, but even faster. The couch behind the vampire puffed as her rounds hit it, explosions of stuffing filling the air, but the vampire was still moving, and she was still firing. Barnes crouched down — *good idea but poor execution.* The television in the corner shattered into a thousand pieces of glass and plastic as the vampire turned lazily in place, her bullets missing it by an easy inch or more. Easy, because she was sure the thing was moving *just* enough to not be hit. It could have moved more, she was sure of it, and she began to feel real fear. *That old man has doomed us all.*

Danny had made it to the vampire, grabbed onto it — but no. She hadn't, she'd almost done it, Carlisle had *expected* her to, but she'd ... missed. Fumbled the catch, and was tumbling across the room, caught by a backhand that hit her almost as an afterthought. It bought a precious few seconds, that tangle of bared teeth and missed punches, and a new magazine was snug in the base of the Eagle, the weapon hungry for more, shouting at the vampire each time she pulled the trigger. Everard stepped in — *he's forgetting the damn coffee again, and why am I thinking of the coffee, we're all going to die* — roaring at it, his eyes bright and yellow and fierce. The vampire stepped around his swings like Everard was an unruly toddler, all windmilling arms with no purpose. A single punch hit Everard square in the chest, sending him tumbling across the room, crashing into Jessie, who was leveling a weapon, some kind of automatic rifle, but it didn't matter because they both went down in a tangle of limbs and unchecked anger.

The vampire turned to Carlisle, took a step towards her with those silver mirrors for eyes looking right at her, into her, like she was lunch, like she was nothing at all. The Eagle clicked empty, the slide racking open, smoke curling from the weapon. The vampire took another step. Right then, *of course right then*, Miles stepped between them. Brave, stupid Miles. She felt something in her chest, a feeling like *no, not this one, not this friend, take me instead, I was the one that started shooting at it, it was* me, *don't you see, that made it angry*, but it didn't matter what she felt, because Miles was there. Between her and her fate.

It didn't matter, the vampire ducked under a swing, picked Miles up like a sack and tossed him across the room, right into Danny. They went down into a pile. It wouldn't take long before Danny was back up, but Carlisle guessed that didn't much matter. Because then, right then, the vampire was in front of Carlisle, a hand at her throat.

The Eagle had been removed from her hand like a child's toy, and she felt herself lifted by that hand, her neck popping as all her weight went through it. She choked, gagged, her hands clawing at the vampire, looking for a pressure point, anything, but nothing worked, it was like the thing felt no pain, like it didn't have a nervous system to work with.

Like it was already dead.

She felt the room starting to go dark, the pressure on her carotid artery doing more than the loss of air. She'd probably suffocate in a minute or two, but she'd be out in less than ten seconds with that kind of pressure, and then she'd die, and not even see the end as it hit her. *You never thought you'd die in your sleep, Carlisle, but here you are.*

The vampire let her fall, and her hands found her own throat, gasping for breath. It held up the Eagle, looking at it, then pulled the weapon apart in a few quick motions, the pieces of the gun falling to the ground at its feet. It crouched down in front of her, and she felt its hand on her chin, pulling her gaze up.

Those terrible mirrors for eyes were gone, and it was just some guy in front of her, a guy named Jeremy, and he looked sad, looked like he'd just kicked a puppy by accident. "Do you see?" he said. "Do you understand? Intel won't do it. You need to learn, because the rest of them, they won't stop." He let his hand fall from her chin, stood up, and held his hand out to her.

Carlisle looked around. Saw Everard, looking thoughtful. Danny, like she wanted to kill someone, but also like she thought she couldn't, not this time. Miles, holding the back of his head with a hand, wincing. Pearce, her weapon held low, her face blank, like she was waiting to be a soldier again. And poor Rex, who'd stood still as a post, struck dumb. Barnes, back up but arms crossed, a look of astonishment on his face, like he'd just learned something he didn't have the mental cubic inches to process. Adalia, still asleep, and that kind of thing just wasn't natural, but there it was. Her eyes went back up to the hand held out to her.

"This is how you do it, isn't it?" she said, not taking the hand.

"Yes," said Jeremy, and it was Jeremy again, not the vampire, not the thing made of speed and power and death. Just Jeremy. "We're … just built a little better than the rest."

She took its hand, felt herself hauled up like she was four years old again, weightless, and she tottered a little on her feet. "And you … want to teach us to fight."

"Hell," he said. "No. You already know how to fight. I think, well, I think together we can work out where the strengths are, what the weaknesses are."

"Together," she said, the word tasting bitter for some reason.

He saw it in her face. "Hey," he said. "He said we were looking for a cure. We were looking to fix it."

He was obviously Everard. That was just the kind of thing he'd say. Carlisle thought about that for a few seconds. "Yeah," she said. "Yeah, we're looking to fix it."

"Then we do that together," said Jeremy. "I … look, I don't want to rain on your parade, but you had the drop on me and I still kicked your asses. But. But I think, together, that won't happen again. And we can fix it."

Together. With a vampire. Carlisle looked around the room. The Knight, his Sword, and his Shield. The Good Right Arm, the Lost Warrior, and the Guide. Their Prophet Adalia, and Barnes, and then finally back to the vampire. *It wouldn't be so crazy, would it? It's not like we're a normal bunch of people as it is.* "Together," she said.

Jeremy nodded.

"Okay," she said. "I still need that fucking coffee though."

CHAPTER
FOURTEEN

Maksimillian Kotlyarov was nobody's fool. He looked across the counter at the young man who wore a green apron and no smile and said, "Maksimillian Kotlyarov is nobody's fool, *da*?"

The young man looked at him like he was lost, stuck on a raft of *what the fuck* in an ocean of *how did I get here*. "Sir, I'm not sure—"

"I said that I wanted a big breakfast," said Maksimillian. "Like a real *Amerikanskaya*. A breakfast that one man would have trouble lifting."

"Sir—"

"And you have given me," said Maksimillian, "a single bagel. With a coffee of ordinary size."

"It's—"

"And," said Maksimillian, holding up his cup, and pointing to the writing on the side, plain old *Max* written in a hurried hand, blue pen somehow softer than the strong black strokes he'd been expecting, "you have not spelled my name correctly."

"Hey," said a man beside Maksimillian, "just order something else."

Maksimillian turned to look at the man. Just an ordinary man, looking more tired than he should, which made him more ordinary than anything else in this city that cared little for its people. Not that cities cared, they weren't actually alive, thinking and breathing, but it felt like that sometimes. It felt like this city took people, chewed on them like a dog with a bone, and left them less than they had been. Maksimillian put his cup on the counter, tossing the paper bag holding his tiny — *tiny!* — bagel alongside it. He clasped the man by the shoulders, gave him a small shake, and said, "My friend, it is not that simple." He let the man go, looking at the astonishment on his face. "I know you see this. You have come to this city — you have traveled far, *da*?"

The man looked lost. "I'm from Queens."

"Exactly so," said Maksimillian. "You give your lifeblood to this city, and it casts it aside, makes you work long hours, for little pay."

"I guess, but—"

"And just imagine," said Maksimillian, "that the thing you want, just to start the day again with a little, how do you say *nadezhda*, is this word hope?"

"Hope's a word," said the man.

"Hope," agreed Maksimillian. "You want to start the day with this hope, so you come to your favorite breakfast spot, for a delicious breakfast of unimaginable size, and good coffee."

"With you so far," said the man, "but—"

"You order the breakfast," and here, Maksimillian turned the man with one hand, pointing with his other at the clerk, "and then this man robs you."

"I—" said the clerk

"You tell him, you say to him, 'I am Maksimillian Kotlyarov, and I need a breakfast of enormous size. The sort of breakfast two men would eat.' He asks you," and Maksimillian shook the man gently, for emphasis, "whether you would like cream. Of course you do!"

"I do kind of like cream," said the man, nodding. "It's not good for me, but—"

"But it gives hope, *da*?"

"Yeah," said the man, "I guess it does." He was sounding more certain, almost a little angry.

"So you tell me, like a true friend, to order something else." Maksimillian let the man's shoulder go. "I tell you, also as a true friend, that I can't let this go. That I must get satisfaction."

"And this asshole," said the man, jerking a thumb at the clerk, "sold you short?"

"He did," said Maksimillian, nodding.

"Hey," said the clerk. "It's not like that—"

"Buddy," said the man, "you best put this back together, and by back together, I mean you better come out with a decent sized breakfast for the man here."

The clerk blinked, swallowed, blinked again. "I—"

"And this time," said Maksimillian, "you should spell my name right. It is not Max," and he used a finger to jab at the letters on the cup, "like some kind of pet dog. The woman with the green hair, she spelled it correctly."

"Ady?" said the clerk. "She—"

"She is no 'Ady,'" said Maksimillian. "That is not her name, any more than mine is the name of a pet dog."

"For Chrissakes," said the man at Maksimillian's side, "at least do the man the courtesy of spelling his name right."

"It's fine," said the clerk. "I got it."

"Where is the woman with the green hair?" said Maksimillian, leaning across the counter. "I feel, it is like these sorts of mistakes — honest mistakes, simple ones, but important mistakes, mistakes that rob the day of hope—"

"Hope," agreed the man at Maksimillian's side.

"*Da*. I feel as if these mistakes would not be made if the woman with the green hair were here. Where is she?"

"Didn't come in today," said the clerk. "I think she's going to be fired." He swallowed, blinked again. "I shouldn't have said that. I'm a little—"

"Lost, without hope," said Maksimillian, "like the rest of this city. Perhaps you should order a large breakfast also."

The clerk thought about that. "You know, maybe I should."

"*Da.* Is good." Maksimillian breathed in, his chest expanding, something at the top of his back clicking back into place. "Now I know what I am doing with my day. I will go find hope."

~

Maksimillian left the Starbucks with a spring in his step, a number of paper bags held in one hand, a large coffee in the other. He let himself be tugged along by the flow of humanity as they surged this way and that, trying to get to their work, or their gymnasium, or their life coach, or whatever it was that these *Amerikantsy* did in the morning. It was no longer early; many of the city's workers would have started hours before, but Maksimillian had adjusted the start of his days to match those of the woman with green hair.

Didn't come in today was not a good way for the start of his day, whether it was early or late. He was so sure he had stopped the *vampiry* yesterday, he was certain this was not a problem to do with them. It was a problem of another sort, and would need Maksimillian fed, the hunger gone from inside him, at least for a little while.

He sat on a bench, chewing. His breakfast had served its purpose, but it was clear that the replacement clerk for the woman with green hair didn't listen to his customers' needs. Oh, he listened to their *words*, but bagels were not the same as sausage, not here in *Amerika*, not back home in mother *Rossiya* either. Such a simple thing could starve a day of ... hope. And Maksimillian Kotlyarov had just started to feel that sensation again, for the first time in a very, very long time.

After he finished his breakfast, he watched the people stream by. It didn't seem to matter what time of the day or night, there were always so many people here in this New York City of theirs. So many noises, so many things going on. So much of it without hope, or purpose, just churning and churning over and over.

We must know where to begin.

Maksimillian shook his head, hit the side of his head with a hand, shook his head again. "What would you know?"

Silence. Of course. Never anything useful, never anything helpful, just words, voices in his head, voices that told him to kill, to kill his own Pack. He hated that voice.

We are the same.

They weren't. Not the same, not at all. He was Maksimillian Kotlyarov, known as *Maks* to a woman with green hair, and he had hope. He didn't need this voice, he just needed her, to start a new Pack—

We are the same.

—a new Pack that would fix everything. Maksimillian didn't know what she would do, but he knew she gave him hope, and maybe that was enough. It felt like more than enough, as if his cup was brimming over, as if the world was suddenly lighter than air, all because she knew what he wanted. Like she could really see him.

He blinked. What was he thinking? He barely knew her. She barely knew him.

We must know where to begin.

"*Da*," he said. "We must know where to begin. So. We find place. We find where this started."

We hunt.

It hadn't taken long to find, once he'd put his mind to it. He just followed the absence.

Not of activity. There was plenty of that. Police officers, a cordon made of flimsy tape, photographers. It was those last that caught his eye, this scene of a great fight, the building doors broken, the bullet holes in the walls of brownstones outside, and those photographers standing by, taking no photos.

The police, doing nothing much more than walking around, ensuring no one came close.

A great deal of activity, but an absence of action. Like they were all waiting. Like they were hiding.

He had seen this before. The *vampiry* owned all, saw all, controlled all. They controlled the police, or a good enough part of them that this area would just disappear. Oh, Maksimillian knew that it would appear on YouTube, that the many people with phones would tell their friends about it, but in a week's time it would be old news, forgotten, just another small fight in a big city. That was how they won. They hid everything in plain sight, made you think that such horrible things were everyday things, so that you wouldn't question the next time your neighbors or friends or family were killed by them. Just another *shooting* or *robbery gone wrong* or other soft words to hide the terrible truth.

This time was a little different. Maksimillian could almost taste it in the air. A *vampir* had fought here, and it had not won.

They didn't know what to do.

Maksimillian felt the smile grow on his face. This, right here, this ordinary bar was where it began. The trail of the woman with green hair started here. All he had to do was to sit, and watch, and wait.

Perhaps he would get to kill another *vampir*.

We hunt.

The day looked brighter already.

CHAPTER
FIFTEEN

Liselle wasn't really looking around the bar. It wasn't a question of interest, although that was waning fast. She'd been here before, and the only thing that had been worth the visit was a man. A man she'd thrown out of her life, because the alternative wasn't worth thinking about.

Because we need to. Because no one else is going to. Because we can.

She felt her lip curl in something that wasn't really a smile. *John Miles, you can't. And if you try, you'll die. Everything around me dies, don't you see? I was made to end this world.*

No. She wasn't looking around the bar because she didn't want to be reminded. Not of John Miles, or of her purpose. She didn't want to see the broken chairs and tables, the blood, the bullet holes in the walls, and be reminded of what Kaylan had said.

We were made for this.

A movement drew her attention to the door, or the space where the door would have been if it hadn't been splintered and broken. Police were moving back and forth outside, doing nothing much of anything at all. Kaylan owned them, or her vampires did. It didn't matter which it was, as Kaylan owned the vampires; what was theirs was hers. It wasn't the officers that had drawn her to look, it was someone else.

Josef.

Josef was ducking under the police tape, his arms bare in the late morning sun. He walked into the place like he owned it — he may well have — and stood at the bar, a few feet away from her. Consciously or not, they were in similar positions as just two nights ago when she'd met John Miles here, when he'd poured her a drink that reminded her of better times, and smiled at her.

The bottle of Midas Touch was still on the bar in front of her, empty now. It would be cleaned away by the police or time or both, but she could still remember the beautiful man who'd put it there.

Josef cleared his throat. "You argue with our sister last night?"

Liselle sighed, reached into her clutch and pulled out a cigarette. She regarded Josef over a long tongue of flame as she lit it, breathing deep before she blew smoke at the ceiling. "You know Kaylan."

"I know Kaylan," he said, nodding. He leaned over the bar, grabbing something — a bottle of Johnnie Walker. He picked a glass off the bar top, considered the inside of it with a squint, and then poured some of the golden liquid into it. A sip, a wince, and then he put the glass down. "She still want to end the world?"

"Someone's killing her vampires," said Liselle.

Josef considered that for a moment. "It's not me. I gave up on that years ago."

"As did I. There's too many of them, and they spread like a disease." Liselle snorted. "Of course they do. Maynor had a hand in making them. The first of us, the weakest, but she still needed him for ... the *recipe*."

"Don't get me wrong," said Josef. "There's a certain something about really, you know, punching them until they ... stop." He air boxed with a closed fist for emphasis, a few jabs at an imaginary opponent. "She's breaking the rules. You're breaking the rules. Maynor's breaking the rules. I'd never have thought it was me, *me*," and here he slapped his chest for emphasis, "that was on the straight and narrow."

Liselle smiled at him. "Old friend," she said. "You are straight and true."

He snorted. "Don't start with that shit," he said. "I'm just a kid, having fun."

"You stood by me," she said.

"Because you were right. You were right then, and you're right now. Being right doesn't fix it though." Josef frowned. "I should be in Mogadishu. There's another war brewing there. Needs some attention."

"So go," Liselle said. "You can't fix what's here, any more than I can."

"Then why are you here?" said Josef.

Because we need to. Because no one else is going to. Because we can.

"I..." Liselle thought for a moment. "Because I need to be. Because no one else is going to do anything."

Josef arched his back, then pushed the glass around in front of him. "That doesn't sound like the Liselle I know."

She almost smiled. "It doesn't sound like the Josef I know," she said, "to not go to the nearest war."

"Wars start and finish themselves," he said. "I've been doing this so long, it doesn't really need a hand on the tiller."

"Don't you get bored of it?" she said, leaning towards him. "Don't you want it to stop?"

"Depends on why you do it." He frowned at his glass, noticed it was empty, and snared the Johnnie Walker to remedy the problem. "Back when this all started, I was on the front lines."

"I remember," she said. "I was there too."

"Yeah," he said. "Different faces, though."

"Different faces," she agreed.

"I thought the job was to make War. I thought it was all about making them," and here he jerked a thumb over his shoulder to the world outside, "fight each other. But they do that *all the time*. I couldn't stop it if I tried. That's not the job." He drained his glass again, poured a refill. "When the last Seal is broken and it all comes tumbling down, I want to talk to the Father. I want to ask him why."

Liselle put a hand over Josef's. "The job," she said, "is getting to know them while you do it. We see them at their worst. It's when they're at their best."

"I know," he said. He was looking across the room into a corner, but his thoughts were somewhere else. "I know."

"Josef," she said. "We need to stop her."

"We've been trying," he said, "for thousands of years. She gets stronger and stronger with each person that dies. Because everybody dies, but not everyone starves to death or fights in a war."

"That's not really it, and you know it," said Liselle.

"It sure feels like it," said Josef. "I tried to get in a brawl with her a few years back and I lost almost all my teeth."

"She made them wrong," said Liselle. "I'm sure of it. She's taken death away from them, the very right to die. But Maynor's part, I think there's something there." She frowned. "Kill the head of the snake, and the tail dies."

"Sure," said Josef, "but all the old ones hide away. How are we going to get them angry enough to come out? Once we get them out, and wipe the floor with them — if we can — how do we stop her doing it again? Just wiping the slate and putting new pieces on the board?"

Liselle thought for a moment, remembering a man with a beautiful light inside him, but with maddening words, words that had made Kaylan incensed. She remembered a woman with green hair who said *STOP* and how Kaylan had, for a moment, stopped, right in her apartment.

And she remembered how she'd thrown them out.

"Liselle?" Josef was looking at her. "Liselle, do you know how we can do this?"

"No," she said, knowing she meant *yes*.

"I see," said Josef. He looked at the bottle of Midas Touch in front of her, and then at the empty space where John Miles had stood two nights ago. "The man that was here. Who is he?"

"He's nobody," said Liselle. "Forget him."

"And if he's nobody," said Josef, "how do we get access to him?"

"You can't have him," said Liselle. She leaned towards Josef, gripped his arm tight, so tight that he looked at her. *That's right. Hear me.* "You can have all the humans on this world except that one. Take them all and burn them to ash, but leave that one for me."

Josef nodded, put his hand over hers, and sighed. "Liselle. Liselle, do we need him?"

"No," she said.

"I see," he said. He sighed again. "What can he do?"

"Nothing," she said.

He looked down at his glass, then let her go. He — *gently, like the friend he was* — shook her hand off. He stood, squinted out into the daylight beyond the door of the bar, then turned back to her. "Then we must find him."

LISELLE LOOKED at the front of the building, a plain warehouse among a hundred other plain warehouses scattered all over New York. This one was more run down than some, less run down than others. There was something about it that drew the eye, if you knew where to look. A black car parked out front, tinted windows dark against the afternoon sun. The hood was up, pieces of metal scattered across a work table next to it, a woman bent over the machine, working on something. A big roller door, secured with heavier chains than you'd need for simple security. A smaller door, ready for humans, but made of steel and thick glass.

This is the place.

It wasn't those tiny aspects that drew her eye. It was the light she imagined was within. John's light. It would ever draw her. She already missed it, being close to it, and hated herself for that.

142

The woman with her head down in the car pulled herself out. She had a baseball cap on, a ponytail out the back, grease smudged on her face. She wiped her hands on a rag, looked at Josef standing next to Liselle, then back to Liselle. "Help you?"

"Is he here?" Liselle took a step forward, looking at the woman. No obvious sign of hostility, no reaching for a hidden weapon, just a *help you?* with a cautious tone. "Is John Miles here?"

"Fuck sake," said the woman. "Carlisle said, but I never thought … are you pregnant?"

Liselle frowned. "No."

"You sure?"

"Yes."

"Cool," said the woman. "Say. This guy with you." Eying up Josef, some flicker of recognition crossing her face. Like she knew him, but couldn't place from where, like he was a supporting actor on her favorite show she'd seen on a forgotten channel years ago. Not that Josef was hard to remember, with his tattoos, his muscle, his attitude. He made a statement, they all did. It was how they were made. "I … who are you?"

"Major," said Josef, "you know me better than you know yourself."

"I'm retired," said the woman, stiffening at the term *Major*. "I retired a long time ago."

"That's a lie, and you know it," said Josef. "You just changed teams. Still fighting the good fight. Still giving your service."

"Who *are* you?" said the woman.

Liselle stepped in front of Josef. "I'm Liselle, and this is Josef. We want to speak to John Miles."

"It's nice to want things," said the woman.

"You know me," said Josef. "You just don't want to remember. Because of what it cost you. No one knows what they mean when they say *thank you for your service*. No one. I was there when you were first deployed, boots down in a mud hole in Asia. You can't even remember the name of the village you razed to the foundations but you remember me. I was there when you got your first command. Always an officer, born and bred. You were meant to lead, and here you are, leading from the front in a different war. I was there when your heart left with your son. I helped the men and women around you get you back to the world to see ... what was left of him, at the end. I was *there* with *you*. Right behind you."

The woman took a step back, stopped, stood up a little straighter. "Who did you say you were?"

"Name's Josef Hackett," said Josef, "but you can call me War."

LISELLE FOUND herself in a large room, a converted warehouse of a sort. It wasn't clear what it used to hold - cars, maybe, or packing crates, or any of the thousand other things humans put into boxes on shelves and forgot about. It wasn't warm or cold. It was dark, or at least gloomy, and her eyes strayed to one of Kaylan's children. His eyes glinted at her like mirrors, then softened, his shoulders relaxing. *Curious. The Night stands with the living dead. These are strange times.* She looked about the room, seeing the Alpha, his strength and certainty. His Mate, nothing borrowed there, all ferocity and power held true by the needs of the Pack. The Knight and Sword.

Turning, Liselle looked at the rest. An older man, his time left in Father's Eden growing shorter. Kaylan would be able to tell how long for sure, but Liselle knew that he wasn't some age-addled octogenar-ian. This man was used to helping people with his strength, and his strength was more than physical. Another man, counted in middle years by the standards of this time, used to commanding people — she could see it by the tilt of his head, and dismissed him as unim-portant. The woman named Carlisle stared back at her, bold as brass, still frightened of the dark, and Liselle felt pity for her. *So strong. So tireless. So afraid of what might happen.* And there, the woman with the green hair, just now rising from a couch, the cloak of sleep slip-ping from her, the power and might of the Universe falling into place around her. *Adalia*, as if such a simple name could contain everything that she was.

Josef was still outside with the Lost Warrior, the woman who was trying to make up for the death of her son by fixing the world.

Liselle cleared her throat. "Where is John Miles?"

"Nah," said Carlisle.

"What?"

"He's not here," said Carlisle. "That's what I meant to say."

"Major Pearce said he was in here." Liselle looked around again, as if he should have sprung fully formed from one of the walls.

"*Major* Pearce needs to finish fixing that carburetor," said Carlisle, "or whatever the hell she's doing with that truck. Car. Whatever. And since she's not — right this particular second — in this room, we'll just say she's dealing with out-dated intelligence."

Adalia's hand had found its way to Carlisle's elbow. "It's okay, Melissa."

"You saying that because you know?" Carlisle's words were careful, gentle almost.

"No," said Adalia.

"Cool," said Carlisle. "He's not here. Leave a number, I'll ask him to call you." She was staring at Liselle, not moving an inch, not in posture, and not in attitude. Silence. No sound, no voices, it was as if everyone was holding their breath.

Then, that one beautiful voice, the one she wanted to hear most. John Miles. "What'd I miss?"

Carlisle's shoulders sagged, and she rubbed at her face with a hand. "Fuck's sake, Miles."

Liselle turned. Her eyes saw the beautiful light at first. She squinted, saw the man beneath it all, fresh from a shower, toweling his hair dry. She couldn't help but smile. "John."

"Hey, baby," he said. Then he frowned. "Why does Melissa want to hit me?"

"I don't want to hit you," said Carlisle. "I—"

"You need to leave," said Liselle. She cast a glance behind her, almost like she could see through the door to where Josef was. "A storm is coming."

"Now there's the truth," said John Miles. "And we gonna bring the *rain*." He grin faded as no one else joined in. "Wow. I need a beer. Anyone else want a beer?"

"I'll take a beer," said the Knight.

"I want one," said the vampire, "but, well, you know."

"Sure," said John Miles, then, "sorry."

"It's cool," said the vampire. "I'll just suck on some blood and try not to gross you out."

"You do you," said John Miles. "Anyone else for a beer?" He tossed a bottle through the air and Liselle caught it out of reflex, the *Midas Touch* label starting to frost slightly. He frowned. "Uh. You need a bottle opener? It's just, it would have been less cool if I'd thrown the bottle at you with the cap off."

She smiled at him, twisting the cap off. This shell might have lacked the strength to wield her birthright sword, but she could still manage the little things. She flicked the bottle cap back at him. He'd already lifted the trash can, and her cap rattled into the bottom. They shared a smile.

"Nothing but net," said John Miles.

"Do you ... do you two know each other?" said the Knight.

"Val," said John Miles, "this is Liselle. My girl."

"Your ... what now?" Val coughed on his beer.

John Miles ignored Val, pointing to the rest of them out in turn. "Danny. Melissa—"

"Call me Carlisle." Carlisle still hadn't moved from where she stood beside Adalia.

"—Melissa, you've met Melissa. Jessica's out front. You've met Adalia too."

"How has she met Adalia?" said Danny, her eyes flashing.

John Miles blinked, then said, "And that there is Sam Barnes. Head of Biomne."

Liselle nodded. "Who is the vampire?"

The room went very quiet. The vampire's mirrored eyes reflected the light, little glints of silver. He frowned. "The blood line, that was a little joke—"

"You are one of Kaylan's children," said Liselle. "I can smell it on you."

"Shit," said Adalia. "*Shit.*"

"What?" said Danny, all hard angles and tension. "What is it?"

"I'm late for work," said Adalia. "I'm *really* late for work." She slung a bag over her shoulder and slammed through the front door. Her footsteps were lost quickly as she broke into a run — Liselle could imagine her green hair flowing out like a mane behind her.

John Miles looked around the room. "This is going better than I'd hoped."

CHAPTER
SIXTEEN

Maksimillian saw the woman with the green hair leave the warehouse, her expression harried and rushed — again. As if she were hurrying for a date with destiny. She walked past the the Lost Warrior out front — even without the name, Maksimillian could tell the woman was a fighter from the way she stood, the way she looked around her, the set of her shoulders. As if everything about the soldier was designed to say, *come at me, world. Those who are behind me, I will protect. Those beside me are my sisters and brothers. But to those against me, I will show no mercy until my life's blood is spent.*

He nodded. Maksimillian knew exactly how that felt. He had been a soldier once. But he wasn't here for the soldier, or for the man she was talking to. Maksimillian pulled his cap a little lower, focusing on the man. Of course, he wasn't a man. He was well known to Maksimillian, almost like they were old friends. He was War.

The woman with the green hair kept such strange company. It was no wonder Maksimillian felt the need to protect her, to be with her. Adalia was special, and the Universe collected around her, light and dark arrayed on all sides.

There was nothing else for it. He would have to ask her out for a drink.

Adalia kept moving, barely pausing as she drew near to War. A glance, a promise, and then she was past, moving into the crumbling edifices of the Bronx. Maksimillian sighed. She was by herself, and this was no neighborhood for a woman alone. He slipped out from the shadow of the warehouse awning he was standing under — hiding, really — and kept pace behind Adalia. Walking casually, as he had been taught.

We needed no teaching.

Perhaps that was true. The Night knew things, it was the very best of hunters. But here, in this city of humans, there were ... tricks, techniques that could be used to be hidden in plain sight. The Night could be almost invisible. But he knew how to be visible and unseen at the same time. A turn of the head here. A certain kind of walk there. The right kind of pause, the right way to vary the speed of pursuit. All designed so the—

Prey.

—followed couldn't tell they were being followed at all.

Her path seemed odd, and Maksimillian considered the feeling, this *oddness*. It wasn't that she was walking in a strange way, but that her route was wrong. *Ah.* He put his finger on it: she was walking a path that was safe for a single man but not a single woman, a path between tall buildings without much street traffic. A path she might not have chosen if she wasn't so hurried, the messenger bag jouncing against her side, her face turned to the ground, her head-phones blocking out all noise. It was as if she didn't *want* to see what was around her.

He was pulled up short by a movement, a pair of men stepping out of a doorway. These were not *vampiry*, but as a guardian angel he was not fussy. Nothing special about the doorway other than it was recessed, dark, a place for bad men to hide bad deeds. One of them had a bandana across his face, the other a ski mask. It was all very

Amerikanskaya, props for show, as if a mask could hide what you did from the creature inside you.

Our Pack is dead.

Ah, now this was a time to hurry. Maksimillian forgot about staying hidden, put the shadowed path behind him and began to run. The one with the ski mask — *in this heat? At least he is dedicated, this Amerikantskiy* — had stepped behind Adalia. A strong hand wrapped around her mouth, and Maksimillian could see in her body language the usual things. *What is happening? Is this happening? What should I do? Should I* — and right there, she began to struggle, stamping back with a foot. The man with the ski mask stumbled, almost losing his grip, green hair flying wild.

That was when the one with the bandana — with a red-white pattern, it was the unexpected the details you noticed at a time like this — slammed a fist into Adalia's stomach. Maksimillian could see her body wanting to curl over around the pain, but she was held up by the man in the ski mask. Bandana pulled his hand back for another strike, and that was when Maksimillian reached them. He didn't even slow down, running at full pace, upright, into the man with the bandana. Maksimillian felt the shock in his body, saw the other man rebound away in an astonishment of limbs. He would not, this *Yanki*, be getting back up in the next five seconds, which gave Maksimillian plenty of time.

Turning, he saw Ski Mask holding Adalia, tight enough to break her, he was sure. Adalia's eyes were wild, full of fear, whites showing as she looked everywhere, anywhere, for an escape. So easy to forget she was just a young woman, when Maksimillian saw so much more. Ski Mask was holding Adalia like a shield, her body across his. Sensible, if one was going to get in a knife or a gun fight. Maksimillian could see his eyes too, the hardness there, the excitement of the hunt, as if this were Prey he was going to enjoy. The problem with his approach is that Maksimillian had neither a knife nor a gun. He had just his two strong hands, curled into fists.

"Hey, back off—" started Ski Mask, before Maksimillian punched him in the face. The strike was strong and true, his fist going past Adalia's startled eyes, connecting with a wet crunch. Ski Mask was falling, dragging Adalia with him, but Maksimillian grabbed her arm, held her upright.

"Will you be okay for just one more minute?" Maksimillian looked into her eyes. "There are things to be done."

She nodded. "Maks? What are you—"

"Is no time," he said. He turned back to Bandana, saw that the man was climbing to his feet. Unsteady, but still trying, a little fight or foolishness still inside his frame. Maksimillian took three steps, almost a little run up, imagining a kicking tee underneath Bandana's midsection. This gridiron wasn't really Maksimillian's favorite, his true love was baseball of course, but he liked many sports, and understood many of their moves and tricks. Maksimillian's foot caught the other man in the ribs, Bandana's whole body coming off the ground in a crunch of broken ribs and an explosion of air.

There. Now the man wouldn't get up for many, many more seconds. He could—

Kill.

—finish this at a more leisurely pace. His fingers curled, and he could feel the savage not-grin on his face.

"Maks?" A touch, there on his arm. He almost whirled, almost clawed, but—

Pack.

—held himself still with a massive effort. "*Da?*" He let his breathing still, the noise of distant New York starting to come back to him. The groaning of the two men at his feet. The tremor of Adalia's heart.

"Maks, they—"

"*Da,*" he said. He thought about earlier, as he'd been following her, as he'd been trying to decide what to do with this strange situation he found himself in. Was now the time? It was ... *difficult* to remember the rules. He wanted to ask her out for that drink, but knew that it wouldn't sit well with either of them. "I was just walking, my morning ritual, *da*? And who did I see ahead of me, but you! Adalia, I thought to myself, does not look like she wants to go with those men."

"I did not," she said. "I don't know what they wanted."

"Money. Your phone. Whatever is in that fine messenger bag." Maksimillian shrugged. "They were hungry, and you were—"

"Prey," said Adalia, looking down at her feet. As if she knew what the word really meant. Well, perhaps she did.

"If is not too forward, perhaps ... perhaps I could finish my morning ritual? With you. Walking, to wherever you are going." He frowned. "I do not know if this would be better or worse. I admit, even after all this time, *Amerikanskaya* rules are difficult to understand. Is girl, alone. Should I help? Should I not?"

"You should help," said Adalia. "Please. I'm ... late for work."

"Ah," said Maksimillian. "Is Starbucks?"

"Starbucks," agreed Adalia.

"I could use a spiced pumpkin latte."

"Pumpkin spice latte," she said, almost absently.

Maksimillian smiled. "And perhaps, a second breakfast. Big enough for two men."

CHAPTER
SEVENTEEN

Adalia walked to the familiar front doors of the Starbucks. A haven, where nothing bad ever happened. Nothing bad, of course, didn't mean that customers weren't assholes or that she never got dirty shoes. *Nothing bad* meant that no one died. Not yet. Not ever, she hoped, because a pumpkin spice latte just wasn't worth shooting someone in the head over.

Yet. She did make a mean latte.

Her hand rested on the door, and she felt that familiar tug, into the Other Place. She didn't have a name for it, not after all this time, and like always, she ignored it. Every time she'd used the Other Place, people died. The world changed. Horrors happened, like something out of a bad movie, or a good movie with a bad ending. It wasn't that horrors weren't real, or they wouldn't happen without the Other Place. It was that when she went into the Other Place, it was her fault.

Like with Just James, the sweet boy who'd sacrificed himself. She could have stopped him; the world would have burned but Just James would have lived. She didn't know it, but a small, scared smile touched her lips for a second. Just a flash, a moment that no one could really have noticed, more a tic than a real expression. Just James, the boy who'd died to save the world. Because of her, or for her. And because of the Other Place.

The tug warned her. She'd felt the tug before the mugging, right before Maks came to, to what, to save her? She still had the stun gun in her bag, the one Uncle John had given her after Melissa had tried to teach her to use *real* guns. Melissa had said *You've got to learn to protect yourself*, and then had gone quiet and walked away when Adalia had said *I protected the world and nothing came of that but a lot of ugly*. Uncle John had seen the whole thing, watched Melissa walk away, looked at Adalia, and had left for an hour or two. When she'd next seen him, he hadn't said anything, but there was a present on her pillow, a wrapped box with a crudely tied bow and bad handwriting that could only have been his. Inside, the stun gun, and she'd kept it with her, because the stun gun didn't kill people, or make people kill themselves, or raise ghosts from the dead. It wasn't like the Other Place. Simple, ordinary, like her job. Here, at Starbucks.

The door opened in front of her, a harried looking woman pushing past talking too loud and too fast into a phone. Adalia noticed that it was some kind of flip phone, and had a passing thought — *the 90's want their phone back* — before she slipped inside. Into a room of warm air fragrant with coffee. Of people about to get their first little bit of happy for the day — even if it was a pumpkin spice latte.

She stepped behind the counter, and snagged an apron from a hook. It was green, all of them were green, and she loved that — not the color, because it was just the wrong shade, and clashed with her hair. The *normal*-ness of the thing, worn a little where it went behind her neck. Clean, not new but completely fine. She was about to step up behind the big coffee machine, dials and steam ready to go. About to nudge Penny aside, and say *thanks for covering for me*. But she got a look from Penny, her friend's eyes flicking towards the back.

Ah. Fuck.

The back. It wasn't like a dragon lived there, nothing scary really, just Mr. Lawrence. Mr. Lawrence had given her this job, and he'd said that there were a hundred people just like her waiting to take her place if she screwed up. She'd said she wouldn't screw up, because how hard can making coffee really be, and then for one reason or another she'd been screwing up ever since. Mostly, because she was late, but often because she was tired, or like today, tired *and* late. She rubbed the side of her face with a hand, smoothed her apron, and stepped into the back.

It wasn't a long, vaulted corridor of doom, filled with traps and guards. It wasn't even a corridor — just a small room, a few bags of beans over there, a couple cardboard boxes of various breakfast goods nestled alongside. A door with cheap veneer stood closed, the *MANAGER* label a little off-center in the slider, like someone had slid it in place and never straightened it, not in the year or so she'd been here. Mr. Lawrence was full of details, about when she was two minutes late here, or when she used too much product there, but he didn't seem to have a lot of detail around the way things looked, the way he dressed, or the label on his door.

She knocked, heard something she assumed was *come in*, and twisted the handle. The smell of his office was just south of bad, old mold covered with new cleaner, some blinds covering a window to the alley out the back. They were broken, the metal twisted in some places, and Adalia figured the blinds hadn't been opened in a hundred years. They kept any semblance of natural lighting out, just shafts of fractured sunlight sneaking in. A single bulb lit the room — not that it was dark. The opposite, overly bright light spreading through the room, like Mr. Lawrence didn't want anything to hide. Certainly not the truth about where you were for those two minutes you were late for your shift.

"Mr. Lawrence, I..." she said, not even sure what story she was going to tell this time. *You're never going to believe this, but my Uncle called me at three in the morning, and my friend Melissa and I had to go to this crazy woman's house. Melissa shot another woman after I fought with her using the power of my mind, like a Jedi — you've seen Star Wars, right, Mr. Lawrence? — and then I passed out. I woke up too late and then I was mugged on my way here.* It was a good story, worthy of her own B-grade movie, and that was just what had happened between dinner last night and breakfast this morning. Except she hadn't had breakfast.

"You're fired," he said, after looking up.

Fired. It was like a stone sat in her stomach all of a sudden, a heavy rock made of fear. The worst part was she wasn't sure why she was afraid, because she could just step into the Other Place, see the strings, the ones that were all around them all of the time, and pull on just one or two. Just one or two — maybe even three — and Mr. Lawrence would think this was a funny joke, and she wouldn't be fired. The right string, and he'd even give her a raise, even though last time she'd asked him he'd said that a raise *wasn't in the blueprint*, whatever that meant.

You can't do that. Every time you step into the Other Place, someone dies.

Not even that was why she was afraid though. She cleared her throat. "Mr. Lawrence. I—"

The way he looked at her made the words die inside her, like a spring that dried up in an instant. Mr. Lawrence wasn't angry. He wasn't sad. He was tired. She could see it right there, she didn't need to use the Other Place at all. He wasn't tired of not enough sleep, he wasn't tired because he was working too hard. He was tired *of her*. He cleared his throat. "Ms. Kendrick—"

"Please, Mr. Lawrence. Give me another chance." She looked down at her hands, saw how they had tangled into each other, her fingers white. "I like it here."

There. That's why she was afraid. Because she liked this place, with the worn green aprons and demanding customers. She liked that she worked in a place where she got to meet people like Maks. The everyday nature of the place — the simple fact that there were no werewolves or *vodou* masters, no zombies or private armies.

Private armies. There was something there, a memory that tickled the back of her mind from a long time ago—

"Ms. Kendrick, you've been late every day this week." He frowned. "I don't really like firing people, you know. But when people cover your shift, when we're short on people, when we don't even know what time you'll come in, or even if you'll come in..." He trailed off, thought for a minute, then cleared his throat. "I have a friend who works at the police. If there's something..." He left that there, an almost-question, and she felt a brief flicker of hope. She could jump on that, say that *yes*, there was a problem at home, that her boyfriend—

There it was, Melissa's face in her mind, she could see it clear as day. Melissa, who used to be a cop, but wasn't anymore because of Adalia. Melissa would find out about the lie, and she'd be so disappointed. Not as disappointed as if she'd gone into the Other Place and made Mr. Lawrence change his mind. Not that Adalia ever would, not ever again. She'd said to herself that she wouldn't use the Other Place, because she still remembered Just James, and what his kiss had tasted like.

Adalia sighed. "No, Mr. Lawrence. It's not ... it's not like that." *I think I helped save my uncle's life last night, and I'm just so tired, do you see, Mr. Lawrence?* "Thank you for thinking of me, but ... well. You've given me so many chances. I understand." She turned away so he wouldn't see the tears in her eyes, see how the stone in her stomach made her feel. She didn't want him to feel bad for trying to look after his business.

She had a hand on the door, ready to leave — to run, really — when his voice stopped her. "Adalia?"

She didn't turn. "Yes, Mr. Lawrence?"

"Adalia, I've arranged your final pay. It's ... it's for the next two weeks. I've put my friend's card in your envelope. Just in case."

Two weeks. Two weeks of money she hadn't earned. And a card, in case she needed help. Oh *man*, did she need help, the whole Pack did, but not this kind of help. She leaned her forehead against the veneer of Mr. Lawrence's office door, and thought about what to say. *I know why you had to do this*, she could start with that. *It's people like you, who are basically nice people in a bad job, and you try and be nice even when it's hard, that's why we're doing this.* That could be the next bit. *Please take your family and leave the city because everyone will die.* A punchy final line, if a bit over dramatic. She sighed. "Thank you, Mr. Lawrence. Thank you."

The door slipped closed behind her, and she pulled off her green apron as she passed the bags of beans, the boxes of breakfast supplies. She passed Penny, touching her friend on the arm but saying nothing. Penny had left a coffee beside the machine, a coffee for Adalia, "Ady," written in big black pen on the side with an unhappy face next to it. There was another cup, "Maks," written on this one, and Adalia was sure that it held a pumpkin spice latte. Adalia almost broke down then, but picked up the cups, felt their heat through her hand, and breathed. Just breathed in, and out. Once, twice, and then the tears were gone, the need to cry gone, like they'd never been there. The only thing that remained was the stone in her stomach.

She grabbed her envelope on the way out, and as Mr. Lawrence promised there was two weeks' pay — a little more really — and the business card of a detective in the NYPD. Adalia might see if Melissa knew her, but then she'd have to explain what happened today. She looked at the card again, the embossed logo of the police department in the corner, and traced it with her thumb. She sighed, flicked the card into one of the big trash cans next to sweeteners and stirring sticks, and stepped back out into the world. The world, outside of Starbucks, where werewolves and vampires were real.

Maks was still there. Maks, the man standing in the flow of New York's morning sidewalk traffic like the Rock of Gibraltar, not moving an inch as people rushed around him. Maks, who'd been there for *her* this morning. Maks, who hadn't asked for anything except a pumpkin spice latte. She handed him a cup, and he took it in silence, his face contemplative.

"I got fired," she said at last. "I can't believe I got fired."

He nodded. "This spiced pumpkin latte, is not as good as before. Did you make it with sadness?" His accent was thick, and she loved it, the sound it made, so different from how everyone else talked. Like he was proud of it, like he didn't need to hide it. She wanted to be that person, with nothing to hide.

"Pumpkin spice latte," she said, smiling a little. "I didn't make it. Penny made it."

"Ah," he said. "Penny? She is not as good as you."

The Starbucks stood at their backs, eyes within staring at them. Or at least, that's what Adalia thought, all those people staring at her shame. Of course it wasn't true — Mr. Lawrence hadn't put up a sign that said *I'm firing Adalia today*. But she'd walked out sadder than she'd walked in, and people noticed that kind of thing.

Didn't they?

Maks was looking at her, like she was the only part of this street that mattered. She liked that. Many good things had come out of Starbucks, but better than her final pay had been meeting him. She felt around inside her head for something to say that wouldn't sound like she was whining about being fired, which was all she really wanted to do. "I was four hours late."

He barked a laugh. "Four hours? Is extreme, even for Millennial generation."

She ran a hand through her hair. "I think maybe more than four hours? I don't know. I mean, I was mugged, and then..." Her voice trailed off. "Last night was weird."

Maks frowned at her, looking like he wanted to say something. She *wanted* him to say something. She wanted him to ... she wasn't sure. *Something*, though, not nothing, like he was doing now. *She* almost said something to get *him* to say something, and then he swallowed. "There is story here, no?" He nodded, more to himself than to her. "In Mother Russia, we believe good stories go best with vodka."

Adalia looked at him from under her hair. "Are you ... are you

159

asking me out for a drink?" The stone in her stomach was warring with something else, something light and soft and happy.

He considered that for a few seconds. "My English," he said, "is not always good. Is vodka "drink" in this country?"

"'*Da*,'" she said. "We have vodka."

He beamed. "*Da*. Then I am asking you out for a drink."

She laughed, and it felt *good* to laugh, like she hadn't in about a thousand years. It occurred to her that maybe she hadn't, hadn't really laughed at all, and that she'd needed that more than a drink. But a drink would do. She shook her head, hair waving about her face, and then smiled at him. "Yes. Let's go for a drink."

SHE FELT like she'd chosen the bar, but after they'd got there she wasn't so sure anymore. Maks had held the door open for her and she'd stepped into the warm dim interior like she was coming home. The wood panels probably smelled of cedar once, or maybe they hadn't, but either way it was okay. It was a proper Irish bar, a place she'd been to before with Uncle John. Uncle John had explained it was real because there weren't any *fake fucking shamrocks, right, nothing green, and no leprechauns.* There were taps in the bar, different beer brands, and she'd remembered Uncle John ordering one with Guinness written on it, and looking like he hated it for the entire time it had taken him to drink it.

Adalia had chosen this place because she'd felt it was somewhere you could be alone with your thoughts, or take them out and show them to a friend. She looked at Maks from under her hair. *Friend* wasn't right, was it? Not really. She didn't know him that well, but she was honest in her own head and ... felt like she needed to know him much better. They found a booth, which wasn't hard because there wasn't a huge number of people wanting whiskey at eleven in the morning. Maks ordered a bottle of vodka. A *bottle*. The bartender — a young guy with an open face and an accent that might have actually been Irish — had looked between them, thought about arguing, probably something like *why not something a little more cheerful*, looked at Maks and the size of his shoulders, and had brought them back a bottle and two small glasses.

The glass of vodka sat on the table in front of her. She felt herself relaxing, that happy soft thing in her stomach still there, and settled back into the leather embrace of the booth's seat. The Other Place tugged at her again, but she was sure it just wanted to show her the stories in the wood of the tables and the clear alcohol in the glass in front of her. Adalia reached out a hand for her glass, then paused. "Do you ... do you just drink it?"

Maks frowned at her. "Is vodka. What else?"

"You don't ... water it down?" She sniffed at it. *Hard* was how she would have described it, perhaps that one word under a photo of herself making a face on Instagram. "It seems rough."

Maks picked up his glass, gestured towards her oh so briefly, then tipped the contents into his mouth in one smooth motion. He made a face, not of disgust but of disappointment. "Is *Amerikanskaya* vodka," he said by way of explanation, as if he had to apologize to her for the quality of a Russian drink in an Irish bar in America. "I do not understand. This country is great, *da*? Good at many things. Especially good at making foods to fatten a person beyond normal size."

"Very much beyond normal size," she agreed. She still had not touched her drink.

"*Da*. Is strange, no, that this skill at making amazing foods does not stretch to alcohol. Alcohol is easy thing to make. Like walking and laughing. Simple." He poured himself another glass, swallowed it back, and made the same face as before. Yes, definitely disappointment. "Is not best grade, no?"

Adalia pushed her hair back, leaned forward to snare her own glass, and slammed it back. She felt the fire of the liquor as it went down her throat, something hot in her nose, and felt her eyes screw themselves shut as if that would in some way help. The cough came unbidden, her lungs turning traitor. "How do you even..?"

"Is good, *da*?" He poured more into her glass. "Is good for taking away the feelings of the body, so you can think about the feelings of the soul."

"Maks," she said. "Maks, I feel like I know you." The Other Place tugged at her again, and she pushed at it, suddenly angry. *Leave me alone! This man is not for you. He's for* me. She looked into his dark eyes.

Maks didn't seem to notice anything strange about her, or see that flash of anger. He brushed his hair away from his face, still considering what she'd said. Probably trying to work out if it was a corny pick-up line, which it wasn't, but made her feel like she should just vanish into the floor and never be seen again. "I have, how do you say, familiar face." He drank again. "Perhaps is vodka. Makes friends of enemies."

She thought about it, swirling the liquor in her glass. Thought about Mr. Lawrence, who was trying to be good in a job he wasn't very good at. She thought about Just James, who had sacrificed himself so she could sit here in this bar. "I am not a good person, Maks." She thought about the Other Place, and the men who'd mugged her this morning. Or tried to mug her. Was it still a mugging if they didn't get what they wanted? "I think ... I think those men, they were ... they were the Universe. Do you believe in karma?"

Maks' face darkened and he looked into his glass, as if it held a better answer than what was going on behind his eyes. "*Da.*" His eyes met hers, and she saw something there, something familiar, and warm, and it made her want to touch him.

"I ... did a terrible thing, once," she said, instead of touching him. Then her hands reached across the table, found his anyway. It felt natural and strange at once, and she felt forward, but also so alone, and she just wanted to touch him to not feel alone. To not be alone. She wanted to touch Just James again, but Maks was here, and his hands were warm. "I ... let a good man die."

"This good man," said Maks, face serious. His fingers held hers for a moment, then pulled back — not breaking away, but leaving space between them for something else. "Tell me his story."

She pulled her hands back, held them in her lap. "Well, see, we were in this crazy fight, and—"

"No," he said. "*His* story. Not yours. Vodka likes honesty." He offered her a small smile.

"Oh," she said. "You know, I've never told anyone about him. Not really. Not even Melissa." She chose her next words carefully, not wanting to have more corny lines from a bad romcom come out of her mouth. "Do you believe in love at first sight?" No, that was terrible. *Terrible.* She held up a hand. "Hold up. This is *his* story. Because I think he loved me from the moment we met."

"Ah," said Maks, and then sat waiting. Like he understood. Like he wanted to touch her too. It helped.

"He was brave, Maks. He knew that I was ... different. That I could do things. That I could see the future, or shape the hearts of men, or break the way that gravity works. I could do any of those things, and all of them, and he wasn't frightened by it. He saw it, and followed me, and burned himself up so that the rest of us could be free. Do you see?" Her eyes were wet, but there were no tears. She wasn't quite sure how this was supposed to work, and figured she hadn't had enough vodka. "After that day, after that brave man gave up his everything to save *me* ... you know, it was me, me, not the world, but *me* he was saving. And I let him. I knew what was happening. I could have stopped it. Everyone else would have died, but I could have saved him. I didn't."

A waiter was making his way towards their booth, but Maks warned him away with a look, like it was second nature.

She took another sip of her vodka, no grimace this time as she got used to the cool dry burn of the spirit. *Vodka likes honesty.* She couldn't be honest with Mr. Lawrence this morning. Maybe she could be honest with Maks. Maybe something more. "I have a ... gift, Maks."

"A gift," he said. "From the way you are speaking, is sounding like you would like to return it." The joke fell flat and hard, neither of them smiling.

"I don't use it anymore. Not really." Her hair had fallen over her face. "Oh, from time to time I get to wheel it out, like a performing seal. I get to do something that the Universe needs. But the rest of the time, I don't … I can't touch it. It makes me sick." *I said I never would, not ever again. And I can't even do that right.*

"Do something?"

"Yeah," she said. "I can," and here, she waved a hand at the bar around them, "see what people are made of. Or, I don't know, change the way someone works. I met a man once, who had the best name. Marcellus Samuel Kentucky. Another man had taken away Marcellus Samuel Kentucky's free will, and a man with a name like that deserves all his free will, like he's earned it forever. So … so I gave it back to him."

"That does not sound bad," said Maks. He turned his glass this way and that. "That sounds like—"

"He wanted to die for me as well," Adalia said. "I made him leave. But he wasn't the one I wanted to save."

"This gift," said Maks. "Could it … what can it do?"

"Everything," said Adalia. "Do you know, Jessie—" of course, Maks didn't know who Jessie was, but the vodka was talking now, the words just tumbling out "—was trying to fix this old car a year or two back, it had been taking her weeks, and the thing just wouldn't start. It was always a 'busted alternator' or 'cracked distributor cap' or other things I don't even know about. And so I looked at the car, and I sort of … fixed it. I just made it work."

"How?" said Maks. "Car, is broken?"

"I made it what it should have been," she said. "I don't really understand cars, which is the funny thing."

They sat in silence for a while. Maks leaned forward. "Could you turn water into wine?"

She jerked back like he'd slapped her, the soft warm thing in her stomach vanishing. Or hiding. "Don't *ever* say that."

"I—"

"I'm not a, a, what do you want me to be? Why does everyone want me to be something else?" She stood up. "I'm not that. I'm not that. Don't make me be that!"

Maks held up a hand, relaxed, like she hadn't just shouted at him loud enough for people out on the street to hear. His eyes were warm, found hers across the table. "Is saying, *have no horse in this race*. You know it?"

She nodded.

He nodded back. "Is not my story." He poured more vodka for her, refilled his own glass, and suddenly she was sitting again, like all the air had left her. "You are still excited from this morning, *da*? Not enough vodka, is problem."

She watched him for a moment longer. "I'm sorry," she said. "You probably don't believe me." Her hands found his again, and it wasn't as weird as it was last time, like the Other Place wanted her to do it. Or Maks wanted her to do it, because it might have been that his hands had found *hers*. Her head was feeling light from the vodka, or something else, but probably the vodka.

"Oh," said Maks, "I believe you. Many things in this world. Many strange things. Many wonders. Many terrors."

"'Many terrors' is right," she said. "What should I do?"

She wasn't really asking him, but there was no one else to ask. She watched his face as he answered, but he wasn't looking at her. He was looking into the distance, like he remembered he'd left something on the oven. "Whatever you want." He shrugged. "Is all we have, in this world, do what we want."

"What if what you want is bad? What if someone dies?"

"Someone always dies," said Maks. "Here, in *Amerika*, is much concern about what is right about the wrong things. Is talk shows on television about what is right. Is fears about what is right thing to wear. Is fear about who is right person to talk to. In Mother Russia, is simpler. Is not whether someone dies. Is more important that *right* someone dies."

She was quiet for a time, sitting across the table from him, the vodka between them. "I just want to work at Starbucks," she said, almost like a wish.

He blinked at her. "I'm sorry," he said. "My English. You said—"

"At Starbucks, I made minimum wage, but I didn't need to make decisions. My Mom, well, she said that it would be good for me, to learn to be like everybody else. Val, too. Even Melissa. She said something about 'building character.' Only Uncle John wasn't on board. He said it ... well, he said something that wasn't like Uncle John at all. He said that I should do what was in my heart." She looked down. "So I did all of that, because what was in my heart was to be *normal*. I don't want to choose, Maks. I don't want to choose who lives and who dies. I just want to make a good latte."

"No," said Maks, and for the first time there was something hard in his voice, but his hands on hers were still gentle.

"What?" she said.

"No," said Maks. "Is ... is wrong." He pointed at the vodka in front of her. "Drink."

"I don't—"

"Vodka holds truth," said Maksimillian, "and you are not speaking truth to me."

"I am!"

"No," said Maks. "You are speaking a lie you want to be truth." He downed his vodka, refilled his glass. "The car you fixed, you say you don't understand cars. Maybe so. But you," and he pointed with his glass at her, "you understand what a thing should be. You, Adalia, are a person. With purpose, *da*? Your purpose is not to make lattes. Your purpose is something else."

"To save the world?" Her words were bitter.

"Is possible." He shrugged.

"I've already done that," she said.

He looked at her, held her eyes. "Is possible world still needs saving."

"What do you care?" she said.

He thought about that. "Is good question," he said. "I do not have good answer. I have seen much of the world. Many things."

"'Many terrors,'" she said.

"Just so," he said. "But also, many wonders. Is worth saving?" He held his hands up like scales, moving one up, then back down. "Is great question." But he was looking at her like she was the answer to a different question. Like he was hungry for her too.

She drank more vodka, reached for the bottle, and poured a generous splash. "It is a great question."

"The world," said Maks, his eyes holding hers for longer, "has you in it."

Her hand stilled as it held her glass. "Yes," she said. "I don't know if that's good or bad."

"Is good," he said. "Is very good."

She looked at him from under her hair. "Would you..." She paused, realized she was touching his hands again. But that was okay, wasn't it? "Would you like to get out of here?"

"*Da*," said Maks. "Very much."

CHAPTER
EIGHTEEN

Liselle drew a long pull from her cigarette. "So you want to teach them to fight," she said at last.

The vampire — who insisted on calling itself *Jeremy*, as if that were its name — nodded. "Yeah." The vile thing looked at its feet, old sneakers on below denim that was faded and patched. "You could help."

"Josef can help," said Liselle. "He can still lift his sword."

"And you can't?" It snorted, almost a laugh. "You just lack the proper motivation. Like the rest of them."

The two of them had walked through a door at the end of the big main room of the warehouse, arriving in what was probably a garage. A large cage stood open and empty, and there was a refrigerator with blood, and a few different vehicles. A Jeep. An expensive limousine. A tractor. She understood the blood, she understood the cage even, but she didn't understand why they'd need a tractor. A big roller door — closed, so that the vampire didn't burst into flames — sat between two windows, makeshift blinds blocking the Father's light.

"What do you know of motivation?" She rounded on it. "You

wear their shape, but hold all the worst parts of their hunger and viciousness. You're driven by base need. I have seen a hundred thousand lives of men. I know what drives them all."

"I think, you know, that it's weird you'd open yourself up like this. I'm not even, what are they, like a counselor. A shrink."

She wanted to hit it, to destroy it. She wondered if she still had the strength. "I used to be the strongest, next to Kaylan."

"You're only as good as your last album, that's what they say in the biz," the thing said to her. "Look, it's pretty simple. We can stand back here while they talk about us out there. Maybe we can hit each other. I don't think either of us want that."

"I want it maybe a little."

It nodded. "Okay, maybe one of us wants that."

"It's your nature," she said. "You're made of death and disease."

The thing spread its hands. "Totally. We've always been a little on the treacherous side." It licked its lips like it was tasting the memory of something. "You know. Knifing our friends in the back and eating them." It turned from her, its back exposed. She could take her sword, drive it through. It would be a mercy.

A mercy for whom?

The thing was still talking. "Look, I'm not for big speeches. They want to learn to fight. I don't mean with guns and knives and sharp sticks, they've got all that. I mean how to fight things that move faster than the eye can see. That can turn into a cloud of fucking locusts. That are stronger than Krazy Glue. I can show them that."

She looked at him, brushing hair from her face. "Why would you do that?"

He snorted again. "I think you know why."

"The end of all things," she said.

"It's not a super cool thing to have on your tombstone," said the thing, eyes flashing in the gloom. "If there was anyone left to make you a tombstone. If tombstones still existed."

Nothing will exist. She looked at this vampire a little more carefully. Perhaps it was different from the rest. *Perhaps it isn't.* "Having you here," and she didn't say *with John Miles*, "is too great a risk."

Its teeth glinted like ice. *It's smiling. It's trying to smile.* "You'll just stand by while he dies? That it?"

"Who are you?" she said. "Really."

"I'm just a kid from the wrong part of town." It shrugged. "I don't know much about these werewolf motherfuckers, right. They're extinct, or that's the line from Vampire High Command. But the stories they tell, they're about these assholes being wrecking machines."

"Yes," said Liselle. "But ... there are so few of them left. They pick all the *wrong* fights."

"But for all the right reasons," said the vampire. "You going to help them, or you going to see them snuffed out?"

"I—"

"Look," said the thing. "You're on the team or you're off the team. Doesn't even have to be *my* team. Pretend I'm not here. Hell, if they win I won't be here. And ... yeah okay, I think we both want that. But since you're on Team *Apocalypse*, you should tell them what they're up against."

"I can't," said Liselle. "Kaylan—"

Bullets punched through one of the makeshift blinds, and the vampire was *on* her, so fast, *by the Father, I hadn't remembered, and now it will destroy this shell and kill John Miles*, but it had grabbed her and was sheltering her with its body. Bullets hammered into it, she could feel each impact as it held her close, the blood stench of its breath, their faces so close they could kiss. The shooting stopped, and a man's voice shouted, "Reloading!" from outside.

The vampire looked at her, the mirrors of its eyes meeting hers. "Do you see?" It wiped blood from its lips, something punctured internally. "Do you see what they're up against?"

"I see," she said. And, through the Other Place, she heard Josef.

LISELLE.

I LISTEN.

THEY COME, LISELLE. KAYLAN SENDS MY CHILDREN AGAINST ME.

The vampire stood her up, and — so fast, so fast she could barely see — ran to the workbench. It picked up a hammer in one hand, a pry bar in the other. It looked at her, lips red. "Your sword."

"I can't," she said.

A man came in through the window, a rifle in his hands, a flash of sunlight making the vampire hiss and cower. She took in the little details. Body armor, but no flag. A camera on the side of the helmet. His equipment, everything from his clothes to his weapon, were black, anonymous, faceless. A private army. Kaylan had bought a private army.

The man's eyes were still adjusting to the gloom, and he pointed the rifle at her. When this shell died, she wouldn't have the strength to come back for a long time, perhaps not ever, and that would stop the end of everything. She closed her eyes, welcoming it. There was a wet crunch, and he eyes snapped open. The vampire had thrown the hammer at the man, the tool punching through the armor vest the man wore, out his back, and splintering against the hard cinder blocks of the wall behind. The man's rifle barked a few shots into the air as he fell, lips moving as he tried to voice words. Perhaps a request to the Father. Perhaps a request to his mother.

The wall exploded in light and noise and heat, shards of stone and brick flying all around her, the air pulling at her hair. She felt something sharp lick at her cheek, something hit her shoulder, and she stood before the Father's light.

The vampire screamed as flames flickered on its skin then burst forth in a blaze. Kaylan's children couldn't stand before the Father's sight, not for long. And here she was, thinking to deal with one of these abominations? She heard John Miles in her head. *Because we need to. Because no one else is going to. Because we can.* Then she remembered what this vampire, this *thing*, had said just moments ago. *I can show them.* And she remembered it standing in front of her, in front of this shell, ready to die for a Pack that wasn't its own.

Oh, Father. Forgive me.

Liselle took three steps towards the vampire, grabbed the flaming thing, and threw it towards the back of the room. It burned a bright line through the gloom, guttering out as the Father's light stopped touching it. Where it came to rest, smoke poured off it like a tire fire, but she was already turning away, towards the breach in the wall. Men were running through, running in to hurt her, to hurt them all. To hurt John Miles.

The first brought its rifle to bear, and she caught it by the barrel. The knife edge of her hand came down against the barrel, shearing through in a flash of heat and light. She stopped her movement, reversed it and slammed her palm's heel into the man's chest. He broke, shattered inside, his body tumbling back through the breach. The man next to him had his rifle pointed at her, at her face, and he pulled the trigger. *They would hurt John Miles.* Her head moved out of the way, once, twice, a third time, this last as a bullet kissed the other cheek, to leave a mark to mirror where the stone chip had hit her. Then she was on him, hitting him once, twice, a third time, faster than his rifle could spit bullets, breaking his shoulder, his chest, his skull under a helmet made of something too flimsy to hold back her fear and her anger.

A third. This one with a stupid expression, his rifle trying to track her, but tracking nothing but air. She tore it from him, smashed him again and again and again until the useless thing fell apart in her hands, the mewling thing at her feet nothing but red flecked with bits of white.

They would come here. To hurt John Miles.

The fourth, then. This one fast, for a man, and strong too. For a man. His gun she tossed aside, then pulled off his arm, then his leg, and left him to bleed dry against the hard earth. The fifth was trying to run, but not even her black horse could have run fast enough. She grabbed the man as he stumbled, snagging his leg, and tossed him into the sky, his body tumbling end over end over end until he was lost from sight.

To hurt John Miles.

She stalked back through the breach, to stand over the smoking ruin of the vampire. It looked up at her, charred lips cracking, bits of carbon flaking off. "Your ... *sword.*"

"I can't," she said. "It's too heavy."

The thing craned its neck to look through the breach, at the bodies strewn outside. It looked back at her. "Too ... *heavy.*"

Gunfire came from the other room, and she thought, *John Miles.* She left the thing to smolder in the dark, hitting the door at a run. It fell from its hinges, and she saw—

Josef. Standing in the middle of it, a red sword of fire in his hands. It was burning so bright, she hadn't seen it burn like that for a thousand thousand years. But he wasn't using it, he was standing still, the eye of a hurricane, as soldiers — his 'children' — moved around him. Jessica Pearce was at his side, a large rifle nestled against her shoulder, turning like a human turret, firing at any that came too close. Val and Danny fought, still human — still human! *By the Father, they were masters of the Night — eyes a bright yellow as they fought by strength and fist. Their blows pounded through armor to the soft meat within. Carlisle was behind a fallen table, covering Sam Barnes with her body, her sidearm speaking with the promise of dead men at any who came too close. The old man Rex was locked in a wrestle with a huge, muscled man, and was winning. There were so many soldiers. So, so many. Their gunfire raked at Val and Danny, who shifted moment by moment to things that were huge and clawed and back to people again. And then back, as the Night called to them.*

These soldiers sought to make the wolves lose control. To kill their own Pack.

And there, standing — not in cover, not crouched, not hiding — was John Miles. He held a rifle, and he was—

By the Father. He was trying to protect the werewolves. By shooting those shooting at them.

Liselle could see how it would happen. Saw that moment shift on the head of a pin, where one soldier saw John Miles, and then another. Saw John Miles standing like a hero from a bad action movie, firing his rifle from the hip, unarmored, uncovered. An easy shot even in the heat of battle.

"No," she said. And she heard the vampire's words: *your sword*. It was too heavy for her, but ... what about the Night?

She reached into the Other Place, felt for the hilt of the familiar weapon. Closer than a friend, the grip more familiar than a lover's face. She felt the fell blade, felt its hunger. It wanted to come forth.

They are given power over a quarter of the Father's Eden.

She called to it. Called with her heart.

They are to kill by famine, by plague.

The sword answered, falling from the sky. It screamed with fierce joy as it fell, shattering the roof of the warehouse, to bury itself blade-first in the hard concrete floor. Smoke billowed out from where it landed, licks of flame hinted at from inside those dark clouds. A black blade, as tall as she was, with a hilt designed to be held by huge hands. Flames of ink roiled off it. She had named it Scourge. *Her sword.*

They are to kill by the wild beasts of the earth.

All action had stopped in the room, soldiers stunned, Josef's mouth agape. She met the lambent eyes of Val, and he reached a hand to rest on the hilt of the black sword. She heard Scourge sing as Val tried to pull the sword from the ground. His muscles bunched, and the sword quivered, but he — even *he* — wasn't strong enough. Scourge was heavy. To wield that sword was to hold a quarter of the fate of the world in your hand. It's what she'd been trying to tell the vampire. She'd hoped that the Night would have been strong enough, and the shell's heart jumped and skipped. *Father, is this what fear feels like?*

Rex had started to move, and a soldier's rifle tracked his movements, and there was John Miles, in the way. Shielding the old man with his body. Because John Miles had seen the rifle, and there wasn't enough time for words. There was a gunshot. It only took a single round. One of Josef's children, afraid after the fall of Scourge.

A soldier with too much adrenaline seeing two people moving, thinking it was a charge.

She saw John Miles looking down at his stomach, the red blooming there.

"No," she said.

She saw John Miles stumble, the rifle clattering from his hand. Saw him fall to one knee.

"*No*," she said.

Saw him fall against the earth, his life's blood leaking out of him, bright red against his T-shirt.

THEY ARE TO KILL BY THE SWORD.

Her hand was around the hilt of the black blade, and she felt the shell around her crack for an instant, something too big for it to contain wanting to pour forth. Her hand remembered this blade. Scourge had been born in her heart, and it was black, black as night, black as the clawing hunger of a belly empty for weeks. Black as justice.

Black as vengeance.

She strode across the room and cut with the sword, the man she hit split in two, his skin shriveling and drying out. A second man cut in half, his essence also going into the black blade, his body emaciated in less than two beats of a human heart. More black flames licked along Scourge's length, hungry, so hungry. The third soldier then, and the fourth, and the fifth, and then to the sixth. The seventh, and eighth were the same, and how they deserved it. How they had *earned* their end. The ninth died trying to scream, but just a croak came from a throat suddenly parched with a thirst of a hundred year drought. The tenth. The eleventh. The twelfth.

The thirteenth stood in front of her, a young man, who said, "Please." Then he died, the water leaving his blood, the flesh leaving his bones as the black sword cut him in two.

"Liselle," said Josef. "They are mine."

"No," she snarled, the shell's voice too small to hold all her hate. "They are *mine*." A fourteenth. A fifteenth. And then she was outside, under the light of the Father, and still more stood against her. She pushed a car out of her way. She paused to draw a breath, and Josef was there. Her friend, her brother.

"Liselle," he said. "This is how Kaylan wins."

She walked past him, a sixteenth firing from a weapon that was tiny and ridiculous. You may as well shoot the ocean and try and stop it. He died, sucked dry and empty, his body falling to dust as it broke against the ground. Seventeen, eighteen, and nineteen were inside one of their tiny vehicles, and the black blade cut through it, harvesting them all like winter wheat. She felt their screams against the blade of the sword, felt the hunger of her grin, the answering need from Scourge.

"Liselle," said Josef. He hadn't walked to join her in the harvest. His sword was gone, that red blade of War. "Remember."

Liselle paused, wiping sweat from her forehead. The tip of the black blade rested against the earth, smoking and burning the Father's earth. She looked around her at the bodies. What was left of men who'd taken John Miles from her. She looked up the street at the milling humans, ripe for the harvest.

Liselle. Would you be bent by their will? You, who call Death your sister?

Why those words came to her now she didn't know. They were from her old friend, dead more than two thousand years. He was a kind man with gentle eyes. He had made such beautiful things from wood he found. This carpenter had said she could choose. Choose to *not* be what she was made for. She had agreed at the time and wept as he died. But that was before. Choosing to let them live made no sense in a world empty of John Miles. She should have stopped it those two thousand years ago, atop Golgotha, when humans like these had taken the last person she'd dared to call *friend*.

She could choose, all right. Her fingers tightened around the grip of the black blade.

"Baby?" The voice was weak, almost like she'd imagined it. Like it was a trick of Kaylan's, and she shouldn't look, or she'd fall for some elaborate trap. Although this felt more like Maynor's work — it more like him to be so cruel, to twist the knife at the end. She turned anyway, sword leaking smoke on the ground, because to see even a mockery of John Miles was something she needed very much.

There he was, John Miles, standing in the Father's light. He was hunched around his stomach, blood weeping through his fingers, his face so pale. But it was him, she could tell because of that beautiful light that shone so bright it almost hurt to look. The black blade tumbled from her fingers, dissolving into smoke that vanished into the earth like water into desert ground. Liselle grabbed John Miles close, held him to her.

"Baby," he said, "baby, it's cool."

She kissed him, or tried to. He stumbled, and she had to hold him up. "Are you real?" she said, meaning *look at what I've done.*

He looked over her shoulder, then back into her eyes. "This is going to sound all wrong, but it's not you, it's me."

Her heart sank. It was what she'd done. He was, what did these humans call it, leaving her. *Breaking it to her easy.* "I—"

"No," he said, putting a finger on her lips. "It really is me. I just got shot. And while I'd ... on a usual weekday ... be up for a few rounds, if you know what I mean, I think I need to put more blood inside me. I've seen the movies. The blood coming out is what kills you."

She laughed, and he laughed, and then he winced, and she was crying and didn't know why.

～

"Fucking awesome," said John Miles. He said *awesome* in a way that suggested it was anything but. They were in the garage, breached wall and all, and John Miles was lying back on a stretcher. Not even a makeshift stretcher, a real one, as if they had expected they'd need it. And *lying back* wasn't exactly right — it was tilted up, more like he was reclining on a particularly mobile armchair.

They probably had expected it, at that. They were all there, all except for Danny, who had left after the attack — a touch, a kiss with Val and then she had gone. *Hunting*, thought Liselle. The Night was always hunting.

The old man, Rex, had connected John Miles to bags of blood hanging above the stretcher. Blood was going in to one of his arms, and John Miles held a beer in his other hand. Rex had frowned at that, and John Miles had said *you've got to die of something* and Rex had said *it looks like that's what's going to happen* and John Miles had said *okay, race you* and Rex had looked like he'd wanted to punch him. But then Rex had done the strangest thing, for all her long years Liselle would never understand them. Rex had said *thank you*, and put a hand on John Miles' shoulder.

Bandages wrapped around John Miles' waist. Aside from the blood bag above him, he looked completely relaxed. At home. Some of that may have been the 'cocktail' that Rex had added to the transfusion, a small vial of clear liquid that joined the red flow keeping him alive.

Val put a hand on John Miles' shoulder. "It's a part of the plan."

There were torn and shredded blood bags on the floor, and what was left of the vampire was feeding on more, sitting on the edge of another stretcher, blood streaking down its face. Black flakes of carbon were littered on the stretcher and the floor around it, and its hair still smoked. The room smelled like barbecue. It finished licking the inside of the blood bag, mirrored eyes looking up. Liselle stood still for a moment, just watching it. *You've got to decide if it's in the tribe or not, Liselle Vitols. The time for trust or death has come.* She looked at the blood bag she held, then handed it to the vampire.

"Hold the phone," said John Miles. "Me getting shot was part of the plan?" He tried to get up, looked like that would make him less relaxed, and leaned back.

"That specific detail wasn't written down—"

"Because it hurt. It hurt when it happened, and it still hurts now."

"Oh for Chrissakes, Miles," said Carlisle, from where she leaned against the wall. "It's barely a flesh wound and you've got enough benzos inside you to float an elephant."

"Not a specific part of the plan," said Major Pearce — *Jessie.* "But I think we can work with it." She was holding one of the soldier's helmets, turning it this way and that in her hands.

"Fuck you guys," said John Miles. He coughed.

"The plan," said Val, "was to kill them all. They're panicking, and we can use that. They've slipped up."

"You've done no such thing," said Liselle. "They haven't 'slipped up.'"

"Hi," said Val. "Look, thanks for the assist back there, but—"

"There was no silver," said Liselle. "Kaylan makes no mistakes."

"Yeah," said Jessie. "I see two possible situations here. The first is that we're not the target, the second is that we're the target."

"My tax dollars," said John Miles, "go towards funding this kind of 'military intelligence.'"

"You don't pay taxes," said Carlisle. "You'd need to earn a salary—"

"I'm the only one with a real job," said John Miles. "I work at a bar."

"At a bar that's destroyed," said Carlisle.

"Back to the situation," said Jessie, her voice professional, smooth, crisp. Hands behind her back, just like she was addressing the troops. Liselle saw Josef watching her from a corner, eyes hooded, but his posture said *admiration.* This woman was one of his chosen. She held up a finger. "First option is that they came to poke the bear. I don't like this scenario because there's no win in it, aside from trying to get under our skin, and I think we can agree we're a bit beyond that. This isn't our first rodeo, it isn't their first rodeo."

"We're all professional cattle herders," said Carlisle. She looked down, working the action on her sidearm. "Nice."

Jessie gave her a look, then held up two fingers. "Second, they came for something particular, and we can assume that this objective was successfully realized." She held up the helmet, tapped the camera on the side.

"They came for intelligence," said Sam Barnes. "They came to find out who we are, and how many. They came to ... to see if I'm here."

"It is my preferred scenario," said Jessie. "And if so, it's a part of the plan."

"Okay," said John Miles. "I'll bite. How?"

"Because they shot you, of course," she said, her lip quirking.

"Asshole," he muttered.

"Okay," said Val. "They're clued up, they know we're here. They'll be coming for us, claws out."

"Teeth," said the vampire.

"What?"

"We don't really do claws," it said. "We're all about the teeth."

"Got it," said Val. "So the question is how we use this."

"Kaylan will come for you," said Liselle. "She will come when the Father's light fades. Tonight. She knows she is many, and you are few."

"Cool," said Val. "I was thinking something along those lines. So now we ... do what? Wait for her to come?"

"Never a fan of waiting," said Carlisle.

"Neither," said Rex.

"That's because you've got so little time left," said John Miles.

A vein bulged in Rex's forehead, and he took a couple of breaths. "It's okay, son," he said. "I understand. It's hard, being the bait."

"Wait," said John Miles, "what?"

"Well, you can't move," said Jessie.

"I can move," said John Miles. He tried to get up, fell back again. "It's only a flesh wound, right Melissa?"

Carlisle eyed him, went back to working on her sidearm.

"Val?"

Val shrugged. "Everyone's got a role in life, John."

"I hate you guys."

Val turned to Liselle, then to the vampire, and then back to Liselle. "I figure one of you has to know. Where are they?"

"Everywhere," said Liselle.

"More specifically," said the vampire, "there's a huge fucking nest right under Madison Square Garden." It shrugged, more black flaking off its shoulders and back. "I don't know how many of the tunnels and shit under there were OEM, and how many are ... let's say, not listed on the original plans. But it gives them a good place to ... recruit from."

Liselle laughed. It started as a chuckle, then turned slowly into a belly laugh.

"What's so funny?" said the vampire, looking at her sideways.

"The Garden," said Liselle. "Father's Eden. Don't you see? Kaylan ... she always had a dark sense of humor."

"Great," said the vampire. "I'm so pleased my eternal damnation is hilarious."

"You still have a problem," said Josef.

"We've got a lot of problems," said Val. "Which one were you thinking of? In particular."

"They are faster than all of you, and stronger than most." He shrugged. "If there are just five down there, you've got a challenge."

"Bombs," said Jessie.

"I'm sorry?" Josef leaned forward.

"It's a device that uses an exothermic reaction—"

"I know what it is," he said through his teeth, as if he didn't expect his children to talk back at him. Liselle smiled at that — his children were *warriors*. What did he expect? "I don't see the relevance."

"We've *got* bombs," said Jessie. "Well, explosives, anyway. Since they're underground, we'll just need to crawl on in there. The plan was to find the nest—"

"Vampire High Command," said the vampire.

"Vampire High Command," agreed Jessie, "that. And just blow it up. All that's changed is the timetable. We need to move now, before they do. Before night comes, and they swarm over us like an unholy tide of darkness and," here she looked at Jeremy, "teeth."

"At a high level, it sounds promising," said Josef, "but you've got to get *inside*."

"Yeah," said Jessie.

There was a moment of silence. Josef looked around, then met Liselle's eyes as if to ask, *who the hell are these clowns?* "Okay," he said. "How are you going to get inside?"

"The Universe will provide," said Val. "I hope."

"The Universe?" said Josef.

"Yeah," said Val. "Danny's gone to pick her up from work."

CHAPTER
NINETEEN

Danny (11:03): Sweetie? We have The Emergency we talked about.
    [Message can't be sent]
(11:04): Adalia?
[Message can't be sent]
(11:15): Adalia? Call me when you get this.
[Message can't be sent]

～

Danny (11:16): Melissa, I can't get hold of Adalia.
    [Message can't be sent]
(11:17): She's not answering her phone.
[Message can't be sent]
(11:18): Jesus does anyone have their phone on.
[Message can't be sent]

～

DANNY (11:20): John.
  [Message can't be sent]
  (11:21): FFS.
  [Message can't be sent]

❦

"WHAT DO YOU MEAN," said Danny, "she 'got fired?'" She leaned across the counter, staring hard at the young man standing there.

"I ... What I mean is ... I—"

"She was fired," said a man, thinning hair, *bossman* written all over him. He was standing at a door leading to *the back*, the mythical place of extra stock and secrets retail customers weren't supposed to know about. Even at Starbucks, they had *the back*. "I fired her. I shouldn't even be telling you this, but..." he gestured around at the customers, people with wide eyes, a few panicked expressions. He sighed. "I guess I hoped running a Starbucks would be easier than this." Danny wasn't sure if he was talking to himself or to her.

"You fired her?" Danny blinked. "But she's a good worker." The response was reflexive, a mother's response, pure and simple, and—

She is Pack of our Pack. Blood of our blood.

—the desire to protect was strong. "She ... she says she makes a good latte."

"Possibly the best in this city, or this country," said the man with thinning hair. "But she needs to turn up to work for that skill to be useful to me."

"I don't think you understand," said Danny. "There's a situation—"

"I understand perfectly," said the man. "She's not here."

Danny was over the counter in a single vault, hand tangled in the man's shirt as she lifted him off the ground. She snarled at him, teeth bared. "I was saying," she said, wanting to *bite*, "that she is in danger. *Put that fucking phone down.*" She didn't turn to look at the young

184

man she'd spoken with earlier, but heard the phone he'd been about to dial drop to the ground. "I'm her mother."

The man with thinning hair's eyes were wide with terror. "If I knew where she was..."

We must pick up the trail.

Danny dropped the man like a discarded backpack after a day's long hike, smoothed her jacket, and turned back to the store. Vaulted the counter again, looked around. Smelled the air.

"I..." the young clerk's voice faltered.

Danny looked at the young man. "Yeah?"

"There was this bar. Not that she would, you know, be drinking underage. Not what I mean." He looked, if it was possible, more nervous. "It's an Irish bar."

Danny leaned against the counter. "Which bar?"

∽

Danny (11:30): She's not at work.

Val (11:31): She's at lunch?

Danny (11:31): She got fired.

Val (11:32): !

Danny (11:33): Why didn't she call us?
(11:33): Where has she been?

Val (11:34): Did Starbucks know where she went?

. . .

DANNY (11:34): Tell the rest to turn their phones on.

DANNY (11:35): It's Starbucks not the r u
(11:35): FBI* fucking autocarrot

VAL (11:36): I'm coming to help look.
(11:36): Why didn't you text me first.

DANNY (11:37): They said she was going to a bar.
(11:37): Your phone is never on.

VAL (11:38): The FBI?
(11:38): My phone on now.

DANNY (11:39): Starbucks.

VAL (11:39): John wants to know if it's an Irish bar.

DANNY (11:40): How did he know.

VAL (11:41): It's John.

DANNY (11:42): Yes Irish bar.

. . .

VAL (11:43): [HAS SENT YOU A MAPS LINK]
  (11:43): ily

~

THE IRISH ACCENT WAS FINE, and the ambience was fine, but the attitude wasn't. "What do you mean, you don't remember?" Danny gestured at the nearly empty bar around them. "The whiskey get to your head? Leprechaun come in here and steal your memory?" It was unfair, and she knew it, but *dammit* she was in a hurry.

The man's mouth opened and closed a few times, then he said, "Here now, that's racist, that is."

"Which part?" said Danny. "The part where I accused you of being an alcoholic or the part where I talked about creatures from your home country?"

"Mythical beasties are one thing, but—"

"They're not mythical," said Danny. "I had an Irish friend in college. She said you were all alcoholics."

"You sure she wasn't Australian?" said the man.

"Accent sounds nothing the same," said Danny.

"You Americans don't have the best ear—"

"Where," said Danny, "did she go?" She leaned forward against the bar.

"What I were trying to say, love," said the barman, "is that we've had no single lasses in here. Not a one."

Danny blinked at him. "She was with someone?"

"Were a young lass in here just before. Lad with her too, strong fellow, Russian unless I miss my guess."

"A Russian?" Danny swallowed, closed her hands into fists, opened them again. *Why don't I know who she is with? She's my little girl.* "In an Irish bar?"

"Russians know quality liquor, that's for certain," said the bartender. "Ordered vodka, though, which seemed a crime at the time, but they had some serious talking to do. Left together, not a half hour gone."

Danny closed her eyes, breathed out, opened her eyes again. "That's useful, thank you."

"What's more useful is knowing where they went," said the barman.

"I agree," said Danny, "but I'll take what I can get."

"The young man," said the bartender, "said he had a room at the Renaissance."

Danny tried to process that information. So many things all at once. First, the Renaissance. Where they found Jeremy. Second, that her little Adalia had gone with a strange man to a hotel room.

He is only strange to us. We do not have his scent.

She wished she knew where *mother* ended and *creature of the Night* began.

She is Pack of our Pack. Blood of our blood.

"You're right," said Danny. "It doesn't matter."

"I'm sorry?" said the bartender, but she was already turning to leave.

～

DANNY *(12:10): She's at the Renaissance.*

VAL *(12:11): Autocarrot?*

DANNY *(12:12): No*

VAL *(12:12): !*

. . .

Danny (12:15): In a cab.

Val (12:16): Meet you there.

Danny (12:20): ily2

~

Danny stalked along the corridor of the Renaissance. It hadn't changed in the couple days since she'd last been here. Dark panels. Mood lighting. Closed doors. She wished she had planted a TrackR on Adalia, but Adalia wasn't a child anymore.

But she was fragile. So fragile, and so precious.

She wasn't sure she was on the right floor, or wouldn't have been without her daughter's scent. The air held a faint memory of it, clean and pure. The air told her other things, like there was a smoker somewhere on this floor — in a smoke-free hotel, no less, there'd be an extra charge in that person's future — and, perhaps more importantly, no smell of blood. It would be tricky to strangle — Danny shuddered at the thought — Adalia without her turning the Universe against her attacker. Any other means of killing her would have to be quick, and almost certainly bloody.

We will find her. She will not be dead.

There was another scent in the air, familiar and strange at the same time. Like something she'd forgotten once, a long time ago. A memory on the very edge of memory. Someone she knew? Someone she'd met? She shook her head. *You need to stop stalking people through hotels. It's becoming a habit.* At least this hotel wasn't full of zombies and *vodou* monsters.

Adalia's scent was strongest *here*, outside this door. Danny rested a hand against the door, thought about tearing it open, knocked instead. And waited.

Nothing.

Danny knocked again. She heard Adalia's voice — *alive!* — from inside. "Just a second." There were footsteps, and then the door opened. Her daughter stood there, white hotel robe on, hotel slippers on, green hair tousled. "Mom?"

Danny crushed her in a hug. "I was so worried."

"Mom? What are you ... what are you doing here?"

"There's been a thing. The Emergency. Get your things." Danny frowned. "Why are you in the Renaissance? Never mind. We can talk about that on the way."

The elevator pinged from up the corridor, and Danny saw Val step out. Her face broke into a smile when she saw—

Pack mate.

—him walk towards her. She turned back to Adalia, and felt the smile fall from her face as she saw who was behind her.

No.

That other scent. The one she should have known.

This one is dead.

The one who she'd killed.

NO.

She bared her teeth, pulled Adalia out of the way, into the hall with her, and sank into a crouch. "You're dead."

"*Nyet,*" said the man. "*Pochti ves' put'.* But not all the way."

"Mom?" said Adalia. "What's going on?"

Val was at her shoulder, standing—

Pack of our Pack.

—side by side with her. He looked at who was in the room, stiffened, and then shook his head. "Hello, father."

"*What's going on?!*" wailed Adalia.

This cannot be.

But here he was, the snake in the grass. The great deceiver. The source of all of their pain. This time, Danny would make sure he was dead.

Volk.

CHAPTER
TWENTY

"You know how much I like road trips," said Carlisle from the back seat, "but riding in the kiddie seat is my favorite."

The big Hummer rumbled along. Rex thought it sounded like it was fueled by the spirits of the dead the way it roared when you put your foot down, but Jessie said it was just dead dinosaurs. It was optioned from the shop floor, leather seats, tinted windows, *hardpoints* — whatever those were — and a twelve-speaker sound system. Hell, it even had little TV screens in the back seats. Apparently this wasn't *military issue*, but Jessie still insisted on calling it a *Humvee*. "Well, you keep trying to backseat drive," he said.

"So you put me in the back seat?"

"I called shotgun," said Jessie, in the passenger seat and looking smug behind her aviators, "and you hate driving in Manhattan traffic."

"I hate Manhattan traffic too," said Rex, "but I'm not currently carrying a firearm, so that makes it safer for me to be in charge of the wheel of this thing."

"Chrissakes," said Carlisle, but subsided.

"Does everyone get a gun who wants one?" said Sam, from beside her.

"No," said Carlisle.

"Why?"

"It's against the law," said Carlisle, "but more important than that, I do not want to be shot by some rookie on our own team."

Rex could see Sam's disappointed look in the rear view mirror, but the man took it with good grace. "Well, at least I can get us in."

"We hope," said Jessie. "It's in the plan."

"You're sure he's ... what did Jeremy call it?" said Sam.

"'Vampire High Command,'" said Jessie.

"You sure the kid's not going to be at Vampire High Command?" said Sam. "You know, in the Garden."

"Not the MO," said Carlisle. "It's where they take people to turn them into blood suckers. Charlie's a little young. You don't want the head of Biomne to be a thirteen-year-old kid. Forever."

"So you figure he'll be here. At my apartment."

"Well," said Carlisle, "it's a little unorthodox for a kidnapper to take the kidnapped back to their own home, I'll admit. But if the kid's bait — no offense — then you need a trap. The best trap is your house. But it's a little moot."

"How so?" said Sam.

"Because they said so in the messages on my phone." Rex caught the turn of her head as she looked out the window.

"*What?!*"

"What she's trying to say," said Jessie, "is that they know who we are, and that you're with us. Remember. They just got a bunch of intelligence. They're trying to draw us out any way they can."

"I ... but I—"

"You've had a lot on your mind," said Carlisle, her voice distracted. "Jesus, you've got a nice place." She wasn't wrong, Rex's phone guiding them up alongside a 5th Avenue apartment, a doorman out the front wearing a red jacket and an implacable expression. Next to him was a burly man, jacket bulky enough to be hiding all kinds of mischief, tattoos down one side of his face.

"Hang on," said Sam. "We're going into an actual trap set by actual vampires? And who's that guy out the front?"

"Which guy?" said Carlisle. "The PMC asshole or Pee-Wee Herman?"

"Pee-Wee Herman is Bruce," said Sam. "He's my doorman."

Rex put the brake on and turned to face the back seat. "Son," he said. "Do you want Charlie back or not?"

"More than anything," said Sam. "But—"

"Son," said Rex, "we're going to get your Charlie. We're going into that building, we're going to get your kid, and we're going to bring him to you."

"I see," said Sam.

"It's not entirely selfless," said Jessie. "You're conflicted. You're thinking about whether you can make a deal with them."

"I—"

"Or maybe you're not," she said, "but we're ... we're just going to snip that problem off. Nip it in the bud." She started connecting things to a large rifle — her *Light Fifty*.

"Christ, Pearce," said Carlisle. "These aren't vampires. They're people."

"PMC assholes," said Jessie. "PMC assholes who've taken a kid."

Carlisle thought about that, then nodded. "I get your math. But it's a little loud."

"I know what you're thinking," said Jessie, "but I brought a solution." She pulled out a tube about as long and as thick as Rex's forearm. "Quick detach suppressor. Subsonic ammunition. You'll know about it if you're next to me, but it won't interrupt the Netflix show in the apartment next door."

"My apartment's a whole floor," said Sam.

"Or the Netflix in the apartment above."

"Penthouse," said Sam.

"Or," she said, teeth gritted, "below."

"Okay," said Carlisle. "Let's go. You want the guy next to Bruce?"

"Bruce is Pee-Wee?"

"Correct."

"I'd prefer not to fire this thing outside." She sighed. "It's quiet, but it's almost as long as I am tall. The less time it sees sunlight—"

"Got you," said Carlisle. She pulled out her sidearm, attaching her own silencer. "Everyone seems to think you want to shoot people when you order a silencer," she said. "I get the weirdest looks."

"I know, right?" said Jessie.

Carlisle holstered the gun and then she slipping out the back door, moving fast and smooth towards the door to the apartment. The PMC guy had time to put out a hand, started to say something that was probably *you can't be here* before Carlisle was on him. She grabbed his outstretched arm and twisted her whole body, the man's elbow snapping the wrong way. He was starting to scream as she twisted back the other way, catching him under the jaw with the heel of her palm. He went down like a sack of flour, if sacks of flour came in at 250 pounds, just kind of stretched out on the sidewalk. Carlisle was already talking to Pee-Wee — *Bruce, dammit, they've got me doing it too* — pointing down the street. Bruce took off at a run.

Carlisle slipped inside, Sam's card opening the door with a click, Jessie already out of the passenger seat and moving behind her. The two of them vanished inside.

"Uh," said Sam, "shouldn't we follow them?"

"We are," said Rex. He didn't move. There was a scream from inside, cut short. You know, they were right: you really couldn't hear the guns.

"But we're still out here."

"Son," said Rex. "We've got two people in there with various forms of weapons, mostly high caliber. You and I? We're what you'd call enthusiastic amateurs. They, well, they are the pros. They are going to punch a hole."

"Two people," said Sam. "Against how many?"

"Not sure," said Rex. There was a shower of glass from above them and a man in a full combat vest fell screaming to the sidewalk. He landed hard, then tried to move. The movements were weak, like his brain hadn't got the message from his body that it wasn't okay to stand. "Hang on," said Rex. He got out, walked over to the man. "Hey," said Rex, "what happened?"

"Two women," said the man, eyes not focusing, "they were fast. One of them had a ... I think it was a fifty cal. So I just ran, you know?"

"Okay," said Rex.

"The other one caught me on the way past and then I was falling," said the man.

"Sounds good," said Rex, and hit him hard, in the face. The man slumped back onto the sidewalk. Rex winced, shaking his hand.

There was a crack of masonry and Rex looked up. One of the walls had puckered out, brickwork raining down. A second hole appeared next to it, then a third. Silence. Rex pointed up for Sam's benefit, the man having joined him on the sidewalk. "Jessie doesn't usually miss twice."

"How can you tell it was Jessie?"

"Her gun's more likely to punch through brick and drywall and people all at the same time," he said. "C'mon. Time to head up."

"Uh," said Sam. "Shouldn't we give them more time?"

There was a hard punch of sound, maybe a shotgun. It fired twice more, then silence. "No," said Rex, "I think we're getting towards the likely end of the journey here. We need you up there. For Charlie."

"Right," said Sam. He seemed in shock. "Why?"

"Well," said Rex, "let's say you were a thirteen-year-old kid. Let's say you were in a house with a bunch of soldiers, and your father was missing. And then these two crazy people came in and started shooting everyone."

"Okay," said Sam.

"What I'm saying is, do you have a safe room?" Rex sighed. "I think you have a safe room. Where Charlie probably is, with a couple of holdout soldiers. We need you to get that room open."

"Okay," said Sam. He didn't move.

Rex sighed. His earpiece crackled, then Jessie's voice came over it. "I think we're clear."

"Safe room?" said Rex.

"Yep," she said. "Standard biometric lock with a PIN on this side."

"We're coming up," said Rex.

THEY WALKED through the foyer leading to the elevators. Rex eyed the stairway, a big open-air affair taking up a ridiculous amount of space for a place in Manhattan. The kind of thing Howard Hughes would have put in, and with the age of this place it might just have been he.

Sam was walking towards the elevator. "Are we going up?"

"Yeah," said Rex, "but not that way." He was still staring up at the magnificent stairway.

"The stairs?" said Sam. "I mean—"

"Son," said Rex, "if I was the head asshole of a PMC holding this building I'd have put a bunch of surprises in the elevator. It's what, ten floors up?"

"Fourteen," said Sam, looking uncomfortable.

"Fourteen," said Rex. "Look at it this way. You'll be getting your step count up."

"I don't use a FitBit," said Sam.

"'Course not," said Rex. "Steps still go up."

They started to climb, passing a body on the stairs. Woman, forties, scar on her face, hole punched right through her armor jacket. Rex stepped over her, looked back at Sam, who was pale but not green. *Good.* It'd be bad to have him throwing up by the time they made his kid.

Their first problem came at them with a scream and a knife on the fifth floor. Rex had time to notice *trim beard, nice lines, I have to go to a barber to get that kind of thing going on* before the man was on him. The knife was huge, almost a short sword, but Rex was too damn tired and over these stairs already, and just kind of helped the guy a little by stepping sideways. The man tumbled over the railing, scrabbling at the edge before falling down. Rex looked over, saw the man at the bottom, neck at an unnatural angle, and tapped his earpiece. "You missed one."

"On five?" Carlisle sighed. "He locked himself behind the stairwell door. I figured he was making a run for it."

"Any more?"

"There's one on eight. You want that I come and get you?"

Rex rubbed a hand over his face. "No. Just, I don't know. What do you kids do? Text me or something."

"Right," she said. "Sorry. Like I said—"

"You thought he was making a run for it."

"Right, right."

Sam was watching Rex's half of this conversation. "Trouble?"

"There's another one on eight. Maybe." Rex frowned. "Could be more. I mean, how many people live here?"

"You know," said Sam, ignoring the question, "I'd have expected more. I'd have expected the police to turn up by now, to be honest."

"Pretty sure they own the police," said Rex. "Not in a bought-and-paid for kind of way. In the all-the-guys-in-charge-are-vampires kind of way."

"Figures," said Sam. "Wouldn't they come and try and arrest us then?"

"YouTube," said Rex, looking up at the staircase and then blowing air out. "Son? Let's go. Charlie's waiting."

They passed a barricade on six made of sandbags and boxes and pieces of furniture. It looked like it had been chewed by a large dog, ripped wood and fragments of material scattered among the bodies. *'Light' Fifty my ass*, thought Rex. "We're getting warmer."

Sam was close behind, almost too close. *Nervous. I get it.* "Uh, how come these ... what are they, military?"

"PMC," said Rex, then, "Private Military Company."

"Right, there's a lot of them," said Sam. "And just two of us."

"Four," said Rex, then, "or, uh, three. Son, I don't mean to be unkind, but—"

"No, it's fine," said Sam. "Last time I saw a PMC was when Elsie Morgan was in charge of Biomne. Some real serious dudes."

"Were they," said Rex, "trained by werewolves?"

"Not that I know of," said Sam.

"Only eight floors to go," said Rex, as if that settled everything.

"Son," said Rex, "son, you need to open this door." He released the press-to-talk button on the outside of the panic room. As far as panic rooms went it looked impressive, at least from the outside. Big black door, made of some kind of metal, probably steel or kryptonite or some such thing. Joins so fine you couldn't fit a pin in them. Anti-duress system so it couldn't be opened from the outside if someone had locked themselves inside. All brushed to a polish, blurry reflections of Rex, Sam, Jessie, and Carlisle in the dark metal.

"We've got re-enforcements inbound," said the speaker.

"Son," said Rex, pressing the button, "I don't know if you've been paying attention, so I'm going to break this down for you." He looked over his shoulder; Jessie nodded encouragement. "We don't really care."

"You might not care," said the speaker, "but you ain't coming in. It'll be dark soon, and then you'll care."

"Let's say," said Rex, "that the night holds some special terrors for you."

"We're not talking about special terrors," said the speaker. "We're talking about fucking vampires. I saw what they ... look, you're here, you know."

Rex thought about that, then nodded. "We know."

"So you kind of understand, we can't let you in. Hell, we just need to wait."

"That's one possible option," said Rex. "It probably won't end well for anyone, because we've got werewolves on speed dial, and son, I'm going to be honest but I cannot *believe* that these words are coming out of my mouth, five years ago I'd have slapped my *own self* silly. But son? We've got *werewolves* on speed dial. And let's say your special vampire friends get here, and these wheat threshers we call werewolves get here, and they're all going crazy outside. How long do you suppose this door is going to stay shut for?"

"Long enough?" hazarded the speaker.

"And when it's opened, who do you think's gonna be on the other side?" said Rex.

"Hold on," said the speaker, a different voice this time. "You're saying that we got two choices. One, we open the door now, and you shoot us, or we shoot the kid, or whatever."

"Okay," said Rex, nodding. "I'm listening. Work it through, son."

"Second option is we wait until dark, and then *maybe* the bad guys open the door and kill us all, or we shoot the kid."

"I'm still listening," said Rex. "I mean, we can argue about who the bad guys are, but I'd like to see where you're going with this."

"So the way I'm thinking," said the speaker, "is that we stand a better chance if we wait."

"It's a nice theory," said Rex, "but I think it's predicated on a poor assumption."

"Predicated?" said Carlisle. "Are you going for a high Scrabble score? You should put an X in there or something."

Rex sighed. He pressed the button again. "What I'm saying is that we're the good guys, because we're not stealing children, and the vampires are, by an actual and very real definition, the bad guys because a) they steal children and b) drink the blood of people, turning them into other unholy monsters." He paused, licked his lips. "And, if I was an unholy monster, there would be a time when I'd like to see all witnesses erased."

"One second," said the speaker.

Rex stepped away, rolling his shoulders. He nodded to Jessie, who frowned. "Don't get shot," she said.

"I didn't walk up fourteen flights to get shot," he said. "It hurts the whole intent of my cardio regime." He looked at the huge rifle stock poking out over her shoulder. "So, Jessie. Getting shot, and all. I'm just thinking, and this isn't meant as a criticism or any sort of advice where it might not be needed, but I'm thinking that you're the one with the gun, so perhaps, and again — no criticism — but perhaps you could try really hard not to shoot me in this next bit."

Jessie looked at him, then looked at Carlisle, who shrugged. Jessie turned back to him and said, "We wouldn't be having this conversation if you could hit a target at ten paces."

"Just don't shoot me," said Rex. "This is a bit more serious than a trust fall."

She gave him gun fingers and then jogged away, her Light Fifty tapping her back as she went. Carlisle watched the two of them. "Daughter you never had?" There was something wistful in her voice beside the usual sarcasm.

Before Rex could answer, the speaker broke into life. "Where'd the other one go?"

"Which one?" said Rex.

"The one with the M107," said the speaker.

Rex looked at Carlisle. She shrugged. "It's what her gun's actually called," she said. "It doesn't come in a box with 'Light Fifty, Little Psycho's First Gun,' on the side."

Who knew. "Thought she would make you nervous," said Rex. "Or the gun would. We asked her to back up a little."

"We're coming out," said the speaker.

"Wise choice, son," said Rex, and gestured Sam back, and a little to the side. Wouldn't want the money getting hit along with the talent now. The man seemed entirely too nervous. Jumpy, and jumpy people got shot. Sam gave a tight nod, walking back in the same direction as Jessie, but along the wall.

"But we want you to put your guns down," said the speaker.

Rex just laughed. "Son," he said, "up until now I've been doing you the genuine and honest courtesy of assuming you're not stupid. Do not, and I repeat, do not make me believe that was a serious error."

They waited. After a length of time that felt like twelve minutes but was probably only that many seconds, there was a series of *clunks* and as some hidden mechanism in the door unlocked. There was a hiss, then the door slowly slid sideways. It revealed two soldiers, one with a boy — *Charlie* — held in front of him like a tiny human shield. One of the man's hands was holding Charlie and the other was holding a sidearm at the kid's head. The other man had a rifle pointed at Charlie's head. The one using Charlie as a shield said, "Now, here's what's going to happen."

Carlisle's eyes had turned hard, too hard, and that wouldn't end well, so Rex crouched down so he was at Charlie's height. "Charlie, is it?"

Charlie nodded, sniffing. Red eyes, probably over the tears stage and into full on therapy-for-life stage by now.

Rex tried a smile on. "Son, it's going to be okay. Can you shut your eyes for me?" He looked up at the soldier. "You ever think it's wrong to use a kid as a human shield? I think it's wrong. Do the right thing, and we'll all make it out of here. All of us. But. You need to put the kid down, and you need to do it soon, because what we've got here is a hair-trigger situation. Mistakes can get made. Put the kid down, live. Keep holding the kid, well."

"You're not in charge," the one using Charlie as a human shield said. "I'm in charge. I make the rules. *I'll* tell you what's right. This kid? He's my insurance. Anything happens to me, I'll *end* him. Like I said, here's what's going to happen. Hey. Are you listening to me?"

"It'll be okay," said Rex, looking at Charlie. "You've just got to shut your eyes."

Charlie nodded, then screwed his eyes shut. His lips were moving, like he was whispering to himself.

"I said—" said the man holding Charlie, before his head

exploded into airborne slurry. No more than a quarter second later the man next to him spun around like a top, blood spraying from where his shoulder used to be, arm flopping by a tiny piece of skin, and then a third bullet pierced him dead center, tearing his spine out in tiny, bony fragments. Carlisle was already moving, catching Charlie, holding his face to her so he wouldn't see, wouldn't see anything more, and she said something into the boy's ear. Rex couldn't be sure, but it might have been *got you*.

Sam was there, and he grabbed Charlie from Carlisle, and he was crying, and hugging his kid.

Rex looked at the two of them, at Carlisle's face, now softer, and then back towards where Jessie crouched. Behind a couch, her Light Fifty's barrel smoking. He walked back to her. "Feels good, doesn't it?"

"It's why we do this job," she said. "To save the world."

"Yeah," said Rex. "Because the world's full of families."

She nodded, racking her Light Fifty and slinging it over her shoulder, the suppressor almost touching the ground. "Yeah," she said, with a smile. "Because of that."

TWENTY-ONE

*P*ack.

Val stood next to Danny in the doorway, Adalia a little behind them. Adalia was trembling, Val could sense the tension, the fear and confusion, pouring off her in waves. Danny by contrast was hard, all angry edges and sharp corners, teeth ready to rend, to bite, to end—

The betrayer.

—this thing that stood in front of them. This enemy from before, the one who'd made him. Volk. Truth be told, Val could use a little of that action too. He couldn't remember that night he'd been ... *made*, as if the Night was manufactured in a factory. He'd been drunk, pretty much like always back in those days. Feeling sorry for himself, except he couldn't really remember that either. Just: a bar, too many drinks, and then waking up the next day. Hungover. Everyone else in that bar had died except for him.

You're just lucky. Val reached out a hand and touched Danny's elbow. He leaned close. "Not yet." There might be time to get some answers. They could remember a lot about what had happened to their makers, and their makers before them, and so on. But not everything. Sure, they could get some of their skills — fighting, flying machines, how to act, even be a poet. But the reasons, the feelings behind those lives were lost, leaves in an autumn fall.

The betrayer killed his Pack.

Danny's head turned, quick and angry, to look at Val. Her eyes were so yellow, so bright. When she spoke, it sounded like she was trying to force the words out around the animal trying to escape from within. "He is everything that is wrong with the Night. *You. Know. This.*"

Val's eyes moved towards Adalia, saw the confusion there, the panic of the violence she could see coming. She could see it, almost smell it, but didn't understand it. Violence had been a part of her life for more than ten years, and that was on Volk. On Volk, and—

We protect our Pack.

—on Val, if he had to be honest. Because he could have just loaded everything up into a truck and moved to Alaska with Danny and Carlisle. Followed her there. Made it right, like patching up an old roof that only leaked a little in the rain. Val looked at Adalia again, at that hurt and uncertain guilt in her face. *That's the problem with being the Universe's conduit at the age of twenty.* Or maybe it was just one of those problems with *being* twenty. He almost laughed then. *Damn, but you sound like Rex.* Val turned back to Volk. "You're dead. You're supposed to be dead."

"*Nyet.* Is difficult, no? To kill one of us." The other man shrugged, his bathrobe not quite closing over his muscled frame. He still looked the same as he had last time Val had seen him. Square jaw and two-day stubble. Moved like a dancer. Not a gray hair on his head, still with that youthful twinkle in his eyes as if he was laughing at some joke only he could hear. And maybe he was. Even after thousands of years, he'd draw the eye of any woman in the market. "Is lucky."

"You're lucky? You bet," snarled Danny.

"*Nyet.* Is lucky that Maksimillian Kotlyarov is still alive. For your sakes." Volk shrugged. "You war with the enemy of the Night. Not much Night left. *YA posledniy* ... I was last one. Is difficult, but not impossible. The *vampiry* have killed us before. They have always killed us."

Val narrowed his eyes. Volk ... or Maksimillian? The difference was crucial. What a man called himself. What the world called him. What his enemies knew him as. He looked at Adalia. "Do you know who this is?"

"This is Maks," she said. She looked like she was close to tears. "How ... what—"

"Is familiar face," said Volk, gesturing at himself. "Adalia, she make best coffee in whole city. Maksimillian Kotlyarov needs good coffee, good breakfast." His eyes lingered on Adalia. Val saw emotions bunch and hustle across the man's face shutter-quick. Yearning. Loss. Envy. Possession. Something else Val couldn't put his finger on. "Life too short for bad coffee, *da*?"

The deceiver knows nothing of love. It was lost to him long ago.

Danny rounded on Adalia. "How could you not *see*? How could you not *know*?" She flung an arm towards Volk. "This isn't Maksimillian or Maks or whatever you think he is. *Why weren't you looking?*"

Adalia took a step back from Danny's anger. *Universe's chosen she may be, but she's still her mother's daughter.* "I ... I don't want to look," she said, her voice small. "Someone always dies."

"Well, congratulations. Someone's definitely going to die now." Danny turned towards Volk, took a step.

Val touched her elbow again. "Not *yet*." He looked at Adalia, saw her stunned face. "Adalia, this guy? He's not who you think he is." Val knew he needed to choose his words with care. "It's a little more complicated than that."

"Who is he?"

"I am, how do you say," said Volk. "I am man who made you. I gave you wondrous gift."

"You gave us," said Val, "a curse."

The Night is the Night.

"You look good, for man with curse," said Volk. "I remember you. I remember fat man, tired man. Old, before your time. Carrying something with you. Is first man I saw after crash. After van." He paused for a moment. "Is good question, *da*? Would you take curse and save world? Or would you leave gift, how do you *Amerikantsy* say it, on table? And table, along with world, die. All gone."

"Don't," said Danny, "make this something fucking *noble*. You ... came for my *daughter*?!"

"*Nyet*," said Volk.

"Then why is she here?" Danny's hands were bunched into fists.

"Is long story," said Volk.

"Sum it the fuck up," said Val. "Small words. Short sentences."

"Power calls to power," said Volk. "*Ona derzhit mir v svoyom serdtse*. The Universe, *da*? Great wrong must be put right."

"You mean the vampires," said Val.

"*Nyet*," said Volk. "I mean me."

THE HOTEL ROOM felt small with three werewolves and the power of the Universe in it, but it was better than arguing in the hall. Val knew they weren't going to kill Volk, not then, not right away. Danny seemed to know it too, although she paced like a caged beast, back and forth, back and forth, by the door. Guarding.

Still. The power of the Universe sat by herself, arms hugged to her sides, head down, not looking at any of them, but especially not looking at Volk. Val's eyes strayed to the bed, sheets in disarray. The clothes scattered in a loose trail from the door to the bed. He looked at Volk, then at Adalia.

Then at Danny. *Ah, fuck.* "You're good at stories," said Val. "Why don't you tell one."

"*Da*," said Volk. "Is long ago. You remember."

"Pieces," said Val. "Tiny bits. I remember ... killing. Always killing."

"Just so," said Volk. "Do you remember my family?"

"You have no Pack," said Danny.

"Not just Pack," said Volk. "*Semeynyy*. My birth family. The village where I was born. Do you remember the face of my mother? Is hard, after all this time." He shrugged. "I had to kill her first."

Adalia's head jerked up. "You ... your *family*?"

"*Da*." Volk looked at each of them in turn. "Imagine a time when there were no *vampiry*. Just you, and the Hunt. You have been on this world a little while, seen a few things, but have not become great in purpose or deed yet. You hear a story about a man who can turn water to wine. You love stories, but this one is different. *Osobennyy, da?* So you travel to meet this man. You never meet him, but you see him. See him killed. See the Four, turn against each other. See two of them, turn against us all."

"The Four?" said Danny. "Who the fu—"

"*Vsadniki apokalipsisa*," said Volk. "You would call them Pestilence, War, Famine. And Death."

"You're saying," said Val, "that the Four Horsemen of the Apocalypse—"

"Horse*persons*," said Danny.

"—*Riders* of the Apocalypse, you're saying you met them." Val blinked. "The harbingers of doom. The ones who will end the world."

"*Da*," said Volk. "Is not best part of story." He shrugged. "You remember this."

"No," said Val. "Only pieces. Tiny bits. I remember ... I can fly a helicopter, but I didn't remember your name."

Volk shrugged. "Is always so. The Night? Is fickle. Is chance." Volk looked out the window, a floor-to-ceiling pane of tinted glass. Manhattan stretched out below them. "The ones who thought to fight the *vampiry*, they taught me to fly. Gifts, in their own way."

We give favor to our chosen. This one is no longer our chosen.

"Wait," said Val. "Someone else is fighting the vampires?"

"*Nyet*," said Volk. "Not anymore. All gone. All gone, except for one final gift. Is present, for the head of all *vampiry*."

"And what is that gift?" said Danny. "More fucking curses?"

"If only so easy!" Volk grinned at her, his eyes twinkling a little. After a moment, he grew thoughtful. "We share memories. I have long time to think. To remember, *da*? Always thinking. The Night, it chooses who it wants. The *vampiry*, they kill the Night. So I, Maksimillian Kotlyarov, have spent my life killing any who would change. To be like us. To be hunted. To become the Night."

"Those you've bitten," said Danny.

"*Da*," said Volk. "Also, I kill *vampiry*. Is not choosy. But those like us? I save them from horrible death. I give them quicker death. Easier death, before dying becomes hard."

"That's messed up," said Val. "With an army—"

"You did not see how they killed my friends, my family," said Volk, the twinkle gone from his eyes over a grin that had become fixed. "The *vampiry* came to my village and tried to turn my Pack. Turn them against me. They had to ... I had to..." He paused. "Is over now. All down to us."

"There's no 'us,'" said Danny. "You're fucking hamburger."

"Is over two hundred *vampiry* in this city," said Volk. "I lose count, *da*? So many. But if you take the head of snake," and here, he made a scissors motion with his fingers, *snip snip*, "then the rest will die."

"Who's the head? These two ... Riders?" said Val.

"*Nyet*," said Volk. "Is not easy to kill Riders. They live in shells, fall for a time. Get back up again. *Nyet*. We kill the first of their children." He looked at Danny, then at Val. "Three of us is not enough. But we will do it."

"Four," said Adalia, her voice a croak.

"Won't they just make more?" said Danny.

"Depends on what Universe say," said Volk. He looked at Adalia, like a cat that got the cream. "Is good, *da*?"

"The Universe," said Adalia, her voice getting stronger, full of spite, "does not want to look." She looked at Danny, eyes hard. "But apparently even the Universe doesn't get a choice."

"It's just that—" said Danny.

"*Nyet*," said Volk, either to Danny or Adalia, Val wasn't sure. "The Universe gets no choice. The Universe *is*."

"Then let me look at you," said Adalia, standing.

Volk's eyes turned fearful for a second. "*Nyet—*"

"*I see you, Maksimillian Kotlyarov*," said Adalia. Val's blood ran cold as her voice took on that sound of raw power, of infinite purpose. He found himself taking a step back, swallowed, and stood his ground. If she was using her gift—

We will guard our Pack.

—after all this time, the least he could do was stand at her side. Adalia was still speaking. "*I see your life, stretching back before time. I see your fights and your hates and your petty fears. I see your need to end yourself.*" Her lip curled. "*I see your many lies, the trail of the dead, and I know that you speak of fixing the world with a liar's tongue.*" She staggered, then held herself upright. "*I see you, Maksimillian Kotlyarov. There is something hidden ... there. Something you would hide from me. There is no hiding. Not anymore.*" Adalia strode towards Volk, put her hand on the side of his face, soft enough to be a lover's touch. Volk screamed, but couldn't move. "*There. There it is. I see...*" she stumbled back, her hand over her mouth.

Danny was there, catching Adalia. Val looked between them, not sure what to do. Comfort Adalia? Help Danny? Hit Volk?

He really wanted to hit Volk, so that was probably the wrong call.

Not all wrong things are wrong.

Maybe not. He cleared his throat. "I feel kind of like a fifth wheel," he said, "so I'm just going to ask the dumb question. What's he hiding? Is it going to kill us all?"

"No," said Adalia, her voice a whisper.

"Great," said Val. "What is it then?"

"This is why I don't want to see," said Adalia. "You ... you don't understand. It's never something good, what I see. It's never good. It's always bad."

Danny was holding her, whispering to Adalia, and to Val it was like years were flushed away, Adalia just a little girl wanting her mother. He looked at Volk. "I tell you what." Volk was pale, but looked at Val. "Why don't you tell me, or I throw you out the window?"

"Were it so easy," said Volk.

"I think it'll be easy," said Val. He gritted his teeth, the anger—

He has hurt our cub.

—just barely in check. "I think it'll be really easy."

"Is last secret," said Volk, with a faint smile. "Is how you can be stronger than *vampiry*. When the Night is angry, is no limit to strength. Remember how they killed our Pack."

"Don't," said Val, his teeth wanting to tear flesh, "change the subject."

"Please," said Adalia. "Please don't kill him."

Val turned to her. He wanted to say *why not* or *he's caused so much pain* or even *he deserves it like no other, if only you knew what he'd done* but of course she knew what he'd done. She'd seen it. He felt his anger ebb, felt his fingers uncurl. "Why not?"

"Love," she said.

THE GLADE WAS much as Val remembered it, soft light dappling through the trees, a cool breeze touching his skin to dampen the heat of the day. Except last time he'd come here, he'd had to kill himself to get in. The glade still looked the same, but it felt different. It felt more like home now, like he was welcome. Like he hadn't forced his way in.

The creature paced under the trees, restless. Massive, clawed, fangs. Yellow eyes blinked from the shade. Val's body back in the cab, winding its way through Manhattan to the Bronx, while his — *spirit? soul?* — stood here. Danny and Adalia were in the cab with his body, Volk — or *Maks*, as Adalia called him — still at the Renaissance. Still alive.

You are learning much. You needed death to enter here before.

"I'm a quick study," said Val. "Look, shit's got complicated. I wanted to ... talk."

He is the betrayer. He has always been the betrayer.

"I get that," said Val, "but ... well, I figure that having an emotional bond with Adalia might help with that."

The creature looked out at him, lambent eyes staring. It said nothing.

"You don't think so?"

He is the betrayer. He has always been the betrayer.

"Well, shit," said Val. "You're stuck on repeat."

We must always protect Pack. What hurts our heart doesn't always kill us.

"Feels like it sometimes," said Val.

Feels like it sometimes.

Val started to pace, leaves crunching underfoot. "When we made our deal," said Val, "we thought—"

Our deal has no value.

"You what now?"

Our deal is a thing of fancy. We do what is right. It paused. *What is right has changed.*

"Sure," said Val. "So what do you think we're doing?"

Our deal was to make the whole world our Pack, as if that would solve all problems. What is right is to save the world.

"Before our deal?" said Val.

What was right was to save our Pack.

"You're very confusing," said Val. "But I like to think I helped change your mind."

We are the Night.

"Also very repetitive," said Val. "Now we know that saving the world is the right thing to do, how do we save our family?" He frowned. "How do we save Adalia from the hurts of the body and the mind?"

It looked out at him, saying nothing again.

"Throw me a bone here," said Val.

You ask me questions as if I'm not a part of you. You ask me questions as if you don't know the answers.

"I ask you questions," said Val, "because, after all of this, I trust you."

You trust the Night.

It was Val's turn to say nothing, just staring at the creature.

Little human, it said after a moment, but there was a hint of fondness there. It turned back and forth. *We must keep the betrayer close. He has killed his own Pack before.*

"So we work with him." Val shrugged. "Then what?"

The Night is the Night.

CHAPTER

TWENTY-TWO

"When you said, 'We've got bombs,' I was wondering where you were going with that," said Rex. "Because I was sure we didn't have any stashed away."

Jessie shrugged, face impassive below her aviators. Her hands were relaxed on the wheel, which was something when you were driving a Hummer. It was even more of a thing when you'd just been in a firefight. Rex was shaking like a leaf and he hadn't fired a shot. Jessie spared him a glance. "We do have bombs. We just don't have them at our operations facility."

"The warehouse."

"The operations facility, right," she said. "Ginger's got them."

"Is Ginger a cat or a dog?" said Rex. "It's hard to tell, the name could go either way. I used to have a neighbor, she had a cat named Ginger. It really confused me because the cat was black."

Jessie cast a glance his way. "Ginger is a six-foot-four Colombian."

Rex thought about that for a bit. "Colombian."

"Yes."

"Like the black cat?"

"Ginger dyes his hair," said Jessie. "It's not the worst nickname I've ever heard of."

"What is pretty bad," said Carlisle, "is how I'm in the back seat again. I thought we took turns at this shit."

"I'm in the back seat too," said Charlie, from the middle seat beside her. Sam tousled his hair. Rex turned to look at the kid. Yep, ordinary kid. Hadn't exploded into flames when they'd walked outside, so the bloodsuckers hadn't turned him into a vampire or whatever else they could do. *Locusts.* Jeremy had said they could turn into locusts, like that would be a thing you'd ever want to do. Mind you, sucking the blood from people to leave them to wander the earth as one of the eternal damned was probably a thing Rex wouldn't want either.

"I'm curious," said Rex. "What kind of Colombian arms merchant has a warehouse in Brooklyn?"

"A successful one," said Jessie. "He can pay more for rent than we can."

"Killing people pays well?" said Sam.

"It's more that selling weapons pays well," said Carlisle. She looked down at Charlie, as if choosing her next words with care. "Killing people doesn't have a supply-demand problem. It's a commodity business." Rex approved — corporate robospeak was more likely to be meaningless to the kid.

"Whereas," said Jessie, "getting access to military-grade equipment is difficult. Especially if you're Colombian. Although Ginger is a US Citizen."

"Is that why he dyed his hair?" said Rex. "To fit in?"

"Six-foot-four doesn't fit in anywhere," said Carlisle. "I can't see the red hair helping."

The Hummer rumbled along while they sat in companionable silence, before Charlie said, "Do these TVs work?"

"No," said Carlisle.

"Sure they do," said Rex, giving her a hard stare. "And Melissa—"

"You introduce me as Melissa to one more person," said Carlisle,

"I'll..." she looked down at Charlie. "I'll have a further series of conversations with you."

"Is your name Melissa?" said Charlie.

"It was, once." Carlisle looked out the window.

"And it still is," said Rex. "You can call her what you like. And to show there's no hard feelings, Melissa—"

"God dammit—"

"—will show you how to use the TVs. Won't you, Melissa?"

Carlisle gave him a murderous look. "Sure." She gritted her teeth. "Love to."

Rex turned back front, smiling. He closed his eyes. "Let me know when we get there."

GINGER'S WAREHOUSE wasn't too much different from theirs. Sure, the outside was a junkyard, piled with old car carcasses, huge bins full of wire or other components, and over there a line of rusting whiteware (brownware?) stretching off into the distance. But Rex could tell that was just window-dressing for the main event. The warehouse itself was a big-framed structure at the back, huge doors closed against the overcurious eye that might have made it far back enough to get a look inside. Inside it was just like theirs: big spaces, couches and chairs mixing with each other, a few televisions, a small kitchen area.

The kitchen area was a little less refined than home.

Home. Is that really what their place was? From where they planned to take back the world?

Felt like it. *Home.*

This place was Ginger's *home* — you could tell. A half dozen fit-looking people — four men, two women — sat around a table, cards in front of them. They'd been laughing when Jessie had led the way inside. Jessie's smile widened under her aviators, and then one of the men — a huge, olive-skinned man with bright red hair — stood up, ambled over, and scooped her up in a bear hug. Rex winced at that, but Jessie just laughed, and said, "Put me down. Seriously."

"Major," he said.

"Not anymore," she said.

Ginger — it couldn't be anyone else — nodded. "Rumor's true, then?"

"Not a rumor if you've got paperwork behind it," she said. "Discharged."

"Still a Major," said Ginger. "Still got a team." He nodded at them, then his eyes widened as Sam entered with Charlie. He cast Jessie a look. "You trying to recruit them young?"

"Not in charge of this lot," said Jessie. "Just following orders."

"Doesn't matter if you're in charge," said Ginger, ambling towards the kitchen area. "You're always following some asshole's orders. Beer?"

"Could use one," agreed Jessie. She looked at the other five seated around the table. "Diego. Vincent. Mallory. Nice to see you. Who are your friends?"

"They're not friends," said one of the men. "Friends don't cheat at cards."

"Mallory, you're just sore because you haven't won a game in three weeks," said one of the women. She crossed to Jessie, shook hands. "Emily Lindle."

"Jessica Pearce," said Jessie. She worked through the introductions — by the end of it Rex wasn't sure what his own name was, but he'd picked up that Ginger's troop were all ex-military. No ranks were exchanged, probably didn't need to if you knew the steps to the dance. Emily Lindle. Thomas Mallory. Bryn "call me Brindle" Vincent. Abigail Finch. Sawyer Diego, a hell of a name if anyone had asked Rex, but no one had, so he kept that one to himself.

"Major," said Ginger, "I got your note. What you want doesn't really make a lot of sense."

"In what way?" said Jessie.

"It's a lot of explosive," he said. "A lot."

"Is there trouble sourcing the material?" she said.

"No," said Ginger. "Got you covered there. Shipping it's another thing, but we can work through that. It's just ... I wanted to make sure there wasn't a rounding error. Decimal point in the wrong place, that kind of thing." He shrugged. "It's like you want to blow up Manhattan."

"Naw," she said. "Just a piece of it." She saw his look. "It won't come back on you."

"Are you ... are you seriously planning an operation *in the city?*" Ginger blinked. "Seems a little bold, if you don't mind me saying."

"Better if you know less," said Jessie, "if you don't mind me saying."

"I don't," said Ginger. "Probably can't extend you credit on this one though."

"Wouldn't even dream of asking," said Jessie. She jerked a thumb over at Sam. "He's paying."

Ginger made a big show of looking him up and down. "He doesn't look like he's carrying a briefcase of hundred dollar bills."

"In the truck," said Jessie.

"It's more than a briefcase," said Sam. "Say, Ginger."

"Yo."

"Can you sell me something else?" Sam shrugged. "Everyone seems to have a gun, and where we're going, I figure I need one."

"Tell you what," said Ginger. "For the amount you're paying, I will put in a gun — with enough bullets to keep you happy for an entire weekend — in for *free.*" He said this like it was a big deal. Probably was, for an arms dealer.

"What kind of gun?" said Sam.

"The kind you're likely to enjoy." Ginger squinted at Sam. "You got one you prefer?"

"I don't know anything about guns," said Sam.

"AR-15," said Lindle. At least, Rex hoped it was Lindle, otherwise he'd gotten very confused. "Semi-auto, good at a distance, solves many problems."

"No, no, no," said Brindle. "Semi-auto, that's good for a pro, but I figure a new guy wants to put more bullets into the air, better chance of solving a single problem. Or multiple."

"I agree," said Finch. "Looks like you need an M4. Same basic gun as the AR-15. Shorter. Pull the trigger until you want the bullets to stop, at which point you release the trigger."

"Hey," said Rex, speaking for what felt like the first time in an hour, "and I don't mean to be rude here, but, uh, you need to use words. No one understands what you just said."

"I understand," said Carlisle.

"Me too," said Jessie.

"What I mean," said Rex, "is that unless you are in the trade, that's just alphabet soup."

Ginger laughed. "He has a point." He nodded at Sam. "Here's the deal. One of those guns fires once for each pull of the trigger. Other one keeps firing for as long as you hold the trigger."

"That's the difference?" said Sam.

"Well—" started Lindle.

"That's the difference," said Ginger, glaring at her.

"I'll take the one that keeps firing," said Sam.

"Great," said Ginger. "What are you hunting, anyway?"

"Big game," said Jessie. "About that."

Ginger raised an eyebrow. "Don't be asking for a discount. We're friends. We ain't that kind of friends."

"More of a bonus potential," said Jessie.

"I'm listening," said Ginger.

"We could use more help," said Jessie.

"She means," said Carlisle, "that we need more people to help us blow something up. And while we're doing that, we're expecting a bunch of other people to try and kill us all in a miserable hail of gunfire. We'd like to not die, and so, by hiring some extra help, we're hoping to alter the statistical chances more in our favor."

"You're not really selling it," said Lindle.

Mallory stretched. "Usual rates?"

"Usual rates," agreed Jessie.

"What's the target?" said Brindle.

"Got to know if you're in or out," said Jessie. "You understand."

"I understand," said Ginger. "Anyone want to make a little cash, stick around. Everyone else, take a walk for a half hour." No one moved. Ginger made a *go ahead* motion with his hands. "The floor is yours."

Jessie crossed her arms. "It's tricky to explain," she said.

Rex cleared his throat. "Here's the thing," he said. "What we've got is a bunch of vampires living under Madison Square Garden. They all want to end the world. Earlier today we rescued that kid—" and here, he jabbed a finger in Charlie's direction "—from them, because that guy—" and he jabbed a finger at Sam "—is his father and owns the world's largest drug company. They wanted to make the kid a vampire and put him in charge in a couple years. They own everything, control everything. They've been hunting our friends for years, and their families before that, because our friends are werewolves, and werewolves are about all that's kept the world together. We're going down under The Garden, pack it with explosives, and blow them all into orbit."

Everyone was staring at him. He shrugged. "They'd have to find out sooner or later."

"Vampires," said Ginger. "Werewolves."

Diego spoke for the first time. "Fucking awesome," he said. "When do we start?"

CHAPTER
TWENTY-THREE

When John Miles was a child, he'd thought the world was pretty cool and nothing so far had done much to change his view. He sat in the back of Sam Barnes' limousine, drinking Scotch out of a crystal tumbler, looking at the back head of a vampire — who was driving — and sitting across from War, one of the Riders of the Apocalypse. He was next to a beautiful woman he'd met at a bar who turned out to be War's sister, which was crazy, right, and she was Famine. Except she'd stopped starving people to death a couple thousand years ago after she met Jesus Christ, who sounded like an okay guy as well, except most of the stories about him were wrong. Apart from the one about being a carpenter.

Yeah. The world was pretty cool. It might have been something to do with the benzos, but the Scotch had a soft, comfortable flavor in his mouth, like a Twinkie. He didn't eat Twinkies, not since he was about four, but maybe now was a good time to rekindle that passion.

"I'd have to say," he said, "that Sam has a good quality Scotch here. Fragrant rose wood. Lavender. Hint of ... I'm going with caramel."

"Sounds like a shampoo," said Jeremy.

"Tastes better," said John. "I mean, I don't drink a whole lot of shampoo."

"Not a lot?" said Jeremy. "Which is the best brand?"

"I don't like where this conversation is going," said John. "I'm a little under-prepared."

"You're drugged out of your mind," said Jeremy. "Here's the thing. Night's falling, so I can be out here with you. Hit the town, paint it *red*, if you know what I'm saying. But the thing is, the rest of my less morally inclined brothers and sisters will also be out. I'm just letting you know so you can make the call on whether you want to do this thing sober."

"Seems more fun my way," said John. "Man, the world is a pretty cool place."

THE PLAN WAS to pick up some of their own intelligence. The A-team was out getting Adalia from work, which was taking a whole lot longer than a trip to Starbucks usually took John, and the other A-team was out buying munitions or bombs or explosives or whatever the flavor term of the moment was. So here he was, with the vampire and half of the Horsepersons. Still, any team with John Fucking Miles on it was definitely A-grade, top-shelf, like the Scotch.

The problem with the Garden was that there was about a hundred entrances to it. The trick was going to be working out which one to go in, get down, lay the bombs, and get out. Jessie had handed him a camera, an expensive one by the looks, a lens stuck on the front of it big enough to get action shots of Mars with. He was supposed to pull up outside The Garden, take some photos, and head on back to their lair — *God damn but we have a real lair this time, it's got a garage and a weights room and everything* — and talk it over. That sounded more fun when there was a better ratio of benzos to blood in his system, so when Jeremy pulled the stretch up on 8th John gave

Liselle a kiss and then just kind of stepped out, camera in hand. There was the scream of a horn as a yellow cab went by a little too close, and from John's frame of reference, a little too fast. John took a breath, realized he wasn't holding the camera anymore, and looked down at the pieces of it broken on the road.

Here's to hoping it wasn't that expensive.

Jeremy was at his elbow. "You cool?"

"I'm cool," said John. Holy shit, but they moved fast. How'd he even get out here? He was *driving* two seconds ago. "Who's driving the stretch?"

"Details," said Jeremy. "What are you thinking?" He was pointing at the Garden. "It's an icon, right?"

"I'm thinking," said John, "that someone with a very small penis designed how it looks from the outside. Let's go." He swayed a bit, pulled out his phone, ignored the notifications about a hundred messages no one had time to read, and took a photo. "I'm figuring we should probably take the train when we come back."

"To Penn?"

"Yeah," said John.

"With a hundred boxes of explosives, assorted assault rifles, and a couple werewolves?" said Jeremy.

"Makes it sound a little more tricky when you say it like that," said John. He pushed through the crowds, got through the doors, and started taking photos with his phone as he walked around. He looked at Jeremy. "I don't suppose you've got a couple pointers on how to identify a vampire from a distance?"

"Aside from the PlayStation tan?" said the vampire.

"Lots of pale assholes spend too much time in front of their televisions," said John.

"Okay," said Jeremy. "Quick check on vampires. They're usually the ones who will run towards you screaming for your blood."

"Usually?"

"Sometimes they just walk over," said Jeremy, "like those two there." He pointed at two pale figures walking towards them, bright lighting doing nothing to flatter their pallor. The male had some kind of tattooed tear on its face, full Goth black lipstick, and a leather jacket covered in metal studs. The female was dressed in pink — pink leather jacket, pink hair in pigtails, pink hot pants, and a pink belt. No studs, just pink.

"Uh," said John, and took another photo with his phone.

"Really?" said Jeremy. "A photo? Shouldn't you be running and screaming?"

"I thought they did the running and screaming," said John. "Besides, you're here."

"Did you not get the part where I'm not a real vampire yet?" said Jeremy. "Did you not see two of them?"

"There's two of us," said John. "You, with the vampire stuff, and me, John Fucking Miles."

"We're going to die," said Jeremy, just before the vampires made it to them. The male stepped close to John, while the female stepped close to Jeremy.

The male leaned in close, sniffing. Taking in John's scent. The studs on its jacket twinkled in the light. It said, "You are so far from home." Its breath reeked.

The female grinned, teeth all sharp points. "We can make them a new home. Here." Her pigtails bounced.

"Hey," said Jeremy. "About that."

"Worm," said the female. "Be still."

"Cool," said Jeremy.

"Being still is being silent," she said. She ran her tongue over her pointed teeth. "Being silent is better than being dead."

"It's just—"

"Silent," she said again.

"I'm already on the team," said Jeremy. He pointed at himself. "No beating heart. Hate sunlight. You know how it is."

The male grinned, giggled, then coughed. "And you have brought us a gift. We'll be sure to let Anatolie know who brought him a new recruit." He grabbed John by the arm. *Fuck me*, thought John, *this guy's been using Fat Gripz or some shit, because that is some serious grip strength. Serious.*

"Say," said John. "I don't suppose we could talk about this?"

"There's nothing to talk about," said the male. "There is just an end that lasts for eternity."

"That's not super appealing," said John. "Look, can I phone a friend here?"

The male started walking, and John had to follow. It was like being towed by an uncaring tractor, one that held your arm so tight that the bones rubbed together. They were getting further away from the entrance; John was being pulled towards a dark doorway, one that no doubt went into a hole of concrete and stone and brick that made up the underbelly of the Garden. Which would, no doubt, be away from the sun. John wasn't sure — he didn't have the list — but he was positive this wasn't part of The Plan™. The Plan™, the one that that Val had somewhere in his head, and that Jessie drew all over with a Sharpie. The Plan™ seemed to have survival of the team as a primary outcome.

"Look," said Jeremy. He was craning his head around the female, who wasn't letting him follow. "I'll call you. After. Okay?"

"After?" said John. "What the fuck?"

"It'll be cool," said Jeremy. "Don't eat the yellow M&Ms."

John looked at the male holding him. "Yellow M&Ms?"

"They're Anatolie's," said the male.

"Anatolie's a vampire?"

"*The* vampire," it said. It looked back at him, eyes glinting like mirrors.

"Look, hold up," said John.

The vampire paused. "You are taking this very well for a man who's about to die," it said.

"This is not the worst situation I've ever been in," said John. "Before I get out of it, can I ask a question?"

"Get out of it?" The thing laughed, lids closing over those mirrored eyes for a moment. "We have all the time in the world. Ask."

"If Anatolie — whatever, nice guy I'm sure — is a vampire, what does he do with yellow M&Ms?" John smiled. "You know. Because of all the blood. And eating ... is it drinking or eating?"

"Drinking," it said, smile gone.

"Drinking all that blood, right, and the M&Ms, well, they just seem out of place."

"Everyone needs a hobby," it said. It giggled again, more forced this time.

John looked back at where Jeremy stood with the female vampire. They were talking about something, the female shaking its head.

"Look," said John. "You seem like a nice, uh, guy. Just following orders. I'm going to break it down for you. In about ten seconds everyone who's a vampire in this general vicinity will be dead—" and here, he held up a hand to stall any interruptions "—and I'll be running away through a crowd of screaming people. So you've got ten seconds to let me go, get clear, and enjoy a few more days."

The male sniffed at him again. "Are you ... are you *high*?"

"A little," John admitted.

"I remember those days," it said, then made a sound like *uurrrk*. It opened its mouth, and blood came out, black as night. It started to paw at its chest, and then it's ribcage exploded in a shower of gore. The spray hit John in the face, but he'd already closed his eyes and — very important, not often said — his mouth. He wiped his eyes clear in time to see Liselle's hand coming through the vampire's chest. The male looked down at the hand, then up at John, surprise on its face a moment before its torso and legs were torn away from each other. Blood rained on the ground, larger bits of meat falling with chunky *plop* noises.

Liselle looked at him. "John Miles, you should run." She frowned. "But first..." She stepped in and kissed him, hard.

"What was that for?" he said.

"The kiss in the car was insufficient," she said.

"Cool," he said, then, "there's more." He nodded over her shoulder.

More was a little vague, even for him, but it did the job. Liselle turned, took in the vampires boiling towards them. She dropped into a crouch. *No sword*, thought John. *Still, doesn't seem like she needs it.* He watched her meet the wave of vampires as they broke against her — the first to hit her leaping through the air, hands hooked into claws, teeth bared. She met the leap with what looked to John like a karate chop, except that it crushed the thing's skull, sheared through half its rib cage, and pulled clean out the other side. The one next to her saw what had happened to the first, and exploded into—

Well, shit. An actual cloud of insects. Probably locusts, like it said on the side of the box. They swarmed past Liselle, reforming behind her into the vampire, but she was already turning, her hand out, and it reformed around her fist. She pulled it back, tearing the thing's heart out of its reformed chest, turning away as the body staggered behind her.

Problem was, they weren't *dying*. Sure, they looked all fucked up with nowhere to go, but even that first asshole she'd torn in half was struggling along the ground, leaving a red-to-black smear behind him. John looked around, and there — glimpsed between the screaming people running around and getting underfoot — was a souvenir place. John sprinted to it, or started to before the hole in his torso gave a sharp stabbing pain, even through the benzos, so he slowed to a jog. No one was minding the register at the souvenir place anymore; presumably they'd run off to get underfoot with the rest of the people screaming and trying for a way out. John looked around, checking the racks and shelves. About a thousand different types of baseball cap. There, a huge selection of key rings. A tower of stacked coffee cups, which he knocked over on principle, before he found what he was after. Right next to the embossed paper and postcards was a stack of pencils. He grabbed a fist full then jogged back out.

Found the male he'd been grabbed by — easy enough to track with the huge trail of red-to-black blood across the ground, deeper into the Garden. John leaned down with the pencil, stabbing it into the thing, right into its heart.

At least, that's what he tried to do. The pencil broke. *Cheap shitty fucking souvenir pencils—*

"Seriously," said Jeremy, at his side. "You ever tried to stab someone with a pencil? Never going to work." He slammed his hand into the other vampire's back, tearing out the heart, and holding it up. "Here."

John pulled out another pencil, skewering the heart with it. The vampire on the ground tried to scream — back arched in silent agony — before it died. They smelled worse after they died, if that was possible.

"There's a thing," said John, after a moment.

"Your girl," said Jeremy, watching Liselle building a pile of vampire pieces. "Where'd you meet?"

"Bar," said John.

"I like her work," said Jeremy. "Let's go stab some more hearts."

"You could do the whole thing," said John. "Just take the pencils."

"Couple of things," said Jeremy. He counted them off on his fingers, one of his hands bloody to the middle of his arm from where he'd punched through the other vampire's back. "First, on general principle I feel uncomfortable around the only real thing that can kill me."

"Pencils?"

"Wooden stakes," said Jeremy. "Size really doesn't matter."

"Second thing?"

"I want you to feel included," said the vampire, eyes reflecting the room around them.

Josef — *motherfucking* War, thought John — entered. He was still dressed in his singlet and jeans, but he held a blazing sword, red as the new dawn. He didn't seem to move with any particular hurry, but he was at Liselle's side in a moment. They stood back to back as vampires circled them.

"We should probably go," said Jeremy.

"Do you know where we're parked?" said John.

"I mean, outside," said Jeremy. "Away from so many things that want to kill you."

"Us, you mean," said John.

"No, pretty sure they don't really want to kill me," said Jeremy.

"You make a good case," said John. The main entrance they'd come in through was a mass of panicked people, and mixed in with the mass were a whole heap of vampires tearing them apart as food. John pointed to their left. "There. Fire exit."

"It'll set off alarms," said Jeremy.

"I don't think that'll make a huge difference," said John. He set off towards the doorway, then cast a glance back. Josef was swinging his sword — blade as long as the man was tall — through vampires. As the blade touched the vampires, they were consumed by flame, faces an anguish of pain as the sword cut them down. John slowed, then stopped. "What the *fuck* is that sword?"

"It's a holy weapon," said Jeremy. "Didn't you go to Sunday school?"

"Not a huge participant of any kind of school," said John.

The vampire's eyes reflected the fight, the red of the sword a tiny mote of ember in them. "It's called Fury," he said after a moment. "It is one of the four blades that will end this world. You've seen one other. Scourge. You ... you should hope you never see all four."

John looked back at War, wielding Fury against the horde of vampires. "Man, those guys are *so* fucked." He glanced at Jeremy. "Present company excluded, I mean."

Jeremy looked at him, then back at War fighting back to back with Famine, who was tearing the eternal damned apart with her bare hands. John saw something in the vampire's face, something almost wistful, and said, "No, it's okay. Present company included. Eventually. But we should be going."

John slammed a hand against the emergency door's bar and it opened into the cool night air. An alarm went off immediately, red flashing lights bathing the interior of The Garden's entranceway. A vampire looked over at them, its face desperate, and burst into a cloud of locusts. They swarmed towards John and Jeremy.

This could be bad. John watched the swarm of locusts get closer, saw Liselle's face turn fearful as she saw the vampire's locust cloud getting close to John.

John wasn't too concerned. He'd seen the vampire's face. That was fear right there, fear and a powerful need to be elsewhere, and he expected the vampire's only desire was to be gone. To escape, to live — probably not the right word, but hey — to fight another day. And, also probably, to warn all the other vampires. A cloud of locusts surrounded John, he could feel them on his skin, in his hair, the sound of the swarm a buzzing that drowned out the alarm. His hand was still on the emergency door's release bar, so he pulled that back shut with all his strength.

About half the swarm had made it out, the other half splatting against the closed door. He saw the vampire reform outside, half of it anyway, a ruined line across its stomach where it just ... *ended*. John pushed the door open again, and he and Jeremy walked outside.

Jeremy punched through the ribcage of the half-vampire outside, and said, "Got another one of those pencils?"

John stabbed through the offered heart with a pencil, then wiped his hands on his jeans. He took his phone out, taking a few more photos. He paused. "Seriously, who's with the stretch?"

"I'd be more worried about where it's parked," said Jeremy. "This town's *brutal* for towage."

They stood side by side outside the rapidly emptying no man's land in front of Madison Square Garden and watched War and Famine clean up the last vampire witnesses. "That wasn't so hard," said John. "We should just send them in with the bombs."

"They can't go inside," said Jeremy. "It's Kaylan's land. Kaylan's forbidden them to enter."

John nodded, remembering how Liselle had returned the favor to Kaylan at her apartment, right before Melissa had turned Kaylan into a pillar of lightning leading up into the sky. "Damn."

"It's okay," said Jeremy, clapping John on the shoulder. "We've got John Fucking Miles."

CHAPTER
TWENTY-FOUR

"What that whole fuck-up taught us," said Uncle John, "was that we're woefully under prepared to invade the nest of a vampire swarm."

"We prefer terms like 'extended family' or 'blood relatives,'" said Jeremy the Vampire. "Also, you're still high."

Uncle John looked like he wanted to argue, *on principle* as he'd often say, not that it had ever made a lot of sense to Adalia. After the cab ride back to the warehouse, which Uncle John called their *lair* or *secret hideout* and Melissa called *home base* and Jessica called *ops*, and which Adalia just called *home*, she'd sat hugging herself, waiting. Her mom had paced like a caged creature, always about to say something. Not just looking like it, but actually about to, and never doing it. Now that Adalia had stepped back into the Other Place, properly into the Other Place rather than just looking through the door like she had for the past *forever*, she could tell things. Things like whether Uncle John was going to live after being shot (he was), or whether Liselle Vitols was really a Horse*person* (she was).

She could also tell when people were about to speak, and sometimes what they were going to say. It didn't matter that her mom hadn't said anything. Adalia could see the words hanging around her like a cloud, things like *how could you not know* or *did you really have sex with that* thing. Adalia wanted to ask those questions too, really wanted them to be said out loud but she was afraid of the answers, even though she already knew what those answers were.

At least she thought she did.

Then Uncle John had arrived back, which always made her feel better, because even without the help of the Other Place she knew that Uncle John didn't expect a single thing of her. Not really. He expected her to help do the dishes after Val cooked, because if Uncle John was going to do dishes then even the Universe was too, and she knew he expected her to do the right thing, although with Uncle John's moral compass that gave a little bit of wiggle room. This time though it didn't make her feel better, because she'd done a terrible thing, a thing so terrible that she couldn't look her mom in the eye, or Val, or ... or *any* of them. She felt sick, sick to her stomach, like she'd been used, like she should have known better.

She'd tried, of course, walking away from the anger of her mom's silent pacing, making straight for the showers. The shower area at *home* was big, with a bunch of shower roses, and plenty of hot water, all lined up. There were his and hers sections, which made Uncle John disappointed, and Melissa happy because Uncle John was disappointed. When Rex had been putting the showers together he'd said something like *no one likes a cold shower or bad water pressure*, right after he'd turned them on for the first time. Like he knew the kinds of things that would turn the warehouse into *home*, make it feel like a place Adalia could belong.

Or a place where she could hide, like she'd been doing.

Hiding had let her down. This wasn't some big epiphany on the heels of being lied to by a guy she really liked only to find out he was a mass murderer. She'd known this for a while, known it for sure after she'd been fired from Starbucks; she just hadn't said it out loud, or at least as *out loud* as the inside space of her head was. But now it was out, and that feeling of tremendous *happiness* she'd had, lying in sheets smelling of Maks, his arms around her after they'd made love, all of that was gone. It was worse than if she hadn't felt it in the first place, because the feeling felt like betrayal, and it tasted like deceit, and that heavy weight was back in her stomach and it made her angry and sad.

What made it worse, the worst thing in the world, was that after she'd looked inside Maks, stripped away the lies with the burning sight of the Other Place, she'd seen that he was alone, and that he was in love, and he was in love with *her*, which wasn't right, and couldn't ever be right. Because she didn't want a mass murderer to love her, and she didn't want to love a mass murderer.

The Universe's power was supposed to be able to fix the world, but all she was able to do with it was break things worse than they'd ever been.

But she'd tried having a shower. The water had been hot and strong and clean, and she'd scrubbed at herself with soap and a coarse brush until her skin had gone from pink to red and then from red to sore. All that had done was to make her feel sore *and* guilty because being with Maks had felt so good.

So she'd come back out and sat on the couch and ignored her mom, who was still pacing, and accepted a sandwich that Val made for her, although she wasn't hungry. And he'd cleaned it away, after she'd taken only one bite after about thirty hours of it sitting beside her, and put a hand on her shoulder and said *I'm sorry this happened to you*, which made her feel dirtier and worse, and want to cry again.

It was a good sandwich, too. Val always made good food, like he had two superpowers: making good food and doing the right thing. She wished she'd been able to do the right thing when it mattered. The right thing would have been opening her eyes, looking with the Other Place's burning sight, and then screaming when she'd first seen Maks come into Starbucks with his boyish grin and his dark curls and his stubble, his eyes only for her.

Now Uncle John was back, with the vampire Jeremy. And War and Famine, who seemed okay for things that weren't really people.

Adalia felt something green and worm-like in her gut when she looked at Liselle, with her beautiful skin, and her perfect features, and her amazing clothes, all like she'd just stepped out of a fashion shoot for *Vogue Paris*, and added *jealousy* to the feelings curling around that stone in her gut. She knew it wasn't fair, because Liselle was perfect, like an angel, except she was also terrible, like the doom of the world, but that didn't make it better. It made it worse, and made her feel more jealous, and sick, and angry, because Adalia couldn't even be the doom of the world right, she was pretty much just going to screw it up for herself, and for her mom, and Val, and Melissa, and probably Uncle John too, despite him saying that the *universe owes me one*.

She wished Melissa was here.

Adalia snapped back to the present as a chair scraped across the floor, loud. Right in front of her. She looked up, and there was Uncle John, wincing, but still pulling the heaviest chair they owned across the floor, and sitting down in front of her, like she needed someone to talk to, only she *didn't*, she just wanted to be left alone.

"I want to be left alone," she said, before he said anything, which was difficult in and of itself because he was usually the first to say anything, which was annoying, and made her feel angry again.

"Cool," he said. "There's only one problem."

She squinted at him. "Just one?"

"I've made a list," he said, nodding, "so we can compare. Later. Right now, there's a number one, or at least top five, issue."

"Is it the vampire?"

"No."

"The fact that there are other vampires?"

"No."

"That we're up against Death and Pestilence, and that the other two on our team, who are War, and I don't know, I guess she's Famine," and here Adalia wanted to say *except she's beautiful and perfect and I hate that*, "are here but are outgunned?"

John thought about that for a second. "Outgunned?"

"Yeah."

"Hadn't thought of it that way," he said, "because *I'm* here. But no. That's not it."

"What is it then?"

"The problem is that you've been served an ice cold glass of pickled assholes, and you don't have a beer. Get your coat." He stood up. "I'm starting to come down from the benzos so really, you're doing *me* a favor."

OF COURSE VAL had wanted to come, and so had her mom, and Famine and War. The only one who hadn't wanted to come was Jeremy the Vampire, who had said *bars make me thirsty* and they'd looked at him and Uncle John had said *cool* and changed the subject.

But when Val had tried to get *his* coat, and her mom looked like she was ready to go because what with all her pacing she hadn't even taken her jacket off, Uncle John had given them a look. Adalia didn't really understand the look, but Uncle John had also said *you are doing this all wrong*, and her mom looked like she wanted to punch him, but Val had just laughed and told him to *turn your fucking phone on this time.*

They'd caught a cab, because Uncle John hated Uber. Adalia suspected this was because of Skyler Evans, who Adalia had thought was pretty excellent, but she didn't want to look into the Other Place to check on what Uncle John was thinking. Because this was Uncle John, and you didn't look at Uncle John with the Other Place. There were rules.

She wasn't sure if she *could* look at Uncle John with the Other Place, for one. But the real reason was that she knew she only had to ask him something, and he'd tell her the answer. He was ... Uncle John.

They'd arrived at the bar, the kind of place that didn't need a doorman because there wasn't any point, what with the run down nature of it, and the tired waitresses, and the grimy bar top, and the patched leather stools, and old booths at the back with faded beer ads hanging above them. The kind of place that was desperate to get customers of any kind. Uncle John had ordered two beers and two other drinks in shot glasses, brought them to their booth, and put a beer and a shot glass in front of her.

The beer was a Coors, which she hadn't had before, and the shot glass was full of something green called *Chartreuse*, which she also hadn't had before, and after she drank it all, never wanted to have again. Uncle John looked at her, and the look on her face, and said, "Right. That's as bad as it gets. It's all downhill from here."

"Why did you buy that?" she said.

"You know, I really have no idea," said Uncle John. "Except that it's so bad it usually takes my mind off anything else."

"The Coors is nice," she said.

"There's also that," he said, taking a sip from his own bottle. "Chartreuse is so bad it makes anything after taste like the tears of Jesus."

"Why are we here, Uncle John?" she said.

"Because," he said, "you feel terrible."

"Don't you mean I look terrible?"

"No," he said. "I mean that a guy lied to you and your mom is pissed and you feel like you did something wrong."

"But I did—"

"No," he said, again. "I mean a guy lied to you." He took another sip from his beer.

"You don't know what happened," she said, looking down at her hands, green hair slipping over her face.

"Don't need to," he said.

"Because I can't do anything wrong?" she said. Her voice took on a nasty, mocking tone, but she couldn't help it. "Because you've done wrong things before?"

He looked at her, saying nothing. He took a sip from his beer, then shrugged.

236

"What?" she said. "That's all I get, all the wisdom? Bad beer and a shrug? I just ... I don't know what happened. I want to know what happened."

"I'm not here for wisdom," he said. "Wrong guy. Not my wheelhouse."

"What good are you then?" she said. She didn't mean to say it, it just came out, and she saw the flash of hurt in his face, but he swallowed that along with another mouthful of beer.

"Not much good at all," he said, starting to peel the label off his Coors. "I'm just a guy who's got a few good friends. I sit around playing video games and," he said, flashing that megawatt smile she'd seen so many times before, "looking damn pretty."

She laughed, and realized she was crying, and laughing through the tears. "Someone needs to," she said, thinking of Liselle. "I can't do this, Uncle John. I can't ... I can't even save myself. He's in love with me, and I chose not to see what he really is because I needed someone. How can I save the world?"

"World might not need saving," he said. "Not by you."

"But why do I have this power if—"

"Doesn't matter," he said, signaling for another round. She saw her bottle was empty and didn't know how that had happened. Maybe it had evaporated. "Only matters what you want."

She looked at him from under her hair, waiting for their beers. They arrived with a *clunk* as the waitress put them down harder than was necessary, her makeup not able to hide the years under it. The Other Place whispered at her, just a little, and she could see the waitress had three kids, and she was working this job and another one at a Subway, trying to put food on the table. She saw the line stretching back from the waitress, and her job at the bar, and the Subway, to dark meeting rooms where people talked about *profits* and *maximizing revenue with available resources*, and saw the unpaid overtime, and how desperate life was at the very brink of survival. She watched the thread stretch back to a vampire named Constanta, and from her to one named Anatolie. She skipped back more, all the way to the top

237

of the thread, and saw Death, the Death that waited for them all, wearing a woman's face and speaking with a woman's voice. *Kaylan.*

All of that, in a heartbeat, and then the moment was gone as the waitress turned away, too tired to wait for a smile of thanks. *What was in the Chartreuse?* Adalia watched her go, then looked at Uncle John. "I want the world to stop hurting," she said.

He looked thoughtful. "That seems like a big problem to solve," he said.

"It's just that, I don't know, if you can do something and you don't, aren't you to blame?"

"No," he said. "Not a big Spider Man fan, either."

"What if you try, and screw everything up?" she said.

"Would people die?" he said.

"All the time," she said.

"Bit more iffy, probably still not your fault," he said. "Look, you remember how Val hauled his ass through Chicago looking for bad guys to fight?"

"I remember," she said.

"You remember how he didn't always get it right?"

"I remember," she said.

"But he got it more right than wrong," said Uncle John.

"But that's Val," said Adalia. "I'm not like him." She licked her lips, tasting Coors. "He does everything right."

Uncle John looked at her, then burst out laughing. "He definitely does not do everything right."

"It looks like it," she said. "He's saved the world a couple of times."

"Nah," said Uncle John. "Right place, right time. For instance, the first world-saving event I can remember, it was actually his girlfriend who ran a bloodthirsty Russian werewolf off. Second time? You saved us all."

"But—"

"Facts," said Uncle John, "are not always my strong suit. But I was there, Adalia. I was *there.*"

She looked down at her beer. Empty again. How did that keep happening? She was silent for a while, a piece of time that felt like forever even to her, and then said, "I want another beer."

"Okay," he said.

"And then," she said, "probably another one."

"I can see where this is going," he said, "and I'm on board."

She flicked back her green hair, daring a smile for a moment. "And then," she said, "I am going to save the world."

"Rock on," he said. "How are you going to do that?"

"One person at a time," she said. The waitress arrived again with their drinks, and Adalia reached out, touching the woman's wrist. She felt the age of the woman, not just the years on Earth, but the extra time she carried because of all her worries. She stepped sideways into the Other Place, just a little, just enough to see properly. *"Mira Rusk, I offer something. No trades, because you give all to your children, whose names are Terrence, after his father, and Samantha, and Ollie, who is only small but sees you age day by day. Mira Rusk, I see how you work here tirelessly. There are six numbers you must remember. They are twelve, twenty seven, forty, nine, three, and thirty."* Adalia slid two one-dollar notes onto the table. *"Mira Rusk, do you remember?"*

"I ... I remember," she said, stumbling back, before hurrying away.

"That was," said Uncle John, "pretty fucking cool."

"Yeah," said Adalia, and she was crying again, but it felt better this time.

"She's going to win with those numbers?"

"Yeah," said Adalia. "Yeah, she is."

"What were those number again?" said Uncle John, and Adalia laughed, and it felt good, good and clean, and right.

She was going to save the world. She was going to save the world. She was going to *save the world*.

But first, another beer.

≈

OH GOD. Her head.

That was the first thing that came through the fugue of sleep, except it wasn't sleep, it was more like a high functioning coma, medically induced, if doctors were allowed to use alcohol to induce comas. There was probably something in the Hippocratic Oath that would stop them, because while it was fun at the time — *it was fun, wasn't it? A memory of her drinking something clear from a shot glass, someone saying "Salt before the tequila! Before!" as the music pounded around her* — there was this awful recovery window where everything was bad.

Beer bottles should have some kind of warning label.

Different sensations started to filter through the pounding on the inside of her skull. Her face was pressed against a coarse fabric. She was going to have a fine mesh pattern pressed into her cheek for hours — *hours*. The fabric smelled like wet dog, which wasn't good because she'd probably smell like wet dog too. And, curious, wet dog wasn't a usual smell for her bed at home, which tended to smell more like lavender if she could get to the wash first, because if Rex did it things smelled like Old Spice which was great for him and bad for her.

Adalia was sure that if she tried really, really hard she could open her eyes, but that felt like a lot more effort than the potential reward. Probably bright light, which would make her head hurt more, and her mom with that look, the one that said *you've only got yourself to blame.* She might have been unfair about what her mom would have said, but her hangover didn't care about fair. It cared about bright lights and a world of what-ifs that might never happen. She wished she had a real friend, someone who was normal, who lived in a world without werewolves and vampires and ghosts and insane power hungry maniacs. Someone she could have a coffee with and say to her friend something like, *is your mom like overprotective all the time* and her friend would nod, and pass over a beer—

Her stomach lurched.

—pass over a coffee, and say, *yeah, she does that, it's weird you know, because she made it through being 20 also and seems fine and didn't burn the whole world to the foundations.* Her real friend, the one who was now speaking in low tones because she knew what hangovers felt like, and who had a sensible name like Mary, Mary would be able to make a sandwich without a gun on the kitchen counter, and Mary would know whether green hair went with the jacket she was looking at in Macy's, except it wouldn't because nothing went with puffer jackets. And that's what Mary was *for*, she was a good friend, uncomplicated, and would have her own small problems, which they would talk about, sometimes just texting, and that would be okay.

Adalia's stomach lurched again, and this time it wasn't Mary's fault. She could hear water dripping from somewhere, not like a tap left on — Jessie did that a lot, which was annoying, like she didn't quite turn it off all the way, and didn't realize she was doing it — but like a slow trickle of water. Not like it was running into a sink, with the sound of water going down a drain, just water running, not a lot of it, the kind of way water might if it was trickling down a wall from a crack or something. Which was weird, super weird, because there wasn't a lot of water flowing down walls back home, which implied that she and Uncle John were staying at someone else's place, which made sense, because Uncle John — like Mary — knew a lot about the looks her mom gave, and didn't like them either.

Was it time to open her eyes? The rough fabric on her cheek wasn't getting any softer, which wasn't great. She heard a metallic *clink*, not very loud but close, although that was difficult to know for sure since she was lying against one of her ears as well, which meant that she was lying on half of her hair, which was going to be a problem for Day After Adalia to fix, when she was hungover, and Day After Adalia didn't have the steadiest of hands.

She opened her eyes.

This isn't what I expected.

The rough fabric she was laying against was a wool blanket, brown and green, which wasn't a great combination, and it wasn't made better by being on a bed that wasn't Adalia's, in a room that wasn't Adalia's. The room wasn't huge, not like a prison cell tiny but small enough that it felt cozy with the bed she was on, and the concrete walls, and Uncle John chained against the wall opposite her. Day After Adalia looked at Uncle John for a few moments, not processing what she was seeing too well, because it was unusual to see Uncle John unconscious, with a bit of matted blood in his hair, and his face so gray, and chains on his wrists leading up to a ring bolted to the wall, a big ring that looked rusty. This was important, because Uncle John might have been the kind of guy who'd try being chained up just to see if it was more exciting, but the chains would be clean, and there'd be a safe word involved, probably *armadillo*, and this didn't look like that kind of setup at all. At. All.

The good news was that the light wasn't bright, a single dim bulb set into the ceiling, still bright enough to look like the Eye of Sauron but not bright enough to hurt too much. This particular Eye of Sauron flickered a bit, like the power here wasn't that good, but stayed on, which was better than good because there were no windows. Day After Adalia started to get up, slow and steady which was good because everything was a little on the spinny side, and took the room in. Her cot — not really a bed, just barely promoted over a camp stretcher — was against a wall. Uncle John was chained against the opposite wall, right next to the door. The other two walls were bare, one of them having a crack running all the way along it, water seeping out and running down to the floor, where it vanished through another crack. Everything was old concrete and older brick, and she felt that the air would have been too cold for comfort if the alcohol wasn't still setting her blood on fire and making her thirsty.

Whoever had put her here had thought about that, because a small bedside table, no more than a metal shelf on four legs, sat next to the cot. It had a bowl of candy, and two water bottles. She grabbed one of the water bottles, draining it in less than three seconds, and then looked at the candy.

Who puts a bowl of yellow M&Ms next to your bed? She wanted a burger, or anything fried really. She took a handful anyway and munched on them, which might have been a mistake, as her stomach wasn't on board, but she kept them — and, blessedly, the water — down. Day After Adalia patted her pockets — they'd left her with her jacket, and her clothes, which all smelled of beer, which was better than it could have been but worse for her stomach than even the Old Spice would have been — and found her phone. Temporary elation melted into disappointment when she saw she had no bars. Not even the hint of a bar, or perhaps the smallest bar hiding somewhere. She wasn't surprised, just disappointed, because this was a prison, what with the chains and Uncle John's matted blood and the blanket that smelled of wet dog, and the prison was probably in a nuclear fallout shelter, and they weren't known for good coverage. Were they?

She was where she was supposed to be though. She could tell by taking a tiny peek into the Other Place. They'd put Day After Adalia in a room in the belly of the city — not a fallout shelter after all — under Penn Station, under Madison Square Garden, and that was the plan all along, to get in here and break the vampires against the wheel of the Night. The order was wrong, because her mom and Val weren't here, and neither was—

—her stomach lurched for a different reason, and she felt confused, like she shouldn't want someone who'd lied to her, even if he loved her, but also hungry and thirsty for a thing she shouldn't have, and wondered if this is what heroin addicts felt like—

—Maks, and the three of them would increase the odds of getting out. Day After Adalia didn't feel strong enough to have a conversation with a cup of hot soup, let alone someone like Kaylan, who was so strong, and getting out of this might need more strength than she could get from a bottle of water and a bowl of yellow M&Ms. She grabbed another handful of them anyway, because they were cheerful, and then leaned forward.

"Uncle John," she said. "You need to wake up."

He didn't move, and so she stepped a little sideways into the Other Place, and saw that they'd hit him hard, so hard on the side of the head that he would be feeling worse than her when he woke up. She looked at the threads that stretched up and away from him, the hundreds and hundreds that connected him in this moment to the other moments that came before and after. Adalia found the one she was after, *that* one, the one that was taught and fragile at the same time, like an old spider's web, with dust and dirt caught into it. She ran her fingers against it, light as a moth's wing. She wet her lips, then leaned forward and breathed against that thread. Saw it tremble, like it was frightened, then strengthen as the dust fell off it, and saw it relax, and she felt herself relax as well. And felt a wave of exhaustion hit her, rested her head on her hands, and tried not to throw up.

"Why…" Uncle John coughed, shook his head, winced, and coughed again. "Why are you leaning forward?"

Adalia leaned back. "You were unconscious."

He nodded, as if that were a normal thing, and for Uncle John and his trips to bars it may well have been. "Why are there chains on my wrists?"

"We're prisoners," she said. "I think."

He nodded again, but slower this time. His eyes strayed over the room, lingering for a while on the water bubbling down the wall, and longer again on the bowl of M&Ms. He shook his wrists, chains jangling, but she could tell his heart wasn't really in it. Plenty of slack in the chains though, letting him move around a little, and he snared himself the remaining water bottle, opened it, and offered it to her.

She shook her head. "I've had one."

"Great," he said, and drained the bottle. "How much did we drink last night?"

"I don't know," she said.

"Was it a lot?" He played with the plastic bottle. "It feels like it was a lot."

"They hit you in the head," she said.

"Oh," he said. "That wasn't very nice."

"No," she agreed. "I … I fixed you. I think."

"Uh huh," he said. "Can you open the door?"

"In a bit," she said. "I don't feel great."

"Do you know where we are?" he said.

"Penn Station," she said. "Underneath it."

"Every time I go into Penn," he said, "there's a legion of panhandlers trying to use me like an ATM. Someone must have seen something."

"It's possible," said Adalia, a twinkle of memory coming to her, "that we walked in here by ourselves. Before they hit you in the head." *Someone had been yelling into her ear — the bar was so loud — about a private club. A place they could go, the guy knew a guy who knew a guy on the door, get them in* no *problem. Boutique place.*

He gave her a sour look. "We drank a lot, didn't we?"

"I don't think I like tequila," she said. "It makes Day After Adalia regret all the decisions in her life. I wish Mary were here."

"Who's Mary?" said John.

"My friend," said Adalia, not really listening to him anymore. She closed her eyes. The Other Place nagged at her, and she glanced into it. Then she sighed, opened her eyes. "They'll come for us soon," she said.

"Who?"

"The fucking vampires," she said, "who else?"

"I was hoping for Val and Danny," said Uncle John, "and if I'm being honest, I'd like to see Liselle again before I die."

"Oh," said Adalia. "She can't come here."

"She can't?"

"No," said Adalia. "We're in Kaylan's House."

CHAPTER
TWENTY-FIVE

Val heard the knock on the door, cracked open an eye, and stared at the red numbers on the clock. *0900*. One of the best things about being one of the Night was never having a problem getting to sleep, or sleeping in general. He seemed to sleep whenever, wherever, Danny too, and when he'd mentioned this Carlisle had given him a look that felt rougher than it needed to be. He'd wanted to grab a little shut-eye before they hit the nest, but sleeping through the night and not getting attacked by a hundred vampires wasn't the plan. They were supposed to move when John and Adalia got back.

Something niggled in the back of his mind. *John and Adalia. John and Adalia.*

Speaking of Carlisle, that knock sounded like her. He kissed Danny—

Pack mate.

—on the shoulder, and she grumbled. "What time is it?"

"Nine," said Val, "which means coffee."

The knock sounded again, and Val slipped out of bed, both feet

hitting the floor at the same time. He stretched — heard an apprecia-
tive growl from Danny — and snared a robe. He pulled the door
open.

Carlisle pushed in past him without even pausing. "They haven't
come home."

"Good morning," said Val. "What a lovely day."

She glanced at him, snorted, and said, "Everard, get your ass out
there. That clown Miles hasn't come home, and neither has the
eighth wonder of the universe."

"They're the same thing," said Val, "if you ask John. Wait. Adalia
hasn't come home?"

"No," said Carlisle.

Val felt his pulse quicken, felt—

Our cub.

—like he needed to start running. Made himself pause, look at
Danny, took in her wide eyes, then said to Carlisle, "Get the rest of
them ready."

VAL'S COFFEE was growing cold. He hadn't touched it since pouring it.
"Give me the rundown."

Jessie nodded, pointing at the board. It was a whiteboard,
magnetic, with scrawls all over it running between photographs that
had been printed and held in place with small colored circles. "Miles
took a few photos of The Garden before he disturbed the swarm.
Doesn't tell us much, except," and here she pointed at a blurry shot
of a doorway, and another, "that they came from there." She paused,
looked at Val, then said, "The picture's not great."

"Photography's not his thing," said Val. "Still, if he'd had more
than his phone—"

"He broke my camera," she said.

"Cool," said Val.

"Not cool," she said, looking like she wanted to say more. "Anyway. Back on topic, we're at the start of the day, which sounds like an excellent place to begin. Jeremy?"

The vampire nodded, taking over from her at the board. "Look, I know what's in there. Been there. Got a room and everything."

"You got any photos?" said Val.

"It's not very cozy," said Jeremy. "It's why I was staying at the Renaissance. That and, of course, they wanted me to eternally damn my immortal soul by turning another person into a blood sucking member of the legion. But mostly because the Renaissance has nicer carpet."

"So no photos?"

"No," said Jeremy. "Got some great pics of the Renaissance, though. The view is amazing at night—"

"The pit," said Val. "What can you tell us?"

"Right," said Jeremy. He pointed to a diagram of what looked like corridors and rooms. "Here's what I can remember of the entrance level. It's not," he said, "to scale."

"Son," said Rex, "I don't think anyone's criticizing your artwork."

"Great," said Jeremy, "because it's not to scale. Anyway, as you can see, there's a main entrance. That's behind a tie shop. Sells great ties, if that's your thing. The corridors branch out a little after that, so I think we'll need to split up."

Carlisle stood up, nudged Jeremy, and took over. "We're pretty sure that Miles and Adalia are there because that's where their phones are. Find My Friends might be the biggest invasion of privacy ever invented, but it's useful in this situation."

"Their phones are on?" said Danny. She pulled out her phone.

"No," said Carlisle, "they *were*. Last place we saw their signal was The Garden."

Val felt something heavy growing in his chest, something that felt like despair. He reached for Danny, held her hand. She gripped his fingers with strength, something angry and hard and scared in her face. When he spoke, he tried to keep his voice level. "So we don't know if they're alive."

No one said anything for a moment, and then Jeremy leaned forward. "If it helps, you can't turn someone into a vampire during the day. Even underground."

"You can't?" said Jessie. "That's useful intel."

"And they don't usually take people back there unless that's the end state. It creates an uncomfortable series of rumors to drag dead bodies out of the same place, day after day. My guess is they're wanting to turn them into information fountains." Jeremy shrugged. "You'd do a lot if you craved human blood and couldn't get it."

"The good news," said Jessie, "is that Ginger and his team have agreed to go in with us."

"Who's Ginger?" said Val.

"Colombian weapons dealer," said Jessie.

"Cool," said Val, feeling a little lost. "How do we know him?"

"I bought a bunch of explosives from him," said Sam. "And a rifle."

"Great, great," said Val. He looked around. "There's not a lot left to say. We need to get our people back. We were going there anyway, but this makes things a little harder."

"A little?" said Carlisle. "Jesus, Everard—"

"I know," he said. "Look, I know."

She glared at him a moment longer before her gaze softened. She looked at Danny, then said, "We'll get them back."

"One thing is bothering me," said Rex.

"Just one?" said Jessie.

"Why'd they let us sleep? Why didn't they take us out?" Rex looked at all of them in turn.

"Ransom," said Carlisle.

"No," said Jeremy.

"I like the ransom angle," said Jessie, "because—"

"No," said Jeremy, again. "See, the reason they didn't attack is because they don't need to."

"Break that down, son," said Rex.

"They have a girl with amazing powers," said Jeremy. "As a point of fact, she is not a hostage for ransom. You guys are. Against her good behavior. While you're alive, they can threaten her with killing all of you, and she might do what they want."

"I'd die for her," said Danny.

"That's exactly what they're counting on," said Jeremy, "or more likely, that Adalia knows you'd die for her."

"And what is it that they want?" said Danny. "What do they want with my little girl?"

"Probably something small, like ending the world," said Jeremy. "I think this provides, uh, a little extra incentive to hurry."

There was a silence. Jessie started handing out headsets. "One of the biggest risks in any extraction exercise is shooting friendlies," she said. "So check your targets." She looked at her feet, then at the board, then around the room. "Get your kit."

VAL STARED AT THE MAN. He felt petty, like he should be in a position to stare down, but Ginger was a giant. Over six feet without shoes, shoulders broad like he was used to pulling carts or the bodies of the dead across battlefields. Hard eyes, topped with orange — *bright orange* — hair. It was the very size of him that made Val want to stare down, to—

We are Alpha.

—be in charge. He crossed his arms. "So, uh."

"You the werewolf?" Ginger said. Like it didn't matter. Like it was a story he'd heard. One he wanted to be true.

"Jess," said Val, shooting a look at Jessie. "Jess? The first rule of Fight Club is that you do not talk about Fight Club."

"It was me," said Rex, looking for all the world like a five-year-old with his hand in the cookie jar. "I didn't think we would be able to get through this with anything less than the truth."

Val raised an eyebrow. "You've always had trouble with the W-word."

"That's because it's stupid," said Rex. He put his hands in his pockets. "God damn werewolves."

Val turned back to Ginger. Looked *up* at Ginger. God*damn*it. "I'm a werewolf, yeah." It still felt—

We are the Night.

—weird saying it out loud.

Ginger cracked a huge grin. "Hell. I mean, hell."

Val blinked. "I expected a little more disbelief, if I'm being honest."

Ginger clapped a huge hand on Val's shoulder. "After what we've been through ... you see a few things." He scratched his nose. "You hear about whole PMCs disappearing after a contract going wrong, if you know what I mean."

"I think I know," said Val, "because I was there."

"Story said," said Ginger, "that there was more than one werewolf."

"There is," said Val.

"How many?"

"More than one," said Val. "Not a whole lot. I'm not trying to be evasive. Yesterday, I thought there were only two of us left. Today, I've found out there's at least one more."

"Not a limited edition anymore?" said Ginger.

"More that the third one's a raving psychopath," said Val, "who tried to kill me."

"That's rough," said Ginger, amiably enough. "I hope you guys sorted that out."

"Huh," said Val. "I'm curious. How would you sort that out?"

"Hire him," said Ginger, not a hint of hesitation in his voice. "It's what I did with Brindle. Guy was trying to kill me. Kidnapped by cultists or something. They told him I was going to end the world."

Val looked at Ginger's posse, with that eye-of-the-storm look he'd seen in Jessie before the action hit. Calm. Professional. Ready to rock, or whatever term they used. "Which one's Brindle?"

"Dude who looks like he doesn't want to meet your eyes." Ginger pointed to a clean-shaven man with a guarded look. "So he comes at me with all kinds of stuff, guns, knives, the whole thing. Tried to blow up my house, too."

"All at once?"

"No, this was over a few weeks. First time I was drunk. Didn't kill him because I passed out, I think. After that it became a habit not to kill him." The big man shrugged. "End of the second week, I tied him to a chair to find out what I'd done to him. He explains that I'm supposed to be this big hombre who's going to end the world. So I tell him, not unless someone else is paying, and we get talking about what a cult is. Then we go to that place where he was living. They'd brainwashed him. Taken him as a child, made him into some kind of assassin."

"Right," said Val, thinking, *if I'd heard this story ten years ago, I'd have thought it was all made up, but here we are. About to go into a vampire nest, with my werewolf girlfriend at my side.* "What'd you do?"

"Killed those motherfuckers, of course," said Ginger. "Look, Jessie's — sorry, Major Pearce — she's told me the plan. We're going in, and we're going in loud."

"Yeah. She's ... my gig isn't attack strategy." Val flexed his hands. "More of an immediate problem-solver. She tell you these guys are fast?"

"She did," nodded Ginger. "I think we're going to address that problem through superior ordnance delivery."

"You what now?"

"Bullets," said Ginger. "All of them, at once."

"Okay," said Val.

"It's sensible," said Jeremy. He was standing a safe distance back from the door. *Too much sunlight out there.* "We can move fast, but there's limits. You've seen The Matrix?"

"I've seen—" started Val.

"Wait, hold up," said Ginger. "Is this … is this tall glass of water here a, a fucking *vampire?*"

"'Tall glass of water?'" said Jeremy.

"Uh, yeah," said Val. "We've got him on as a, uh, consultant."

"'Consultant?'" said Jeremy.

"That's fucking cool, man," said one of Ginger's posse. Val thought his name was Sawyer Diego. Diego's face was all smiles. "Fucking. *Cool.*"

Jeremy gave Val a *where did you find these guys* look. "There's a … look, it's more of a wrinkle than anything, but I figure it's worth mentioning."

"Shoot," said Ginger.

"Well, and like I said, it's more of a wrinkle, but unless your guns fire sunlight, we're going to have a problem."

"How so?" Ginger's face had turned business-like, all humor gone. *Ah,* thought Val, *here's the professional soldier.*

"You'll probably just piss them off," said Jeremy. "We're already dead, right, so if you shoot us, we're not going to get more dead. We're just going to get angry-dead, and I can assure you that's not a thing you want."

"What about," said Ginger, "if we use *more* ordnance."

"More?" Jeremy frowned. "You got a portable wheat thresher there? I think if you put one of us through a mulcher it'll take a while to come back, but last time I checked you couldn't fire those."

"Explosive rounds," said a woman in Ginger's posse. Finch, her name was. Abigail Finch. Val had tried to shake her hand and she'd shouldered past him saying *don't touch me.* "Airborne mulcher, problem solved."

"With a lot of bullets," said a gloomy man Val was sure had introduced himself as *Mallory but don't worry about remembering it we're all going to die.* "I'm thinking belt-fed. Take us from no chance to barely a chance."

"Fuck it all," said the other woman — Emily Lindle. "I hate carrying around the M249. It's heavy."

"If it helps," said Jeremy, "you can leave body armor behind."

"Why's that?" Lindle squinted at Jeremy, suspicious. "Just the kind of thing a vampire spy would say to make it easier to kill us."

Jeremy shrugged. "You can do what you want, but it won't make a difference."

Val nodded. "I'm with him. Won't make a difference. Armor will slow you down, not them."

Ginger nodded, slow and steady, like he was considering rather than agreeing. "I've never seen a werewolf fight. What are you going to take?"

"My sunny personality," said Val. "Jeremy?"

"Yo," said the vampire.

"Can I have a word?"

"I was waiting for it," said the vampire, his eyes glinting like mirrors.

THEY WERE IN THE GARAGE, the blown wall letting cracks of light through around some crates they'd pushed against it. Long-term repairs seemed a bit meaningless at this stage. Val ran a hand through his hair, then said, "I think you should go."

The vampire looked at him through the gloom. Not that the low light was a problem for either of them, but the vampire had mirrored eyes that made Val feel exposed, like he was looking—

We are what we are, but not yet what we can be.

—at himself more than anything else. "I do something wrong?"

"It's not that," said Val. "I can't ... I said I'd find you a cure. I can't do that. So I can't ask you to come with us into a den of vampires on some fool's errand. To save a couple of friends of mine."

"Huh," said the vampire. "You've only just worked that out?"

"What?" said Val.

"You've only just worked out that there's no happy ending," said the vampire, "for any of my kind."

"I'm still working on it," said Val, "but—"

"It's okay," said the vampire, the mirrors of his eyes falling away. Leaving just the man behind. Jeremy rubbed at his face. "I'm not okay with it."

Val nodded. It'd be harder without the vampire on the team, but he needed to be here for the right reasons. "I understand."

"What? No, no, no," said Jeremy. "You don't understand. I'm not okay with being a vampire. It's not a thing you really understand when you sign up, if you're even given a choice." He started pacing. "Look, it's been a ... it's been a good long time since I've had a beer, or seen the sunlight, or thought about parties as anything other than a movable feast. It's ... time for this to end."

"There's got to be a cure," said Val.

"Well, two immediate things come to mind," said Jeremy.

"Shoot."

"First up is, do you think there's a cure for being a werewolf?" Jeremy held a hand out to Val, as if saying *here's exhibit A.* "I get it's not the same thing, but there's some kind of supernatural fuckery at play that took you from being some random guy with a video game habit—"

"John's the gamer," said Val. Then felt sick for having said it, because it reminded him that *John wasn't here.*

"—and into a sometime monster, sometime savior," said Jeremy. "Second, though, is more important. I've ... I've killed a lot of dudes, Val. Murdered people. A lot. It ... doesn't sit well with me, and I'd like to go."

"I ... right," said Val. "Do you want to talk to Adalia first? She knows where the dead go when they die."

"Not really," said Jeremy. "It won't be here, and it won't be Idaho, and that's a two-for-two win."

"Nothing wrong with Idaho, but I get you," said Val. "Are ... is there anything I can do?"

"Oh, man." Jeremy turned and looked at him, really *looked* at him, and smiled. "Don't you see? You're doing it."

IN THE END, it was simple. Two teams. One to make sure they had an escape route. That would be Danny, with Ginger and his team. The other to infiltrate the nest, get John and Adalia, and get the fuck out to the escape team. No explosives this time — Sam had cringed at that, because of the eye-watering expense, but Jeremy had assured him that there'd *be another time.* No explosives wasted, just deferred, but the important point — Jeremy had stressed this — was not to put explosives next to the people you wanted to save. With a touch of luck they'd get a chance to kill the head vampire and save the world, but the priority was getting their—

Pack.

—friends back. It was difficult choosing who went where — Danny wanted to be the one going in, and Jessie had explained that was exactly why she shouldn't. She'd do something stupid because it was her daughter in there, something that would get them all killed, and that would be the worst outcome.

That was probably the hardest part of planning: explaining to a desperate werewolf why she couldn't go where she wanted.

Ginger's team were packing light machine guns, big black hunks of metal that put a lot of bullets into a target. Apparently they jammed a lot too, which is why they all had one. Emily Lindle and Sawyer Diego were also carrying flamethrowers after the *we can turn into a cloud of locusts* comment from Jeremy. Carlisle had waved the big guns off, sticking with her sidearm, but had grabbed a second sidearm — this one a smaller gun with a drum on the bottom. She'd said *I hate Glocks* but picked it up anyway. Jessie had — a little reluctantly, Val had thought — stowed her usual rifle in a box and was hefting one of the machine guns, belts of ammunition worn around her like macabre scarves.

Rex had arrived back after dropping Sam and Charlie off —
somewhere safe, he'd said — and was picking through the weapons.
He'd ended up selecting two — a shotgun and a grenade launcher —
because, as he said, *two is better than one, especially when you can't hit
shit.*

It was all going to be easy from here on out, right?

CHAPTER
TWENTY-SIX

This wouldn't do at all. Not at all.

Maks looked out over the city with all its little people, the tiny humans doing their tiny things, repeating the same stories, the same mistakes, over and over. It was a tragicomedy of the highest order, and he felt like he — *Maksimillian Kotlyarov* — was the prime actor. Front and center, and everyone was watching. To see him rise, or fall, on this last great performance.

And that scrabbling *whelp* had come and taken the Universe from him. Dragomir had asked him to guard her, but this was more than that. Adalia was the woman with the green hair and he'd been looking for her his entire life. He just hadn't realized it. She'd been whisked from this room. He touched his lips where he felt the burn of her first kiss, and imagined he could still taste her. No matter that the whelp claimed to be her *father by choice*. What did fatherhood matter? Maksimillian had been father to a thousand damned souls, and had ended them all. Better that than the fate that awaited them at the end of a vampire's kiss.

It irked Maksimillian that the whelp could become the Night at will, that he didn't have to die—

You have ever tried to tame me with your madness.

—to become what Maksimillian had earned the *right* to be. No, this wouldn't do. Maksimillian was the Alpha. Maksimillian was the head of his Pack.

Pack is more than one.

"*Molchi,*" he said.

Better to tame the wind than ask for my quiet.

"What would you know? Thousands of years and all you've been is a scratching tick at the back of my mind. *Pochemu ty ne ostavish' menya v pokoye?*" Volk scratched nails against his face, felt tears of blood trickle and stop almost at once. No, not *Volk*. He'd said that name was dead, hadn't he? Gone, gone forever, after he had promised.

What had he promised? What had the great Maksimillian Kotl-yarov promised?

You want to stop the hurt. We suffer, you and I.

"I made no such promise. We deserve it." He pressed a hand against the glass, leaned his forehead against it. Felt the cool of the city outside this window, fifty, a hundred floors below. If he jumped, he wouldn't die. It would hurt for a little while, and Volk would walk away, would—

Maksimillian. Kotlyarov. He must remember his name. The woman with the green hair — he could always remember who he was when he was with her. He hadn't known it, but he'd been looking for her for thousands of years. He closed his eyes, and said, "Adalia." That was it, not *Ady* like a cheap toy, a friend for Barbie boxed in pink. Adalia, with her green hair and her easy smile and her knowledge, but not understanding, of everything.

You will make the Night new again.

"I will ... make the Night new again," he said. "Why? Why would I do that?"

The silent forest.

Yes, yes, he'd forgotten. So many things he'd forgotten, but he'd fought the she-wolf, mother of the woman with the green hair, by tooth and claw they had fought, until her muzzle was wet with his blood. She'd thought him dead, but it took a lot to kill the great Maksimillian Kotlyarov. The silent forest had watched as he'd clawed his way out, what was left of him slipping into a small town. He'd fed, and healed, and hid.

And promised.

Because it wasn't supposed to be like this. That was it — he remembered now, the night that Volk had been born. The night he'd killed his own Pack, every one of them, taken by the vampire swarm. He'd saved them. He'd killed them.

He'd lost them.

We killed our own Pack. We suffer, you and I.

"Then we must get her," said Maksimillian — Maksimillian, again, for the moment. "So we can finish what they started."

～

Maksimillian Kotlyarov (10:32): I am hunting.
   (10:33): I would welcome you at my side.

Val (10:35): Who is this?

Maksimillian Kotlyarov (10:36): You know me, whelp.

Val (10:37): Volk?

Maksimillian Kotlyarov (10:38): Volk is dead. Your mate killed him. I am Maksimillian Kotlyarov, and I will find the woman with the green hair.

• • •

Val (10:39): You can't fix what you've done.
  (10:40): What we've done.

Maksimillian Kotlyarov (10:45): She can. She will.

Val (10:46): And you and I will have a reckoning.

Maksimillian Kotlyarov (10:47): I welcome it. Maksimillian Kotlyarov will see you at the end.

~

Now we hunt.

His feet were silent as he walked the city. The sun was bright, the air clear, and there would be no stopping him. He had sent his last messages, threw his phone into a passing trash can. The act gave him a momentary pang — teaching the thing to not autocorrect *Maksimillian Kotlyarov* to *Malayan Lakewood* had been a thing requiring much patience and time. Time: he had plenty before, and not enough now.

He knew where their nest was. The Garden. These *Amerikantsy* had the best names for things, as if calling an arena where man fought man something poetic would change its fundamental nature. He knew of the obvious entrance, the one where they sold those fashionable neck ties for busy men who attended many meetings. He would not use that entrance, because being obvious was not something Maksimillian Kotlyarov liked to be.

Maksimillian Kotlyarov liked to be violent.

We are the Night.

~

THE TRICK with not being obvious wasn't to go at things head-on. Volk would have gone head-on, and would have died too soon. Maksimillian Kotlyarov would die at just the right time. So: no using any of the usual entrances. Stick with other routes.

The air was thick with the stench of too many people. Too many people living too close to too little water. The Hudson River was home to the occasional dead body, a liquid that wasn't pure enough to be called *water* flowing along it. Maksimillian spent a few moments looking out over it, then up at the sky. This was to be his last day above ground, alive, in the blazing light of the sun. An hour from now, everything would be different.

He turned around, jogged across the road to the sound of horns, and faced the fence surrounding Hudson Yards. It stood above his head, but height was the only obstacle. There was no razor wire, no guards patrolling. There would be cameras, because the *Amerikantsy* loved their surveillance. Cameras were not a problem. They might call police, or they might call heavily armed police. They might alert the *vampiry*, and that might mean *vampiry* to kill. It wasn't a problem. *Kulake vse pal'tsy ravny*, as they said in Mother Russia.

Yes. Many teeth await us where the sunlight fears to go.

Maksimillian crouched down, then jumped the fence into Hudson Yards in one bound. There was no fence made by tiny humans that could cage the mighty Maksimillian Kotlyarov.

CHAPTER
TWENTY-SEVEN

Adalia ate the last of the yellow M&Ms, still feeling sick but also feeling unable to help herself. They were *there*, and they *wanted to be eaten*. It's what M&Ms were for, right? Mary would have agreed, if she were here and not a figment of Adalia's imagination. Mary probably would have eaten the bowl herself. They would have had a good-natured squabble about who would have the last one.

Uncle John cleared his throat. "Any chance you could get the door open? Chains off? Something?" He looked down. "I'm feeling a little constricted here, and I'll admit to feeling confused."

"About what?" she said.

"Why'd they chain me up and not you?" He shook the chains at her. "Look, it's just us, so I've got no problem admitting this. I think if something comes through that door with fangs and a real attitude problem you're better equipped to deal with it."

The door made a clank, the interior handle rotating. John took a step back. Adalia would have as well, except she was already on the bed, and there wasn't anywhere else she could go. A tall, thin woman stepped through. "It is because," said the woman, "you are a hostage."

"Oh," said Uncle John. "She's not?" He jerked a thumb at Adalia.

"You are a hostage," said the woman, "against her good behavior."

"Right, right," said Uncle John. "I'm stuck here, she can't get away?"

The woman gave a crooked smile. "Something like that." She looked back to Adalia. "Anatolie awaits."

"Who's Anatolie?" said Adalia, feeling fear touch her. It was an almost familiar feeling now.

"Anatolie," she said, "is the husband of Constanta."

"Who's ... look, I don't want to spend a lot of time working through this," said Adalia. "Who's Constanta?"

"I'm Constanta," said the woman.

Adalia blinked. "You don't ... you don't talk to a lot of other people, do you?"

"No," said Constanta, with a smile. It wasn't a nice smile, like her face had forgotten how to be kind, and had read a book on expressions that it didn't really understand. "They are food."

"I'll just, uh, hang here, I guess," said Uncle John.

"You do that," said Constanta. "We'll come get you when we're hungry."

Adalia pushed herself off the bed, squaring her shoulders. She'd read somewhere that if you adopted the pose of someone brave, like a Wonder Woman hands-on-hips posture, you would actually feel braver.

It wasn't working.

Uncle John smiled at her. Now *that* was how you smiled, all warm, and full of the way you loved someone. "I'll be okay," he said.

"Oh," said Adalia. "I know." She shrugged. "This isn't how it ends for you."

"It's not?" said Uncle John. "Wait. How does it end?"

Constanta closed the door behind them, shutting off Uncle

John's voice. He sounded nervous, but not nervous for himself. He was *never* nervous for himself. He sounded nervous for Adalia, which was fine, because in that room he wouldn't die. As long as he stayed in that room, she was pretty sure he would be fine.

The woman — Mary would call her a *giraffe*, and they'd laugh — led the way down a corridor. The place was underground, carved out of the rock and stone of Manhattan. It felt cold, and a little damp, and Adalia didn't like it very much. They passed doors opening as they walked by, curious eyes set in pale faces watching them. There, two women kissing. There, a man and a woman bit at each other, drawing black blood, licking it clean. There, two men giggled as she walked past, and were drawn back into their room by a third.

"Every day's a party day, huh?" said Adalia. It's what Mary would have wanted her to say.

"It is that or ennui," said Constanta, not turning. She was graceful, in the way you'd expect someone to be if they'd had a thousand years to practice walking. She led the way to a huge room, or vault, or cave, or something. Adalia wasn't quite sure what to call it. It had hanging chandeliers, as if to make it nobler, although it didn't help because it still smelled like a dank locker room. There were twenty or thirty vampires lounging on couches, on chairs, or in small groups. Adalia knew they were vampires in the same way she knew water was wet without touching it. There was a dead person chained to a table, blood puddling on the wood under him, a little more blood dripping down from the gashes on his wrists to stain the stone floor. Adalia saw the floor was also stained in many other places, dark blotches of brown or black, like a spreading fungus, and she thought, *how many people have died here?* That wasn't the worst of it though. The worst was a *today's-theme-is-silver* thing going on. Silver knives on the tables. Silver swords hung on the wall. Other more creative weapons — like a bat with silver nails hammered through it, which was an interesting touch — were scattered around. Leaning on tables. Held in the hands of vampires. That kind of thing.

She could look into the Other Place to see how the blood got there, or how the dead person had become dead, or how the silver weapons had been used, but she didn't want to know. Not really. Sure, she could *guess*, and her imagination was doing a good job — *just great, thanks brain!* — of suggesting things. But seeing it for real? There should be a limit on the number of horrible things you got to know in your life, and she was pretty sure she was over that limit. Mary would have nodded, and agreed.

The focus point of the room was a huge chair — *no, that's a throne* — and a man was lounging in it. His skin was white, like it hadn't seen the sun for thousands of years, and his eyes were blood red. He looked up as Adalia entered, first looking at her, then to Constanta. When he spoke, his voice was rich, like honeyed oak, like a lover Adalia wanted to have at some stage, if she made it out of this. Except this guy was a vampire, and she didn't want to have a lover that was a corpse, so maybe that voted him off the island. "She's awake."

"She's awake," said Constanta, her perfect walk taking her to the man's side. She kissed him, long and slow, then turned a lazy look towards Adalia. "She's been awake for a little while."

"Good," said the man. He stood. "I'm Anatolie."

"Uh, hi," said Adalia. "I'm Adalia. I'd say it's a pleasure to meet you, but ... I'm not sure that's true."

Anatolie laughed. "No. For you, it doesn't seem like it. But it could be." His accent was strange, like a hundred different accents on top of each other.

"Is this," said Adalia, "where you offer me some kind of deal? I," and here she wiggled her fingers, "do something for you, and you let us go?"

Those blood-red eyes watched her across the room. She hadn't noticed it, but the rest of the vampires had cleared away, like water seeping down a crack, leaving the room vacant, Adalia in the middle. That wasn't uncomfortable *at all*, was it? Not the part where they were silent, not the part where they put her in the middle, and not the part where she had just lost sight of thirty vampires, because thirty was a lot, but it was a horrible number to not know where they were. Like a spider in the corner of your room: if you could see it, everything was cool, but if you couldn't, it'd be in your hair in ten seconds.

"No," said Anatolie. He blinked those blood red eyes at her.

"Oh," said Adalia, feeling a little surprised. "That seemed like where this was going."

"He means," said a woman's voice, horribly familiar, "that you will do something *for me*."

Adalia turned. There, walking into the chandelier's light, was a woman. Raven hair, dark eyes. Angry, angry, *angry* face. Adalia felt herself take a step back. "But ... but we ... but Melissa *shot* you."

Kaylan Gleicher stepped into the light. "Oh, child," she said. "You can't kill Death." And then she was on Adalia, a hand like iron around her throat, a thousand times quicker than Adalia could have made it to the Other Place. Her face pressed close to Adalia's, her breath smelling of lilies. "But you *can* kill a person."

CHAPTER
TWENTY-EIGHT

Danny was standing in the back of the M113, something Ginger had called an *APC* and something Jessie had called *conspicuous*, bracing her hands against the roof. The sound of sirens was never far off. The inside of the van smelled like sweat and tension and gun oil and death. She looked at Jeremy. "I have no idea how I got stuck with you."

"It's because I'm so much fun," said the vampire, eyes mirrored in the gloom of the van. "Also, driving a van into The Garden is an easier way to get me inside in broad daylight without—" and here he paused as the van swerved around a corner "—me looking like a Pop Tart you've left in the toaster for an hour." He frowned. "The fillings are like spill-off from a reactor, you know? That shit'll melt your skin. Especially raspberry. It's like no earthly berry."

"Impact in five," said Ginger. He was looking at a tablet device, tracking their progress. Mallory was at the wheel — *do these things even have wheels?* — the man having said he *wanted to see death coming.* The sound of sirens got closer for a second, then they blasted through an intersection in a churning crunch of metal and the roar of the APC's engine. Ginger looked up. "Barricade," he said. "Police are onto us."

"That's the idea," said Danny. "They look at us, they won't be looking at—"

Pack mate.

"—my Valentine." She was balanced light on her feet, the APC shuddering around her like a thing alive, the machine's engine roaring as it chewed through the streets of Manhattan. There was a bang, loud, loud, *loud* and the APC bucked, but she kept her feet.

Ginger looked up again. "Mallory?"

"Rammed us," came Mallory's voice. "It's fine."

"Fine?"

"Just a car," he said. "I don't think they'll have much that can get in our way before — wait."

"Sitrep, Mallory," said Ginger.

There was a massive crunch, and the APC lurched into the air for a moment, crashing back down on its treads. Danny could imagine the rent tarmac under the machine as it plowed on.

"We're good," said Mallory. "Bigger barricade. Helicopter."

"There was a helicopter on the road?" Ginger's face and voice were tense. "Unusual."

"No, no, in the air," said Mallory. "Get someone on the gun."

"Got it," said Danny. She put a hand on the hatch, then looked at Jeremy. "Cover your eyes or whatever."

The vampire looked at her, sucking air through his teeth. "They're just cops."

"I know," said Danny. "They're—"

They interfere with the Hunt.

"—in our way." She saw the vampire pull a tarp over itself, and she dogged the latches leading to the roof. Hauled herself out, the wind blasting past her like the shout of freedom. She looking around, seeing everything at once, the streets rushing past in a blur. A person with a phone, recording them, passed in an instant. Two squad cars pulling around a corner, smashing into each other, gone too like they'd never been, their only memory the sound they left, falling away fast behind them. Danny looked up, saw the helicopter. Police, rotors *thud-thudding* against the sky. The APC had a big gun, and she crouched on the roof next to it. Grabbed it, put her back into it. Felt the metal bend—

By rock and stone. It will yield.

—and give in her hand, and then she was holding the gun, APC running wild underneath her like a mustang, and she pointed the gun into the sky, laughing. She lined up the helicopter — *they're just cops, they're just cops* — and pulled the trigger. The gun roared, angry and loud and full of the rage of men, lines of tracer fire climbing into the sky. Dancing, like a hundred fairies rising to the light, ready to fight the sun. The helicopter sheared through the air, the tracer fire cutting around it, always around—

They will run like the Prey they are.

—the engine of it taking on an urgent note, and it pulled away, lost against the tall fingers of buildings around her. She released the trigger, the weapon feeling light, hungry for more. Another squad car rounded a corner ahead, she didn't even notice the sirens but saw the lights. Hauled the big gun around, pulling the trigger, feeling it buck and wrench against her like a living thing. The rounds tore up the road, lances of bright destruction that found the engine of the police car, the machine dying in a bright spray of metal and fire.

Another car was closing behind them, she hadn't even seen it, the lights off, but she felt the sting of a bullet hit her in the shoulder. She turned—

They challenge us.

—to see an officer leaning out the passenger window, firing at her. She ducked, moved, the APC under her shifting like water, then tossed the machine gun down through the hatch. She took two strides, launching herself through the air—

Bite the neck of the beast.

—to land on the hood of the police car. Saw the eyes of the

driver, so wide with surprise or fear, it didn't matter. Danny punched a hand through the windscreen, grabbed the wheel, and—

By rock and stone.

—pulled. Pulled, felt the hood bend under her, felt the muscles in her arm strain, and then the wheel was free, and she tossed it aside, tumbling away into the streets. She spun, leapt, snared the side of the APC, and watched the police car spin out of control to crash, and then it was gone into the distance like it had never been.

Danny pulled herself back onto the roof, stuck her head through the hatch. "We good?"

"Two minutes," said Ginger. "What's going on out there?"

Danny grinned. "Nothing important," she said. She stood, breathing deep as the APC roared under her, still feeling alive. So alive.

They were running hot and fast and loud the wrong way down 8th, somehow here through swerves and dodges, the peals of horns and tires and screams and—

We are the Night.

—panic looking like a wave they were cresting as they sped along. Ahead, she saw The Garden, ugly, full of death, and smiled. They would bring death of their own. These crawling insects had killed and killed and killed her brothers and sisters and—

Our Pack.

—mothers and fathers for thousands of years, and today they would fall. Today she would taste blood. She reached down into the hatch, grabbed the machine gun.

The APC wasn't slowing, and Danny dropped to a crouched as the wall of The Garden grew larger and larger, faster and faster. A half a second before they hit, she leapt, tucking herself into a ball, flying through the rain of glass and metal as the APC entered. She landed on her feet, slowing her run to a standing position. *There*, the door the vampires had boiled out of when John was here. It was opening, but her finger had already found the trigger, and the gun roared long and loud, pulling with each bullet against her grip. The door dissolved into pieces of wood and metal, and she kept firing, firing, until the weapon clicked, stopped, the barrel glowing in the gloom.

The lights had died when they hit, and smoke and dust curled around her feet. She tossed the weapon to the ground, stalking towards the fractured hole where the door had been. A red mist still hung in the air. She looked into the darkness beyond and smiled. They were—

All will fall who stand against us.

—gone, nothing larger than a Quarter Pounder left inside the entrance. Danny turned, saw Ginger and his team climbing out of the APC, the vampire slinking around the side of the machine, avoiding the light.

Ginger looked at the machine gun on the ground, looked at the torn mount on the top of the APC, and then at Danny. "You're not really a half-measures kind of person, are you?"

"Not really," she agreed. She smiled wider. "Now we hunt."

Mallory joined Ginger at the front. "She's scary," he said. "She can go first."

We are the Night.

THE DOORWAY HAD LED to a hallway, that had led to a stairway, that had led down, down, down into the earth. The walls had shifted from drywall to wood to brick to stone, layers of a tree showing the age of each level as they went. The vampires had been here for a long, long time, right in the heart of Manhattan. Their prey all around them. Danny strode forward, not halting. They entered a larger chamber, about twice the height of a person, a dark tunnel leading forward. Always forward, down, into the dark.

"Hey," said Lindle, hefting her flamethrower. "We should use a little more speed, a little less hurry."

Danny turned back to the woman, saw the soldier pause. "Why?"

"Uh," said Lindle. "You know your eyes are yellow? Like, glowing."

"It's time for hunting," said Danny.

"Uh," said Lindle. "Ok. You go, girl. Uh. It's just, you know, the rest of us can't see so well, and if there really are vampires—"

"Vampires are real," said Jeremy, sliding up to Lindle, a hand on her arm. Silent. Danny would have to be careful. They didn't have a heartbeat she could hear, and there was no wind down here to carry their scent.

Lindle jerked away. "Don't touch me," she said. "Fucking weirdo."

"Fucking vampire, actually," said Jeremy.

"Whatever," said Lindle. "Look, if there are vampires, we're going to need—"

"*CONTACT!*" screamed Mallory, his gun roaring into life. Danny whirled, saw big chunks of stone falling away as Mallory's weapon fired into the dark. It was hard to see through the dust, but *yes*, there was something there, moving fast, running up the walls as bullets chased it. Finch's weapon joined in, the huge gun adding to the noise, bits of stone spraying and raining all down the tunnel. Danny could see the thing down there—

Hated, vile enemy of the Night.

—explode into a cloud of locusts, their buzzing lost against the rage of the guns.

Lindle was moving, her flamethrower coughing once, twice, before a jet of bright white fire roared into the tunnel. She held the weapon on, engulfing the cloud of locusts in cleansing fire. The guns stopped, but the flames streamed on, and Danny could hear a hundred screams of dying things as the fire ate, and ate, and ate the darkness.

Silence. Lindle's flamethrower snapped out, a tiny pilot light still on at the front. Jeremy walked to her side, looking at the chewed and charred stonework of the tunnel. "Did you get it?"

"Fucken' A," said Lindle. "Barbecue."

Jeremy turned to look at Mallory, then at Finch. "And how many rounds?"

"About a hundred of the five point five six," said Mallory.

"Yeah," agreed Finch. "About that."

"Okay," said Jeremy, looking at Danny. "Two hundred rounds and a bunch of flamethrower fuel for one vampire. How many bullets did we bring?"

Ginger frowned. "We just got to hold the line."

"Yeah," said Jeremy. "But we need to get to the line to hold it."

"How much further?" said Danny. "How much deeper do we have to go?"

"All the way," said the vampire, its eyes reflecting her face back at her.

Lindle screamed, and Danny spun towards her. None of them had seen what happened, but she was being dragged back into the tunnel, and she was — *on the roof.* A vampire — same one, different one? — had her, and it was *on the ceiling.* Lindle would be gone in less than a second, dragged somewhere to be killed, to be fed on, to be food for these, these *things.* Danny sprinted into the tunnel, bunched up, leapt—

We will have our kill.

—and crashed into Lindle and the vampire. Lindle fell heavy, hard, her flamethrower tumbling free, the light going out with a click. Danny looked into the dark, yellow eyes seeing all. The vampire was in front of her, crouched, perfectly balanced after the fall. She had time enough to see that before it jumped on her, teeth bared. Danny had her arms out in front of her, the reflex action saving her. She got an impression of the thing, grotesquely extended jaw, teeth, so many teeth, charred skin — *same damn vampire, how do you kill them?* — and then it was biting at her neck, the strength of a train behind it.

She held it away, she didn't know how, it was so *strong*, and they tumbled together in the dark. Danny heard snatches of sound from where Ginger's team stood, guns readying, people not sure of where to fire, and *Oh God where's Lindle?* Danny felt the sound fall around her, snatches of reason coming to her from a place where this impossible thing wasn't trying to bite her throat out.

Crystal clear, she heard one voice above the others. Jeremy. "If you fall, they will kill your child."

The rage hit her then, the rage and the fear and all the hopeless fear of a thousand thousand dead Pack before her, stretching out, a timeline of the dead, and knew—

No more.

—that this thing would die. It would die because Danny wouldn't let her daughter—

No more.

—fall, wouldn't let her lover—

No more.

—die, wouldn't let these people who came into the terror and the darkness throw their lives away—

NO MORE.

—for nothing, for nothing more than a *meal*. She yelled at it, and pulled with all her strength, and the strength of the thing inside her, until her yell grew into a roar, and her hands turned to claws. Roared, and felt the tiny thing she held come apart like taffy. She held the pieces of it up like a prize, and screamed her triumph.

THE CREATURE TURNED LAMBENT, hungry eyes about her. Saw the human—

They aren't prey. They are here for us.

—ally at her feet. She looked at the torn, wet, bloody thing she held, the meat already trying to heal, to become an enemy again. She bit down, began to feed. Tasted the wet salty tang, tasted the squirt of marrow as she crunched. She was so very, very hungry.

"Hey." Another small creature, but she could smell the death on him. He was one of the enemy, the hated foe.

His name is Jeremy. He's here with us. Please don't hurt him.

Her claws flexed and curled, wanting to grab it, to end it, like this other one.

Remember his name. Jeremy.

"Look," said the small creature, "and far be it for me to get between a … a … between you and your meal, but we need to be moving on."

She crunched, and licked her jaws. Looked down at the fallen human at her feet.

"Yeah," said the small creature—

Jeremy.

—said Jeremy. "Look, she'll be okay. She wouldn't be, if you hadn't … you know, done your thing. Go team."

She knew how these things hid their fear behind words that made no sense. How they were always afraid of her. She bit down again, the last morsel going into her mouth. A growl escaped her. So hungry.

"Right. Thing is, there's more." Jeremy shuffled his feet, mirrored eyes glinting her yellow ones back at her. "And if we don't move it, your daughter's going to be lunch. Or, I don't know, something worse." He held up his hands. "Not that I know what 'worse' might be."

Adalia!

Our cub. Our cub is in danger.

Yes. Our little girl.

We will save her.

Yes. She's everything.

Then we will get to kill the enemies of the Night.

Yes. All of them.

She reached to the ground, picking up the ally at her feet.

Lindle. Her name is Emily Lindle, and she tried to burn away the dark for us.

Lifted the one named Lindle as if she was no heavier than gossamer. She turned to Jeremy, lumbered past him with massive feet. Into the light the soldiers had brought.

"Fuck me!"

"What the fuck is that fucking thing?"

"Fuck!"

"Shoot it!"

"Lindle! It's got Lindle!"

She looked at them. Heard their panting, their racing hearts. Laid Lindle, who had tried to burn away the dark for her, at their feet.

The one called Jeremy stood beside her. Ancient enemy of the Night, at her side. He said, "She got Lindle back. Before, you know, the whole teeth thing."

The biggest of them, still tiny, stood forward. "This is ... this is *Danny*?"

Jeremy looked up at her, and she looked back at him. He frowned, then turned back to the biggest. "Not ... quite? Not ... not anymore, I don't think."

"Fucking awesome," said one of the humans behind the big one.

That is Sawyer Diego, who has a cool name.

Sawyer Diego stepped up to her. "Lady? Thanks. For Lindle."

As if Lindle wouldn't be here without her. What is this feeling?

It is guilt. It is shame.

She didn't like guilt. She didn't like shame. She bowed her massive head to Lindle, nuzzled her. The fallen soldier groaned, opened an eye. Looked up at her, eyes widened. Reached a hand out to touch her muzzle. Then said, "Don't touch me."

If she could have smiled, she would have. What is this feeling?

It is happiness.

She liked happiness. It felt as foreign as guilt and shame. Lost, behind the hunger.

"We should go," said Jeremy.

She looked down at him. Licked her muzzle. Made a noise, like a growl, or a whine, or both at once. Because she felt happy, and guilty, and shameful. And fearful, and hopeful. She wanted her Pack Mate—

Our Valentine.

—at her side, so they could find her Cub.

Adalia. Perfect Adalia.

She looked back down the tunnel, and took a step towards the dark. Then cast a glance back at them, these tiny creatures who would throw their lives away to help the Night. She set yellow eyes on the biggest of them. *"Now We Hunt."*

CHAPTER
TWENTY-NINE

"Whose fucking idea was this?" said Carlisle. She pointed her flashlight up the ladder, rusty rungs leading up to a small circle of daylight at the top. The air around her smelled like a sewer, because that's what it was.

"Old tunnels like this are everywhere," said Rex, looking up the shaft. Carlisle was waiting with him at the bottom of the ladder for Pearce. "Hard to work out which way we're coming from."

"I knew it was your idea," said Carlisle. "I *knew* it."

"Heads up," said Pearce's voice from above. The small circle of daylight was occluded by a something, and with a whine a box descended the shaft, knocking against a rung or two as it came down. The *clang, clang* echoed around the dark quiet surrounding Carlisle. It made her nervous. Nerves were to be expected though, because they were in an unmapped sewer system underneath Manhattan. That wasn't the worst part of it, of course: some idiot thought walking around in the dark where there were actual vampires that could dodge bullets was a *good idea*.

Also, it was a sewer. Like you saw in the damn movies, dark *let's-*

call-it-water lapping in the middle of a canal of sorts, something that was probably ancient brick curving up to form a ceiling. A narrow path either side of the *let's-call-it-water*. Rats, or something like rats out there at the very brink of her flashlight's reach. They better not be cockroaches, that's for sure, because a cockroach that size was a thing to be feared.

The box Pearce was lowering hit the bottom, a big black Pelican case, the kind that military people seemed to pack their underwear in whenever they were going to Miami on vacation. This one was a rifle case, the size of which might have prompted a question like *are you trying to compensate for something* if it weren't Pearce lowering it. It wasn't so much a matter of compensation with Pearce, more that the right caliber weapon just hadn't been made yet. She was still carrying around survivor's guilt under her jacket like an old war wound, and that was okay. Carlisle knew what guilt felt like, especially if you were alone in the dark. Especially if you'd done terrible things in the dark.

"Hey," said Rex. "You okay, Melissa?"

"Call me Carlisle," she said, but with a smile. Because it was Rex, and she wasn't alone in the dark. Not anymore, and not ever again.

Pearce, now there was a woman Carlisle liked having at her back. Or her shoulder. Or anywhere, really. Got the job done. She looked like civilian life was working okay for her, *thank you very much*, and maybe that was because her return to civilian life came with vampires and werewolves and an excuse to get out there. Get on the front line of a war that needed fighting, for people that mattered.

Like a ghost from the dark, Everard came back from his patrol. He made plenty of noise coming back, because — werewolf or not — he didn't like getting shot. "We're all good," he said.

"All good like 'there are no vampires' or all good like 'the sewer ends just around the corner?'" said Carlisle. "Because anything in a sewer isn't 'all good.'"

Everard looked back at her, the beam of light from her flashlight making stark shadows of his nose, cheekbones, and chin. He didn't have a gun, just a bunch of wooden stakes in a bandoleer going from shoulder to waist. "You should try having my sense of smell," he said. "To you, it's your everyday garden-variety sewer—"

"There is nothing everyday about a sewer, Everard," said Carlisle. "I'm expecting hazard pay for this."

"Right," he said. "For me, it's a sewer that's a hundred years old, with a little piece of everything that went through here still stuck around."

"Son," said Rex, "that sounds horrible."

"It smells horrible," said Everard. "Anyway. No vampires."

Pearce slid down the ladder, boots scuffing the rails as she descended. Machine gun strapped to her back, barrel down. Leather jacket, but she'd ditched the aviators and hat for the trip underground. Boots on the ground with a functional crunch, she looked at the other three, then wrinkled her nose. "Whose fucking idea was this?" she was.

"It's just—" started Rex.

"Because," said Pearce, "I don't want to die in a sewer."

"Then we better get moving," said Carlisle. "Call me soft like a marshmallow, but I just don't want to die."

"Copy that," said Pearce. She hefted the Pelican case.

Carlisle nodded at it. "You really want to bring it?"

Pearce ran her free hand across the black of the case, almost gentle. "Never leave home without your favorite weapon," she said.

Carlisle's hand found the hilt of the Eagle at her back, the motion almost subconscious. "Yeah," she said. "Let's go get our family."

EVERARD HAD GONE ON AHEAD. Like he knew where he was going. Probably did — what that thing living inside of him let him do was equal parts terrifying and magical.

Okay, okay. It was more terrifying.

Carlisle was on one side of the canal, Pearce on the other. Rex was behind Carlisle, looking back behind them. He held the shotgun in his right hand, the grenade launcher — mercifully pointed towards the ground — in his left. Pearce had ditched the case holding her rifle, swapped her Light Fifty to her back, and let the nose of her machine gun lead her forward. They were both wearing some kind of night vision setup that you either got from having friends in the military or from having poor impulse control while watching infomercials. These were the real deal, genuine Uncle Sam equipment. They weren't lowered at the moment, lenses pointed at the ceiling. Pearce had her own light attached to the machine gun, and Rex's shotgun had a tiny flashlight under the barrel.

Carlisle checked her own loadout. *Okay, you thought it would be a good idea to fight vampires with a seven-round magazine. Not your best move.* But like Pearce had said, you never went into a fight without your favorite weapon. And the Eagle had lifted her on its wings for longer than she cared to remember. It wasn't just a gun. It fit into her right hand like they'd never been apart, like it was tailored for her grip. Or that her hand had ... tailored itself to hold the Eagle. The unfamiliar Glock was in her left hand, the comically absurd drum magazine underneath it. Plenty of drums for the Glock strapped to her, along with spare mags for the Eagle. Her flashlight was clipped to the Eagle, its light leading her forward. She had her own night vision goggles on her head, which made her feel like an idiot, because you only saw things like that in movies, and this wasn't a movie. The number of flashlights felt ridiculous, but Carlisle didn't want to die in the dark. Not today.

Seriously, Carlisle. Two pistols? You're definitely going to die.

Wasn't like it wasn't due, though. She'd fumbled, and fumbled bad, and Adalia had been taken away. *You had one damn job.* That one job was to make sure that young woman didn't have anything bad happen to her. Not because of some stupid words mumbled by a crazy prophet from across the seas. No, not because Carlisle was supposed to be some kind of mythical Shield for the Prophet.

It was because Adalia was her friend, and you didn't let friends get taken by fucking vampires. That one was on Carlisle, and if it took dying to put it right, then that's what it would take. Sure, Miles was there too, and they'd get him back, but he was a grown man — *Man? Man child? Boy in a man's body?* — grown-up person, and he could look after himself. John Fucking Miles always had a way through. Not out, because John Fucking Miles didn't quit. Through, to the end, and beyond.

Gunfire sounded from somewhere, lots of it. Not the soft *pop pop pop* of a pistol in the distance, but a steady stream of noise. Big guns, firing a lot.

It made them all stop walking. Carlisle gave Pearce a glance. "Sound like your guys?"

"Ginger's guys," Pearce said, but her heart wasn't in it. Take the uniform off, and she couldn't formally be *Major Pearce* anymore. But they didn't stuff you into a uniform and make you a Major. You made yourself a Major and then they put a uniform on you. Born and bred to lead, that one. "Yeah, could be. Sounds like they're letting off a few rounds."

"Jessie," said Rex, "does it sound like they're winning?"

"It sounds like they're shooting a lot of bullets," said Pearce. "If we were up above ground, we'd have comms. We could, you know. Ask."

"Huh," said Rex. "God damn underground monsters."

"God damn," agreed Pearce.

Carlisle wasn't paying attention, eyes drawn to Everard as he jogged back to them. "You guys hear that?" he said.

"If you mean all the gunfire, yeah," said Carlisle. "If it was something else, no."

There was something in Everard's expression. Like a desire, or a hunger. *Figures.* If you'd been tracked for thousands of years by a group of psychopaths who were hunting you and everything like you to extinction, sure, you'd want a piece of the payback pie. He turned his head back down the tunnel. Back into the dark, beyond where Carlisle's light could reach. "I should..."

"Yeah, you should," said Carlisle. "Hey."

Everard looked back at her. "Yeah?"

"They'll save some for you," she said.

"Yeah," he said. A shadow of something that might have been doubt went across his face. It could just as easily have been a trick of the crummy light from her flashlight. "There will be plenty for everyone. There're so many of them, Melissa."

"It's okay," she said, waggling the Glock at him. "We brought a great many bullets."

He nodded at her, once, then jogged back up the tunnel. Silent. It was crazy how quietly he could move, like a foot making a noise when you put it down was something that happened to other people.

"OKAY," said Everard. He'd appeared like a damn ghost again, but Carlisle had seen him coming this time. Two yellow points approaching from the dark, his eyes glowing that damn freaky yellow. "We need to start being careful."

"Son," said Rex. "Son, I'm being careful already."

Carlisle flicked the beam of her flashlight down to the bandoleer. A stake was missing. "Trouble?"

"Not anymore," he said, teeth white in the gloom. "But I think we've found the perimeter."

"Do you want to," said Carlisle, "stick around with us?"

"No," he said, and jogged back into the darkness.

They walked further along the tunnel, their lights picking out something against the wall in the distance. It was at a join in the tunnel, a branch leading towards where the gunfire had come from. *Probably* come from. The shape resolved itself into a pale corpse, hanging away from the curve of the wall, legs dangling in the air. It was stuck to the wall with a wooden stake through the heart.

Pearce leaned forward to get a better look. "Guy looks dead," she said.

"Really," said Carlisle.

"No, I mean," she said, "he looks like he's been dead for weeks."

She was right. Carlisle could see it now she was closer, the way the corpse's skin was pulled in as the water left the body. Didn't smell though, or not more than the sewer around them, but to be fair to all parties concerned Carlisle wasn't going to lean in close enough to get a real good lungful. There was a wet tearing sound and one of the legs of the body came loose, sliding out of the pants and onto the ground. The body swayed a little on the stake then, starting slow but picking up speed, fell to the ground, the stake carving a trough through it, up the chest and out the shoulder.

"They, uh, come apart easy after they're dead," she said, looking at the body on the ground. It was hunched over itself, collapsing before their eyes.

"That's because they've been dead for a while," said Everard, almost giving Carlisle a heart attack. He blinked yellow eyes at her. "Stake them and it catches up. Faster above ground, but fast enough down here."

"You know this how?" said Carlisle.

"Not my first rodeo," he said, and was gone again on silent feet.

"That boy needs to explain things better," said Rex after a moment's reflection.

"I don't need those kinds of details," said Pearce. "What I need is to know how many there are."

"There are too many for you to kill," said a voice like honey and silk at Carlisle's shoulder. She spun, but there was nothing there, the beam from her flashlight stabbing the darkness there, there, *there*, but nothing.

She'd have thought she'd imagined it, but Rex's gun was pointed in the same direction. She spared a look at Pearce, and saw two things. First, Pearce was also looking towards where the voice had come from. Second, there was a pale man *right fucking behind her*.

Carlisle spun the Eagle and the Glock around, but the man was gone. There was a splash, a ripple in the *let's-call-it-water*, and then nothing else.

"They move fast," said Pearce.

"Not that fast," said the voice, and all beams of light moved to catch him. One hand against the tunnel wall, one up in front of his face as he inspected his nails. Nails that were sharp, long, unnecessarily long by any standards. He was wet, like he'd just come out of the *let's-call-it-water*, but looked relaxed. Calm. "Just a lot faster than you."

Carlisle pulled the trigger on the Glock, the tiny pistol rattling in her grip, bright sparks of light lancing from the barrel to the man. To where the man *was*, but he was moving fast, up and over, around the ceiling of the tunnel back to the other side. Pearce's machine gun roared, the noise making the Glock sound like a child's pop gun. The woman had couched down to better brace the weapon, the bullets smashing brick and old slime from the walls.

The vampire was still moving, coming at them, and Rex pulled the trigger on his shotgun, fire and smoke blasting out with each round.

They stopped shooting, smoke and dust surrounding them. Carlisle could smell cordite above the stench of the sewer.

"We hit nothing but air," said Pearce.

"I think I got him," said Rex.

"No," said the vampire's voice, from behind them. They all spun. There the fucker was, back up the tunnel. Still wet, otherwise not a scratch on him. "I'll let you line me up this time. It's only fair." There was a glint of fangs. "For each round that gets me, I'll let one of you live. How does that sound?"

"You got it," said Carlisle. Never look a gift horse, or vampire, in the mouth. *Think.* Fucker can dodge bullets, but has to obey laws of inertia and motion. *Probably* has to obey those laws. She held the Eagle in one hand, lining up the Glock right on those smiling fangs with the other, and squeezed the Glock's trigger. The vampire dodged, of course, a flash of mirrored eyes and then it was moving, right down the tunnel at them. Fast, fast, goddamn it was fast, but that's what she was counting on. Her right hand twitched, the Eagle's beam ahead, and she pulled the trigger. The Eagle roared, all defiance as it bucked once, twice, three times. The vampire was moving away from the Glock's rounds, into the Eagle's. It tried to dodge, but was already moving, its feet skidding on something on the ground, and a round from the Eagle caught it dead center, right in the heart.

It stumbled, and Carlisle fired again. Blooms of red broke out on it, two more dead center and the last one in the head, the back of the thing's skull blowing out across the *let's-call-it-water*. The body stumbled, but was still standing.

"How is it still alive?" said Pearce. She hefted her machine gun and fired, the roar of the weapon thundering through the tunnel. The vampire's body shook and stuttered, jerked ten, twenty times as bullets riddled it. Bone and flesh sprayed out the back as explosive rounds tore into it, its arm falling away, a piece of skull blasted into the dark.

Her weapon jammed, and she worked the action to clear it.

Carlisle played her light over the remains. From a distance, of course. Fuck *me*, but it was still alive. Not much in the way of a head left, but she swore what was left of the mouth was smiling. And pulling itself back together, like she'd seen Everard do. Except *not* like Everard. Everard healed, like a normal person, or wolf, or whatever the hell he was, just a lot faster. This thing was pulling pieces of itself back together, blood and chunks of flesh crawling across the ground back towards the body.

She fired the Eagle again, not that she had much hope after the failure of Pearce's weapon. Where the fuck was Everard, anyway?

There was a fireball, an explosion of light and heat and something bigger than noise. A pressure wave hit her, picked her up, threw her back against Rex, who fell back into the *let's-call-it-water*.

Carlisle fell on the floor, saw Pearce thrown against the opposite tunnel wall.

Carlisle's head was ringing, and she couldn't hear anything, couldn't see anything. Fire and smoke billowed from down the tunnel where the vampire had been. She clawed around her, found the Eagle. Slapped the flashlight once, twice, before the beam flickered on. She played the light about, picked out Rex pulling himself from the *let's-call-it-water*, Pearce propping herself up on an elbow. Carlisle's ears were ringing, and she banged her free hand — *where the fuck was the Glock? Where was it?* — against her ear. Hollow thud, not a lot else.

You can die later. Get to your feet, Carlisle.

She reached for the tunnel wall, pulled herself to her feet. Pointed the light back at where Rex was. He was mostly out of the *let's-call-it-water*, grenade launcher still in one hand. *Ah.* Carlisle pointed her light back at where the vampire had been, bits of flesh and wall slime burning with low flames. Her hearing was coming back, the first thing she heard was the patter and slap of bits of vampire raining falling from the tunnel and down.

"I..." she said.

"Rex," said Pearce, then louder, "Rex!"

"I'm okay," he said. "Everyone? I'm okay."

"I can see you're okay," said Pearce. "I'm wondering if I should kill you myself."

"Hey," he said. "We had a situation. I ... it worked out, didn't it?"

"You do not," said Pearce, "fire an explosive device in a contained space."

"Okay, Jessie, okay," he said. "It's just..."

"What?" she said.

"Well, what if there are vampires?" he said. "The rules need to be different."

"No," said Jessie, "because the rules aren't for the *vampires*. They're for *us*. There is nothing friendly about friendly fire."

Everard skidded around a bend, came running back to them. He slowed as he past the ring of burning remains and broken brick that was the vampire. "What happened?"

"Nothing," said Carlisle. She found the Glock, checked the weapon, fed it a new magazine. Slipped another magazine into the Eagle, the sidearm hungry for it as always. She looked at Rex, at the grenade launcher, and then back at the remains of the vampire. Back to Rex. "Kill-stealing motherfucker," she said.

CHAPTER
THIRTY

Liselle looked at the broken machine, smoke coming from within, doors torn open. The Night hadn't done all of this — the damage to the machine from the crash was clear, paint and damaged metal. But something else had come along afterward, something strong and hungry, to tear the doors off, to find the meat within. And finding nothing — because there was no blood — they had damaged the machine beyond repair. There would be no escape using it.

Like all of their kind, humans gave machines like this cheerful names. This was an *APC*, something that rolled off the tongue like children singing their *ABCs*. It meant *Armored Personnel Carrier*, and was designed for taking humans safely to places where they would then die or kill other humans. Humans were always killing. She looked back out through the hole the APC had punched through, saw the police cordon set up outside. Saw soldiers of a type right for this time and place — Josef would have called them the *National Guard* — collecting there as well, with other APCs, and helicopters buzzing overhead. A woman was shouting at them through some kind of loudspeaker, but her words were wearisome. Words like *surrender*

290

and *come out with your hands up* and *just let the hostages go*. There were no hostages to let go, and Liselle never surrendered. The concept of coming out with her hands raised to the stars above was comical. So she ignored them, turning to Josef.

"That's not going anywhere soon," said Josef. He was standing with his arms crossed, a look of contemplation on his face as he examined the APC.

"We must help them, Josef," she said. She didn't say *or they will all die*. She wanted to. She wasn't talking about the messy collection of police and national guard outside. She was talking about the Night, and their Pack.

"Yeah," he said, uncrossing his arms, flexing his fingers, like his was preparing to lift something heavy. "If we don't, they're all going to die."

She laughed. "You know what I'm thinking. Always."

"I'd be a poor brother if I didn't," he said. Josef looked around the inside of the building, took a breath, let it out. "What we really need to do is go inside, and kill every fucking vampire we see."

"We aren't permitted," she said. "It's Kaylan's house."

"Yeah," he said again. "I'm still pissed that she sent a PMC after me. *Me*. My own, against me."

"Your 'children?'" Liselle shook her head. "They're just humans."

"You're telling me that?" He laughed, the sound trailing off to silence. "I just ... wish."

She knew what he wished. For a family, a real one, and children of his own. Of all the Father's gifts, that was one they could never have. A joy denied to them. Except Kaylan, Kaylan and Maynor had found a way. A perversion of the Father's will. They'd seeded His Eden with unholy monsters that ate and bred and hid in the dark like roaches. Liselle didn't say any of that. What she said instead was, "Me too."

"Still," said Josef. "At least you've found one to call your own."

"John Miles," said Liselle.

"John Miles," agreed Josef. He faced her, his face serious. "You can't have him, sister."

"I can have whom I want," she said. She felt a hot stab of anger.

"I didn't mean it that way," said Josef. He looked at his hands, like they were unfamiliar to him. "We're not these shells. We're the End of the World. We are forever, until we Ride. And the end that follows ... that will be forever as well. Anyway. John Miles is a man, and he will be dust in a moment of our time. He will leave you, because he will die, and that will hurt. After the hurt, you will be empty. And alone."

She thought about that, wrestling with her anger like it was a living beast. After a moment, she said, "We are already alone, Josef. I ... I have never loved before. Not like this. There are so many things in the Father's Eden we have seen but never felt. There are so many kinds of love, and ... we have watched. We have sat in their windows as families died, lovers left, friends stood back to back and fought to their last. As betrayal and long years and fierce pride and petty jealousy took them, and took them, and took them back to dust. And now—" here, she laughed, the sound sharp, bitter to her own ears "—I finally feel it. I *feel* it, Josef. It's so wrong to take them. And if I lose him—"

"It's wrong to take them," said Josef, "or take *him*?"

"They are the same thing," she said.

"They are not," he said.

Liselle realized her teeth were bared, her fists clenched. She relaxed, letting her breath out. "You're not wrong," she said. "But you're not right either."

"Maybe not," he said. He seemed to brighten. "Either way, we get to kill a lot of vampires today."

"There are many good things in this world," she said.

～

She tried to go down into the dark, of course. As she walked lower, the air felt thicker, heavier, and then it was solid. Not something visible, but immovable all the same, a point at which she couldn't go past. It was a tie shop, celebrating the chains binding men to their work with yokes of fabric they'd wear around their necks. Liselle couldn't go past the entrance, a simple doorway that was impossible to move past. *Kaylan's House.*

Liselle walked back up to where the broken APC sat. It wasn't smoking anymore, but that didn't make it any less dead. Josef was sitting on the roof of the machine, legs crossed, eyes closed. She cleared her throat. "What are you doing?"

"Meditating," he said.

She laughed. "I've never seen a fish climb a tree, but I've seen Josef Hackett meditate. I would have thought the first more likely."

"I got bored," he said, "because there are no vampires here."

"We just need to keep the path clear," said Liselle. "The APC might be broken, but there is still sunlight. If they can get through here, they can make it into the Father's sight and be safe."

"How," said a voice, "are you going to do that with all of us?"

Liselle turned towards the voice. There were tens, perhaps a hundred of them, mirrored eyes staring out of hungry faces. So quiet, and so fast. "I'm going to do it the way I always have," she said, unsure which one had spoken. *It doesn't matter.* "By the sword."

"We saw what you did last time," said one of them, stepping forward. A man, in a torn business suit. Stained, dirty, brown splotches on a white shirt. Hungry, hungry eyes. "We've watched. We've learned."

Josef stood up on the APC. "What have you learned, vermin?"

"You are strong," the vampire said. "But not very fast." The vampires were spreading out in a ring around Josef and Liselle, so many of them. So many hungry eyes, polished to a mirror finish. They didn't fear the Father's sight as much as they should because the sun was right overhead, no stray beam finding its way inside.

Liselle looked outside to the collection of police and national guard and — of course — reporters.

Her eyes came back to the vampire that had spoken. "We are fast enough."

The creature smiled, gleaming fangs somehow odd against the dirt and grime of its torn suit. "I don't think so."

Liselle saw some of them had crossbows, bigger than you might expect a crossbow to be. Ropes looped to bolts, bolts ready to fly. She had a moment's thought — *they mean to tether us to the Earth* — before one fired. She moved aside, the bolt skimming past her face, rope hissing and slithering in its wake. Like a snake.

She grabbed at the end of the rope as it flew, felt the braiding of the material — *false, fake, plastic* — as it sped through her fingers. It slowed as it ran out of line, the end of the bolt embedding in a wall. Liselle hooked her fingers closed, *yanked*, and pulled the line, crossbow, and vampire holding it across the room. To her. She lifted the creature up by the throat, hefted, and threw. It tumbled through the air, out through the glass, and into the Father's light, where it burst into a thousand beautiful motes of fire, before it became ash on the wind.

The sharp stabbing pain surprised her, and she looked down to see a bolt poking through her chest, barbs extended. She turned, saw a vampire behind her hold a crossbow. Reached for the line, felt another stab through her arm as a bolt passed through forearm, barbs flicking out. The vampire holding it pulled, and Liselle stumbled to her knees. *By the Father, they are brazen!* She rose to her feet, felt another bolt pass through her leg, and her shell cried out with the pain of it.

Josef, my brother.

I am here, my sister.

She looked up, saw Josef, still atop the APC, ropes stretched out from the barbs through him to vampires all around. Through his chest, stomach, arms, legs, one through his shoulder. He looked at her, smiled, blood against his lips. Saw him turn to the vampire with the dirty suit. "You are not fast *enough*," he said, coughing.

"Seems fast enough to me," said the vampire.

Josef was still smiling, reached a hand to the sky. Where the sky would be, if the roof of the Garden wasn't there. There was a crack of thunder, distant, booming, echoing across the heavens. Liselle saw the faces of the police and national guardsmen outside turning up, all looking in the same direction. Saw faces going slack with aston-ishment. Saw the faces of the vampires turn, uncertain, some holding hands up to shield mirrored eyes against the bright sunlight they were forbidden to walk in.

The roof of the Garden exploded in a shower of concrete and rebar and glass, pieces big as cars and small as pebbles raining around. There, a vampire crushed under one. Another shorn in half by a spinning piece of glass. In the middle of it all, still on top of the APC, Josef: standing now, tall, strong, holding a blood red blade taller than a man. Fire, bright red flames burning off the blade.

Not Josef. That is War, and he holds his blade Fury.

Josef threw Fury, the blade tumbling end over end to embed itself in the suited vampire's chest. The thing tried to scream but as it opened its mouth fire poured out, its eyes exploding into flame. Josef reached a hand out, not calling Fury to him but calling himself to Fury. He slipped through the Other Place, closing the distance in an instant, the ropes and cables falling slack to the ground where he'd been. Josef grabbed the hilt of Fury, pulled it out, and the suited vampire exploded in a shower of fire and blood.

He pointed the sword across the room at another vampire. "You are not fast enough," he said again. Threw the sword, again. Pulled himself to it. Again, and again, snapping back and forth across the room, red fire everywhere he hit.

Liselle felt the savage expression on her face, teeth bared. She reached a hand to the sky, felt the barb in her arm pulled, her hand struggling to reach for the heavens.

Scourge. How I've missed our work together. Oh, how she wanted to feel the grip of her sword. But her arm was held by this barb, these ropes. More vampires were grabbing the line, adding their strength to the pull, holding her back.

There was another crack and rumble in the heavens, Scourge answering her call. She could feel the sword as it left a trail of dark smoke through the sky, feel the black burning of the blade as it fell towards the earth. Feel its unending, unquenchable hunger, because she was Famine. Liselle Vitols was a fiction, a shell given to hold purpose.

These vampires thought they knew hunger? She would teach them hunger. The gnawing, empty belly of a baby never fed as its mother died giving birth. The deadly, creeping thirst of a traveler stuck in the desert. The agony of a body eating itself, day after day, as nothing but salted earth stood for miles around. Snow-starved victims of a plane crash, emaciated faces turning on each other with desperate fear. Men and women on a raft in the sea, drinking salt water to their death. A mother so, so hungry that she ate her dead child. Oh, she would teach them hunger.

She was Famine, and no one tethered her to the Father's Eden. She yanked her hand up as the roof exploded in a second place, Scourge hitting her palm with thunderous noise. Vampires were knocked to the ground, some atomized by the Father's light cascading in. She turned black eyes on the vampire nearest her, sweeping Scourge, feeling the blade whisper through the Other Place. Nothing happened for a moment, then the vampire shrieked, clawing its belly, falling on a vampire close to it. Sinking fangs into unsuspecting flesh, hunger beyond hunger driving instinct before reason, action before alliances.

Liselle grabbed at a tether, tearing it from her arm, black blood and smoke falling from her arm. The room around her felt dim, vampires bright sparks of hunger as they leapt and gouged each other. She let the crossbow bolt drop to the ground, swung Scourge about her, the blade hissing and biting as it cut her free. She held it up before her face, closed her eyes. Leaned forward to kiss the blade, then let it go. It fell, dissolving into smoke. That smoke flooded about the room, finding its way into vampires, through their mouths, their eyes, their noses. They screamed, and more clawed and bit at each other.

As they bit each other, they would cough, and choke. Because Kaylan had forbidden them to feed on each other. A safeguard, to keep her empire strong. But hunger, hunger was greater than rules, and it drove madness before it. As they fed on each other, their skin darkened, veins standing out black against their skin. Their eyes would swell, lips bloating, before their bodies ruptured from the inside, dark slime exploding out.

Liselle walked through the chaos, careful, slow, methodical. Her feet were surrounded by Scourge's black smoke. It seeped from vampire to vampire, hated spawn to hated spawn. War swung his Fury, the red fire mingling with the black smoke with terrible purpose. War, and Famine, together.

As it was meant to be.

~

SHE DIDN'T KNOW how much time passed, but there were no vampires standing anymore. War leaned against Fury, and Famine held Scourge over one shoulder.

"That felt good," said War.

Famine nodded, tasting victory. "They are so petty. So tiny."

War looked outside, towards the police and national guard, standing their unsteady ground. "I should speak with them. Warn them."

"Your children will not listen," said Famine. "They are not really your children. They do not know you."

"Then I will teach them," said War. He hefted Fury, striding out into the Father's light. Famine watched him walk, men and women pointing weapons at him. Guns were trained on him the entire time he walked towards their line.

War stopped before he reached their barricades, saying something to them. Gesturing, arms wide. Perhaps telling them that their time was close, or that they should leave. She sighed. It didn't matter. They were all for reaping.

Ah, there it was. The moment where it started to fall apart for them. They weren't listening, of course, weapons still pointed, the discipline of the line still holding. One of the helicopters buzzing overhead cast a shadow. War looked up, and in that moment he was shot. One round turned into a hundred, and his body jerked and stuttered. There was a flash of lightning, stretching from War's body to the heavens, then another, and another, the light and sound massive. Arcs of lightning reached for vehicles, turning them to molten slag. Reached for people, turning bodies into pillars of fire. The helicopter overhead was caught in the bolts from above, liquid metal remains falling in a shower on those who remained alive below.

Famine turned her eyes to the heavens. War was strong, the second strongest of them in these times. You could fire a weapon into a mountain, chip off some rock, perhaps cause an avalanche. But the mountain would remain.

It didn't matter to her. War was gone for the moment, but so were his 'children.' He had to learn that he had no children. He could never have children. Humans weren't for him, couldn't be his family, couldn't be sheltered by him. It didn't matter what a kind man with a gentle voice had said on Golgotha as the life was taken from him. The Riders were made for one purpose: to bring about the end of all things.

Humans weren't for them.

Josef learned it just now. Kaylan and Maynor already knew it. To be a Rider was to know destruction above all. She was happy to see it now, so clearly, with Scourge in her hand and murder in her heart. Humans were chaff, leaves on the wind, dirt in the eddies of an otherwise clear stream.

Humans weren't for *any* of them.

THIRTY-ONE

The gentle clack and rumble of train cars was well behind him, like many of his problems. The future, and only the future, lay ahead of Maksimillian Kotlyarov.

The tunnel was dark, light fixtures infrequently placed. Even when he encountered one, the bulbs were missing, or smashed, as if the light hurt, or was a reminder of the day. And the day was a thing that the *vampir* couldn't tolerate, would erase if they could. It was lucky, *da*, that the sun was so very far away. Safe from their hands and their schemes. Not like—

They made us kill our Pack.

—the people that were close, people that meant something, down here. Like the woman with the green hair. He shook his head. He couldn't get distracted by—

Pack mate.

—feelings, not when he was near to finishing it. He let his teeth show in the dark. Being close, of course, meant that they were close to *him*, to *Maksimillian Kotlyarov*. Close to justice, and revenge, and a return of the Night.

We were ever made to walk alone.

He moved on quiet feet, soft steps making no sound. Not to his ears, and the ears of the Night—

We hunt.

—were the best ears ever made. Maksimillian Kotlyarov knew this to be true. He was bringing them all a surprise. Speaking of surprises, there was something unexpected ahead: a heartbeat. Steady, almost confident in its regular rhythm. He could hear it above the excited rush of blood in his own ears, above the gentle soft trickle of water from somewhere far away. It was a big heart, used to doing big tasks, but big hearts didn't mean generous hearts. Maksimillian had a very big heart, and he—

They made us kill our Pack.

—had the darkest heart he knew. Oh, he was no savior, no hero. That was a job for other men and women who preferred doing the right thing to doing the thing that was necessary. So: this heart he was hearing, it could be good or bad, gentle or hard, sweet or sinister. It was unlikely it was good, gentle, or sweet, as such things had no place in a nest of *vampiry*. Such things only had a place in the sun.

Maksimillian rounded a bend and saw a single man standing. The owner of the heart, leaning against a wall like he owned it. Like he had paid good rubles for this nasty hole in the earth. The man was wearing a tweed jacket, a jaunty cap on his head, a long beard that would be copper in the daylight, and a smile. A huge sword rested against the wall opposite the man. Maksimillian knew that smile, and knew the sword also. The sword was something to be very, very careful of. If it was in the light of the sun, it would be white, not like bones, or even white paint, but white like the heart of the heavens. If the stories were true — and why wouldn't they be? — the sword was made for Christ. This man wasn't Christ though. If the stories were true — and again, why not believe? — Christ was good, and gentle, and sweet. This man wasn't. This man was Maynor Coen, and the sword was Stroke.

"Ah, Maksimillian." Maynor touched the brim of his hat in the darkness. "I was hoping I would see you before the end."

"It is," said Maksimillian, "your lucky day, *da*?" He thought for a moment. "I think it is mine too. I have always wanted to kill you."

Maynor *tsk*'d. "Maksimillian, you can't kill me."

Maksimillian laughed. "Is easy. I take heart, *da*? And tear from your chest." He made a reaching, wrenching motion. "Just so."

"Assuming for a moment you *can*, I'll come back," said Maynor. "You just can't keep a good man down."

"What about a bad man?" said Maksimillian. "As we are both bad, bad men. Speaking to each other, here in the belly of the world. Where all," and he gestured to the walls around them, as if they would agree, "is darkness and hate."

"All four Swords have been drawn, Maks," said Maynor. "Do you mind if I call you Maks? Or would you prefer Volk?"

Maksimillian shrugged. The woman with the green hair—

Pack mate.

—had called him Maks, and it felt right. Better than Volk, who was always a deceiver. Maks was someone who could, in the right light, be a friend. Or if that was too much of a stretch, he could not be your enemy, at least for today, *da*? "Maynor," he said, "you may call me Maks. Do you mind if I, in turn, call you something shorter? Perhaps evil, slime, scum, a crawling roach, something that should be scraped from the bottom of a boot—"

"Maynor's fine," said Maynor, his smile dimming for a moment.

"I feel like," said Maks, "we haven't spent the time to get to know each other. You think I am some lone wolf, *da*? A man with no plan."

"I think you're the end of a very bad mistake," said Maynor. "You carry a weapon that was stolen from me and mine."

"*Da*," agreed Maks.

"I'm here to take it back," said Maynor. "And by 'take it back,' I mean I'm here to kill you. And you, Maks, won't come back."

Maks held up a hand. "May I tell a story? One that perhaps may shed some light on why two bad men like us are here."

"I'm all ears," said Maynor. He made a show of checking his watch — expensive, with many dials.

301

"Is class, *da?*" said Maks. "At school. There is many people in class. Boys and girls, and of course I am there. The man with no plan, as you say."

"I did say, yeah."

"Who is teaching class but Pestilence? One of the finest Horsepersons to ever ride." Maks smiled, hoping Maynor could see his expression. Jokes needed the correct delivery. "And Pestilence, he is teaching important lesson. About cleverness, and having a plan. And in class is poor Maksimillian Kotlyarov, young, inexperienced, and with no plan."

"I like where this is going," said Maynor, reaching for Stroke.

"One moment," said Maks, holding up a hand. Maynor paused. "I have not finished story, *da?* Call it dying wish."

"Fine," said Maynor, leaning back.

"Thank you," said Maks. "Pestilence says to all boys and girls, and of course young Maksimillian, 'Please stand up if you think you are young, and stupid, and have no plan.' After a moment, Maksimillian stands up. And Pestilence nods, and says, 'Maksimillian, are you saying you are young, and foolish, and have no plan?'" Maks smiled wider. "And young Maksimillian said, 'No, friend. I just did not want to see you standing there by yourself.'"

Maynor blinked in the darkness once, then roared, reaching for his sword. Maks knew how this fight would go. First, Maynor would swing at him with Stroke, the mighty weapon cutting through the tunnel's wall on its way to him. The weapon would blaze with bright light, causing blindness. It would go for Maksimillian's heart, seeking to cut out the weapon he carried, to erase the mistake. And then Maks would die.

That wouldn't do at all.

Maks wasn't ready to die. *Yeshche nyet.* Certainly not now, when he was so close. So he moved faster, faster than Maynor, fast enough to reach Stroke a whisker of time after Maynor. Maynor's hands were on the sword, but Maks's hands were on Maynor's. Maks and Maynor were shoulder to shoulder. Maynor was yelling, making all kinds of noises, and struggling against Maks's grip. But—

THEY MADE US KILL OUR PACK.

—anger made Maks strong, stronger than the *vampiry*, stronger than this *Vsadnik*, and he bared his own teeth. Maynor caught a glimpse of those teeth in the dark, a panicked expression crossing his face. Maks held Maynor still as stone, hard as iron, Stroke's blade trembling as they matched will to will, strength to strength.

Maynor seemed to focus for a moment, Stroke blazing bright for a moment, white smoke pouring from the blade, filling the air around them. Maks grinned, and breathed in the smoke. Best for this enemy of his—

Smallpox. Boils breaking through the skin. Polio, terrible weakness stealing a man's ability to even draw breath. The Black Death, migrating up from what was now Asia, killing through pustules, and gangrene, and pain. Diseases born by a terrible mind, all designed to kill, but kill in the worst way: alone. Those infected would be separated, to live out their few remaining days in pain and blindness and despair as their bodies rotted around them.

—to see that the Night did not age. It couldn't be poisoned. It didn't get brittle with time.

And it most certainly did not get sick.

"I like," said Maks, teeth gritted, "that you tried." And he turned, hard and fast, pulling Stroke from Maynor. Felt the terrible weight of the blade, a weight that the Night wasn't meant to carry. So heavy, that sword. But the Night was strong, strongest when—

THEY.

MADE.

US.

KILL.

OUR.

PACK.

—it was angry, the red rage rising to destroy all. Maksimillian felt that rage, that anger built through thousands of years. Thousands of years of not-death, living past everyone. Held Stroke, his muscles bunching with the effort. Held Stroke above his head, and cut down, one perfect cut starting at Maynor's shoulder and exiting through the opposite hip. The weapon flared, white fire blasting out from Maynor's body, and Pestilence fell.

Stroke's blade was buried in the floor. Maksimillian panted, wanting to—

We will kill them all.

—rend something, tear something else, to pull limbs from bodies.

The sky will open.

The sky will open? Recollection, a memory almost forgotten came to Maks's mind, and he threw himself back down the tunnel. Just in time, as the tunnel filled with lightning, strike after strike coursing through the walls. A stray arc hit Maks, the fire of it burning him, his skin shredding off one side, and he screamed with the exquisite, beautiful, pure pain of it.

Darkness.

~

DARKNESS.

Maks sat up, his face, side, both feeling like they were on fire. Not that they were burning, that had already happened, but burns were a funny thing. Not funny as in, *ha ha Maksimillian, that is a fine joke*, but funny as in they were a thing you did not want or need. They would heal, given time, and food.

So hungry.

He pulled himself to his feet, yellow eyes looking through the gloom. A small shaft of light led above ground where the lightning had burned to Maynor's body, taking him back to wherever they went when they died. The sword Stroke was still here, white blade catching the light. It was stuck into the ground on an angle, blade clean, like it had drunk Maynor's blood.

"Ah, Maynor," he said. "When we tricked you before, you were so angry. But you didn't learn. You gave me a sickness I can't die from, and tried to kill me with another sickness. You must get better plan."

Maynor didn't answer, because there was nothing left of him here. He wouldn't be back for a little while. How long was difficult to know, but until then, Maks had his sword.

He gritted his teeth, grabbed the hilt of Stroke, and tore the sword from the earth.

We hunt.

CHAPTER
THIRTY-TWO

The rumble of thunder sounded from somewhere, faint, but still there. A moment later, another rumble.

Adalia watched Kaylan look up at the stone ceiling, Death's face going blank. She was beautiful like Liselle, but terrible too, and Liselle wasn't terrible. Liselle was soft and caring and good, and shouldn't be a Horseperson at all. Pinned here against the wall *by her throat* — held there by Death herself — Adalia could see what it meant to be a Horseperson.

"Uh," said Adalia, having trouble getting the word out. It sounded more like *hrk* than *uh*. "Sounds bad, yeah?" *Srds bd hrk eh*.

Kaylan's head snapped towards her again, dark, perfect eyes examining Adalia. Almost like she was being dissected with them. "Only for you," she said.

It was time for courage. Not the kind of courage that Uncle John had, where he just talked until people got confused, or the kind of courage her mom had, where she would stand against a wall of fire and scream at it. Or the kind of courage of Val, who would hold you behind him so nothing could reach you. Not even like Rex, who was tired of other people not having courage, or Jessica, who wanted to save someone who was already dead. And, sadly, not like Melissa, who would stand still while a hundred people cut her again and again, because someone had to stand there, and if being cut was what it took, then she'd stand there and be cut. And then punch them. It was time for courage like Adalia, except she didn't know what that was.

Mary might know, if she were here.

"Kaylan," she said, "there should be no lies between us." *Klrn urk. Thurk shld be urk nnnn urk lees urk b tween urks.*

A smile played against Kaylan's face, and it reminded Adalia of one of those video games of Uncle John's, where some graphic artist doing 120-hour weeks had tried to make a human face smile, except they were jacked up on caffeine and hadn't seen their kids in about a year. That artist would be sitting there thinking *God damn but I need this face to smile, except I don't remember what other people look like because I'm in this stupid cubicle, but fuckit, it's just got to ship, we'll fix it in post*, and made this thing on the screen smile like Chucky, not just nasty but *wrong*. "Why ever not?" she said. But her grip slackened, just enough for Adalia to be able to speak easier.

"Because it's a waste of time," she said, and knew Mary would be pleased with that kind of answer. "You know I can tell. You're really only lying to yourself. Which just shows you don't really want it." Adalia paused. "Also, you should put me down, because you're not going to kill me, because you would have already if you were going to, which means you're not. This is just awkward, like family photos at weddings, which you won't have been to, and I haven't either, but I'd like to."

Kaylan let her slide down the wall, turning away. She spoke to Anatolie. "*Vay' chay'pen 'aHa'ba lulegh ngeH.*"

"*Ta' 'oH,*" said Anatolie, slipping from his chair. He started giving orders to the vampires around him.

"That is a weird language," said Adalia.

"You will give me what I want," said Kaylan, "or I will tear the life from you, and put it back, only to do it again."

Mary would have huffed here. "Kaylan, no lies."

"I mean it," said the avatar of Death. Which was unusual, right, to be having an actual conversation with the avatar of Death, one of the four Horsepersons. If Adalia hadn't met Liselle, it might have been hard to swallow, but she'd seen how Liselle looked at Uncle John, and knew what that meant. It meant they weren't all terrible, and weren't all perfect, even if they looked like it.

"I know you *mean* it," said Adalia. "I also know you can't *do* it."

"I can—"

"Look, look, look, okay," said Adalia, patting the air with her hands. "I can see the Other Place too. I know the rules. Rules you've ... bent ... by making these—" and here, she pointed at Constanta "—things. I know that once you've taken someone, they can't be brought back. I know where the dead go when they die, Kaylan. I know." She didn't say, *I brought someone back, and it was against the rules, and I'm sure that's why everything is wrong now.*

"What about if I kill John Miles?" said Kaylan.

"Well that's one option," said Adalia, "but I feel like we're getting ahead of ourselves."

Kaylan looked at her, head tilted sideways like she was wondering what manner of creature she was looking at. "Ahead? Of ourselves?"

Adalia sighed. "This will go a lot faster if we just agree some things up front. First, I'm not all 'wow'd'" —and here, she made little air quotes "—by you. I've spent the last ten years of my life, which is actually half of the years I've been alive, running around with a werewolf pack. I have seen *vodou* priests, and zombies, and vampires, and I'm sure I'll see another ten amazing things before I die." She took a breath, sure Mary would be encouraging her on at this point. "Second, you haven't actually told me what you want, so going all Big Bad Wolf and threatening to blow my house down is, what, premature? So could you, like, start at the beginning."

"I want you to take away the terrible effects of the sun from my vampires," said Kaylan.

"You want me to make them unstoppable monsters that will end the world," said Adalia.

"Yes," said Kaylan.

Anatolie sauntered back in, threw a glance at Adalia, then said to Kaylan, "*QaSlaH wej ghom, Ha' qoD tu'lu'. QaStaH police je QI' wovbe'. Wa'vatlh maHvaD* massacred *be'nI' loDnI'wI' je.*" Funny, that one English word in there.

"*HoH,*" said Kaylan.

"*Chay'pen 'e' Qu',*" said Anatolie. "That was my whole thing."

Kaylan waved him away, turning back to Adalia. "Will you help me?"

Adalia looked between Kaylan and Anatolie. "What language are you speaking? I thought I could at least grab a hold of most of them, but this one..."

"It's not common," said Kaylan. "It was Dragomir's idea."

"Who's Dragomir?" said Adalia.

"Dragomir is Viorica's lover," said Kaylan.

"I think I see where this is going," said Adalia. "Say no more."

"I need your answer," said Kaylan.

"About whether I'm going to use the Other Place to make vampires that can walk in the sun and kill everything on earth?"

"Yes," said Kaylan.

"I think we'll have trouble coming to an agreement on that one," said Adalia. "What's the second option?"

"They will still kill everything on Father's Eden," said Kaylan, answering a question Adalia hadn't asked. Or just making a statement, because she liked to hear herself talk. "They're too perfect. Too good at killing, and making other vampires. And always hungry for more, because of how we made them."

"Mis-made, maybe," said Adalia. "Liselle didn't help you, did she?"

"She is soft-headed," said Kaylan.

"Figures," said Adalia. "You'd want Famine on the team to make sure the whole hunger thing worked right. Anyway. Second option?"

"Everything still dies, but slower, and I kill you, and John Miles, to start with. Then I kill Danielle Kendrick, and Valentine Everard, and Melissa Carlisle, and Jessica Pearce. I will save Rex Aubrey for last, because he believes he has lived a good and useful life, and that will hurt him most of all. If you help me, you still die, but I promise. I'll leave you until the very end. You will live the longest of any ... humans. You will live out your allotted span. Together."

"Two things," said Adalia. She really hoped Mary had her back on this one. "First, if everyone is going to die anyway, except us, who will live alone in a barren wasteland for a few more years, well, you're not really incentivizing me here. Second, and I mean this from my heart, you're a *real* cunt."

Kaylan's slap caught Adalia on the side of the face, left her head ringing, the taste of copper in her mouth. She was on the floor, and didn't remember how she got there, and one of her teeth was loose. More than one? Definitely one at least on the side Kaylan had hit her, and she couldn't see out of that eye. Adalia spat on the ground, because she wanted to throw up but didn't want to in front of Kaylan, so that was a kind of compromise she could live with, and saw a tooth and some blood there, and that wasn't good.

Kaylan towered above her, all beautiful and terrible. "It's not whether they die," she said. "It's the manner of their death that should concern you. Death can be soft, and kind, a release at the end of a life well lived. Or it can be done alone, in terror and pain."

"Why," said Adalia, "are you so beautiful?"

"Because Death is beautiful," said Kaylan. She turned to Constanta this time, and said, "*Qem* John Miles."

Adalia didn't know what that language was, but she could guess at the intent. She wasn't 100% sure what was coming next, but she did know Kaylan was *still* lying to her. To her!

Death wasn't beautiful. Not at all.

THIRTY-THREE

The lights were too bright, the shadows too dark. Everything jarred. Just the way she liked it.

We need to help them stay alive. Because they came here to help us.

She growled, and the big one with orange hair took a step back. She watched him check himself, reverse and retake that step. If her face could have done so she would have smiled. He—

Ginger. His name is Ginger.

—didn't lack courage. So many of the humans failed to be brave when tooth matched claw, when fangs found flesh and the hot, sweet salty hot within. It wasn't who would win. That was always known. The biggest took the prize. It was how you won or lost that made you worthy of the hunt.

Our daughter is small. Do you judge her by her size? She has done amazing things. She freed us from a cage made of silver—

Hated, vile metal.

—when we were lost. Do you remember?

She remembered. There were many things she didn't remember. Her memory felt like a cloak of animal skins patched many times against the cold and wet of the world. The further back she went, the less she could recall. Fragments. Some memories were too painful—

You talk of courage, but you can't look there. Can you?

—to remember. Some were bright like the sun. Paws padding silent against the earth as she hunted. Teeth bared as she struck—

Those memories are base. You can do better. Look where it hurts.

Where it hurts? The dark place in her mind.

Yes. The place where Volk is.

That one was crazy. The oldest living of them by far, and it had driven him mad. To remember everything was to go mad, like that one.

Yes. It drove him mad. But if you see how, maybe we can stop it happening to us.

No. All she needed to know was that he had killed his Pack, and she would never do that. It was false, like wearing silver or being friends with the vampire, their enemy.

And yet here we are. Friends with a vampire. You remember his name?

Jeremy. The thing wanted to be called *Jeremy*, as if a name could change its nature, make it safe. It was walking up to her now, head tilted up to look at her. She hunkered down on big haunches, better to look it in the eyes. Which were normal, human-like eyes, not mirrored like the hated, burning metal. It slowed as it got closer, cautious, careful.

"So," it said. "So. Uh."

She waited. A low growl escaped, because she was still so hungry. One corpse did not a meal make.

"Right," it said. "Look, there's a thing. The ... we're going to have to go lower, because there's not a clear path from the, uh, sanctum, uh, to here. What would be super cool, and I mean really fucking frosty, is if you could hold the growls *in* and not kill anyone until they open the door. Can you do that for me?"

She leaned forward, and it took a fearful step back. Again she wished for that human ability to smile, but she settled for showing her teeth.

"Uh," it said. "Cool, I'll take that as a big ol' yes." It turned to the orange-headed one—

Ginger. Is it so hard to remember their names?

—Ginger, and said, "You got that?"

Ginger said, "You want us to go further into this nest of monsters so we can help a werewolf get out." He looked at his feet, then back at the vampire. "A *werewolf*."

"Yeah," said the vampire—

Jeremy. Jeremy. Jeremy.

—Jeremy. "That's what I want, because the werewolf is not the problem. It's the young woman and her uncle that I think need our help." He jerked his head back at her. "These things can almost take care of themselves."

She should end it for that slight, but—

Remember how he came into our home and tossed us around like a bunch of toys?

—it had a point. She watched as the rest of the humans—

Soldiers. Who could become friends.

—who wouldn't live to see the end of today picked up their equipment. One of them was still battered around, hurt inside—

Lindle. Her name is Lindle.

—but Lindle was still moving forward, still trying to help. Perhaps more than just the big one had courage, then.

The vampire led the way, holding up a hand at a junction in the tunnel. The walls here were strange, half-rock and half of those small stones that humans set next to each other. Some of the walls were damp, and all of them felt wrong. Being under the earth, where there was no sun or moon, was not the place she wanted to be. Not the place she wanted to hunt, but they had her cub. And she would get her cub back.

Focus.

She shook her muzzle, tongue licking her teeth, and tried not to growl. It was hard, because everything was strange, but it would be easier to get her cub, so she kept her peace.

The vampire was speaking to someone, or something, around the corner. *"MInDu'lIj Da'elDI'."* She knew many of the languages of humans, and this one wasn't familiar to her.

The thing Jeremy—

Good work. You remembered his name.

—was speaking to around the corner — definitely a vampire, because she could hear no heartbeat — replied in the same language. *"Jatlh* Anatolie *ngaQ vI'ogh."*

Jeremy didn't look back at them as he spoke. *"LaH Hegh* Anatolie *qaStaHvIS qul. MInDu'lIj Da'elDI'."*

The other vampire said, *"Lu', lu'. cha'DIch HInob."* There was the sound of bolts being drawn, big locks of metal, and she smelled something on the air. The hated metal. Perhaps that door was lined with it — a thing other humans had done before, to keep her kind out.

Jeremy sauntered forward, and she leapt around the corner, following his tracks. She bounced off the opposite wall, around Jeremy, and lunged at the other vampire. It didn't even have enough time to look surprised before her jaws crunched around its skull. She suckled at the body's blood, lapping at the neck's stump, before crunching into the chest.

"That is fucking gruesome," said Mallory, walking slowly past her. She continued to chew, yellow eyes watching the soldier.

"It's a good solution," said Jeremy. "She won't eat us, and the fucking vampires won't come back from the dead. Win-win, I think they call it."

"Not very win for the dead vampire," said Sawyer Diego.

"Fuck those guys," said Finch. She was the last through after Brindle, closing the door behind her.

She continued her meal. Sawyer Diego walked up to her, said, "Cool, fucking cool," but not like he meant it, and then turned to Jeremy. "What language you speaking? I can order beer in at least seven and I don't even know that one."

Jeremy said, "Klingon."

"Say what?"

"Klingon," said Jeremy. "Look, you get a bunch of people together who are all Millennials and ask them to learn Hebrew or Ancient Latin or whatever and you've got two basic problems. First, every asshole knows them. Grave robbers or, I guess they're called archae-ologists, they know those, so it's not a great method of communica-tion for secure conversation. Second, Millennials don't want to learn Hebrew or Ancient Latin, but you say, 'Yo, our secret club's language is Klingon,' and they're all on board."

"Never thought of it that way," said Sawyer Diego.

"To be fair, you've only just heard about it," said Jeremy. He clapped his hands. "Okay, team. Here's where it's at." He was pointing to the exits from the room. "That one leads to the dorms. Don't go down there or you'll fucking die. That one there goes to the lounge area."

"What's in the lounge area?" said Lindle.

"It's where we torture humans and shit," said Jeremy. "Don't go there either. Finally, this last tunnel—" and he gestured at a wide corridor leading down and away "—leads to the sanctum. If I was Anatolie, I would have them down there. Beyond that's the prisoner wing, so if they're not in the sanctum we can keep going."

"Hold up," said Ginger. "We just got to hold the line. And..." He coughed, looking up at her. She had almost finished her meal, worrying at a thigh bone. "Well, so, what if they're in the, what did you call it, the *lounge* area?"

"Won't be," said Jeremy. "You don't kidnap the secret power of the Universe and then play with them like you're an extra in Saw."

"Never liked those movies," said Ginger.

"Me neither," said Jeremy. "Thing is, we need to go to the sanc-tum. To your other point, there's cameras and alarms all over this place. We'll be balls-deep in vampire scum if we don't keep moving."

"That's not ... that's not a great analogy," said Lindle.

The first vampire burst out of the tunnel—

Dormitory. I didn't know they slept.

315

—to her left, a cloud of locusts that settled on Bryn. The man was swatting and sweeping his arms, then the vampire formed out of the cloud of insects and Bryn was just ... *gone*. A spray of blood, and there was a vampire licking its fangs and smiling, two wet sides of Bryn, one for each hand.

"Motherfuckers!" screamed Lindle, pulling the trigger on her machine gun. The sound was deafening in the small room. The vampire dodged to the side with ease, moving faster—

They are so fast. Be careful.

—than should have been possible. Another one surged into the room in a cloud of locusts, and Mallory caught at least half of the cloud in a blast from his flamethrower. He also caught Lindle in the blast and she screamed, high and keening, as she turned into a pillar of burning fat and meat.

Help her. We've got to help her.

She snarled, grabbed Lindle, and snapped her neck with a twist. The keening stopped. She lunged at a shape, snared a vampire as it was forming, and bit down into it, rending it. *Their* vampire Jeremy was moving around the room with unholy speed, snapping a punch here, a kick there, just enough to push an enemy into the line of fire, to be caught and twisted by explosive rounds or the rush of fire from a flamethrower.

We will die in this room.

A vampire was on her left arm, another on her right, and they were pulling her apart. She flexed, but they were so strong. Another leapt on her back, reared up, and punched a hand through her back. She felt the pain of it as the creature clawed at her insides.

We will die and never see our Adalia again.

The vampires on her arms were pulling harder, and she felt like she might come apart.

They will hurt her worse than this.

She roared, denying it, denying death. Challenging death. Here, under rock and stone below the city, where no sun shone above, no moon hung in the sky, and no stars, she roared out her rage. It gave her the strength she needed, and she snatched the vampires on each arm, smashing them together in front of her into a pulp. She reached a clawed hand behind her, grabbed the vampire that clung there, that clung to the *inside of her*, and wrenched it off. Something inside her came out, and she coughed blood from her muzzle. But she didn't die. And if she didn't die—

She will die alone, our baby will die alone.

—she would kill them all. All of them, every one. A quick tearing motion and the vampire she held was in two pieces. She swiped at another, and it burst into a cloud of locusts.

It will move to the other side. See? See how they move? They vanish only to reappear on our blind side.

Reversing her motion, trusting to the tiny voice inside her, she swung at what should have been empty air. But the vampire's locust cloud reformed, and her claws slashed through it, three separate bloody chunks of the thing falling to the ground.

She ducked, and danced, and fought, all to the hammer of gunfire, the rush of fire, the smell of blood, the tangy sweet taste of it. Through it all, she hurt. Hurt inside, in a way that she had never hurt before. Some brought fire. Some brought silver. Some brought fangs. But she kept going. Over and over again.

Until it was done.

"Hey. She's coming round."

Danny blinked, vision blurry, and coughed. She tried to get up, but something in her chest hurt, wasn't working right, and she tasted blood. Her blood. She was covered in gore, marks and cuts all over her. She wasn't healing. *She wasn't healing.*

"It's cool," said the voice, and she focused. Sawyer Diego. "You, uh, saved us." He looked small in the dim light. Sawyer looked behind him, and then said, "Well, some of us. There's just Ginger and me. And you."

Danny made herself focus. *Get up.* She made it to an elbow, then to a crouch. "Jeremy," she said.

"Gone," said Sawyer Diego. "There's about a hundred bodies in here. I haven't checked 'em all yet. But ... yeah, he's gone."

She could see the pain in his face. Not for Jeremy, but for the names he wasn't saying. "I'm ... sorry."

"Yeah," he said. "Hold the line, right?" He handed her some clothes, a pile of what would have been blood stained rags in other circumstances.

She accepted them with a nod, started pulling them on. Cold, and wet, and sticky. "I'm sorry," she said again. "We'll hold the line. But when we're done, we'll remember them. Bryn. Mallory. Lindle. And Finch." She had to catch herself against the wall, a wave of blackness sweeping over her. *She wasn't healing.*

She was dying.

"You know their names?" he said. He seemed surprised. "Most people don't ... *invest*, you know?"

We will remember those who fight for us.

She sagged a little, with relief or pain she wasn't sure. *You're still there.* "I'm not most people," she said.

"True," he said, "true."

Ginger walked over, some of his saunter gone, but anger replaced it, making him stiff. He hefted a machine gun, held it to her. "Here."

She took it from him, stumbling a little with the unexpected weight. "Thanks."

He gave her a skeptical look. "You going to be okay to hold that? You seem ... a little knocked around."

"All your people died," she said. Danny didn't want to answer his question, because of what the answer meant.

"They did, except for Sawyer Diego," said Ginger.

"Told you I'd be the one to make it out alive," said Sawyer Diego.

"I don't think any of us are making it out alive," said Ginger. "But we'll die the right way. Which means you got to hold that gun, fire it at the bad guys, and keep firing it until it's empty, you hear me?"

So tired.

She looked at the gun. Felt the pain in her chest, how much everything hurt, like it hadn't in a long time, if ever. Like she was going to just ... *stop* ... if she fell down again. *It's okay. Sleep now. I'll carry us for a little while.* "I hear you," she said. Her Valentine was down there, and would bring her Adalia with him when he came. She turned the barrel towards the tunnel Jeremy had said led to the Sanctum. *"Let them come."*

CHAPTER
THIRTY-FOUR

He pushed the vampire's body into the water, watching it sink. Odd — most bodies didn't sink that fast, not that soon. Didn't much matter, it was dead enough for now, but a weird fact he might have time to think about later. If there was a later.

There will be time enough, tiny human.

Val smiled in the dark. *Still there.*

Still here.

Carlisle walked up behind him. "Hey."

"Hey," he said.

"You good?"

"Never better," he said. He gave her a glance, smoke smudges on her face, some of her hair singed. Still standing strong, both guns held like she meant to use them again before the day was done. "You?"

"I'm almost middle aged," she said. Her mouth quirked.

"That's a killer," he agreed. "You got enough left to open that door?" He nodded at the big door in front of them, a massive wheel set in the face of it.

Hated, burning metal.

"Silver?" she said.

"Yeah," he said. "It makes me feel funny in my tummy."

"Copy that," she said. She turned over her shoulder. "Rex."

"Hey," said Rex, approaching them. He still had a shotgun and a grenade launcher, but the grenade launcher wasn't pointed anywhere but down.

"Door," she said.

"It is," he said.

"I mean, you should open it," she said.

"Why me?" said Rex.

"Because you're so big and strong," she said. "Also, because you almost killed us all. And also, because if there's anything going to come out of there and eat our faces, I want first shot. It's only fair."

Rex considered that for a second. "Okay," he said. He looked at the Glock she held. "Don't shoot me."

"I'll try not to," said Carlisle, "but I make no promises."

"Rear is clear," said Jessie, sauntering up. "I feel like an asshole, carrying both these guns." She hefted the machine gun. "This one seems to be all you need for this kind of evening."

"Cheer up," said Carlisle. "I've been on worse dates."

"Me too," said Jessica.

Rex was at the door, hand on the wheel. Val watched as he gripped it, then placed a hand on Rex's shoulder. "One second."

Rex sighed. "What is it?"

"Let me go in first. After, you know, you open it." Val shrugged. "I'll probably survive the longest."

"Son," said Rex, "you misunderstand. I'm not opening this door and going through. I'm just opening it. After that, I'm off the clock."

Val gave him a grin. He clapped the man on the shoulder. "Thank you."

"For what?" said Rex.

"Everything," said Val.

"Sure," said Rex. He put his hands back on the wheel, giving it a turn. The metal groaned, something mechanical inside the door *clank*ing as he turned the wheel. After a few rotations it looked like it freed up, spinning. Rex stood back, then held out a hand in an *after you* gesture. "Your nightmare awaits."

We are their nightmare.

"Something like that," said Val, putting his hand on the safe—

Not silver. Not hated.

—metal of the door and pushing it open.

IT WAS A SHORT TRIP, not because the walk was easy — it was — but because there was a lack of guards. No vampires. No humans. No super-powered aliens, robots, or overlords from another dimension, all of which would fail to surprise Val at this point. What *was* a surprise was Volk, who was waiting at the top of some stairs with a giant sword resting against the wall next to him. Val could hear him before he smelled him, and smelled him before he saw him. You never forgot the scent of your maker.

Pack father.

"Kinda sorta," said Val, looking up the stairs at Volk. "I'm not real comfortable with this whole situation."

"Talking to yourself again?" said Carlisle.

"No. It's ... fine, yes, that's what I'm doing," said Val.

"You want me to shoot that asshole?" she said. "I brought silver rounds."

"*Nyet,*" said Volk. "You did not. If you had, I could smell them. And I do not smell them."

Carlisle gave Val a sour look. "Hard to put one past you fuckers, isn't it?"

Val spread his hands in a *what-can-you-do* gesture. "Just being generally annoying comes with the job description."

"*Da,*" agreed Volk, making no move. Which was a promising sign

322

as far as Val was concerned. The sword he had was familiar, like his should know it from somewhere—

The air was hot, the crowd yelling for blood. Not for his blood, but the blood of a man who made beautiful things. That man was tied — no, not tied, nailed — to a cross, blood streaming from his wrists. Maksimillian crouched some distance away. Curiosity had drawn him here, and curiosity kept him here. The wind had whispered to him, telling a story of a man who could work miracles.

This man was in no position to work miracles. He was dying, and if he didn't die fast enough the crowd would tear him apart.

Between the crowd and the man on the cross were four people. The crowd brayed and surged, but the four people didn't move. One held a black blade high, the other three holding similar swords but of different colors. They were cloaked and hooded, but some trick of the weather stirred that hot air for a second, just enough to tug the hood of the one holding the black blade. Maksimillian took in the perfect features, the cruel lips—

Liselle. Val knew that face, just not the way she wore it. The Liselle Val knew wasn't anything like this one, all anger and justice and vengeance.

—holding a sneer. She turned back to the other three, her voice hard, and loud, carrying across the crowd and their hate and fear. "בואי, אחים. בואי, אחותי. אנחנו נכה אותם מעדן. זה הזמן." *The language wasn't unfamiliar, the meaning clear.* Come, brothers. Come, sister. We will strike them from Eden. It is time.

The other three raised their blades. Red for War. A pale sword, translucent, for Death. And purest white for Pestilence. They readied their charge. The man on the cross raised his head. "אתה יכול להיות הרבה יותר מזה." *You could be so much more than this. He said other things, about choice, and about saving being harder than destroying, and how it was here that could be the end of all things or the beginning of everything. Maksimillian wasn't listening to his words, but the effect was clear.*

Curiosity had brought him. But astonishment kept him here. These were the Riders, and this dying man was using words, words without any special power, to stop them ending the world. To stop those terrible swords from falling. Because when all four blades were bared to the sun, the world must end.

"Huh," said Val. "That's Stroke, isn't it?"

"*Da*," said Volk. "I have seen it before. This you know."

"I know it," said Val. "I ... remember it. What I'm a bit puzzled about is how you're able to lift it."

"That," said Volk, "is easy and hard. It is hard to kill your Pack, *da*? But once you have, the anger it gives you will move mountains."

"Good talk," said Val, after a moment. *Still crazy — check.* "What are you going to do with it?"

"I will kill Death," said Volk.

"That ... seems an oxymoron."

"What is this 'oxymoron?'" said Volk. "This *Angliyskiy* is difficult to fathom. Even after so much practice."

"It means you're a moron," said Carlisle. She looked at Val. "What are we doing here?"

Val looked past her, back at Rex, and Jessica, and then back to Volk. "Like the man says. We're going to kill Death."

Carlisle studied him for a cool second. "This motherfucker," she said, "tried to kill you at least twice I know of."

"Third time's the charm," said Val. "I'm not really cool with it either, but I see nothing but poor options. First, we can try to kill him, which would be difficult at the best of times, and harder since he's got Stroke."

"Stroke's that sword?" Carlisle looked doubtful.

"The same," said Val. "It's the sword carried by Pestilence, one of the four Horsepersons of the Apocalypse."

"Where's Pestilence?" she said. "Isn't he going to come looking for his sword?"

"*Da*," said Volk. "I hope for this! Killing Maynor Coen once was not enough for Maksimillian Kotlyarov."

"The second option," said Val, before they burned more time they didn't have, "is that we go with him, and ride this crazy bronco all the way. And because a business case always needs three options, our third option would be to turn around and go home."

"I'm not going home," said Rex. "Son? I'm not going home."

"Me neither," said Jessica. She was looking up at Volk, measuring.

"No," said Carlisle. "I don't have a fourth option."

"Then we will kill Death," said Volk, "together."

Pack.

"I THINK YOU SHOULD GO FIRST," said Val, "because you have the sword of Pestilence. That's kind of an ace in the hole, right?"

Volk looked at him sideways. "*Nyet.*"

"No?"

"*Nyet,*" set Volk. "Is not good tactics for enemy to see sword first. Better for them to see unarmed man."

"I'm hardly unarmed," said Val. "That's like saying a saber-toothed tiger is unarmed."

"They're extinct," said Rex.

"Not helping," said Carlisle.

They were all bunched up outside a door, this a plain wooden one. They were talking in hushed whispers. Which made Val feel like he was ten years old again, sneaking around outside school, which he'd failed at, and got grounded (who grounds a ten year old? And what does that even mean?). It had left him with a deep discomfort of hushed whispers. What gave him deeper discomfort right this particular second was the smell. Silver, and—

Hated. Burning.

—lots of it. Behind this door was the Fort Knox equivalent of *all the silver*. Going in there wouldn't be happy times. The vampires knew their strengths; here they were underground away from the burning sun, and they had the metal that could kill werewolves. As if being a vampire weren't enough, because they could suck all the blood out of a werewolf and kill that way. Val did not want to go through that door.

Then he heard John's voice. John, saying something like *go fuck yourself*.

Val straightened, took a quick step, and kicked the door clear off its hinges. The wood splintered, the frame falling loose, the door itself tumbling into the room beyond, shedding wood chips as it tumbled end over end. It collected a surprised person — vampire? — on the way, who fell over. He stepped into the room before the door had stopped moving, grabbing the first person he encountered — definitely vampire — and smashing them against the ground.

"*Da*," said Volk, in the moment of silence that followed. "Is how to do it. See? Is good entrance."

The room was large, and had an unexpected cast of players. There was John, bent backward over a table, another man's — vampire's? — hand at his throat. This wasn't that unusual, Val had wanted to choke John a few times in his life. What was unusual was that Death was here. It wasn't every day that you saw Death. There were about ten other people — *vampires, definitely vampires* — in the room. Adalia was off to one side, looking angry and frightened at the same time. There were a couple of vampires looking at her. It was difficult to tell if they were threatening her or standing guard or making a prayer circle.

Probably not a prayer circle.

There was silver everywhere. Fucking *everywhere*. Swords of it. Maces with heads of silver, with spikes of silver for added effect. Knives made of solid silver, or steel blades edged with silver. A female vampire by the far wall had a glove — *gauntlet, if it's a metal glove it's a gauntlet* — made of silver, sharp edges and needle points. It looked nasty, not just because it was made of silver. Or the vampire looked nasty. Or both.

Some of the vampires looked familiar. One especially so. Jeremy.

"Sup," said Jeremy. He was standing on the other side of the room, looking like he'd just come through the door there. He was covered in blood and gore but none of it looked like it had come out of him. He didn't seem to be carrying anything made of silver.

"In the middle of some important wolf stuff," said Val. Jeremy here, alone, was bad—

Where is our mate?

—because Danny was supposed to be with him. "Aren't you with the evac team? Is Danny okay?" Val took a step forward, and the vampire holding John gave him a cautionary shake. Val stopped.

"She's fine," said Jeremy. He looked around the room. "Looks like everyone's here."

"You know this ... thing?" said the vampire holding John. He was looking at Jeremy as he said it.

"The dude you're holding, or the dude who kicked the door in?" said Jeremy.

The vampire holding John looked at John, then at Val, then back at Jeremy. "Both."

"Dude you're holding is an extra in the action game of life," said Jeremy. "I know him."

"The werewolf?"

"He's a werewolf," said Jeremy. "Look, Anatolie, I've come for a chat."

"You are in no position to make demands," said Death.

"Kaylan," said Jeremy. "Been a while. Look, I know you don't grok people so well, so here's a thing. I haven't made any demands."

"But—"

"It's cool, demands are coming," said Jeremy, winking at her. He looked at Val. "Did you come in here with any sort of plan?"

"I was going to kill everyone," said Val, shrugging. "Seemed the right thing to do."

"It's a good outline," said Jeremy.

There was a rumble from above, and everyone looked up. A moment later, the roof blasted in in a shower of rubble. Death's sword, blade so pale you could see through it, was stuck blade-first in the floor, vibrating slightly in the shaft of light from above. Kaylan reached for the hilt and took up her sword. "I think I will take the first option. I am Death itself." She held her pale sword in one hand. She swept the blade to point at Val. "I will take you up first."

Volk pushed past Val. He hefted Stroke, then slammed the blade into the ground. "*Nyet*," he said. He looked back at Val. "Next part is very important. Very. Do you understand?"

"No," said Val.

"What you must do—" said Volk, and then Kaylan was on him. She came across the room in a beam of pale light, latching on to Volk with one hand. Pale wings, softer than moonlight, were at her back, and she lifted Volk off the ground. Her sword—

Ending. That blade is called Ending.

—Ending was held up and behind her, ready for the strike. Everyone started moving, running and screaming and yelling. Carlisle was already moving towards Adalia, the two vampires in front of her running to meet her. Rex was at her side, a step or two behind. Val knew they were outclassed, that they couldn't win—

Believe in our Pack.

—but knew they were the best choice for an impossible job. He turned, started sprinting towards John, ducking under the fight above him as Kaylan and Volk wrestled in the air. She was screaming at him, and he was changing, turning from man to the thing they shared, the thing that was both more and less than a man. Volk had sunk claws into her in turn, and they were moving around the room through the air, borne up by Kaylan's pale wings.

Val arrived at John and Anatolie as the vampire was baring fangs. Val grabbed at the creature, wrenching him free of John, kicked the back of Anatolie's knee to make the vampire stumble. Anatolie shattered into a thousand locusts, and reformed ten paces away. He snatched up a silver sword, the blade long and thin. *Great. These fuckers are fast, and he's got the fastest possible sword you can imagine.*

"Yo," said John. "Good timing. Do your thing."

Val gave a tight nod, lunging after Anatolie. The vampire was quick, like liquid light, moving from place to place. Val jumped and turned and ran after, always a step behind. Each time he paused, Anatolie would land a hit — a lash against his face, a cut with the swords razor tip against his leg. Each time, the cut burned like fire, pure pain, and he bled more. Not healing as the silver tore and jabbed and stabbed at him, over, and over, and over again.

Faster.

He picked up a chair, threw it, and the vampire dodged. Another vampire, the female with the silver gauntlet, snapped at him, and he wrestled with her — *avoid the damn metal* — and threw her at Anatolie. She dissolved mid-air into a locust swarm, the cloud coalescing somewhere behind him. Still with the gauntlet.

Rex was wrestling with a vampire, and it looked bored. Rex was putting everything into it, but it was like watching a five year old try to bend a steel bar. Carlisle was caught up by another, and it brought lips in to kiss her neck, and Val could see it almost smile. Almost, as the Eagle dipped under its chin. It bit down, and Carlisle was screaming, and then the Eagle roared, and roared, and roared, and the top of the vampire's head was gone. Dropping Carlisle like a used rag. She didn't get up. The vampire playing with Rex saw this, reared back to strike Rex, and there was a massive shot, and another, and another, and huge holes appeared in its head, its shoulder, and its chest as it fell back. Val saw Jessie on one knee, the barrel of her Light Fifty smoking. Adalia was at Carlisle's side and screaming *no, no, no* over and over.

Kaylan was smashing Volk against the ceiling, but the werewolf seemed to not notice, snarling and snapping at her. It managed to get its feet under — or is that above — it, bracing against the roof the next time she tried. Put a massive claw around Kaylan's throat, and with a roar threw her at the ground. She landed in a spray of stone, but Volk had launched himself after her as soon as he'd thrown her. Almost like gravity didn't matter. He landed on her, the stone under her cracking, lines spreading out from the impact. He bent down, biting deep, and tearing. Tearing at Death's shell.

Anatolie was back at John's side, hefting Val's friend up. Val found himself standing, panting, by Stroke. Anatolie looked at him, shook John, and gave a mocking smile. Drew back teeth. Jeremy was by Volk, moving like a dot of calm in the ocean's storm, fangs bared, and was about to lean in, to bite ... *Volk.*

Father. He is our maker.

Val couldn't make it to either of them in time, but with the right weapon ... he could save one. Could see the look on John's face that said *it's cool, you can't save the world with me, so make the smart choice,* and the look on Jeremy's face that said nothing but hunger and loss and endless torment.

What had Volk meant to say? He had wanted to say something about what was coming next. What was important. That he had a plan.

Blinding, crippling pain made of pure fire stabbed through him, and he looked at a hand coming out through his chest. The female vampire, behind him. Silver gauntlet punched through his chest. Val choked on blood. Felt his strength stutter like a broken machine. Time, though, for one last act. Val's hand was on Stroke, the sword lifted as if it weighed no more than air. Born of strength of desperation, he made the only choice he could. The choice that was the smart one.

He threw the sword at Anatolie, the vampire sliced in half as the big blade turned end over end across the room. *Save John.* Because the smart choice was always the right choice, and the right choice was his friend, his real family. And damn the world. And then he fell to the floor, strength spent.

Jeremy's fangs bit into Volk's neck, the blood spraying out. The werewolf howled, and shrank, and emptied, until there was a weakened, naked man. Maksimillian Kotlyarov, at the end of things, nothing more than a dying man.

Adalia was screaming, and tried to run to Volk's side. Rex was holding her, holding her back from the edge of danger, or madness, or both, and Adalia was still screaming and trying to break free.

Jeremy's head came up with a gasp and he took a deep breath. Blood ran down from his mouth, and he licked his lips.

"Dragomir Balan, you are my good friend, *da*?" said Volk, eyes up at Jeremy, before looking at Val. "This is plan." He laughed, and coughed.

Jeremy clapped Volk on the shoulder. "This, my Russian friend, is a motherfucking *plan*."

"I have small regret." Volk looked at Val. "Regret is not killing Maynor Coen again. Please, do for me." Then he leaned back, and Jeremy sank fangs in again. Volk's eyes moved to Adalia, and he said something so soft and quiet only Val could hear. He said, "*Moya lyubov' moya zhizn'*." And then said nothing else ever again, as Jeremy drank until Volk was dead.

Kaylan was rising from the floor, moving on broken limbs. She tried to claw at Jeremy, but the vampire stepped away.

Val's vision was fading. He was almost done, he knew it. Tried to get up anyway, slipped back to the ground, where the stone was cool, and things were quiet. He hadn't saved the world this time. The most important time, but that was okay, because Danny was still there, and she would get it done, and Adalia would be free, and John would make it out, and Carlisle would make sure they were all safe. He blinked.

"Dragomir," said Kaylan, "what have you done?"

"I've gone and fucked everything up for you," said Jeremy. "Absolutely, completely, totally everything." He laughed, then coughed, and spat blood. "You made me first, but you didn't *ask*. You took me, and then you made me kill *my* family. You and Maynor. You came to me. Do you remember?" He nudged Volk's body with a toe. "You made him — through me — kill *his* family. It was only right that the two of us kill *your* family. Bring a virus here, that causes blood to explode." He coughed again, his nose streaming red. "I needed him to get her—" and here, he nodded at Adalia, "—in here. To ... see to you. I could have stood in the sun at any time, you know? But you need to be *fixed*, Kaylan. You're *broken*."

"No," said Kaylan, then, "*NO!*"

Jeremy looked at Adalia, who was still crying. "I—" he stopped, coughed again, and then sagged to his knees. He gave a shrill scream, and then his eyes melted in their sockets as the virus Volk had carried all these years did its work. His chest sagged under its own weight, and all the blood in him dissolved, gushing out to the ground. The vampire above Val started screaming, then she tumbled into a red shower of chunks. There were other screams, of terror, and agony, and loss, as all the vampires under Jeremy—

Dragomir. The First.

—died. It was enough.

Val closed his eyes.

CHAPTER
THIRTY-FIVE

No, no, no, *no*. No.

Melissa was on the ground, and her heart wasn't beating. Adalia could see it through the Other Place: There wasn't anything left in her. Val was on the floor, and he was *dying*. Adalia heard a sound, a kind of keening, or a wail, or a cry, and realized it was coming from inside *her*. She was making the noise, and she couldn't stop.

She wished Mary were here. Except Mary was made up, she wasn't *real*, and what was real was Death, right *there*.

Maks was also real, and he was also dead. There, on the ground. And he'd said *my love, my life*, and then he'd died. She didn't know what she felt about that, but the noise coming out of her was related to that, and that made it harder to stop.

Uncle John was next to her, and his eyes were sad. Like all of him hurt but he couldn't let it out. He put a hand on Adalia's shoulder, then reached down and picked up Melissa's gun. Melissa, who wouldn't be empty and gone, except that the universe had made her into a Shield, and being a Shield had brought her here and thrown her at vampires and she *died*.

Uncle John was walking towards Kaylan, who was standing up, and he lifted Melissa's big gun, pointing it at Kaylan's head. His hand was shaking.

Kaylan smiled at him. "You can't kill Death, John Miles."

"I don't know," said Uncle John. "What if I shoot you a few times and see how it makes both of us feel?"

"What if," said Kaylan, "I brought my sister here? What if you saw her now?" Her smile was bitter, her face angry.

"Liselle?" said Uncle John.

Adalia heard it through the Other Place. Kaylan said *Sister, come*. Nothing happened for a second or two, then the ceiling ruptured inward, stones as big as chairs and small as pebbles showering the room. Adalia covered her eyes against the dust, blinking to clear her vision. There they were: Death and Famine, next to each other. And it was *Famine* and not *Liselle* this time, nothing soft left in her. Terrible, and beautiful, and not human, not at all human. Not anymore.

Famine looked around the room. Nudged Jeremy with her Louboutins, then leaned on her sword, like she was leaning on the edge of midnight. "They all lie. And they must all end. We should have done it two thousand years ago. Not with vampires. We were each given power over a quarter of the Father's Eden. We were told to kill by famine and to kill by plague." She tapped a manicured nail against the black blade. "We were to kill by the sword."

"And you said no," said Kaylan. "You let the words of our friend cloud your purpose, instead of letting his death confirm it."

"We weren't," said Liselle, sparing Uncle John a look, "made to love."

"Baby?" said Uncle John.

"I'm not your 'baby,'" said Liselle. She hefted her sword. "You are a tiny, feeble thing, and your time has come."

Uncle John's face went blank, but his eyes looked more hurt. Adalia wanted to hug him, or make this go away. But these were the Riders, and she was ... well she was just a person, and she couldn't make them do what she wanted. She wasn't strong enough, and they'd hit her on the head and now she was believing in people who didn't exist, like Mary. All of this was because Adalia hadn't been using the Other Place. Because when she did, people died. She couldn't win, because people died either way. She didn't want this power, she just wanted to be Adalia, having coffee with Mary.

You just need courage, Adalia. Not your mom's courage, or Val's, or Melissa's. Just your own. Mary's voice was soft in her ear, and she turned to look. There she was, in the Other Place. Just like Adalia had imagined her. Cheeks that dimpled when she smiled. Skin like dark honey. A ribbon in her hair. Adalia looked at her. She wanted to say *it's not that easy*, but all that came out was sobs, because something in her chest hurt, and hurt, and kept on hurting. She looked at Melissa's body, then back at Mary, as if to say *see?*

Your courage is to believe, said Mary.

Adalia believed. She did. She knew about a lot of crazy or weird or amazing things. The biggest of those was that someone as wonderful as Melissa would die for her. Because Melissa was strong and brave and smart and funny, and Adalia just made people get hurt. Melissa was amazing. More amazing than Horsepersons, or werewolves, or even vampires.

No, said Mary. *You need to believe.*

She wanted to say, *I do, Mary. My failures are all really real! Mary, I believe in them.* But her chest still hurt, and she couldn't get the words out.

Mary leaned forward and whispered in Adalia's ear, the tip of the Other Place brushing the side of Adalia's skin. It almost tickled. *My lover*, said Mary, *was a lot like you. A lot different too. But he didn't believe. He made beautiful things, and the people around him became beautiful as well. But people are people, and some of those people that didn't know him well came to fear him, and they killed him.* Her face was sad, but it was a remembered pain from a long time ago. *I think you would have found a lot to talk about. When you find yourself, call me. You know how. I'd like to have that coffee.* Then she was gone, like she'd never been there, because of course she hadn't. But one last word was left. *Believe.*

Adalia realized no one else was moving. It was like time had stopped. Liselle's sword was held out, pointed at Uncle John. Kaylan's face was stretched into a terrible smile, almost a rictus, because she'd made her sister want to kill the one she loved. And what else was Death for? Like Jeremy had said — Adalia didn't want to call him Dragomir, because he hadn't been Dragomir for a long, long time — Kaylan was broken. But there weren't any threads for Adalia to pull, nothing binding Kaylan or Liselle here. With them it was strength against strength, and Adalia was just a twenty year old woman with green hair and a broken heart.

She looked down at Melissa again, then at Uncle John. *Oh. Okay.* Maybe that would work. Adalia walked over to Liselle and touched her on the arm. The one that was holding Scourge, like she wanted to ram it through Uncle John. Adalia leaned in close, her lips next to Liselle's ear, and said, "Liselle, I'd like to show you something."

THE EARTH WAS BARREN. Nothing would grow in it ever again. She had seen to that.

Liselle held Scourge in her hand and victory in her heart. Father's Eden was finished, like it should have been. They had done their jobs, their eternal vigil rewarded. They had stood together, swords bared to the light, and then swept it all away. Not even roaches were left.

Still she came here. She didn't know why. There was a stone sticking out of the blackened earth. It was a headstone, the last one standing in what had been a beautiful open space, grass once growing over it. A tree had stood just over there, its boughs shading anyone who'd come to sit for a time. Liselle hadn't come to sit, or even to see it, because it was put there for humans, and the humans were to be killed. Like they had agreed. Like they were made for.

Liselle crouched down, wiping a hand over the sand and dust and ash that covered the face of the stone. A piece had broken off. What was left was chipped at the edges, cracked down the middle when some disaster had struck. It might have been fire, the old tree burning until a branch broke. Liselle could imagine how it would have happened, the crackle of flames and then louder crack as the wood broke. She found the broken piece of the headstone, lifting it. Examining it.

If she put it back like so, it would make a rough rectangle. She placed the broken piece back on the rest of the stone, balancing it. She didn't know why she took such care with it. It was just a piece of stone.

"It's not just a piece of stone," said the young woman next to her. Liselle didn't know when Adalia had arrived. "It's a headstone."

"I don't care what it's called," said Liselle, standing up in a rush.

"No, probably not," said Adalia.

"I don't care who's under it," said Liselle, brushing her hands clean of ash. Not all of it would come free, and her hands stayed black and gray in places. Dirt remained in the lines of her palms.

"I wasn't talking about who's under it," said Adalia.

"Good," said Liselle. "It's done now."

"Yes," said Adalia. Her green hair blew about her face in a rush of wind that smelled of smoke and burning flesh. "You did it."

"Yes," said Liselle. "I did it. It's what I was made for."

"Do you know what he was made for?" said Adalia. The woman with the green hair crouched down, started working at the grooves on the tombstone with the end of her sleeve. Getting the dirt and grime out of what was written there.

"I don't care," said Liselle.

"Then walk away," said Adalia. "If you don't care, walk away. When you leave here, it'll all be over. I won't be here. You'll go back to wherever you came from. And he," Adalia touching the top of the stone with a gentle hand here, "won't mind. He's dead. He's where the dead go when they die."

Liselle turned, started to walk away. Something stopped her. Something in her chest, a hollow feeling, except it was heavy, anchoring her. She'd felt something like this once, at Golgotha. But not this empty. Not this harsh. Not this big, or this heavy. "Why ... what am I feeling?"

The woman with the green hair continued to clean the stone. "You know, he loved you. It was the light you saw inside him."

"Don't be stupid," said Liselle. "You can't love something like me. I ended the world."

"He loved you anyway," said Adalia. "He loved you like birds love soaring on the wind. He loved you like the stars love the sky. He loved you like the sea loves the sound of waves."

Liselle wiped something wet away from her face. There should be no rain here. Not anymore, Father's Eden barren and dry and empty. "He was a fool."

Adalia stepped away from the tombstone, and they both read what it said in silence. No date, because that wasn't important when the world had ended. Just a name, and an epitaph.

JOHN FUCKING MILES

GAME OVER MAN

ALSO THIS REALLY SUCKS

"Yes," said Adalia. "He was a fool. He was my friend, and you killed him first. I couldn't stop you then, because I wasn't strong enough. They gave me all this power, but it wasn't enough." She shrugged.

"Why are you here, Adalia Kendrick?" said Liselle. She wiped at her eyes again.

"Oh," said Adalia. "Mary said I had to believe. I didn't realize she wasn't talking about me. I wanted to show you this. Before it's too late."

"Too late for what?" said Liselle. But she was talking to the wind. The woman with the green hair was gone.

Liselle turned to leave. The headstone's broken piece wobbled, fell off to fall back on the black earth. She knew she'd done nothing wrong. She'd done what she was made for. She wasn't made for love.

She didn't know why her chest ached. She didn't know what that noise was. She hadn't heard it before.

She was crying, and she didn't know how to make it stop. Because everyone was dead. And she had killed them all.

∾

ADALIA LEANED AWAY FROM FAMINE. Famine jerked back, like she'd been given about fifty thousand volts. Scourge fell from her hand to *clang* against the stone floor. Famine was crying, crystal tears falling from her eyes. Where they hit the ground they broke into tiny pieces of glass.

"What did you do to me?" said Famine. She raised her hand to strike Adalia.

"Nothing," said Adalia. "I didn't do anything."

"What did I do?" said Famine.

"Nothing," said Adalia. "Not yet. But you will. In just a second, everything will go back to normal. And you'll have to decide who you want to be."

"Who ... I want to be?" said Famine.

"Sure," said Adalia.

"Who is that?" said Famine.

Adalia held her hand against Famine's chest, where all the hurt was. "That's your choice, Liselle."

"I am Famine. Liselle is a lie."

Adalia frowned, feeling a different kind of sad. "That could be. Or it could be that Famine is a lie. You've played around with this for a while. Two thousand years, right? Two thousand years ago you said that you wouldn't end the world, but you've still got your sword. Like a backup plan, in case you didn't like what happened. That's not a *choice*, Liselle."

"Stop calling me that," said Famine.

"Okay," said Adalia. "I want it to be over too, you know? My friend ... Melissa, she's my friend. She was brave, and strong, and she died for me. For *me*. Val is dying right now, and I can't stop that. There are rules."

"There are rules," agreed Famine.

"What makes me sad," said Adalia, "is that all he wanted to do was to ask my mom to marry him. And he didn't, because he was fighting a war that you started."

"Kaylan started it," said Famine. "Kaylan made the vampires."

"You've got a sword," said Adalia. "What stopped you and Josef? You didn't join her, but you stood the fuck on the sidelines. And now, here we are. You're about to kill John Miles."

"I—"

"No," said Adalia. "The time has come for choices. I'm with these guys." She took a breath, and then another. "What about you?" And she let go, and time started again.

CHAPTER
THIRTY-SIX

Liselle looked at the sword in her hand. Her partner, through all the long years of this world. It had never let her down, its blade always sharp, ready. It was her that had faltered, her hand that was weak, her hand that wouldn't do what was necessary. She looked down the black blade at John Miles, and said, "This can't ... *be*. It can't ... be like this."

She saw his face, the imperfect lines of his bare humanity. The rough clay that he was made from, bitter elements of the universe. Saw that beautiful light coming from him when he looked at her. The light she'd seen from no one else because they feared her, or hated her. And who wouldn't? A smile was on her face, but it was full of the bitterness of life.

He sighed. "I know, baby." But the light didn't dim, and he didn't move.

Kaylan looked at them both, then said, "I will make it easier for you." Her pale sword drew back, swept towards John Miles. John Miles, who closed his eyes and waited for it.

Why is he doing that?

Oh, said Adalia through the Other Place. *You don't know?*

No.

It's because he knows that being alive is hard for you. That it hurts you. When you love someone, you do things that aren't very smart.

The crash when Scourge and Ending clashed shook the room. Kaylan's eyes widened in disbelief as she looked at Liselle. Liselle, who was holding Scourge. Who had blocked that deadly strike.

By the Father. I make my choice. She drew back Scourge and swung at Kaylan. Sister against sister. Famine against Death. Their swords rang as they hit, each blow enough to crush stone and rock and the soul of the world. *My sister would take my love from me. She would end the world, and with it end John Miles.* Liselle slashed and hewed with Scourge, that black blade that had never failed her.

It didn't now.

Kaylan was beaten back, took to the air on those almost invisible wings. Liselle grabbed at her foot, dragged her back down to the Father's Eden. Where they would fight, for the fate of the world.

THIRTY-SEVEN

Rex looked at his hands. They'd always seemed to be such strong hands. Could tear a coin in half, something John Miles — with all his fitness and weight training and protein shakes and compression clothes — couldn't do. And yet Rex had failed to arm-wrestle a weedy kid who looked like he'd stepped off the back of a milk carton, and because he'd failed to do that simple thing, Melissa was dead, and Val was down and probably going to die. It seemed a strange thing to be thinking of, all these dead or dying people, what with two powers of the timeless universe slugging it out like a couple of drunks at a bar right next to them.

Although it might have been just the right thing, because thinking about dead and dying people was a motivator, and they needed to motivate themselves right out of here. Death and Famine's fighting had punched a massive hole in a wall, and sound and light and heat were coming out of it. From where they fought, sister against sister.

God knows where Danny was, but if she wasn't here, she was probably dead too.

"Old man," said Jessie. "We have to leave." She had her *Light Fifty* held loose and ready by her side.

"Yeah," said Rex. He stopped looking at his hands and started looking at Melissa. Spared a glance for Adalia, who had tears running down her face like they'd never stop falling. *Not like you were any different when your wife died. Wife, friend, brother or sister, doesn't matter. All feels the same. All feels wrong.* His hands might not be able to wrestle a skinny vampire kid, but they were good enough to carry a dead friend out from under the earth and back into the sun. He grabbed Melissa, threw her over his shoulders in a fireman's carry. The motion was like a memory of a memory, so natural it was like he'd always known how to do it. Maybe he had. Pulling people from burning buildings had felt like a thing that needed doing. Pulling Melissa's body from here also needed doing. He shrugged her weight — so light, so empty — and looked at Jessie. "Jess. She makes it out."

"She makes it out," agreed Jessie with a slow nod. "We all make it out."

"But not alive," said Adalia. She made a noise that broke Rex's heart, the start of a wail that she cut off before it could get started. "Not alive. Can I ... I need to carry her."

Rex nodded. Showed Adalia how to lift her, like Melissa were still alive, how you needed to be gentle. The woman with the green hair lifted her friend's body, face set, eyes sad and hard at the same time. Rex gave her a nod, reached out a thumb and wiped a tear away from her face. "I'm sorry. I ... I'm sorry."

"Me too," she said.

There wasn't more that could be said. Not with two Horsepersons of the Apocalypse swinging iron at each other. Rex hauled Val up — *good goddamn this boy weighs a ton, first thing we do outside is put him on a diet* — and started skirting the edge of the room. He was careful not to brush anything made of silver, none of the swords or knives or goddamn forks or whatever they had in this crazy place. Out, and up. Not through the sewers, which would have been easy, but up those stairs. Where Jeremy, damn him, had come from. Where Danny might be. Where help might be.

He stepped around that crazy Russian's body. Rex didn't understand what that was all about, except he seemed to have *history* with the rest of them. History would be put in scare quotes, but it didn't matter because no one would tell him anything like always. Adalia paused, looked at the crazy Russian's body, and her face went hard, but her eyes stayed soft. Rex cleared his throat. "Do we need him too?"

"No," said Adalia.

"I got him," said Jessie. She hauled the Russian's body up, slung him over a shoulder. Like whatever he weighed wasn't a problem, not *today*. "You realize that I can't shoot like this?"

"Still got ol' faithful," said Rex, waving the grenade launcher in the air.

"Move," was all she said in response.

She was right, of course. It wasn't the time for snappy lines. Rex looked across the room at Miles. "Son! Move it!"

Miles looked at him, and then at the hole in the wall, and then at the gun in his hand. *Melissa's gun.* "I'll stay, I think."

"Son," said Rex, hefting Val's weight. "Son, your friend isn't getting lighter. We need you, John. Do you hear me? For the first time ever, someone actually needs you. We got hurt people. We've got—"

"Dead people," said Adalia.

"We've got ... we've got *people*," said Rex. "We've got to get them out. We've got to find them all, and get them out."

Miles looked at the gun in his hand again. "I was ... I was thinking that someone needs to stay. To see ... just to see."

"No, son," said Rex. "No one needs to see."

Miles sighed. "Okay. Okay. We need to get out?"

"Son, that's what I've been trying to say. We need to get out."

"No problem," said Miles. "We go that way." He pointed Melissa's gun at the stairs leading up. Looked at Rex, holding Val, and then at Adalia, holding Melissa, and Jessie, holding the crazy Russian. "You want me to go first, huh."

"If it wouldn't be a bother," said Rex.

Miles winked at him. There was something false behind it, like he was a recording of another man, but it'd do for now. "Don't get your pacemaker overloaded," he said. "John Fucking Miles is on it."

REX SPENT the next few minutes watching John Miles' back. The man was acting like a cop from a movie set, holding Melissa's gun in front of him, turning fast around corners, crouching low. He cleared his throat. "Son? It's going to take us a while to make it up here if you're acting like a damn G.I. Joe."

"More of a Transformers man myself," said Miles. But he straightened up, walked as normal as any overgrown boy-child could, and lead the way at a faster pace.

They came to a door, top of the stairs, ajar an inch or two. A dim light was coming from the gap. Miles put a hand on it.

"Wait," said Rex. "What if there's bad guys?"

"'Bad guys,'" said Miles. "Seriously?"

"You know," said Rex. "Vampires 'n' shit."

"Pretty sure the vampire situation has resolved itself," said Miles.

"What's going on?" said Jessie, from the back of the line.

"We're going through this door," said Miles, and opened the door. Led the way through.

Rex was close on his heels and saw three people he knew. There was Danny — *alive, thank God, don't think my heart could take another one today* — on the ground, awake but pale. The giant, Ginger, was on his feet. And the one with the weird name, Huckleberry Finn or Tom Sawyer — Sawyer Diego, that was it — right next to him. Two other men Rex didn't know were there, guns pointed at the three he did know.

There was a collection of bodies in uniforms similar to the ones worn by the men pointing guns. The bodies were by a door leading out, and *out* meant *up*, which meant an end to these tunnels, and which by Rex's inference meant a path of escape. The fact that the bodies were there in uniforms implied they were what Jessie would have called *PMC assholes.* Brought in to shore up the line.

One of the men with the guns said, "Freeze."

John Miles still had Melissa's gun. He looked at it, looked at the two men, and then raised the weapon and fired twice. Headshots, each time, both of the men with guns falling to the ground like marionettes with their strings cut. The giant man, Ginger, looked surprised. He looked at the fallen men, then at John Miles. "Took you for an imbecile, genuine football bat guy. You know, the kind who wouldn't know which end of a gun to point," he said. "My apologies."

"No harm no foul," said Miles. He cast a glance at Adalia and the terrible burden she carried. "I had … uh. A good friend taught me a few things. Speaking of imbeciles though, how'd a couple of hard motherfuckers like yourselves let a couple of rent-a-clowns like these get guns in your face?"

"Ran out of bullets," said Sawyer Diego, nudging a fallen machine gun with his toe. "We had a lot going on. Before, you know?"

"I get you," said Miles. He was leaning down next to Danny. Her eyes kept going to Val's body. "Hey," he said. "Hey. He's still alive."

She was looking at the red wetness on Rex's jacket. "But not for long."

Miles sighed. "Not really my area. What is my area? Doing dumb shit. So I'm going to do more of that by leading the way out." He stood back up, offered her a hand. "Can you stand?"

Danny got a hand under herself, tried to get up, fell back. Rex watched as Miles took her arm, lifting her up, steadying her. Danny nodded her thanks.

Miles was looking at Ginger and Sawyer Diego. "You guys good? Need a rest stop or anything?"

Ginger was rooting among the fallen. He hauled out a short ugly weapon that looked like a cross between a rifle and a pistol. The big man grinned. "I'm done resting. Time for some air up top, no?"

～

THE NEXT FIVE minutes felt like an hour.

"Firing!" Hard hammer of automatic weapons. Then, "Reloading!"

"On it." A shot, the Eagle's angry roar. Again. "One down."

Staccato of bullets ricocheting from around Rex's head. He ducked down. *More time in the squat rack after this, old man.* Val was heavy, like carrying two or three men heavy. He wasn't getting lighter either, no matter how much he bled.

Sawyer Diego's voice. "Down! Down! Down!" An explosion, dust in Rex's eyes. He couldn't hear. He couldn't see.

Then, a hard rush of something that would have been loud. Jessie, and her *Light Fifty*. It really pulled at your hair when fired that close. Rex felt the force of the weapon, rubbed his eyes clear. Saw her on one knee in front of him. A shield against the bullets.

Not for me, he wanted to say. But she was already up and running low. Dropped again. Fired, fired, fired.

"Check weapons."

"Last mag."

"Two for me."

"Empty."

"I'm good," said John Miles, and fired again. The Eagle's muzzle barked light down the corridor.

Jessie was back, grabbed the crazy Russian's body. Nodded at Rex. "You good?"

"I'm good," said Rex, before a storm of fire came back down the tunnel. They all ducked. Hunkered behind whatever there was. Rex looked down, saw he still held the grenade launcher. Looked up the tunnel, at the bright points of light where the enemy was firing at them.

Enemy. They weren't *enemies.* They were just men, but they were in his way. In *their* way, stopping them from getting their friends out. Jessie had said to never use a grenade launcher in a tunnel, but sometimes you needed to break the rules. He hefted the weapon, pointed it down the tunnel, and pulled the trigger.

CHAPTER
THIRTY-EIGHT

urts.

Val opened one eye to darkness, smoke. The smell of cordite and blood. Burning meat. Saw yellow eyes on the ground next to him.

Pack mate.

She reached a hand towards him, and he touched hers in turn. Linked fingers. She said, "I love you."

He said, "I love you." Closed his eyes. Opened them. "There's something I've been wanting to ask you."

"Okay," she said, blinking yellow eyes at him. She was dying. They were both dying. He could feel it, something wrong deep inside. Something that you didn't come back from. So much silver. So many vampires.

Hurts.

"I wanted to ask you five years ago," he said. Heard footsteps coming towards them, the heavy crunch of boots on broken stone. "I wanted to ask you the day I met you."

"Okay," she said, and closed her eyes. They didn't open again.

This isn't a good time. It will never be a good time. It's the only time.
"Will you be my wife?" he said.

She didn't say anything. Couldn't say anything.

Val pushed an arm under himself, felt a terrible grating from inside his chest. Felt more of his life leave him. Where was he? How had he got here? Looked around. Saw Rex first, the old man right next to him, blood all over his shirt, eyes closed. Over there, Jessica, a hand moving weak as a moth against the ground, looking for something. Adalia, tossed against a wall like a doll, a trickle of blood coming from one ear. Melissa's body. John, always there, always by his side, but not this time. John, lying on his back, rock and dust all over him.

A broken Knight. A useless Right Arm. A shattered Sword, a buckled Shield. A blind Prophet, and a Guide who couldn't see. A Warrior that was truly Lost. All to save the world. A world that wouldn't know what they'd done. That would keep turning through the heavens, where people would get up tomorrow, go to work, live their lives, all without knowing how close it had come to ending.

He closed his eyes again. It would be okay.

Hurts.

"Yeah." He opened his eyes, licked blood from his lips. A soldier was coming closer, gun at the ready. He found Jessica first, raised his rifle like he wanted to finish her off. Val summoned up some strength, put it into his voice. "Hey. Asshole."

The soldier looked at him, rifle moving at the same time. Walked closer as Val beckoned him on.

Val spat blood, got an arm under himself. "Who you with?"

The soldier didn't say anything.

"No, it's cool," said Val, then coughed again. "I just ... I wanted to know."

"Would it matter?" said the soldier.

"I guess not," said Val. "How many of you guys are left? How'd we do? You know, final score."

There was a pause, then a chuckle. Why couldn't Val see? Of

course. His eyes had closed again. He opened them, saw the soldier's face. Something familiar about it. "They're all gone," said the soldier. "You got them all."

"Oh," said Val. He closed his eyes again. It was easier to speak without looking at the end. "Except you."

"Strange way of putting it," said the soldier. "Since I'm on your side."

Val opened his eyes. Looked at the soldier again. The gun he carried, blood red. The face, one that had seen many wars. Time, and time, and time again. "Oh," he said. "Josef."

"Yes," said War.

"Would you," said Val, "do me a favor? One last … one last thing, for the Night."

"What could one like me do for one like you?" said War. "You have conquered heaven and hell. You have saved the world."

"Not … not yet," said Val. He touched a hand to the hole in his chest, felt the wetness there. "But maybe we've done … maybe we've done okay."

"The Night always does more than is asked," said War. "It's what made you … *makes* you so troublesome."

"Sure," said Val. "Look, could you get them out?" He tried to point, but let his arm fall, like he had a choice about it. "Just get them out. To see the sky."

"Of course," said War. "That, I can do." He put a hand on Val's shoulder. "Sleep now, wolf. It is enough."

CHAPTER
THIRTY-NINE

Adalia woke up with the sun on her face and clean air in her lungs. She took a breath, almost a gasp, and sat up. Looking around, she saw Uncle John, and Jessica, and Rex. And ... and Melissa.

They were outside The Garden. What felt like a hundred miles away was a cordon, a bunch of military-looking people behind it. Helicopters buzzed overhead. Adalia couldn't tell if they were trying to get a good set of photos for the news or if there were snipers ready to shoot them. Although probably not snipers, because it would be easier to shoot from a window or something. When that man shot JFK, he wasn't in a helicopter.

She shook her head. She couldn't hear out of one of her ears. Her mom wasn't here. Val wasn't here. She wanted to cry. Her phone buzzed, finally getting reception again after all this time. She swiped the screen, read the email. Then she did start to cry.

FROM: The.Maks@gmail.com
    TO: The Woman With The Green Hair

. . .

AFTER FIVE THOUSAND years you think I would learn to write words. Words of meaning. Nothing I write can undo what I have done. I met a man named Pushkin once, and he wrote this wonderful thing. I give it to you, as I gave you my heart.

YA VAS LYUBIL: LYUBOV' yeshche, byt' mozhet,
  V dushe moyey ugasla ne sovsem;
  No pust' ona vas bol'she ne trevozhit;
  YA ne khochu pechalit' vas nichem.

YA VAS LYUBIL BEZMOLVNO, beznadezhno,
  To robost'yu, to revnost'yu tomim;
  YA vas lyubil tak iskrenno, tak nezhno,
  Kak day vam bog lyubimoy byt' drugim.

YOUR MAKS.

SHE KNEW what the words meant. She knew all the languages of men, of heaven and hell, of angels and demons. It was the words that made her cry. She wondered that she had tears left.

I LOVED YOU: love is still, perhaps, in my heart;
  But do not let it bother you anymore;
  I do not want to sadden you.

I LOVED YOU SILENTLY, hopelessly, tormented by timidity, then jealousy;

I loved you so sincerely, so tenderly;
May God give you another to love you so.

SHE CLOSED HER PHONE, felt her chest wrack with sobs. With the unbelievable pain of living. Death would be the kinder thing now. Death would be an end to this. If only she didn't know where the dead went when they died.

The ground started to shake, and about fifty feet away the street exploded upward in a shower of asphalt and stone and concrete and dirt. Death was in the air on those almost-invisible wings, her face a mask of terror and pain. She held no sword, had no fight left. She was *running*. She was climbing for the sky, and made it about two stories up before a streak of black speared her through the middle.

Scourge. Thrown from in the hole. Kaylan fell hard on the ground, wings flapping like a broken toy.

Liselle climbed out of the hole, dusted off her clothes. Looked at Adalia, then walked over to Kaylan's fallen body. Tore her sword out, leveled it at her sister. "And this is how you kill Death."

"Hold up," said Adalia, wobbling a little as she hobbled towards them. Kaylan's face was lit with hope, Liselle's was a blank mask.

It was Liselle who spoke. "She needs to die."

"Yes, but no," said Adalia. "You can't really kill Death."

"She has taken so *many*," said Liselle. "She means to end the world."

"I think we're on that," said Adalia. She looked over her shoulder, at where Uncle John lay, next to Jessica, and Rex. And … and Melissa. She turned back to Liselle. "He needs you. They all need you."

Liselle looked doubtful. Shoulders strong, sword held rock-steady in one hand. "If I leave here—"

"It's just *Death*," said Adalia. "She can't do anything that's not going to happen anyway. Go on."

Liselle nodded and walked away. Walked towards the man she loved. Adalia watched her go, then turned to Kaylan. "So."

"Thank you," said Kaylan. "I'll give you—"

"Shut up," said Adalia, thinking, *Melissa.* "Just shut up."

"I can bring her back," said Kaylan. "I can bring back your friend. You only have to—"

"I said *shut up!*" said Adalia. Thunder crackled and boomed far above. Her teeth were clenched. She held up her phone. "Do you know what he said to me?"

"I—"

"*I SAID SHUT UP!*" screamed Adalia. The world fell silent, the horns of Manhattan quiet, the helicopters above making no noise. Men and women behind the cordon fell silent. There was no noise. The air was still, as still as it had been the moment before the world began. Adalia wiped tears from her face, leaned down. "He loved me."

Death looked at her, but said nothing.

"Jeremy said you were broken," said Adalia. "What did he mean?"

Kaylan started to get to her feet in this little bubble of the world they shared, just the two of them. Outside the bubble, everything was still. "*Dragomir* was flawed."

"*Jeremy* was your first. He made the rest. And you say he was flawed?"

"Because," said Kaylan, "he saw the things I saw. Each person dies. Each one. And they do terrible things! They cheat, and steal, and hate. They *deserve* to die. It's time, time for all of them. It's what I was *made for.*"

"Oh," said Adalia. "Is that all?"

Kaylan blinked at her. "What?"

"Death isn't beautiful," said Adalia. "Death is terrible. It's what comes before Death that is beautiful. I want to show you."

"What can you possibly show me that I haven't seen?" said Kaylan.

"You've seen it," said Just James. "You weren't looking." He looked like he always had, hands stuffed into his pockets. He gave Adalia a shy smile. "Hey."

"Hey," she said back, and stopped, because otherwise she'd start crying again.

"It's cool," said Just James. "It was my choice."

"It's not okay," said Adalia. "But she needs to see."

"I know," he said. The buildings behind Just James were visible through him, like he wasn't all the way solid. Which, of course, he wasn't. He was a dead boy who'd died for her five years ago so the world would live. And she'd dragged him back from his rest because she needed his help again. "But still."

"But still?" said Adalia.

Just James leaned close, kissed her on the lips. She tasted the memory of him, the beautiful wonder of this boy. She closed her eyes and leaned into him. Held him, while he held her back for what felt like a year and not long enough at the same time.

"Who's the kid?" said Emily Lindle. She had a hand on her hip, and was staring at Kaylan like you'd look at a roach in your cereal.

"Just James," said Just James. He reached out a hand. "Pleased to meet you."

"Don't touch me," said Emily Lindle. She walked to stand next to Death, shimmering slightly in the air. "You the bitch we had to die to stop?"

"You died for money," said Kaylan.

"I died for Ginger," said Emily Lindle, "because he pulled me out of an internment camp. I owed my life and soul and everything I ever was after that moment to him."

"Me too," said Bryn Vincent, stepping out of the air. "I mean, I wasn't in an internment camp. Who says 'internment' anyway, Lindle?"

"Shut it," said Emily Lindle.

"Sure," said Bryn Vincent. "My friend, that big ol' ginger-haired bastard. That's why I died."

"Am I late?" said Abigail Finch.

"You're right on time," said Thomas Mallory. He clapped Abigail Finch on the shoulder.

Adalia stepped back from all of them as they started to form a circle around Kaylan. She felt a hand on her shoulder, so faint she thought she might have imagined it, but looked anyway because it was that kind of time and place. There was a woman she didn't know. "Oh," said Adalia. "I'm sorry. I ... I didn't call you."

"No," said the woman. "He was my Valentine first, you know?"

"Oh," said Adalia, looking at her shoes. "Rebekah. You must be Rebekah."

"Yes," said Rebekah. She walked towards Kaylan. "We all died for someone else, Kaylan. We didn't die for you. We didn't lie, or cheat, or steal, or stab each other. We died to make the world more beautiful. Because death isn't beautiful, but the people we leave behind are." She looked over a shoulder at Adalia. "Tell him I loved him. Tell him I still love him. Tell him—"

"He's gone," said Adalia. "Val's gone, Rebekah."

A smile touched her lips. "Then why isn't he here?"

"*Da*," said a voice, and Adalia whirled. *He* was there. Her ... and it made her start crying again to admit it, but *her* Maks. "No. No tears for Maksimillian Kotlyarov. Only vodka."

"Only vodka," she agreed, and cried anyway. She felt his fingers on her cheek, her chin, and then his lips against hers, and then he was gone. Adalia crumpled to the ground, alone, alone, alone again. There was no one left. The dead had come, and taken Death. Taken Kaylan to where the dead go when they die. To show her what a life worth living was for.

WHEN SHE STOPPED ROCKING BACK and forth, the first thing she saw was a pair of Louboutins. Adalia looked up, saw Liselle's hand stretched out towards her. She took the hand, let Liselle help her to her feet. "Thanks."

"Oh," said Liselle. "You don't have to thank anyone."

"If ... Liselle. If I hadn't—"

"Hush," said Liselle. "We've asked so much from you. But I've one more thing I'd like to ask. You were right. All my life, I've held something in reserve. And it's ... it's held *me* back." She held out her sword, the black blade Scourge. "*I would like to make a trade.*"

CHAPTER
FORTY

"Hey, Sam," said Adalia. "Sam, it's me. Adalia."

The voice on the other end of the phone seemed surprised. "Uh, hey, Adalia. Uh, hey."

"Hey," said Adalia, phone pressed to her ear. God, she hated talking on the phone. Of all the things the device could do, with its apps and messages and Yelp reviews and pictures to share and social media feeds, actually making *phone calls* seemed redundant. Also, she'd said *hey* already. *You can do this.* "Sam? We saved the world again."

There was a pause on the line. "Yeah," said Sam. "I figured you had. Because there were storms, and lightning in Manhattan, and the streets blew up. Charlie ... well, Charlie thought it was fun."

"He's spent some quality time with a bunch of vampires," said Adalia. "Give him a little while to find his feet. Sam? When I was about his age, I spent some quality time with a sociopath who ran a drug company. I turned out okay." She scuffed a toe against the sidewalk.

"Pharmaceutical company. We prefer 'pharmaceutical' as a

term," he said. "Otherwise it sounds like we're making heroin for children."

"Fair enough," said Adalia. The light was bright, just the way she liked it. The streets were busy, about a hundred people running around looking frantic. A bunch of police had tried to take a statement. A bunch of soldiers had pushed them around. No one had taken her phone from her yet. "Look, I need a favor."

"Anything," said Sam. "Seriously? Anything. You ... Charlie's *home*, Adalia." There was a pause. "Where's ... where's your mom? Where's Mr. Everard?"

"They're ... not here," said Adalia, and tried to sound casual about it, like it was expected, or normal, just a thing. Like she could accept it. Except she couldn't, especially not what had happened to Melissa. She hoped Sam wouldn't ask about her. "They're ... gone."

"Maybe they're home too," he said, but he said it with soft words, and they both knew that it was the truth and a lie at the same time. "What favor?"

"Okay," said Adalia. "I've got a list."

"A list?" said Sam. "You came prepared."

"First time for everything," said Adalia. "I think we'll need a lawyer, a couple of SUVs, and a cabin in the woods. I was going to Airbnb that last one, but my card's maxed out."

"What kind of lawyer?" said Sam.

"One that hunts and kills without mercy," said Adalia, looking at the police and soldiers around her. "One that's ... get me a good one, Sam. The best."

"I've got just the one on speed dial," he said. "We need them when we sell heroin to children. I can get you a couple cars as well. But a cabin in the woods?"

"Yes," said Adalia. "It's for Melissa. There should be a field of wildflowers around it, and the sun should hit it in the mornings. There's a line of trees just far enough away to look cool, not frightening. There's no cell coverage. Can you see it?" She didn't say anything else.

After a while, Sam said, "I can see it. Give me thirty minutes." He clicked off.

She spun her phone in her hand, then stuffed it into a back pocket. Wiped at her eyes, because the lawyer wouldn't care about her tears. She smoothed her green hair, then went to find Rex.

"This is the world's smallest convoy," said Rex. He was driving, trying his best to make conversation while Adalia did her best to look out the window and ignore everything. It wasn't working. She would stare out the window, and try to listen to the radio because she couldn't get the stupid Bluetooth working on her phone so there wasn't anything else to listen to, and then she'd think about Melissa, who was in the back of the SUV, wrapped in a blanket.

She sighed. "I ... um," she said.

He nodded, not looking at her. "Yeah," he said. "I get that."

"It's just," she said, then stopped.

"It is," he said, hands on the wheel. She watched his hands for a while, relaxed but in control. She turned her face into the sun coming in the window, and sighed again. She felt safe, for a second. But only for a second.

"She's dead," said Adalia, trying the words out. They didn't taste right, didn't feel right. Couldn't be right.

"She is," said Rex. He seemed to deflate a little. "I ... I'm not good at this. People dying, you know? It's not ... I'm just not good at it," he finished. His hands were tensing on the wheel, fingers turning white.

It was Adalia's turn to nod. She reached out a hand to touch his arm. "Rex?"

"Because," he said, "I'm so damn old. I ... it should have been me. It's my turn. I've ... it's not fair, and I'm sorry. It should have been me."

"Oh," she said, and let her hand drop. They sat like that for a while, the seams in the freeway *thump thumping* underneath the wheels of the SUV. After quite a long a while, because the sun was warm and making her feel sleepy, she opened her eyes. "I'd bet Jessica thinks the same thing."

"But Jessie—"

"And Uncle John," said Adalia. "Because, you know, he and Melissa, they were really good friends. Really good. The kind of good that comes once or twice in a person's life. They never said it to each other. They should have told each other. But they didn't, and then Uncle John got taken with me, because Death herself wanted me to make vampires stronger, and Melissa came down to where it's dark to get us out. And she died."

"But—"

"And the weird thing is," said Adalia, "None of you are right. You're not. The only one who's to blame is *me*. I ... I could have stopped it all, Rex. Don't you see? I ... it's *me*. I'm why she died." And she was crying again, and she hated that too, because it didn't seem to stop or hurt less at any particular moment.

Rex's hand was on her shoulder, awkward and warm and strong all at once, and she cried more, until she stopped crying. She didn't know how long they'd been driving, and it didn't matter. The other car, with Jessica driving and Uncle John and Liselle in it, was behind them. Making sure Melissa got to where she needed to be, for ever and ever.

"So," said Rex. "So."

"Yeah," said Adalia, wiping her eyes for the hundredth time today. "Yeah."

"It feels like a lousy way to win," said Rex. "Like, losing's worse, but ... I don't know."

"Losing would have been worse," said Adalia. "There'd be vampires everywhere, or the world would have ended."

"You sure?" said Rex.

"Pretty sure," said Adalia.

"Jeremy was an asshole?"

"Jeremy was wonderful," said Adalia. "Maks was an asshole. He was a liar. And..." And she rubbed her eyes again.

"Maks was a man in love," said Rex. "Men do strange things when they're in love."

"Do not," said Adalia, "tell me that boys will be boys, or so help me I will turn you into a woman for just one day."

"No," said Rex, still calm, measured, relaxed. "Didn't mean it like that. Didn't want to give any excuses or reasons. Just said it's a thing."

"Okay," said Adalia. "But still."

"Sorry," said Rex.

"Okay," said Adalia. "It's like this. Jeremy was actually an ancient vampire named Dragomir. He was the first one ever. Kaylan and Maynor—"

"That's Death and Pestilence?"

"Yeah, those two. Kaylan and Maynor made the vampires, but they didn't make them right. I don't know why. I guess it's because Horsepersons were made to destroy the world, and trying to *create* something, even to destroy, was beyond them."

"I think," said Rex, "that unholy monsters can't take the light of the sun, because God is watching."

"If that makes you feel better then go with that," said Adalia, watching trees outside the window. They were getting outside of the city, away from the people. Closer to their destination. And then they'd have to put Melissa in the cold, cold ground. "What I know is that Jeremy and Maks knew each other."

"From where?" said Rex.

"From when Jeremy hatched a plan to steal a terrible blood virus from Maynor. Or from where he caught Maks and gave him the virus. Doesn't matter." Except it did, and she should look. Really *look*, back at where it started. But if she did that, she'd need to see Maks again, and she didn't want to cry any more. "I think Pestilence made a kill switch for the vampires, and Maks caught it, but werewolves don't get sick, so he was just a carrier, like Val, or my mom. Except Maks wanted to die, more than Jeremy, because Maks had killed his whole family, but he wanted revenge more than he wanted to die. And Jeremy, he, he … arranged everything. So Maks could die and get revenge at the same time. So Jeremy would die with him. So I would see Kaylan. Because I would … fix her."

"He could have died at any time," said Rex. "Took them all out just by walking outside. Seems like you didn't need to be there at all."

"Kaylan would have started again," said Adalia. "Now she's where the dead go when they die."

"Can't she get out?" said Rex. "I'm nervous about that."

"I'm not," said Adalia, thinking of Just James for just a second, and the Maks for just another second. "I'm not at all. She will *never* get out." She realized she was clenching her teeth, the anger burning on top of the pain, and that was good, if only because it made her feel different for a moment. Adalia rubbed her hands on her legs, then licked her lips. "I … he wanted me to *fix* her."

"Hell," said Rex. "I could have told him that was impossible. You can't fix stupid."

Adalia laughed, and Rex laughed. She gave him a fond smile. She didn't know how she had so many wonderful people around her. She didn't deserve them. She deserved to be where the dead went. To look out from the Cliffs of the Damned — which was a weird name for such a peaceful place. It was a sobering thought, and she stopped smiling. "He wanted me to fix her so she wouldn't start again, Rex. I couldn't do that, but I can put her somewhere she can't get out of. Because the people there? They love us, and they love this world, even though they're all dead. She will be there forever, and forever, and forever."

"Sounds bad," said Rex.

"It's not bad enough," said Adalia.

THE CABIN WASN'T QUITE big enough, but it was a long way from Manhattan, and cars, and people, and that made it perfect. Adalia was sitting across from Mary, and there was coffee in front of both of them, two off-white cups that had been used a thousand times before, chips on the rims. It didn't matter. The table was in the middle of a field full of wildflowers. The sun on her face and her hair was warm. A butterfly wove between them, Adalia watching it as Mary watched her.

"I didn't know you were real," said Adalia.

"I didn't know that it mattered," said Mary. She took a sip. "Hmmm. Good coffee."

"I made the best coffee in Manhattan," said Adalia, and tried to stop herself from crying. She looked out at where Uncle John was chopping firewood. No shirt, of course. And there was Liselle, pretending not to look. Focused so intently on the book she held that she couldn't possibly have been reading it. It helped. Adalia held back the tears.

"You saved the world," said Mary. "How does it feel?"

"Pretty terrible," said Adalia. "I thought us coming to a cheesy log cabin in the woods would help."

"Did it?" said Mary.

"Not really," said Adalia, "but the wildflowers are nice."

They sat in silence for a while, then Mary leaned forward. "This wasn't what you thought having a friend would be like, was it?"

"It's perfect," said Adalia. "It's just..." She trailed off, turning her cup in her hands.

"It's just," agreed Mary. "My lover, he wanted to speak with you."

"I don't want to," said Adalia.

"I know," said Mary. She laughed. "He never was very good with people. Good at making beautiful things though."

"Unlike me," said Adalia. "All I do is make the world uglier. Everyone dies."

"You ... can break the rules," said Mary. "He did. For a friend."

"He brought himself back from the dead, or so the stories say," said Adalia. "Other people too. Lazarus. Lazarus of Bethany."

"That's right," said Mary. "Lazarus was his friend."

Adalia cocked her head at Mary. "I thought he was some kind of follower. You know. Like a cult."

Mary laughed. "Not all the stories are written down exactly right."

"I guess not," said Adalia. "How do you think they'll write this one down?" She was watching as Rex walked out of the cabin, helping Jessica, hand around her waist. Or she was helping him. It didn't matter.

"It depends how you end it," said Mary. "You took the trade. That was a good start."

Adalia wondered about that. About the trade Liselle had begged her for: her sword, her constant, eternal companion. *Take my sword,* she'd said, *and make me like you.* She meant *make her mortal* so she and Uncle John could grow old together and die. She was already like them in all the other ways that mattered. So Adalia had taken her sword, made it go away, and also taken her name, Famine, and made that go away. Left her as Liselle Vitols. It felt good to have such a stylish aunt.

"Is it over?" said Adalia. "It feels over."

"Then why am I here?" said Mary.

"Because I need a friend," said Adalia.

"You have many friends," said Mary.

"Not the one that matters," said Adalia. "Not Melissa."

"Ah," said Mary. And then nothing else.

"What happens," said Adalia, "if she is my Lazarus?"

"I don't know," said Mary.

"Your lover died," said Adalia. "He died, because he broke the rules."

Mary set down her cup. Put a hand on Adalia's. "He died because he didn't ask for help. He died because he thought people were different. He died because someone needed to, and he was beautiful that way."

"That's great news," said Adalia. "Because I'm not beautiful."

"Adalia Kendrick," said Mary, "would you like to make a trade?"

"Very much," said Adalia.

CHAPTER
FORTY-ONE

"Fucking Christ," said Carlisle. "I feel like I've been dead for three days."

"Five," said Miles, at her bedside. "You've been dead for five days." He was grinning, but there was something sad there too.

She caught onto that straight away. Because apart from her neck, which hurt, and the rest of her, which hurt more, there was something ... *empty* inside. "Where's Adalia?"

"Yeah," said Miles. "About that."

～

CARLISLE LOOKED out over the field of wildflowers, at the small table and its two chairs. The half-empty coffee cups, gone cold. "What do you mean, she's gone?"

"She's gone," said Miles. He had a hand over hers, held it. Not like they were lovers, because first Liselle was *right there* and second because she would have punched him in the face. He held it like they were the best of friends, and he had something frightening to say. Both of those were the truth. "She was talking to Mary—"

"Who the fuck is Mary?" said Carlisle.

"Mary of Magdala," said Liselle.

"Cool," said Carlisle, thinking *bullshit, but what do I know*. "She was talking to this Mary girl? And why are we in the woods?"

"Adalia was going to bury you out here," said Miles. "Because she said you'd served enough. Because you deserved somewhere peaceful to rest."

"Seems fair," said Carlisle. "But I'm not dead."

"Not anymore," said Miles, and then he started laughing. Laughing, and crying. And then just crying, and he was holding her. Carlisle felt herself stiffen, then relaxed, and put a hand on his back.

"Jesus, Miles," she said. "It's okay."

"Is it?" he said. He pulled back. "Is it?"

Carlisle looked around the field. Took in Rex *like a fucking Tyrannosaurus*, and Pearce, and Liselle, who was just like them now. Broken and perfect at the same time. And Miles, the big dumb strong fool crying at her side. Felt around inside her for where she'd always known Adalia was. But wasn't, anymore.

Carlisle started to walk. Left the porch of the log cabin, feet getting stained wet with dew as she walked among the wildflowers. She came to stand at the table where Adalia had been, and knew it to be true — Adalia was gone. Lifted Adalia's cup and picked up the scrap of paper that was hidden under it.

Melissa. I'm sorry if I made it worse not better. It's all I seem to be able to do. I couldn't bear a world without you. —A

Carlisle sat down on the grass for a while, not realizing she'd just dropped. Felt a head full of questions, questions that probably didn't need answering. Not really. She read the scrap of paper again, then said to no one in particular, "But what if I can't bear a world without you?"

No one answered her.

After a while, she needed to get up. Not because she wanted to stretch her limbs, but because her ass was getting wet from the ground. Who moved a table into the middle of a field to have coffee, anyway? She took in Miles, still on the porch, but with Liselle beside him. Rex would be around somewhere, maybe he and Pearce headed up into the hills with that big gun of hers. Still her family, but smaller now.

She caught a glimpse of something at the tree line, huge shapes, yellow eyes, and stumbled back. She almost tripped — *damn* all the parts of her that hurt — but caught the edge of the table. When she looked back at the tree line, there wasn't anything there. There probably hadn't been anything there. Those two were gone. Weren't they? And if they weren't gone, they wouldn't be here, now that Adalia—

Carlisle looked down at her hands, and found them to be shaking. *Come on, Melissa. You can face it. There are harder truths than a beautiful person going to a more beautiful place.*

They wouldn't be here now that Adalia was gone. Would they? No. They'd be off, together. They'd saved the world enough times. Hell, they'd saved a broken down old cop, a retired firefighter, a reprobate who played video games, the CEO of a powerful corporation. They'd even saved Famine, turned her into a real person. Although — and here, Carlisle rubbed her face — Liselle had always felt like a real person anyway. Some big problems, just like the rest of them.

No, they wouldn't be here now. They'd be—

Running free.

THE END.

～

YOUR TIME with the Night's Champions has ended. But the fight is far from over.

You've walked the path with the Pack, faced impossible odds, and stood against monsters born from myth and nightmare. But the shadows that fell weren't the end of the story. They were just the beginning.

A new darkness stirs in Valhaven. A warrior stands ready. And this time, the battle isn't just for survival—it's for the fate of the gods themselves.

Turn the page to meet Isolde.

A hunter. A survivor. A woman who won't stop until the chains of fate are broken.

The dawn is rising. And with it, a war unlike any before.

THE THREE FACES OF FATE

A SUPERNATURAL THRILLER ADVENTURE

PROLOGUE

"Social media is on fire today following the latest round of cryptid sightings after Alex Macy, a twenty-three-year-old homemaker, posted a video of a goblin raiding his trash.

Government sources have been quick to respond, further denying this as a conspiracy of misinformation and claiming involvement from the Chinese Ministry of State Security. A CISA spokesperson released a statement: "This is another deepfake. You can make videos like this with a pocket calculator."

Despite the statement, this isn't the first time we've seen information like this appear. Ten years ago, Madison Square Garden was destroyed. Sources at the scene claimed a "brutal battle" between vampires and werewolves, with the werewolves eventually emerging victorious. But what many find strange is that despite the chaos and destruction, no footage or records of the event seem to have survived, and no one has seen a werewolf since. It's as if the entire incident was wiped from existence.

What happened during that fateful event still remains a mystery to this day. Could this be a government cover-up? Many are now asking that very question as more and more unconfirmed sightings of cryptids continue to surface on the Internet. The lack of evidence surrounding the Madison Square Garden incident only adds fuel to the fire, leaving us all to wonder what exactly happened that day and why the government is so determined to keep it hidden from the public.

This is Emily Chen, Valhaven Observer."

THE IMBECILE

The waterfront at night was no place for the young, the old, or anyone in between. Fog clung to the oily black sea, unmoving against the cool shoreline. The city noise kept its distance. Nothing moved; to move was to become prey.

So why is this cretin out for a stroll?

Astra kept her distance, hunched on a warehouse roof like a gargoyle against the clouded sky. She was used to the night, its darkness a comfort and its chill a balm. The grave mist that hovered over the water was an old friend: one that welcomed monsters but also her, the monster of all monsters.

The imbecile she followed was handsome, in a rakish way. His hair was longer than fashion liked, and Astra imagined it strawberry blonde, although the night hid that from her. Nice jawline, if you were into that kind of thing, with a trimmed beard that suggested wisdom his actions certainly didn't.

He walked with sure steps, his face open and curious. Not afraid, as anyone who knew what lived down here would be. Not hunched or furtive. Just another night stroller, out for a walk in murder central. A satchel hung from one shoulder. He had good boots on, none of the slick-soled leather nonsense of city fashions, below a pair of worn but serviceable jeans. A longshoreman's jacket and scarf completed the hipster vibe.

A sound like footsteps on stone came from Astra's right, echoing briefly between the warehouse buildings before falling silent. If you hadn't hunted in the dark for the last eight years, you might write it off as random noise, maybe just a trick of cooling stone. Astra hoped it wasn't cooling stone. She hadn't come all this way to fight rocks.

The sound came from the direction of the city. If they were after the handsome imbecile, that's where they'd be coming from. To his credit, the imbecile froze, head tilted, listening. Astra didn't move her body but tilted her head, watching.

Nothing. *These assholes are good at hiding; I'll give them that.*

The imbecile didn't run. He just shrugged the satchel strap higher on his shoulder, shook his head, shoved his fists into his longshoreman's coat, and headed farther up the wharfs.

Astra waited a few moments. It started to rain, the patter of it *tinking* on her armour. She didn't mind the rain. She'd slept under it often enough. Below, two shapes darted from around a corner, padfooting after the hipster imbecile. She grimaced behind her mask. *Just once, it'd be nice not to be right about the murder thing.*

She didn't know *what* the thugs were, only that they wanted blood more than money.But she wasn't sure *why* they wanted the sticky red wet. Vampires were all gone, so it wasn't that. Werewolves too. But so many other nasties were out there, mould blooming in the grouting now the vampires weren't around to stamp them down.

Time to find out what kind of fungus this is.

She rose, ghosting along the warehouse roof, feet whisper-light. The roof's edge neared, and she urged her body to move faster. Then she was at the edge, vaulting the distance to the opposite roof, where she landed cat perfect. Astra slowed, listening and watching. The rooftop was empty, hers alone. She liked old haunts like these. No one thought to look up. Not even monsters.

Astra kept low, but didn't hurry. Furtive movements drew the eye more than assured ones. She climbed up the sloping roof, casting a weather eye in through skylights she passed. Nothing inside but racks and boxes. As she made the pinnacle of the roof, the rain started in earnest. Her armour husbanded the little light that made it to her and gleamed in anticipation.

Down the other side, and sure enough, there was the imbecile. He'd shored up underneath a light pole, confirming the strawberry blonde of his now wet hair, and broadcasting to any predator that prey was waiting in full illumination, night vision ruined.

Astra froze like a gargoyle again, waiting, and watching. There, around the corner of the warehouse, came the two thugs. They'd cast aside the padfoot pursuit and were all swagger and balls. The imbecile hadn't noticed them. The fool was fussing with a document in a clear plastic sheet protector, turning it this way and that under the light.

Best come down behind the thugs. Stay hidden from the imbecile. She sprinted to the roof's edge, grasped the gutter, and swung over. She dropped to the pavement behind the thugs, her feet splashing in the water. They turned, cat-quick, and she got her first good look at them.

Human... *ish.* Grey-green skin wouldn't pass muster in the daylight, and neither would those saw-like teeth. Astra wanted to think *goblin*, but they were too tall—and too damn muscular. The one on her left wore baggy jeans and a bomber jacket. The right one committed the cardinal sin of double denim but redeemed himself slightly with a pair of Beats studio cans slung around his lean neck.

Both wore red hats. Bomber Jacket's was a red ball cap. Double Denim had a beanie.

They looked her up and down. Bomber Jacket raised an eyebrow. "What's with the mask?"

"What's with the face?" Astra lowered her stance, then glanced to Double Denim and kept her voice low and conspiratorial. "Does Dre know you're ruining his brand?"

"It's *Doctor* Dre. He's got a Ph.D. from UCLA." Double Denim showed too many teeth in a hungry smile. "Are you some kind of hero? Gonna knock us off?

"I didn't know creatures like you could spell UCLA. That's a lot of letters all at once." The mask hid Astra's surprise. "I'm not going to kill you. If I did that, there'd be no one to tell the rest of you that humans were off the menu."

"Hey," called the hipster, his voice still safely around the warehouse corner. "Is there anyone there?"

Bomber lunged for her. She'd actually expected Double Denim to make the first move, but the strong silent type clearly wanted it more. She waited for the charge, ducked under his swing—*sweet Christ, he's got claws*—then rose in a savage *hiji age*, her elbow connecting with Bomber's chin. Teeth sprayed, clattering against her mask.

She slipped sideways, dodging Double Denim's curiously inept front kick. Astra stepped in nice and close and acquainted Double Denim with her knee, then slipped back from his groaning swing. Three paces took her back to the wharf's edge. Fog hid the water below, but she could hear the lapping of it against the wharf piles.

Bomber said something that could have been *fucking bitch* if you accounted for the missing teeth, then came at her in a rush. She braced, grabbed his bomber lapels, stepped to the left, and *twisted*. It was a textbook *tai otoshi*. Bomber sailed into the water below. Double Denim came next, but Astra wasn't waiting this time. She darted in, chopped a *shuto* to the throat, and while he gagged, grabbed his beanie, then said, "Leave the fucking hipster alone."

Then she heaved him after Bomber. He slipped through the fog with no further fuss than the splash he made.

"Hello?" The hipster imbecile's accent was something from Europe. Scottish? Irish? In a different setting it'd be cute. The kind of thing her other self might want to listen to. His voice was steady, not the quavering of someone afraid of having his head kicked in.

Astra spied a drain pipe heading skyward. She tucked the beanie into her belt, then scampered to the pipe. She curled her fingers behind it, put the soles of her feet against it, and made a good approximation of vertical primate walking. In a moment, she was over the edge of the warehouse roof, play-acting a gargoyle once more.

The imbecile came around the corner of the warehouse. He still held the clear plastic sheet protector in one hand, but had the foresight to wield a flashlight in the other. Astra shrunk back, not wanting to expose even the hint of her mask to a stray beam.

But no, like everyone else, the imbecile didn't look up. He walked to where Astra had fought two might-be-goblins-on-the-protein, and crouched, before tucking his plastic sheet protector into his satchel. He found something gleaming in a puddle, and picked a tiny object up, turning it about in the light of his flashlight.

He'd found Bomber's teeth. He didn't gag or toss them away in disgust. No, the hipster imbecile picked up another fragment of tooth, then tucked both away in his satchel.

Then he stood, looked around, and said, Irish brogue in full effect, "Ah sure, would you look at that now? I do hope I get the chance to thank whoever's out here someday."

Astra stayed still. She didn't need his thanks. Her duty was a blessed reward.

The hipster imbecile sighed, scuffed his toe in a puddle, hunched into his scarf and longshoreman's jacket, then—showing the first sign of intelligence all night—headed back the way he'd come.

Astra waited until he was gone from sight, then pulled the beanie from her belt. It was a horrible red, and her fingers smeared some of the crimson away as she touched it. She lifted her mask for a moment, then sniffed the beanie. *Old blood.* Lowering her mask, she tossed the beanie over the side of the roof, then turned to the city.

Valhaven gleamed right back at her, a city almost waiting for her. Almost.

THE NIGHT HAS FALLEN.

NOW, THE DAWN MUST RISE.

Valhaven is on the brink. The shadows are deepening. And Isolde is about to step into a battle that will shake the very foundations of fate.

You've had a glimpse of *The Three Faces of Fate*. Now it's time to dive into the fight.

Grab *The Three Faces of Fate* now!

https://www.books2read.com/TheThreeFacesOfFate

The gods are in chains. The city is burning. And the battle has only just begun.

Acknowledgments

First thanks goes to you, my readers, for enjoying the *Night's Champion* trilogy. Not only have you made it here to the end with me, but you encouraged me with your emails full of kind words, and your reviews with kinder words. We wouldn't be here without you.

I've said it before, and will keep saying it for a while: writing is a team sport. Sure, there's the hours of self-doubt and alcohol-induced creativity that yield words on a page, but there's also a lot of people who helped make this story. My Team Narrative helped to ensure that this story made sense. You can tip your hat towards Arran, Cheryl, Greg, Julia, Raelene, and Paula for this thing being coherent in any way. My Team Kwality (let me tell you, they *love* that name) were the ones who caught the errors of quality in the manuscript; Anthony, Cheryl, Erin, Jane, and Julia, thank you. This collective group of fine humans continue to humble me by how much effort they put in to making my work worth seeing the light of day. Trust me, the first draft of a novel is not a handsome thing; these people give time, but they also take any future counseling they need on the chin.

Writing *Night's End* was hard due to some excessive life stress during most of the time I was writing it. Turns out, you should *not* take a job on the Death Star! Anything called a *Death Star* is not where you should work. During the time I was serving the Empire, my Writer's Coven kept me aiming for brilliance, not settling for anything less, and consistently called my bullshit on areas that my tired brain could not see. Cassie, Frances, and Kate, thank you. I suck less for knowing you all.

It turns out that writing a Russian character after your Russian human has turned into a pumpkin is difficult. I'd like to extend a fond thanks to Google for their excellent Translate services (https://translate.google.com/) that turned English into Russian and back again. As a side note, a lot of people worry about *net* vs. *nyet* when trying to be all Russian and negative at the same time. As near as I can determine, pronunciation is *nyet* to the English Ear™, but correct spelling is *net*. Fuck correct spelling, because it jars: you'll find it with the *y* throughout. The actual Cyrillic is нет, for all you nerds like me out there. Do not fucking email me about it being *net*, because I have already done enough agonizing for both of us on this one.

The last thank you is the most important: my Rae. You were there with me when the Death Star was destroying planets, and my soul. You've given so much to enable me to write. None of this would be possible without you. You are, above all others, the person I write for.

— R. P.
May 2017, Wellington

ABOUT THE AUTHOR

Richard Parry worked as a senior marketing manager in one of the world's top tech companies. It sounds cool, but it wasn't all cocaine parties. He lives in Wellington with the love of his life, Rae. They have two cats, Harry and Friday, who chase birds. The birds, who have the power of flight, don't seem to mind.

WAIT. DON'T GO!

Thanks for reading my book. If you enjoyed it, let's keep the party going:

📖 Join *Roll for Narrative* for reviews, storytelling breakdowns, and writing misadventures:

https://rollfornarrative.parrydox.com

✐ Lurk, judge, or say hi:

https://www.parrydox.com

P.S. An angel still gets its wings for every five-star review, but I'm told they're on backorder.

🅐 amazon.com/author/richard.parry

🅖 goodreads.com/richard_parry

🅑🅑 bookbub.com/authors/richard-parry-6ffc3911-9f2c-43ef-8ab4-13dc-cd7f5874

▶ youtube.com/@parrydigm

🦋 bsky.app/profile/parrydox.com

in linkedin.com/in/therealrichardparry

ALSO BY RICHARD PARRY

DAWN'S WARDEN

The Three Faces of Fate

The Undefeated Throne

The Fury of the Betrayed

THE SPLINTERED LAND

Tomb of the Six

Blade of Glass

The Storm Within

Requiem's Justice

The Copper Bard

Heartsong

The Hymn of All

THE EZEROC WARS

The Ezeroc Wars universe is big (and growing!). Get the reading guide here: https://www.parrydox.com/ezeroc-wars-reading-guide/

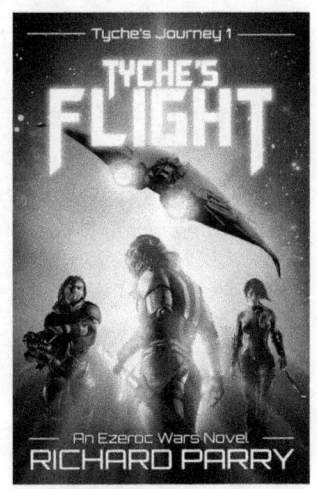

The Empire's Rogues: Volume 1

FUTURE FORFEIT

Not sure where to start? Get the reading guide here: https://www.parrydox.com/future-forfeit-reading-guide/

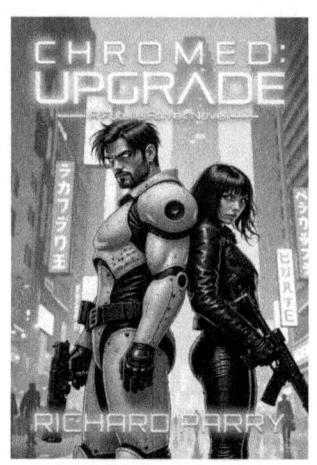

Chromed: Upgrade

Chromed: Rogue

Chromed: Restore

City Stories

Chromed: Consensus

Chromed: Delilah

Chromed: Meltdown

NIGHT'S CHAMPION

www.ingramcontent.com/pod-product-compliance
Lightning Source LLC
Chambersburg PA
CBHW061510020726
47502CB00006B/2011